DAYS of the DEAD
ADIE STURM MYSTERY
new uncut edition

ANASTASIA AMOR

BRODT PUBLISHING

BRODT PUBLISHING
Days of the Dead: Adie Sturm Mystery
new uncut edition
AnastasiaAmor.com
Copyright © 2007 by Anna Brodt
All rights reserved.
ISBN: 978-0-9918062-8-7
Cover art by Anna Brodt
Author photo by Kristen Wells

ACKNOWLEDGEMENTS

Thanks go out to my karate instructor, Julie, for her insight into the fight scenarios, and to Clara Ana and Patricia who filled me in on the *Day of the Dead* and the lives of the rich. Hugs to Bruce for proofing the new edition.

By ANASTASIA AMOR

ADIE STURM MYSTERIES

Corpse for Cozumel
Days of the Dead
The Curse of the Carnaval
Dead Delicious

PARANORMAL FANTASY SERIES
Havana Heat

EROTIC ROMANCE
Exploring Irresistible

Praise for ANASTASIA AMOR

DAYS OF THE DEAD: *ADIE STURM MYSTERY* "…murder, hot romance, intrigue, and suspense…Adie is a modern-day, sexy Agatha Christie…charming and quite captivating…put together well!"
— *ReviewYourBook*

"…You never can tell just what will crop up…a fun read, and will be very welcomed by fans of the series." —*LongAndShort Reviews*

"…Anastasia Amor delivers a page turner that I could not put down until I'd finished it. If you love mystery, romance, and a dose of humor from time to time, I know you'll enjoy reading *Days of the Dead* ever bit as much as I did."—*Michelle Stinson Ross, Florida*

"Adie's back and so are her hotter than hot men…Ms. Amor has written another heated cat and mouse hunt for Adie, and Adie's readers. The scenes between our heroine and her male admirers are just as steamy as book one…Adie's one romance female I can handle, she's not all goo-goo brained over the guys. She's smart. She's self-aware. Adie is liberating and confident,.. a successful mystery romp…" —
ChrisChatReviews

1

Glassy dilated eyes.

Moments ago those same pale blues had been captivated by the clarity of the golden-hued liquid, nectar of the gods, topped with a foamy froth. Its power was unique—giving a fool courage, inspiring witty repartee, transforming a mouse into a lion. At what point had it become the enemy, delivering a bitter message before its ultimate betrayal?

Expect the unexpected is a karate motto. I had expected a rowdy Friday-night crowd going crazy drunk. Singles trying to get lucky. It was Oktoberfest in Kitchener—one of the biggest beer festivals in the world. I was hosting a get-together for my tour group, strangers wanting an unusual vacation with an emphasis on the Days of the Dead. Soon, we'd be in Cozumel finding out how they celebrate death. But Death had decided not to wait, making an unexpected early appearance.

I was standing on a long wooden table demonstrating the sway and toast-your-beer method practiced at the Stuttgart Club. "*Ein prosit, ein prosit, zum Oktoberfest,*" rang out from every table in the place, but I was here only in body.

My mind wandered to the place dreams are made of. *Under a blue Caribbean sky, turbulent turquoise waves pounded on a powdery-white shore. On the beach blanket, a man sat next to me, his sapphire eyes, locked with mine. Windblown hair fell over his forehead. I brushed it away, my fingers lingering in the thick locks. The fiery heat from his body radiated out to me like the tropical rays of the sun. His abs felt firm and flat as I skimmed his velvety-smooth skin. "I have a truffle for you," I whispered.*

"I like chocolate," he said, his voice husky with desire. Soap and ocean breeze assailed my nostrils. His arms wrapped around

me, pulling me closer to him. The electricity of our kiss charged my every fiber.

From my ear to the hollow of my throat, sensuous lips captured my skin—his tongue silken and hot. He gripped the curve of my hip. His fingertips tightened...

"Wait." I pushed him away.

He lifted an eyebrow.

"Find the chocolate."

His eyes scanned my bikini-clad body stretched out before him. "I love treasure hunt," he said softly. His finger played with my strap and the skin beneath before he pulled it off my shoulder. Warm hands stroked the length of my body.

"Hey!" My beer partner shouted, rudely jolting me out of my fantasy. "Adie, it's time!" On the table George thrust his beer stein high.

George was massive. He'd gone Oktoberfest all the way. His white shirt was tucked into gray suede shorts held up by suspenders. Green wool knee-socks hid pale thick legs and practical bulky hiking boots completed his Bavarian outfit. A buzz cut did nothing to disguise an overly square face and monkey ears. His grin was more a gritting of teeth as tiny piggish eyes squinted down at me.

I climbed up on the table and waved my mug around for the tour group to follow my lead, shouting, "*Prosit!*" I wasn't prepared when the impact of my mug sent my beer partner careening backwards off the table, landing on the dirt floor of the canopied *festhalle*.

"George?" I yelled, alarmed. He had dressed the part but was not a beer drinker—or any kind of a drinker. I jumped off the table and hurriedly circled around to the other side. He lay there stiffly, his legs straight out—his face a deathly white. Kneeling down on the ground in front of him, Fern, fingered his shoulder gingerly. "I think he's passed out, Adie." She tossed her wavy black hair back as she looked up at me. I glanced down at the poor schmuck. Bending over, I loosened his collar.

George moaned, opening his eyes wide. "Adie, this place is great, but how about you and me heading out and you know..." He didn't finish that thought. His eyes shut. A snort blasted out, loud as a train whistle. This guy wouldn't see another *prosit* anytime soon.

I waved at the bouncer standing at the doorway. He trudged over and looked inquiringly at me.

"I brought these people out tonight, but this guy," I pointed at George, "couldn't hold his liquor. He's okay, though. Think he just needs to sleep it off. Could you move him somewhere? Please, Matt?"

The bouncer smiled cheerfully. "No problem, Adie. I'll shove him behind the sausage stand for now."

"Thanks, sweetie." Matt was a friend from karate. He did the bouncer stint at the Stuttgart Club during Oktoberfest to pick up some extra cash.

When I returned no one asked about George. They were too busy guzzling beer and gorging themselves with schnitzels and sauerkraut. Fern and boyfriend Bryan had just returned from dancing.

The Dinklemeister Band blasted a polka for the Bavarian Club Dancers—ladies decked out in dirndls, men sporting white shirts and lederhosen. I grabbed a big doughy pretzel from the tray on our table and bit into it, watching my tour group. I didn't need anyone else punching out early.

A solid brunette in a slenderizing black sweater dress and matching boots, a former Miss Oktoberfest herself, Ingrid Fleischer, leaned unsteadily against the table. Her thin scarlet lips twisted in a frown. The blush on her olive skin did nothing to disguise the salad green complexion. Could be she's about to… I didn't finish that thought.

Snatching her arm, I dragged her in the direction of the washroom. "Come on. Let's go." She wavered, but I'm stronger than I look. I manoeuvred her into the crowded washroom the way they do with juvies. Just in time, too. When I pushed her into a stall, she heaved out the evening's meal of sauerkraut and sausage. At that point I left. Ingrid Fleischer, the owner of Fleisher Travel was not my favorite person and the washroom had a putrid smell that would turn anyone's stomach.

I needed clean air. Across from the washroom a cool crisp breeze rushed in through the open door. Wisps of shifting white haze shrouded the darkness—misty ghosts walking. I shivered, hugging myself against the chill of the night.

I was so ready to escape. Back to Cozumel where he lived. Oh, yes… *On an isolated stretch of ivory shore, the sun caressed our bodies. He knew what I needed and wanted to please me in every way—my smoking hot man.*

"It's a treasure hunt."

His incredibly sexy eyes searched mine. He smiled seductively. "No clues?" His eyes shot down the length of my body and back, stopping at my bikini top.

I arched my back and ran a finger down to the valley between my breasts. My skin felt hot and moist. Full sensuous lips kissed my shoulder and journeyed down to meet my finger, torching my restless body. His mouth sucked each fingertip before he loosened the ties on my top. Over my curves his hand, searched for the decadent treasure. As he lowered my top, his mouth found the chocolate resting on the peak of my breast—melting creamy-rich flakes on my nipple. He sucked it up—bit by bit.

"Hey, honey! What's happenin'?"

Jerked out of my trance, I ignored the man—maybe he'd go away. Oktoberfest was full of players.

"Adie, it's me." I felt a hand linger on my shoulder. Shrugging it off, I swivelled around. Gelled dark hair and a facial growth. He was trim in an elegant black leather jacket, white muscle shirt, and designer jeans. He was slick—too slick. The host of Entertainment Tonight had a clone—Bernie Scharf.

"Watcha doin' here, Adie?"

I glanced at Slick. "Same as you, I think, except I'm working."

"That makes two of us. This is the most exciting thing they've found for me since those murders." Slick's gaze traveled up and down my body. "You're lookin' hot, Adie. You still together with what's-his-name?"

"Um-hmm." I wasn't about to tell Slick anything. He was okay as far as reporters went, but not my idea of a boyfriend.

"Where're you sitting? I'll join you."

"Over there by that pillar." I motioned in the general direction of our table. I could see that Ingrid had rejoined the group and was now linking arms with boy-next-door, Bryan, Fern's boyfriend. I was surprised she was joining in after what she'd heaved up.

4

Singing, dancing, and drinking, not to mention eating, was what this week was all about. There was some German culture thrown in somewhere, but it was kept to a minimum I thought, glancing at Slick's *Kiss Me I'm German* button pinned on his t-shirt. That guy had made in Ireland stamped on his pale-freckled forehead, not even a smidgen of Kraut, unlike me. A painful nudge to the ribs knocked me out of my philosophizing mood.

I turned around. Telly, a tiny red-head with bow lips and a perky short hair-cut was Fleischer Travel's manager. She looked flushed—a thin sheen of sweat coating her pink complexion. Telly was cute in a weird way, resembling one of those tiny chipmunks you see in the park, begging for peanuts. At this moment, she looked particularly enthusiastic with her arms thrust out to me appealingly, blue eyes bright with excitement.

"Adie, you've gotta come to the washroom with me," Telly said, propelling me along. "I'm dying to tell someone. You'll never guess…"

"What is it?"

Telly jerked her chin in the direction of the washroom. My curiosity piqued, I went. Remembering Slick, I pointed to the table in the main room. "Over there, at that table, Bern. Tell them you know me."

People were ahead of us. We joined the line against the wall. Telly patted my arm. "Adie, listen to this. Ingrid said I could run the whole shebang."

"What?"

"Ingrid wants to take it easy. She came into an enormous amount of money and guess who gets to be the big boss?"

"You?"

She hugged me and did a little hip wiggle. "Yeah! No more area manager. I'll be CEO of Ingrid's whole operation. That's three agencies, Adie."

I stared at her.

"It's true, Adie. Her boyfriend was very generous. She's got money to blow now that she's redecorated everything and updated all the buildings."

"What do you mean, her boyfriend?"

Telly stared. "You are so naïve, Adie. She's had this old guy on the side for years." She looked away to a woman coming out of a stall. "Not that she particularly likes old but rich is another thing…" She stopped abruptly in mid-sentence, caught my eye and grinned. "How did you think she got to wear those Italian suits and drive that Mercedes?"

"Oh-hh." After considering the recent renovations at Fleischers—marble bathroom ensuites, and upscale décor in all the offices, especially in Ingrid's, I said, "I just thought the travel business was doing well."

"Ha!" She guffawed loudly, thudding me on the back. "You and Morris must be cut from the same cloth. He doesn't have a clue, either."

Ingrid had been married to Morris for eighteen years. Rumour was hubbie had filed for divorce. Unfortunately for him, he didn't know Ingrid played hardball. "What about Maureen? Does she know about the boyfriend?"

"Doubt it. She's a teenager." Telly tweaked my cheek gently and smiled. "She probably doesn't care either. Teens are into themselves, Adie."

I nodded, thinking about my niece, Tasha. Besides being snotty, she was my sister-in-law's clone and that was not good. "Isn't Ingrid sending Maureen to boarding school?"

"For sure. She's not the motherly type. Maureen was an accident, according to her. Boarding school solves that problem. Ingrid wants the support money, Adie, not that she needs it with all the hoarding she does. I wouldn't be surprised if she has off shore accounts," Telly said, swinging a stall door open.

I saw a free one and entered. I started to think about Ingrid and had to disagree with Telly. Ingrid liked the wealthy life style but it wasn't money that turned her crank. It was control. Ingrid liked to control everything and everybody. Her other flaw was constantly changing her mind. She was capricious to an extreme. Telly had better get that job in writing.

But none of that was my problem. All I cared about was the Cozumel trip. Ingrid could be malicious on a whim. She'd better not change her mind about me heading up the tour group. With ice pellets in the forecast, I was counting on this trip.

"Hey! Hurry up in there. I'm desperate!"

I got myself together and swung the door open.

A heavy woman with dyed coal black hair glowered at me. "It's about time!"

"Sorry. It's the beer."

"A little thing like you shouldn't drink." She huffed loudly before slamming the door shut.

I glanced around at the line of women staring accusingly in my direction, but where was Telly? I exited quickly and headed back. From where I stood, I could see the table ahead but my progress was snail-paced with a couple of paunch-bellied beer drinkers crowding the aisle. I watched Bernie chatting to a rumpled-looking Telly, her grubby mustard-stained T-shirt tucked into a pair of gray suede lederhosen. She was smiling but was obviously not a partier like Lola.

In a dirndl and a cleavage revealing blouse, the blonde on the tail end of fifty, polka-bopped in the aisle with every male who pranced by. Lola was fit and looked better than most of the younger women. She wasn't a cougar, just bored with married life. Her partner, Dan, either approved or didn't care. No slouch in the Oktoberfesting mode either, he was happily chug-a-lugging alongside Jim, when he wasn't ogling women. Cheerful bald Dan was wearing a red plaid lumberjack shirt and relaxed fit jeans. He was round in every way, sixty-something, with a pregnant gut filled with fat, not baby. Jim and Tom, geeks with round wire-rimmed glasses and conservative hair-cuts were decked out in denim shirts and skinny jeans. They worked for Blackberry, a local company that specialized in cell phones. These boys had an excuse for checking out women. Neither had a girlfriend. Not that Tom was into any woman here except bodacious Fern. Every time she fluttered her long lashes, and whispered in his ear, he turned beet red.

Ingrid, hands empty, stood next to Telly, apparently ready to call it quits. With good reason, I'd guess. Ingrid's olive complexion had lost its lustre. In fact, her face was a ghostly white. As far as I could see, Fern and her boyfriend Bryan were the only sober ones standing on that table other than nerdy Tom. They'd been sipping when everyone else had been slurping.

Fern was beautiful—long wavy jet-black hair, elaborately lined brown eyes, glossed plump pink lips and a curvaceous figure. Her funky leather-fringed clothes and feather earrings were

Toronto rather than Kitchener. Her boyfriend with the freckles reminded me of a Best Buy greeter or Mark Wahlberg on a good day—light-blue shirt tucked into a pair of tan Dockers.

A few days ago, Fern had traipsed into the travel agency looking to book a vacation. I recognized her from college. When I suggested she join the Fleischer Travel group at the Stuttgart Club for an intro to Days of the Dead in Cozumel, she got all excited. That's what she and Bryan wanted, so I gave her tickets for tonight and booked them with my tour.

I had to get back to my group but it was as busy as a bee hive in the *festhalle* tent. That's the problem with being petite. It's like being a five-year old kid trying to watch a parade between adult legs. No matter how much I pushed and shoved, I couldn't get to the table. I could barely see it. A massive man with tree trunk legs and a head like a hippo blocked my view, rooting himself in my path.

"Excuse me!" I shouted, but I think the din had damaged his hearing. Standing, beer glass in hand, he rocked unsteadily with the music. When hippo lifted his stein up higher, I made my move and squeezed under his arm. Just then two couples polkaed into hippo, who jostled the tour group table. Bernie tottered and fell. His beer glass slipped out of his fingers and crashed to the dirt floor. I rushed over. But instead of getting up Slick started crawling under the table.

Whoah, Slick. You're cut off.

I heard him yelling, "You okay, lady?"

Crouching down beside him, I peeked over his shoulder, not believing what I saw. Lumped in a crumpled heap, Telly's pale blues fixed unblinkingly up at Bernie. Her mouth twitched.

I kneeled down. Her throat gargled and wheezed. "You know CPR, Bernie?"

Slick shook his head. He glanced at the crowd milling around and shouted out, "Anyone know CPR?"

People stared blankly and shuffled.

"Stay with her, Adie. I'll get security."

Tilting her head back, I poked a finger in Telly's mouth, checking for an obstruction, but found nothing. Pinching her nostrils, I gave her a few quick breaths.

At that point the security guard arrived and took over. Paramedics came in next and worked on her. Finally, they put Telly on a gurney and carried her out.

Ingrid grabbed my arm. "What happened, Adie?"

"I don't know." When I stood I noticed my group was gone. As the band announced last call, I asked, "Where is everyone?"

"I told them to get the taxis before everyone else does. Bryan took George with him." Thoughtfully, Ingrid placed a finger at her lips. "I figured it would be best if they left. If something happened to Telly, they might blame the agency. I don't want anyone cancelling."

"But what if someone did something to her? The police would want to question them, wouldn't they?"

Ingrid patted my shoulder. "Don't go drama queen on me." Her eyes swept to the police officers coming through the doorway. "Listen, Adie, tell them she fell off the table. Okay?"

And I had thought she and Telly were tight.

A couple of cops came over—a man and a woman. The brunette Amazon pushed back her shoulder length hair and stared at Slick. "Hey, Bernster! Long time no see."

"Janey." He checked out her statuesque figure. "What's shakin'?"

They seemed a touch overly friendly, considering the circumstances.

Janey smirked. "Whatever I'm hangin' on to." She glanced at us, but asked Slick, "What's goin' on?"

"I fell off the table and saw her lying there."

"You know her?"

"Just met." Slick shot his glance in my direction. "This was Adie's party."

The stocky male cop turned to me. "You know the woman, Ma'am?"

"Yes. Her name's Telly Henderson."

Janey tugged out her notepad. "What happened, Ma'am?"

"I don't know. When I came back from the washroom, she was on the floor."

Janey turned to Ingrid. "Ma'am? Were you there?"

She straightened her shoulders. "Ingrid Fleischer, Fleischer Travel."

9

Janey nodded. "Right. What happened, Ma'am?"

"Everyone was on the table clicking steins. Telly was beside me when this man crashed into our table. She fell."

"We should get going to the hospital." I glanced at the officers. "Kitchener Central?"

Janey nodded. "I'll let you go soon. I need some information for my report, first."

Bernie took that as his opening to leave. He mouthed, "Call me," before waving goodbye.

By the time the cops were finished with us, the crowds had thinned. I hooked up Ingrid's arm into mine and steered her down the hallway to the front of the building. Taxis were lined up outside.

Ingrid swung the door open, talking over her shoulder, "I'm sick as a dog. Going home. You take this one, Adie."

Telly was her employee, but it was useless to argue. I was freelance on contract for Fleischer Travel. I was tired, but Telly was alone and needed someone.

* * *

It was about an hour before they let me speak to a doctor. The news wasn't good. Telly was dead.

On my way out I recognized a slim, dark-haired man in a trench coat at the empty volunteer station. Ilya Kharkov, a detective in major crimes, was on his cell. When he spotted me he shoved his phone in his pocket and came over.

"Adie. What are you doing here?" He pulled out a notebook and pen.

"I'm waiting. The manager of Fleischer Travel was brought here." I found it difficult to voice the rest of it. It was unbelievable. Tonight, Telly had been on cloud nine with a promotion dream come true. Now she was dead.

His eyes scanned his notes. "Telly Henderson?"

"Yes. You're here because of her?"

His dark brown eyes met mine. "Um-hmm. You're leaving?"

"She died and they don't know why."

"I'm talking to the doctor. They should have something soon."

"Could I phone you tomorrow?"

His mouth curled up at the corners. "You can call me anytime, Adie."

My cheeks flushed. "I mean to talk about Telly."

"Sure, sweetheart, but if it's a suspicious death, you know I can't tell you anything."

"She was so happy today."

He squeezed my arm reassuringly. "They'll do an autopsy. Something is bound to come up."

"I hope so."

His eyes, the color of chocolate, glowed warmly. "We've got to start meeting under happier circumstances."

I tried to return his smile, but I was too tired. "Good-night, Ilya." A chill breeze blasted my face as I made my way out. With a drizzle of rain mixed in, it seemed colder than before. By chance, I found a taxi parked near the entrance. After I told the driver where I was going, I took out my cell and punched in Ingrid's number. She was groggy, but miserable enough to start complaining about interrupting her beauty sleep.

"She's dead, Ingrid."

Only then did she stop her rant. "Oh! Was it a heart attack?"

"They don't know." I was done with this woman. "Good night."

"Adie, don't hang up!"

I put the cell back to my ear.

"I want you to come in to work, tomorrow, Adie. It's urgent. We need to…"

I pressed end.

* * *

I was glad to be home. My cats greeted me at the door, brushing against my leg. I filled their bowls and got a glass of water for me before I went upstairs. I made it to bed in record time and deliberately neglected to set my alarm.

Several hours later, I woke to the sound of ice pellets hitting my bedroom window. Outside, freezing rain had coated everything in sight. This meant closings around town. The police would be warning people to stay put.

I rarely go into work on Saturdays. I couldn't believe Ingrid had asked. It's not like I make bookings anyway. I take tour groups on trips out of the country. The job was all about freedom.

Throwing on my leopard-print robe, I trudged downstairs to the main floor kitchen and plugged in the kettle to make some green tea. I usually had herbal tea. Less caffeine. It's better not to wake up some days.

I mulled over the events of last night. Telly had made it to the top and plummeted to the bottom in one night. She was forty-three. As I inserted a waffle into the toaster, my eyes flicked over to my phone. The red light flashed. When I pressed the text, it said voice mail.

The first one was from Slick. *Henderson's death is classified as suspicious. How about that? Call me. 570-2599.*

My mom's voice was next. *Adelina don't go out today. It's icy. Call me.*

The last one was from Ingrid. *I'm sorry. I'll make it up to you. I really need to see you today. Please come in, Adie. It's very important! I'll wait for you!*

Bringing my mug and waffle to the living room, I turned on the TV. A news flash had updates on a recent robbery. The rest was about the ice storm and shut-downs. A list of closings was read but Fleisher Travel was not mentioned. Predictable. Ingrid wasn't about to lose any business no matter what the weather. Maybe she thought people would be more anxious than ever to get away. Telly's death made the tail end of the clip but only as a *suspicious death under investigation.*

I had to talk to Ilya. He would be the man in the know. When I became involved in one of his cases a while ago, he'd almost made the mistake of arresting the wrong person—my gff. I sighed. She owed me big time for enabling her to live long enough to come into a fortune and meet the man of her dreams. Wish my life was as easy. I pressed his contact number and got the operator. She put me through.

"Kharkov."

"Ilya, it's Adie Sturm."

"Hey, sweetheart," Ilya said, his voice husky. "How're you doin'?"

"Tired."

"Yeah, join the club. What's up?"

"Telly Henderson?"

"A suspicious death."

"I know that Ilya, but how?"

"She'll get an autopsy. Three days, we'll know."

"But you must have some idea by now."

"Classified information."

"Ilya, remember what I did for you?"

"You didn't give me that back massage you promised."

"I think you've got your women mixed up."

"It's nice to know you're one of my women."

"Dream on…"

Ilya chuckled. "Yeah, I have those when I think of you."

I felt heat rise to my cheeks. "Come on, Ilya. You owe me."

There was a pause before he spoke. "You probably know the murderer."

"So you're saying it's not from natural causes?"

"Nope. Something ingested, is the doctor's guess."

"And you want me to help because usually the victim is killed by someone she knows—like a boyfriend?" I frowned.

"She was your agency manager, wasn't she?"

He had something there, but Telly and I had been acquaintances at best. I hardly knew anything about her personal business.

"Was she ever married?"

"No."

"Boyfriend?"

"No."

"An ex?"

"No."

"Girlfriend?"

"Hm-mm. Let's see…" Telly had a man's short haircut and always wore dorky track outfits, but that didn't really mean much. "Seriously, Ilya, I don't know. She could have been gay or bi. Telly and I weren't tight. I never heard her talk about anyone, come to think about it. Pottery was her thing. You could check with that pottery place on Victoria Street. Her parents passed in a car accident. Last few years she lived downtown—mingled with a sketchy crowd. No relatives, except a cousin in Hamilton that I know of."

"Thanks. That helps." There was a pause. "You know, Adie, this is the second time you've become involved in one of my cases. Could be you're unlucky."

"I was born December 6th, a day associated with death."

"No kiddin', eh?" He chuckled. "You're one cute vampire. But hey, if you dig into this, you might be lucky for me and we'll find Henderson's killer."

"So you're saying I should help you solve this murder?" Was this cop unusually anxious to keep a civilian out of police matters?

"Yup, right, but on the sly, hun. This case is getting tossed to the backburner anyway because of a robbery and something else really big." A beep sounded. "Got another call. How about we get together Monday and discuss it over lunch?"

"Sorry, Ilya, I'll be in Cozumel."

"Again? This is *deja vu*," he said slowly. "I'm always missing you somehow. When are you leaving?"

"Tomorrow night. Will you let me know about anything you find out regarding Telly? Text me."

"Yeah. But one thing—be careful, Adie. You don't want to end up unlucky and dead."

I set the cell down. Telly was a good person. She didn't deserve to die. She liked animals and always gave to charity. Sometimes she gave me the heads up about psycho Ingrid or a crazy client. No one cared about poor Telly—alive or dead. Outside raindrops speckled the window. I watched them roll down the glass. Tears for Telly. I felt an overwhelming sadness. With no family advocates the police would focus on high-profile cases and forget Telly. It was up to me to do right by her.

With the temperature rising, the ice was melting fast. Going in would ruin a stay at home curled-up-with-my-cats day. Anything to do with Ingrid usually ended up with stress but she had me curious.

I padded up the stairs to shower. While I shampooed my hair, I wondered what Ingrid wanted. I couldn't get over how callous she'd been about Telly, especially since the poor girl had practically sold her soul for that job. But Ingrid had been practically begging. Grovelling would have been even better. She'd owe me big time if I went in. That decided it for me.

I put on a pair of jeans and a sweater. My boots were black with three-inch heels. Not the greatest for walking on ice but I liked to look tall and I'm good in heels. Besides, if I were looking down on Ingrid, it would really irritate the control freak.

14

Salt trucks and rain had cleared the main streets. The travel agency on King Street was located a few blocks from my karate club. As I eased my Beetle into my parking space, I noticed two cars in the lot. One was Ingrid's silver Mercedes and the other was Suzanne's blue Fiesta. No clients. Suzanne was sitting at her desk making a timetable for next week. She looked up when I came in. "Hey, Adie. Whatcha doing here?"

"Ingrid wants to talk to me."

Suzanne whispered, "Adie, she's acting odd and I don't think it's about Telly. By the way, did you know it was on TV?"

"I saw the clip. Is Ingrid making any funeral arrangements?"

"Apparently she tried, but one of the funeral homes phoned. Said Telly had prearranged her funeral. She wanted a cremation."

"With Ingrid leaving for Cozumel, I guess there won't be a memorial service either, or was there a friend that would hold one?"

"Telly was a loner. We might just do something with the people here at the travel agency. I'll phone her cousin." She leaned in closer. "Still it might be better with Ingrid gone. We can do it the way we want. Too bad you'll be in Cozumel. I was thinkin' of a wake."

"She would have liked that." Telly loved beer and pubs. "I hope Ingrid isn't thinking of taking over the tour group and leaving me here."

Suzanne kept her voice low. "No chance of that, Adie. She's been on the horn with her lawyer and is royally stressed. Morris is putting the screws to her."

"Really?" I thought back to what Telly had confided in me. "Do you know anything about Ingrid's stash?"

Suzanne looked around furtively before she whispered, "Two words—Jordan James."

"He's the boyfriend?" Jordan James was loaded—ad agencies all over Canada. He'd been high profile but I hadn't heard anything about him for the last few years. "He's way older than Ingrid, isn't he?"

Suzanne leaned back in her chair and pursed her lips. "In his seventies, I'd think. But don't tell her I told you. If she knows I said anything, she'll lose it. She wants to get rid of me, Adie."

I nodded. Ingrid couldn't do without Suzanne, but she liked to intimidate her employees with threats. "No, don't worry about that. I won't say anything." I glanced down the hall. No sign of Ingrid. Was her office door open? She liked to eavesdrop on Suzanne, and anyone else for that matter. I bit my lip. I had better see what Ingrid wanted. Get it over with—like a trip to the dentist. I headed to her office and knocked.

Ingrid swung the door open. "Sit down, Adie." Ingrid motioned to the plush gray leather chair. She picked up a cigarette and lit it. A large square-cut diamond flashed on her finger. "Drink?"

After all that beer last night, I was not keen. I sat down and leaned back too suddenly, painfully knocking my head on the frame. It was an expensive Italian chair but not exactly comfy, mimicking the tailored suit she wore.

Ingrid had a couple of shot glasses and a bottle of Peppermint Schnapps on the black coffee table. She picked up the bottle and inclined her head inquiringly.

"No, thanks. What did you want to talk about, Ingrid?"

Ingrid stared off into space for a few seconds and then focused on me.

I stretched out my legs on the ottoman and waited.

Ingrid directed her gaze back at the bottle and poured herself a glass of Schnapps. She sipped it slowly before she said, "I was interested in your Mayan frog. Looks old."

Ingrid must have snooped in my office. How else would she know I just got it? "Yes, it's Pre-Columbian." A few months ago in Mexico, I had spent some time with Diego Francisco Bolivar Alvarez. He had a branch office in Toronto. When he came to Canada on business, we went out for dinner. I knew the frog was expensive but Diego had looked hurt when I suggested that it might be inappropriate for me to accept it.

"Spendy, I'd say."

I nodded.

Ingrid studied my face. "Where'd you get it?"

"A friend in Cozumel gave it to me."

"Would your friend be able to get a hold of any other antiquities?"

Diego's family had an import-export business. "Probably."

"When we get there, would you be able to introduce me to your friend?"

"I don't know, Ingrid. I'll have to find out if he's in Cozumel."

Ingrid's lips formed an *o* and she blew out smoke like a row of Cheerios. "Could you call him?"

"Now?"

"I need your help, Adie. I would make it worth your while."

"How?"

Ingrid smiled. "We'll have a tour to Jamaica in December. You've been there, haven't you?"

"Um."

"Like it?"

"Beautiful beaches, sunshine and the bluest ocean in the Caribbean."

"Sara's been dying to go there."

"But, you'd rather contract me to go if I…"

"Exactly." Ingrid inhaled deeply. "Find out if he'll be there."

"I'll check my office and see if I have his number." I got up and crossed over to the door. Ingrid held it open for me.

I wasn't eager to do this. Diego was devastatingly handsome and very rich. But my life was too complicated. He could misinterpret my interest when I phoned him to ask about his whereabouts. I made my way slowly to my office at the end of the hall.

It was small but comfortable with a teak desk and two blue upholstered chairs. On the wall I had framed ink drawings of my cats.

Thinking about Ingrid's bribe, I watched droplets of rain splash my windowpane. October always was a mish-mash of weather—warm some days, others unpleasantly cool. I was glad Ingrid hadn't switched my assignment, at least not yet. If she was upset, my next tour might be to some horrible cold place—like Edmonton. But then again, she had to be careful. If she messed with me, I wouldn't renew our contract. Sara was a novice tour guide and Ingrid knew it. I picked up my cell and slid my finger down until I came to Alvarez and pressed the phone icon. I waited until it rang.

"*Diga*," a deep voice drawled.

"*Hola,* Diego."

"Adelina?"

"Yes." I ran my fingers through my hair nervously. "How are you?"

"*Bien, mi amor.* Happy, now that you've called. How was your castle tour?"

"The history was fascinating. I love Wales."

"You like history, don't you? Do you remember Tulum?"

"How could I forget?" A kaleidoscope of scenarios flashed through my mind—the two of us on the beach, swimming, kissing, and our run-in with death. "Diego, I am flying down to Cozumel tomorrow."

"I will make sure they prepare the condo for you. And I look forward to seeing you."

"That's kind of you, but I'm not sure I will be staying there. My tour group has a reservation at the Don Juan Hotel."

"Not the best place. Must you stay with them?"

"It might be the best thing to do—stay close to my clients."

"Surely the condo will be more comfortable. You haven't seen it, Adelinita. Don't make up your mind just yet. When you get there, give me a call and I'll show it to you."

"So, you'll be in San Miguel? You won't be out of town?"

"Here and there I might be. Business."

"Would you be able to speak to an associate about obtaining some Mayan antiquities?"

"Antiquities? Um, Adelinita, we should discuss this in person. Call me when you get in."

"Sure."

"*Chao, mi amor.*"

"*Chao,* Diego." I placed the phone back onto the receiver and studied my Mayan frog statue. Diego had been so sweet to give it to me. Glancing up, I saw Ingrid leaning on the door frame.

"So?"

"He'll be there, but I didn't talk to him about getting the Mayan antiquities."

"But he would know how to get them?" She fingered the frog gently, and turned it, examining the bottom.

"He'll do it for me."

"You know, Adie, I saw a piece similar to this at an art auction in Toronto. The buyer ended up paying fifteen hundred for it."

"I didn't realize it was that much."

"We wouldn't want this conversation to leave this room, Adie."

I nodded.

"Thanks." She swivelled around and made her way back to her office.

What now? With the city shut down, my karate club would be closed. I might as well go home and pack.

* * *

Rush hour had started. The ice was almost gone and the traffic was light. Soon, I was pulling into my driveway. Once inside my kitchen I realized I needed something to lift my spirits. The weather, Telly, and now the meeting with Ingrid contributed to the black cloud hanging over me. I stroked Minnie, my gray Turkish-angora, thinking a chocolate fix would help. *Pleasure is chocolate.* So which should it be? My mom's chocolate cake or one of grandma's blintzes? One with rich, creamy chocolate and the other with to-die-for, thick, smooth bitter-sweet chocolate. Choices— always choices. I closed my eyes and visualized a slice of chocolate cake.

There was almost nothing I liked more than chocolate, except maybe an afternoon wrapped in a passionate embrace with a man. I clicked in my mom's number as I forked up the cake.

"Hello?"

"Hi, Mom. What's up?"

"Erika called. She's worried about Wolf. She wants to know if he's coming back from Cozumel. Apparently, he's ignoring her."

"Um-mm?" I didn't think I liked this topic of conversation.

"I told her you're going to Cozumel."

"And?"

"She wanted to know if you might check in on him. Get him to call." I closed my eyes, the chocolate melting in the heat of my mouth. I conjured a picture in my mind. Mysterious, sapphire eyes.

"Adie?"

My mom's voice startled me.

"What?"

"Wolf's in Cozumel, Adie. She wants you to persuade him to contact her."

That's asking a lot. I bit my lip, remembering.

"Adie, he's living in a house in San Miguel. The phone number is—got a pen?"

"Yes." I looked at the mug on my table. It held an assortment of pens.

"81-2222. Have you got that?"

"Yes." I scrolled down on my cell to where it said sea god. It was the same number.

"Write this down—Avenida 10, that's the street, Entre 4 y 6 Nte, between the roads four and six north. You should stop by. Erika hasn't heard from him since New Years."

New Year's Eve. Bringing in the New Year together—his full lips pressed sensuously against mine. Rockets had fired and soared through my body. "And if we talk?"

"Just tell him to phone home. You know Erika. She's like a she-lion with her boys and Wolf is so independent." Mom chuckled. "A lot like you."

"Okay, but I may not have time to see him."

"Please, dear. You should recognize him. I know it's been ten years but he doesn't look much different. Maybe a bit more muscular. You remember what he looks like, don't you?"

My heart skipped a beat—he was unforgettable. "Yes."

"Erika said it's such a small place, you might just see him in the town, anyway. You know how close our families have been. Remember how you came up with us to their cottage that summer? The two of you disappeared for hours. I was worried. Thought the boat might have run out of gas. Erika thought you were up to no good. Blamed it all on you. Your father thought you'd…" Mom sighed. "Well, we were never religious enough for Erika but she's a friend, so anyway, sweetie, do this for me, okay?"

I frowned. This certainly complicated matters. "I'll try."

"Have a great trip!"

"Thanks. Take care." Pressing the end button, I rubbed my temples, thinking of my last trip to Cozumel. Steamy hot nights and a tongue that had set my body on fire—too much unfinished business. But life doesn't always deal us a good hand. Sometimes we have to play the cards we've got, no matter what the stakes.

2

George was a big guy. About six-three and super wide like a NFL linebacker. His body took up more than his share of space—his beefy forearm smothered my armrest, long legs indented the seat in front. When the flight attendants told us to fasten our seatbelts and put our seats in an upright position, George wrenched the belt, flipping and twisting it, frustration burning his cheeks red. I took pity on him. After I got a hold of his seatbelt, snapping it shut, I pointed to a black button on the armrest and said, "This button adjusts the seat."

Breathing a sigh of relief, George straightened his chair. "Adie, I'm so glad you're here with me. You might not have guessed, but I've never flown before."

I nodded.

"When will we get there?"

"We should land about six."

George glanced nervously out the window at the engines starting up. His knuckles clenched and white, he sat silently until we ended our ascent and started flying steadily. The pilot came on the intercom and told us the weather in Cozumel was sunny and eighty degrees.

"That's encouraging," I said.

"What time will we get to the hotel?"

"If all goes well, probably sevenish."

"Will you be having dinner with us?"

I was beginning to get the feeling this was not a casual question. "Probably not. I have plans with a friend."

"A female friend?"

I had to nip this thing in the bud. "A male friend."

"Well, let's see. There's Jim and Tom, but they're not exactly your type, I'd think. So with no single males your age on our tour, except me, I'd guess this guy lives in Cozumel?"

"Um-mm."

"What does he do there?"

I had to think fast—which male friend should I tell him about? "He runs an investment firm but his family also holds an import business."

"I'm interested in investments. What kind?"

He was putting me on the spot. "Land."

"Is he good at it? I might want to invest in some property."

"Oh?" I asked incredulously.

George regarded me seriously. "I may not look it, but I have money. I have my own company."

"What kind of company, George?"

"Computer software."

"Oh…" I dug around for my book in the carry-on luggage.

"It probably sounds dull to someone like you."

"Someone like me?"

"Yeah…" His face flushed. "You're sophisticated."

I raised an eyebrow.

"You know so much more about everything than I do, except software, of course. I'm an expert when it comes to computer programming."

I opened my paperback to the first chapter.

"Computer software is where the money's at."

"Um-mm." I blanked him out and read the first sentence.

"I took technology and business management in university. The computer field was just opening up. I mean, well, Bill Gates, Microsoft, and then of course, there was Mac and Apple."

I couldn't be rude to one of my clients, so I nodded my head in the manner that a psychologist would, before I refocused on my novel.

"Adie, one time I saw a special about Gates. You wouldn't believe the stuff he did." He slumped back in his seat. "The vision of the man."

His voice was a boring monotone. George was smart enough but his voice could put anyone into a coma. As he droned on with details, I read. I was near the bottom of the first page when I felt George press his hand on my arm.

"So, do you understand, Adie?"

"Um-mm. There's a radio station on two." I pointed to the armrest, hoping he'd get the hint. He frowned but after he noticed I was back to reading, he picked up the newspaper the flight attendant had given him and opened it to the business section.

After an hour into the flight, we were served drinks and sandwiches. Tearing open the sandwich package the flight attendant had deposited on my tray, I noticed George's eyes on me. I had the uneasy feeling I really had to follow through with Diego or George would catch me in a lie. Maybe, I'd have to find him a woman, as well. With all the money he said he had, surely there would be one out there for him somewhere—ready, willing, and able.

I glanced across the aisle at Ingrid. Her face was pale, fingertips nervously tapping the surface of her tray. Four nicotine free hours on the airline would be hard on a pack-a-day woman like Ingrid. There were two empty plastic glasses with swivel sticks on her tray and she was sipping on another one.

With Telly's unexpected death, Ingrid had put Suzanne in charge. She was competent for someone in her twenties but didn't have the experience to deal with some situations. It surprised me that Ingrid made her manager and went ahead with her trip to Cozumel.

When the flight attendant came to get our trays, I started thinking about going to the washroom and changing. It would be easier to do it now, before we started our descent.

"Excuse me." I waited, but George continued to sit, staring at the flight attendant wiggling her way to the back. He looked zoned out, probably a combination of male hormones and getting up in the wee hours to make it to Toronto. George lived out in the sticks and with the long drive to the airport, he'd be tired. I spoke up louder. "George, will you excuse me, please?"

He angled his legs slightly away. That left me with an awkward climb over a pair of huge knees propped tightly against the seat in front of him. With the carry-on held high, I swung one leg over, my butt brushing something as I stepped into the aisle. Was that his hand? I glanced over my shoulder but George had closed his eyes.

I squeezed by a wheezing barrel-chested fellow coming down the aisle and waited for the occupied light to turn off. It was taking so long, I was wondering if I shouldn't try the washroom at the back of the plane. Just as I turned to leave, the door jerked opened and Fern popped out.

She smiled when she saw me and touched my arm lightly. "Adie, hi! We haven't really had a chance to talk since I booked this trip. Oktoberfest was something else. Thanks for including us. Never had that experience before." She looked suddenly concerned. "So what happened to that woman from your office?"

"She..."

"What?"

"Died."

"Huh?" Fern said, her dark eyes widening in surprise. "Died? I thought she had too much beer!"

"They took her to the hospital and a few hours later she died. They don't know the cause yet."

Fern's brow furrowed. "That's unreal. When Ingrid said we should hurry and get ourselves a taxi, she didn't mention anything."

"We didn't know at that point and I think she didn't want to put a damper on the night."

Fern looked over my shoulder, her eyes shooting daggers in Ingrid's direction. "No, she wouldn't, would she?"

I was taken aback. "You know Ingrid, don't you?"

"Yep." Fern glued her eyes on Ingrid. "It's a long story." She changed the subject abruptly. "When do we land, Adie?"

"Soon. You might want to change, Fern. It'll be hot when we get in."

"Yeah, sure. I have some shorts in my carry-on. I might as well do it now. Thanks, I'll tell Bryan."

Getting changed in the washroom was like being a contortionist in the circus, without the applause. After I checked my hair, I tossed my things in my bag and headed back to my seat.

George had dozed off, his mouth open, whistling snorts coming out of his nose in irregular intervals. I crawled over him carefully, trying not to touch him, but with those massive legs I couldn't avoid it. Relieved that he continued to sleep, I closed my eyes myself, but the train blasts kept me awake. After a while, I pulled out my book and started to read.

When the seat belt light came on, the flight attendant woke George to move his seat into an upright position. He looked nervous, sweat dribbles appearing on his temples and neck. I wanted to feel some compassion for him, but I had to wonder where his hand had been when I had stepped over him. If there was one thing that annoyed me, it was a guy that took advantage of a woman with some unwanted groping.

* * *

My tour group was outside the airport at the curb, waiting to board the shuttle bus. The sun was nearing the horizon, but the breeze was warm—no cold rain or ice pellets.

An island twenty-eight miles long and eleven miles wide, Cozumel rests off the eastern coast of Mexico's Yucatan peninsula. In Mayan, Cozumel meant Place of the Swallows. The hotel zone was on the west coast because of the calm waters and its major attraction, the reefs. Our hotel, the Don Juan was located close to the ferry dock in San Miguel, the island's only town.

Before I sat down, I spoke to our shuttle driver. "*Hola,* I'm Adie Sturm, Fleischer Travel."

"*Buenas tardes.* You have come at a good time, Señorita Sturm. The last few days have been sunny."

"Great." I hoped it would hold up.

"You have everyone?"

I looked up and down the aisle and did a head count. "Yup, we can go."

Our driver was experienced dealing with pedestrians, not to mention the speed bumps called topes that interrupted the flow of traffic along the coast road. It should have been easy to drive with the avenidas and calles at right angles but these streets were often confusing with the one ways. When a bicycle swerved out at the last minute, I was glad I was a passenger and not the driver. In the hotel's adjacent lot, the driver brought the luggage out of the shuttle and deposited the suitcases on the cement.

"Welcome to the Don Juan," I said to my group, as I picked up my suitcase. The hotel was a two-story, yellow stucco building with a red tile roof. The double glass doors slid open and a doorman grabbed some of the luggage, bringing it to the central area near the front desk.

A cozy grouping of wicker chairs with floral cushions was set in the middle of the lobby. Apart from a young couple at the reception desk we were the only group arriving. It didn't take long for my group to register and after everyone was given a room, I announced, "We have a reservation for dinner in half an hour."

Hoots and clapping sounds filled the air. Airline food can only go so far. Jim, the geeky Blackberry guy, called out to me as I followed the bellhop. "Adie," he motioned to Tom, "we thought we'd skip dinner here. Is there somewhere you could suggest where there'd be a little more action?"

"Carlos 'n Charlies. Tell the taxi driver."

"Cool." Jim beamed happily and grabbed his suitcase.

The bellhop's lapel pin read Miguel. His nose held proof of his Mayan heritage, narrow, with a bit of a hook to it. He led the way to the second floor and inserted the key. "You have the ocean view, Señorita." He opened my door for me to enter first. Eagerly, I made my way to the patio to catch a glimpse of the Caribbean. The sky at sunset had a rosy hue that cast a lavender light on the turquoise waves. It was as I remembered it, and with that came those bittersweet memories of the days I had spent with a man I should forget. But his slow sexy smile and his mysterious eyes were impossible to wipe out of my mind.

When the bellhop left, I closed the door and dug in my purse for my cell and pressed Diego's number.

"*Bueno.*"

"*Hola,* Diego, I'm at the Don Juan."

"Are you free for dinner?"

Diego was a godsend—here was my excuse to get away. "Yes, but in about an hour. Is that okay?"

"Certainly. Where should I meet you?"

"The dining room. I'll need to get my group settled in to their dinner first and then I can leave."

"Soon then. *Chao, mi amor.*"

"*Adios,* Diego and thanks."

Time was short and I had a few things to do before dinner. Unlocking my suitcase, I took my usual Caribbean hotel room precaution. My aerosol can of Raid was in a plastic bag in the outside pocket of my luggage. I pressed the button and aimed under the beds before I moved them together. I stepped away quickly—just in the nick of time.

A three-inch cockroach and his buddy raced by, inches away from my toes. I wasn't fast enough to squish the first one but the second one wasn't so lucky. I completed a rendition of the Mexican hat dance before I stopped stomping—Mexican roaches being hard-shelled suckers. I glanced around but the first roach had headed for the bathroom. I threw the can but it bounced right off and the beast kept on running.

Poison acts slowly, but eventually the noxious fumes would overpower the thick-skinned devil until it succumbed to its inevitable death. This brought back thoughts of Telly. Not that she had been ugly or roach-like. She'd been a good person and hadn't deserved to die. Could she have been poisoned? As I wandered over to the window I looked out at the fronds of the coconut palms waving gently, and thought how lucky I was to be alive. Telly had been dealt a joker that shouldn't have been in the deck.

From my suitcase, I dug up silver high-heeled sandals, a matching purse, and a gauzy halter-top dress. In the washroom, I touched up my makeup before I grabbed my key, placed it in my purse, and made my way outside.

The palapa-covered restaurant was nestled between the pool and the ocean. A breeze ruffled the red table cloths. As I stood waiting, the tour group started to arrive.

The maître d' smiled a welcome. "*Buenas noches,* Señorita."

"*Buenas noches.* I have a reservation for Sturm."

"For nine people?"

"Six."

"I have set up a large table over there." He gestured over to the part of the restaurant overlooking the ocean.

"*Gracias.* I appreciate it." I waved to the group to come along.

Fern, Ingrid and I sat at one end. George tried to sit on the other side of Fern but Bryan took the chair before he had a chance. Poor Bryan. Even before our drink order arrived, George pushed up closer and started a monologue. "Nikons are the best, Bryan." George had his camera out of the case and was pointing to the back. "If I hold the button long enough here, I can get the perfect night shot. Of course, it all depends on how long I time it."

Bryan nodded distractedly, as if looking for an escape. The waiter carried our drinks over, ceremoniously setting my order of a strawberry daiquiri alongside Fern's, the drinks tarted up with flowers and fruit.

I waited until the table was served before I stood up to propose a toast. "*A muchos amores y a muchos pesos*!" I winked. "Love and money."

The group clicked their glasses.

"Cool!" George boomed. "I'd like a little of both."

Dan chuckled. "There's plenty of señoritas here, buddy. You go and git 'em."

George glanced in my direction before he guzzled his beer.

I focused in on Fern. "So tell me, girlfriend, why is it that you're not a travel agent?"

Fern turned to Ingrid with a grimace. "You want to tell her, Ingrid?"

Ingrid snickered.

Fern shot her a look. "I worked for Ingrid in her London office."

"And?"

Suddenly, Ingrid's eyes riveted on the entrance of the restaurant. "Holy shit!"

Fern and I stared at a tall dark-haired man walking to the maître d's stand.

"Delectable," Fern whispered.

"Sinful," Ingrid ran her tongue over her lips.

"Like chocolate." My eyes ran down his body.

Ingrid nudged me. "Do you think he's staying here?"

"No." I took a last sip of my daiquiri.

"You know him?" Fern asked curiously.

Ingrid sat up straighter and craned her neck. "Adie! Look, he's waving at us!"

My eyes shot to the man in white. He stared back. A lock of his hair fell on his forehead as the wind picked up. His full lips curved into a subtle smile.

I motioned the waiter for my check. Signing it, I took my leave of the group. "People?"

Eyes looked up at me.

"Sorry to interrupt. There is snorkelling tomorrow morning. Those interested should meet me on the beach at ten. Enjoy your dinner and have a fantastic evening!"

I turned on my heel and headed over to the man at the doorway. Santiago Francisco Bolivar Alvarez—also known as Diego to his friends.

* * *

When I got close, I felt suddenly shy.

"Adelinita." His eyes sparkled, as they fell from my face slowly dropping down to my dress, lingering at the scooped neckline. "Lovely, as always." He lifted my hand and brushed his lips on my wrist.

Not wanting an audience, I pulled him towards the double patio doors. "Let's go, Diego." Amused, he let himself be manoeuvred into the lobby and then stopped.

"What?"

"You seem in quite a hurry, Adelinita."

"I just need to get away from my tour group."

"They're that bad?"

"Some of them." I glanced back through the glass doors. "Where are we going?"

"El Pescado. Have you ever been there?" Diego steered me out of the hotel with his hand on the small of my back. "It's close, a block from here."

"Yes, I know." I thought back to a warm sultry night with another man.

Diego turned to me. "Does that mean you'd rather not go?"

"No, not at all. It's a nice place. Do they still have a band?"

"Yes. Did you like the music?"

"Um-mm. Nouveau flaminco." Moorish rhythms that had transported me to the desert—the heat of the man hotter than any desert breeze.

"That band has moved on to Cancun." Diego flashed a white smile. "But this one has the mood of South America."

"Oh?"

"We could dance." Diego took my hand as we headed along the broad sidewalk on the main street. The rush of the ocean soothed my senses as I breathed in the salt air. Couples strolled past us on the promenade along the busy Rafael Melgar.

"I'm so sorry, Adelina. I should have kept my driver waiting, but I thought he needed a night off and the restaurant isn't far." He glanced down at my sandals. "However, I didn't count on your shoes."

"Don't worry. I can do almost anything with heels."

Diego grinned. "My imagination runs wild, *mi amor*." His eyes swept down my legs. "You look beautiful in them." He stopped and pulled me close. "I missed you, Adelinita." Diego's lips brushed lightly against mine. Every nerve ending I had charged at his touch. Releasing me, he said, his voice husky, "Are you alone on this trip?"

It took an effort to concentrate on his question. "If you call being with a tour group alone, yes."

"Does Wolf know you're here?"

"No, Diego." I turned my head away, upset by his question. "But let's not talk about him, okay?"

Diego smiled. "No need to say more." His eyes settled on a white stucco building. On a wooden sign, a large fish had been painted with the name, *El Pescado* in flowing red and blue lettering. "There it is, Adelina."

Diego held the door open and I entered a dim room lit with candles. Under a thatched palm roof, the restaurant was perched high, overlooking the Caribbean.

"*Buenas noches,* Señor Alvarez," the maître d' said. "*Buenas noches,* Señorita.*" Leading us to the table, he said something in Spanish that I didn't quite pick up.

Soft strains of a tango filled the air as we were seated at a table with a magnificent view of the sea. The moist warm sea breeze tousled my hair as Diego pulled out the chair for me.

"The margaritas are exceptional here," Diego said, as the waiter stood by waiting for our order. I nodded and Diego ordered. "Two margaritas, no salt for the Señorita."

"*Si,* Señor Alvarez," the server said, inclining his head before retreating to the bar.

"You remembered."

Diego nodded. "I remember a great deal about you, Adelinita." He straightened himself up in the wicker chair. "I'm having a party at my beach house on Tuesday. Will you come?"

"When?"

"Around one."

Shopping in the town was the only thing scheduled for my tour group on that day. "Sounds like fun, but I have a little problem—maybe two."

Diego took my hand, his eyes gleaming green in the candlelight. "Let me solve them for you, *mi amor*."

"Would it be all right if I bring two people from my tour group with me? They want to speak with you."

"Why?"

"Well, George has money to blow. He wants to make some investments and Ingrid, she…" My voice trailed off as the waiter arrived with the margaritas. I picked up my glass as Diego clicked mine. "*Salud!*"

"*Salud!*" His hazel eyes shifted to the color of brandy. "You were speaking about this Ingrid. Who is she?"

"She owns several travel agencies. Her interest is in Mayan antiquities."

"Ah-h… You mentioned this on the phone."

"There is a problem with that?"

"Yes and no."

"How so?"

"I could speak to her, but Adelina, it would have to be kept strictly confidential. Perhaps, if you brought her to me at the beach house, I could see what she's interested in exactly." Diego stroked my hand gently. "Don't talk about this to anyone, *cariño*." He glanced around to see if we were being overheard and seeing no one near, he continued in a low voice, "Can she keep her mouth shut?"

"Is there something illegal about this?"

"There's nothing to worry about as long as she's discreet."

I was beginning to kick myself for letting Ingrid drag me into this.

When the waiter appeared to take our order, we both settled on lobster.

After we were left alone, Diego leaned in. "There is something else I needed to talk to you about." He downed his margarita and set the glass on the table. "You know Carmelita has modeled through the years?"

I nodded.

"Well, she's expanded into designing. There'll be a fashion show tomorrow night. Would you be able to see it?"

"Yes, of course. Where?"

"At the Hotel Maria. It's a dinner-fashion show." He reached into his wallet, pulling out a book of tickets. "Take these. You can give them out to your tour group, if you want." He frowned. "I'm worried about her."

A waiter arriving with a bottle of wine put a halt to our conversation. He opened the wine and poured a trace into Diego's wine goblet. Diego drank some water and then picked up his glass. Swishing the wine, he eyed the color before sipping the berry-tinged liquid. When he nodded his approval, our glasses were filled. Another waiter set down our entrées before he retreated discreetly.

When the first server joined him, I asked, "Why, Diego? You don't want her designing or is it the modeling?"

"It's not that." He stroked my hand absently, staring up at the ceiling fan a moment before he continued. "You know she's had her problems with her husband." He gritted his teeth. "Fede is a swine. If she didn't love him so much, I would make sure he was…"

"No, Diego. Violence is not the answer."

"I forget how forgiving you are, *mi amor*." He sighed. "But Carmelita is my sister and needs guidance in the right direction and as her older brother…" A waiter refilled our water glasses and we waited until he left. "…in the absence of our father, the responsibility becomes mine."

I nodded, watching him silently while he sipped his wine.

Lowering his gaze to my cleavage, Diego flashed a sudden smile. "I'm being too serious, aren't I? Did I tell you it was a beach party? You'll look sensational in a bikini."

"Pale and sickly."

"Not you, Adelina. You'll have a golden tan by Tuesday."

I smiled. "You've always been my biggest fan. Don't I do anything you don't like?"

"Just one thing. But I'm a patient man, *mi amor*." He grinned. "But when it comes to you," his fingers brushed a strand of hair away from my face, "I can wait for your love because I know it will be sweeter than honey."

32

I felt a rush of fire flood my body but I ignored it. I changed the subject. "What is it that worries you about your sister?"

Taking a bite of lobster, he glanced at the wine. "First, let's talk about the wine, Adelina. Do you like it?"

I swirled the dark red wine and then took a sip. "Velvety."

He smiled and said, "You have an excellent palate. Let this be a challenge for you. Tell me what you taste?"

"Fruit…raspberry?"

Diego nodded. "Anything more?"

I sipped some more wine. "There's a hint of spice."

Diego smiled slyly. "Correct…black pepper. And the finish?"

"It's a bit bitter, but pleasant," I said, puzzled. "I know this flavor but…" I looked up at the night sky and closed my eyes, focusing on the delectable taste.

"I'm so envious. You have that rare ability to discern the bouquet of the wine." He sat back and stared at me. "A woman with this ability must bring an interesting aspect into lovemaking."

I frowned.

Diego laughed. "Don't be so serious. It's all good."

"Ah-hh! That was my clue, wasn't it? Chocolate…dark chocolate." I glanced at the bottle. "That's so unusual."

"Almaviva 97. Chilean."

Diego was amazing—finding a wine with a chocolate finish. I took another sip before I took note of Diego's furrowed brow. He had gone quiet. "Diego, tell me what's bothering you."

"Well," he said, pulling out a cigarillo and lighting it. "Someone has been sabotaging Carmelita's business." He drew in smoke before he released it into the night air. "Something came to her in the mail."

"What?"

"A dead rat with one of her brochures. Carmelita's head on the brochure was cut off."

I dropped my fork and stared at Diego. "Couldn't the police do something? Your cousin, the commander?"

"Um-mm. I called Hernan, but he said Carmelita made the unfortunate mistake of tossing everything in the garbage." He sighed. "It was all taken out by the maid."

"Oh."

Diego shrugged. "So, what could they do?" He glanced at me. "The cigarillo—it doesn't bother you?"

I shook my head. "Does she have any idea who did this?"

"I was thinking if you perhaps speak with her, she might confide in you."

"And then I would tell you?"

Diego nodded. "I would have Churo guard her, but she insists she can handle it on her own."

"Do think it might be Federico?"

"I don't know what the idiot would gain. Perhaps he wants Carmelita to quit modeling so that he can keep her at home. He'd prefer her waiting on him with a glass of brandy in one hand and his slippers in the other." Diego glanced at me. "She'll be in suite 101-102 at the Hotel Maria before the dinner show. She's getting everything ready. I'll call her and tell her to meet you at the bar at six. Her show doesn't start until seven-thirty. Could you see her then?"

I patted his hand. "Don't worry, Diego. I'll talk to her. And thanks for the tickets. I'm not sure if some of the men in my tour group would be interested in the fashion show but I'm sure they would be happy to have dinner."

Diego smiled. "Remember our breakfast together there? To have a woman like you, feeding me. I felt like a king."

"And you were, well...my hero."

Diego ran his fingers through my hair and searched my face. "Unfortunately, I wasn't your only hero."

"No," I sat back in my chair, "but you promised not to talk about Wolf."

"Of course. I'm curious as to what happened between you, but I suppose whatever it is, might be good for me."

I frowned, not wanting to think anymore, especially about Wolf. "Diego, you never told me anything about the Mayan frog you gave me."

"The frog is Pre-Colombian. It symbolizes the Mayan rain god, Chac—god of agriculture and fertility."

"And you decided fertility was a good idea for me?"

"I like your features—slanty blue eyes," he focused on my mouth, "and such pouty lips. Imagine what beautiful babies we could make."

34

My jaw dropped. "Babies?"

"After you fall in love with me, of course."

I laughed in relief. "I love you already."

He grinned wickedly. "You never take me seriously, but you will someday. Why don't we dance?" He stood up and took my hand.

It was a tango. Smoothly seductive, it was an intimate dance that stirred the senses. It was no wonder it originated in the bordellos of Buenos Aires. Diego's hand felt warm and strong on my waist as he led me in the intricate movements. Walking steps on a diagonal, left crossing right, and a sudden turn. Diego's compelling brandy eyes met mine. I shuddered as his hand stroked my hip and I urged myself to remember it was only a dance.

"Do you want to see the condo?" Diego whispered into my ear as he led me back to my chair.

I wanted to and yet I didn't. Being with Diego? Was I ready to jump into that powerful current?

"Oh, I'm sorry, *mi amor*. I've forgotten—dessert?" Diego's eyes glinted like sparkling emeralds in the candle light.

He'd be the perfect sweet to end my meal. If my body had to choose, it would definitely say yes. He was better than chocolate or at least on par to those to-die-for chocolate blintzes grandma made. But no, I couldn't get involved. "No, thank you, Diego. And, if you don't mind, I'd rather not see the condo tonight. It's an early morning for me with the tour group."

The waiter came over and said something in Spanish. Diego's gaze swept my face. "Of course, *cariño*. You must be tired. A flight is always exhausting. Why don't I call my driver to pick us up?" Diego picked up my hand and kissed my wrist. My nipples perked under the silk material of my dress.

Diego gazed at me as if he knew how my body had responded. "Regretfully I can't see you tomorrow—a meeting in Cancun that will probably run late." He helped me out of my chair.

"You said your party is Tuesday, but you didn't tell me where."

Diego picked up my hands. "My driver will pick you up at the front of the Hotel Don Juan with your guests at twelve. If you change your mind—you have the condo key?"

I nodded. I wondered if he'd take that as an invitation. By the heavy-lidded look he gave me, I knew I'd have to step carefully or plunge right in.

While Diego phoned for his driver, I leaned over the railing, feeling the salty breeze on my face. Even if this was somewhat of a working trip, it was worth it to be here again. The white-crested surf triggered memories—flashbacks of that night with Wolf. Diego's hand on my arm brought me back.

"Come, *mi amor*. He's waiting." He took my hand and led me to the front door. Passing by an elderly woman selling roses, Diego gave her some money. She smiled her appreciation. Diego said something to her in Spanish and she wrapped the stem in cellophane and tied a ribbon around it. With a flourish, Diego handed the blood red rose to me.

"You are like this rose, my sweet Adelinita—vibrant and strong, yet so soft and fragrant."

I bent my head to the flower and caught a spicy scent. "*Gracias*, Diego. I enjoyed our evening."

"And I am pleased you made time to see me."

The limo was waiting for us in front of the restaurant. A massive man with a square head sat in the front seat, his grim expression scary.

Diego held the door of the white limo open for me and I slid across the seat. "*Hola*, Luis!" I called out.

He bared his teeth, in what I supposed was meant to be a smile. "*Buenas noches,* Señorita Sturm."

"We will return Señorita Sturm to the Hotel Don Juan."

Luis nodded, easing the limo out into the street.

It was a short drive, with the Don Juan quickly coming into view. Diego glanced at me, hesitated a second before he drew me close. His hands dropped to my waist, stroking through the fabric of my dress. A delicious shiver of arousal ran down my body as his lips brought mine to life. Sinking back, I wondered what the rest of him would feel like.

Releasing my shoulders, Diego sighed. "I'll look forward to Tuesday, sweet Adelina. Luis will come by at twelve."

I nodded, picking up my rose and my purse.

Diego got out and strode to the other side. He held the door open for me, helping me out. My dress riding up to my thighs received an appreciative glance from my companion.

"I will count the hours." Diego's lips brushed mine.

From there, I floated into the hotel all the way up to my room, thinking how sexually deprived I'd been for the last few months. No wonder a kiss sent me into such a state. But it wasn't just a kiss—Diego knew exactly what he was doing.

3

Bzzzzzzzz. Make it stop. But no one heard me. The buzzer kept on making its irritating noise next to my ear, until I finally dragged my hand over to the knob and shoved it to its off position. I opened one eye to peek at the time. Just as I had suspected, it was nine.

Gathering up all my resolve, I made my way to the bathroom. Mascara applied, I was almost ready. Quickly, I ran a comb through my hair and fluffed it out. Snorkelling would mess it up anyway.

When the phone trilled I wasn't surprised. After all, the tour group members always needed help with something. I picked up the phone.

"Adie, you're still there. Good, come to my room. We'll have breakfast. I hope you like fruit and eggs. I ordered for you."

"Ingrid? Can't this wait?"

"You need to eat, don't you? I know you. You can't do anything without food in your belly. Anyway, it's on its way. Hurry!"

I pulled on a pair of denim shorts and a top over my red string bikini and stepped into my wedged sandals. My snorkelling gear was already in a gym bag. I picked it up and grabbed my key.

Ingrid's room was close, two rooms down. At her door, a dark bearded man wearing a panama hat stood as if listening, his hand resting on the knob. Who was he? Certainly not room service. Coming closer, I noticed her door was open. The man stepped in.

"Excuse me! Are you here to see Ingrid?"

He swivelled around and stared, my image reflected in his mirrored sunglasses.

"Is Ingrid expecting you?"

He coughed and muttered, "Wrong room." Pushing his sunglasses higher onto the bridge of his nose, he turned away and trekked down the hall.

I watched him round the corner before I knocked lightly on the open door and entered. There was a tray with dirty dishes on the floor but no sign of Ingrid. Maybe she'd gone back to sleep.

A shuffling noise behind me. "*Buenos dias,* Señorita." A waiter pushed a cart filled with covered plates into the room. He smiled, glancing at the tray crowded with plates. "The Señorita likes her food. Last night I brought her up a big order."

Eating, drinking and smoking. That's all I'd seen Ingrid do lately. The divorce must be getting to her.

Ingrid called out from the bedroom, "Adie! That you? Is room service here? Have him bring it to the table, eh? I'll be right out."

I signed the bill for Ingrid and pushed the cart next to the table near the double doors leading out to the balcony as Ingrid came into the room, dressed in loose black capris and a low-cut black camisole. Her thick brown hair was in waves to her shoulders.

"Your door was open, Ingrid."

"Hm-mm?" Ingrid's eyes fixed on the covered plates. She sat down across from me, lifted the metal lid covering her eggs and peeked in before she picked up her cutlery wrapped in a red napkin.

"Why'd you leave the door open?"

She looked at me like I'd lost my marbles. "Duh, room service."

I rolled my eyes. "It's not a good idea to leave your door open."

"You are so paranoid, Adie. We're in Cozumel. They don't have robberies here."

I uncovered my eggs and picked up my fork. "I think you should be more cautious, as a single woman alone."

"Unlike you, eh?" Ingrid snorted. "Bet you weren't by your lonesome last night."

I felt heat flush my cheeks. "Diego and I are friends."

She winked. "Diego, eh? That man is sex-on-legs. Not the friend type, unless, of course, we're talking friends with benefits." Her lips parted and the tip of her tongue curled up. "Mm-mm. Yes, indeed, Adie." She chortled, delighted by her wit.

I grimaced and tapped my spoon impatiently.

Ingrid pursed her lips. "What?"

"Someone came into your room. That's why I said you should make sure it's locked."

"Who?"

"A man with a beard and dark hair."

39

"It must have been a mistake. I don't know anyone with a beard," she said dismissively, in between mouthfuls. "I want to talk to you about the antiquities."

I sipped my orange juice and waited.

"Have you spoken to your friend?"

"It's all arranged. He'll send a car to the hotel to pick us up at one o'clock on Tuesday. You'll be my guest at his beach party. He said he'd meet with you privately."

Ingrid pushed her plate away and picked up her juice. "So tell me about your friend. Who is he?"

"You saw him last night."

Her mouth dropped open. "Diego?"

I nodded.

"I can't believe it, Adie. I was just joking before. I had no idea you had what it takes to take care of that sexy man."

I gritted my teeth. "He seems to think so."

Ingrid stopped chewing. "Hm-mm, he does, doesn't he? And he's rich too, eh?"

"Very." I finished the eggs and wiped my lips. "I have to go." I got up from my chair.

"Wait—what's his last name?"

"Bolivar Alvarez."

"Suits him—studly." Ingrid sucked on a strawberry. "I have pictures of the pieces I'm interested in. I hope he can locate them." She glanced up, as I gathered up my bag. "Where're you going?"

"The beach. The tour group's gathering for snorkeling."

I left her sitting there buttering a piece of toast. Taking the stairs two at a time, I hurried to the lobby. A large white board with Fleischer Travel, Days of the Dead Tour, stood near the front desk. I picked up a black marker and printed in Free! Dinner-Fashion Show at 7 pm./Maria Hotel. Tickets at the door, before I made my way down the corridor to the beach exit.

* * *

The ocean was a bright turquoise with dark patches where the reef appeared close to the surface. Crystal white sand stretched out to the water's edge. Large jagged rocks cut up the shoreline near the wharf where the snorkeling boat was moored.

I hadn't booked a boat. No need for that when there was plenty of coral reef twenty meters out. My sandals sank into the hot sand as I made my way to the sports rental booth. Two dark-haired guys stood around looking bored. They perked up when they saw me.

"*Hola,* Señorita! You renting today?"

"*Hola.* I'm Adie Sturm, Fleischer Travel." I glanced at my underwater watch. "A few people from my tour group should be arriving shortly."

"Good morning!" Dan boomed from behind. "I'm snorkeling, but Lola decided she wanted to tan." He motioned to the white chaise lounge chairs by the shore where Lola was stretched out. "She'll save you a chair."

I turned to the guys in the rental booth. "I'll sign for anyone from the Fleischer Travel tour group. It's been arranged with your manager."

"*Si,* no problem," the taller guy said.

I felt a tap on my shoulder and I turned to see George. "Adie, I decided to try it," he said. He was wearing a baggy, orange bathing suit that hung low under his belly.

I looked around for Jim and Tom, but they weren't anywhere in sight. Probably sleeping it off from their night at Carlos'n Charlies. That's what singles usually did. I should know.

Fern said she wanted to try snorkeling. Too bad she'd changed her mind. Something had gone down with her and Ingrid and it couldn't have been good. I had to wonder why she booked with Fleischer Travel, knowing Ingrid owned it.

"Okay," I said to the dive guys, "set these two up. They'll need vests." Then I turned to George and Dan. "Meet me over there." I motioned to the chair where Lola was stretched out. At the line of chairs, I placed my bag on an empty lounger and kicked off my sandals. There were only a few people out on the beach.

"Hey, Lola."

"Adie, hi." Lola looked half asleep. "Nice day, eh?" She stretched her arms over her head. I glanced up at the clear blue sky. No clouds and the sun shone brightly. Perfect for snorkeling. "Sure is. You didn't want to try snorkeling?"

"Maybe sometime, but for now I just want to relax and watch the waves. I'll be here, so don't worry about your bag."

I unzipped my shorts, took them off, and laid them on the chair. "Thanks, Lola. I was just about to ask you." I tossed my tank top. "Enjoy the sun!" Carrying my fins and mask to the water, I met George and Dan.

I told them how to keep the mask watertight and what to do if it filled with water. "Don't swim past the reef, guys. The current's stronger there and you can get sucked out to sea."

It was like a salty bathtub. I sank in and swam ahead, checking back every once in a while to see if Dan and George were following.

Yellow-striped sergeant majors swam by my face, curiously staring with their yellow eyes. Purple fan coral poked out of the sand, swaying gently with the current outcropping ten meters ahead. A silver flash above me appeared like magic. A four-foot needlefish with a sharp tapered snout floated just below the surface of the water. I pointed it out for the benefit of my companions. They swam up to see. Whether they caught a glimpse of it, I wasn't sure, because when I looked back, it was gone. But a moment later, two more appeared on the surface. George and Dan got closer. Dan pulled out an underwater camera and started to snap some shots.

The coral was an undersea garden, a mixture of yellow pillar, brown brain, and staghorn coral. As I swam around, I thought about the people I knew here in Cozumel—people I hadn't seen for a while. It would be a kick to get together with Carmelita, even if what brought us together was upsetting. I watched the purple fan coral sway, showing off its exotic beauty. She'd be like that coral, lovely but fragile. I didn't know her very well but she was someone I genuinely liked. She was a rebel, too, and I could see why Diego would have trouble keeping her out of trouble.

I dove around some brown fire coral and thought of my nemesis, that man-eater, Daniella. Would I see her again? Fire coral stings on contact just like that woman. Daniella lured men in. If only I could attach an anchor around her leg and toss her into the deepest part of the ocean.

A pair of dark-blue angelfish, their scales gilded with gold, reminded me of the snorkeling I'd done with Wolf the last time I was here in Cozumel. He'd quipped about queen angels having responsibility and I'd told him, I'd be happy without it. Ironically, I was back here with more responsibility than ever—the murderer could be in my tour group and I had to find him.

We swam around the reef sighting more and more fish. After we checked out another site in deeper water, I began to feel a chill. The current was strong along the reef and I was tiring quickly. When I waved for the guys to head back to shore, they seemed ready to return.

The salt has a stinging sensation when it starts to dry on the skin. A beach shower would get rid of it fast enough, but first I had to endure a torturous stream of cold water. Dan walked over to the beach bar and called out for two Coronas while I headed over to the lounge chair that Lola had saved for me.

Oblivious to my arrival, Lola was sleeping, a hat slanting over her eyes. When Dan came over, he placed Lola's beer on the plastic table and slumped down on the chair, sipping his beer.

I placed my equipment into my bag and took out my makeup kit and headed back to the washroom to fix myself up. My hair was a salty mess, but I managed to run a comb through it and after some quick touch ups was ready to face the world.

The sun overhead was strong and bright. Waves of heat rose from the powdery white sand. George was standing beside my lounge chair looking a bit lost, but I wasn't about to encourage him. That wasn't part of the job description.

"Adie, what should I try, to drink, I mean?"

"Well, tequila is big in Mexico. Ask for a margarita at the bar."

"Isn't that kind of a girlie drink?"

I tried to be understanding. "Sol, then. That's beer."

He nodded and ambled away.

At last, I was alone or as alone as anyone can be on a busy beach. I sat down, stretching out my legs, relaxing in the heat of the midday sun. My conversation with George must have woken Lola. She shifted in her chair and opened her eyes, gazing out at the sea. "It's so beautiful, isn't it, Adie?"

I nodded, leaning back in my chair, watching the waves gently roll in. The water sparkled a brilliant azure. A boat was anchored on the other side of the reef.

Lola glanced at me. "You look tired from that snorkeling."

"I probably shouldn't have gone anywhere last night."

"You'd have to be crazy not to go out with Mr. Gorgeous." She sighed, brushing her hair off her neck. "You are so lucky, girlfriend. If it was me, I'd have stayed up all night with him and slept in this morning." She waved her hand. "These guys could have gone snorkeling on their own and you could have…" She giggled. "That's what I would have done if I were you, Adie."

I laughed seeing her spacy expression.

"Have a beer, Lola." Dan handed her a Corona. "Forget about those model types. They're too hung up on themselves, anyway. Besides, you've got yourself a real man."

Lola sipped the icy brew, and then suddenly let her hand drop, spilling out beer as she sputtered and pointed. "Adie, look!"

My eyes followed her finger to the water's edge. Whoa! What was this? A tall tanned man rose like Neptune from the sea. His shoulders were wide, his chest muscles clearly defined, and his hips narrow. Pushing his mask back, he bent down to pull off his fins and made his way out of the water to the beach. Tugging off his mask, he ran his fingers through his wet hair, gazing in our direction.

Lola stammered. "Adie, he's…" her eyes fixed on the sea god, "eye candy!" She jumped up to get a better look.

The sea god's eyes met mine.

"We should go, Lola. I'm getting burned out here." Dan shifted in his chair.

Lola stared. "Adie, have you ever seen anything that sexy?"

Getting up, Dan noticed where Lola's attention was fixated. "Lola! Snap out of it." He picked up the beach bag and glowered at her. "First the Calvin Klein guy and now this Nike model? These guys don't go for old broads like you. Can't you see that?" He patted his belly. "This is comfortable fat. You've got some too, you know. Maybe not as much as me but…"

"Yeah, sure." Lola's eyes followed the sea god as he headed to the beach shower. This was too much. I felt a pain in the pit of my stomach. I turned away and lay flat on my stomach, closing my eyes, trying to wipe away his image from my memory.

I heard them shuffle around. "See you later, Adie. Come on, Lola."

"Don't forget the dinner at the Maria," I called over my shoulder.

The breeze felt warm on my back. I reached around until I found my open bag on the sand beside my chair and felt inside the pocket for my sunscreen. I grabbed it and placed it on my chair. I needed sunscreen but I just wanted to lie there, maybe curl up into a little ball and disappear. A crab could do that. If this chair were a shell, nobody would be able to see me and I'd be safe.

"Hey Adie, this margarita is good stuff." George approached my chair. "Adie?"

I ignored him.

A moment later I felt his weight on my chair. I kept my eyes shut. Maybe he'd go away. Suddenly, hands slippery with sunscreen touched my skin. I was ready to smack the man, but he surprised me, skillfully applying lotion on my neck and shoulders and rhythmically stroking it down my back. The sensation of the massage overwhelmed me. I sighed. The tips of his fingers touched my bikini bottom. I was about to protest when he ran his fingers over the exposed skin on the curve of my butt. Here he paused before he trailed his hands down to my thighs. I tingled all over. He could do this forever as far as I was concerned—it felt so good. But no, I had to discourage him.

"Thanks, George. That's good. You can stop now."

I heard him place the sunscreen back in my bag but he didn't get up. Soft lips brushed my neck and his tongue feathered down to my shoulder. Oh-hh! I was *so* aroused. How could this be? George was a total turnoff. I rolled around. Intense blue eyes met mine.

"Wolf!"

"I thought you needed a reminder. The big guy over there is George." His eyes shot over to the bulky man swishing his toes in the water a few feet away. "At least, I think he is." He glanced down at me. "When did you get here, Adie?" Wolf asked softly.

I focused on the sensual curve of his lips. "Yesterday."

He stroked my cheek slowly. "Why didn't you let me know you were coming?"

I shook my head—I had phoned. I sat up quickly, accidentally brushing my hand against his waist. His skin felt velvety smooth, his body firm and hard.

Wolf ran his hand down the thin strap of my string bikini, fingertips lingering on my skin. "Red looks good on you." He kept one hand on my shoulder while the other tilted my chin up. "Talk to me, Adie."

Nervously, I looked away. Over his shoulder, I saw George.

"You okay, Adie? Can I get you something?"

"No, thanks." I glanced at Wolf, who looked amused.

Wolf stood. "I'm a friend of Adie's," he said, extending his hand. "Wolf Du Lac."

"Oh," the big man said, uncomfortably. "George Vandomheit, INP Software." Reluctantly, he shook Wolf's hand.

Wolf motioned for a waiter. A smiling young man trotted up, tray in hand. "*Si,* Señor."

"Dos Equis and a strawberry daiquiri, *por favor.*"

"*Si,* Señor." The waiter looked expectantly at George, who stood there uncertainly, scratching his head.

"And for you, Señor?"

When George shook his head, the waiter left. Wolf bent down and tugged out a pair of dark sunglasses from his snorkeling bag and put them on before he sat down beside me, surveying George, his lips curling slightly upwards at the corners.

"What's that thing you just ordered?" George asked Wolf, curiously.

"Dos Equis or the daiquiri?"

"Er, uh, both."

Embarrassed for George, I said, "Dos Equis is a Mexican beer and a daiquiri is a cocktail."

George glowered. "I thought you didn't want anything."

I shrugged. Who was I to stop a man who catered to my needs?

"I guess the daiquiri is a girlie drink, eh?"

I glanced at George, wondering why I had the bad luck to be stuck with him. "For sure, but some really macho men have been known to drink pitchers of them."

Wolf sat down on my chair, leaning against me, his mouth twitching in amusement.

George watched the waiter returning from the bar with our tray. Wolf had remembered my favorite drink and I couldn't help but be pleased. If a drink could be beautiful, this one sure was—a bubble shaped glass filled with a frosty strawberry concoction adorned with a bright orange hibiscus flower.

After the waiter left, George glared in my direction. "Were you making fun of me, Adie?"

I knew I'd better smooth his feathers. "No, of course not, George. Just kidding." In an effort to lighten up George's sour mood, I smiled and said, "Hey, I've got a joke. Listen to this, guys: A macho dude married a good looking babe. When they came home from the honeymoon he laid down the law. "I'll be hunting, fishing, drinking, and playing cards whenever I want," he said. "And I'll be with my buddies if and when I want. You'll have dinner on the table every night when I come home. You got that? His wife said, "Sure. No problem. I've got a rule for you too. There'll be sex every night at eight—whether you're home or not. You got that?"

Wolf grinned. "My kind of woman."

George's face showed confusion. "Will I be seeing you tonight, Adie?"

"There's a free dinner and fashion show at the Hotel Maria. If you're interested, come at seven."

"You'll be there?"

I nodded.

"Guess I'll go," George said reluctantly. He shifted his weight and glanced at my breasts.

In an effort to get rid of him and his unwanted attention, I said, "George, the sun is awfully strong in the tropics." I studied his belly. "You're getting red."

"You too, Adie," he said, his eyes still focused on my body, "maybe we should both go back to the hotel."

Wolf followed his gaze. "My apologies, Adie. I neglected some parts of you." He picked up his bag and mine with one hand. "Why don't we go inside?"

I grabbed my tank top and pulled it over my head. "Okay," I said, tugging on my shorts before I slipped into my flip-flops.

"Nice meeting you, George. See you later," Wolf said as we walked off.

"Yeah," George growled, watching us.

On entering the sliding doors, I swung around to see if George had followed us. Through the glass, I saw him ambling up, a towel rolled up under his arm. He was almost at the doors.

I didn't want to be spending any time with him but, Wolf was not an option. "I don't want to talk to you."

He smiled. "No? I'm glad. There are so many other things we could do."

I felt myself flush.

"We can't talk here, Adie, anyway. You'll feel better with a shower and some lunch."

True. Food does wonders for me but not after what he'd pulled. He must think I'm stupid. I brought my hand to my neck. The sea salt irritated my skin. And my hair? I fingered a strand. I must look like a sea witch having a bad hair day. Glancing towards the glass doors, I saw George pushing them open. Forgetting everything, I squealed, "Let's go. Upstairs, quick!"

Wolf grinned. "That's my woman."

"Come on!" I climbed the stairs two at a time. When we got to my door, I searched for my key, fumbling around nervously. George could appear any minute. If he knew where my room was, he'd start bothering me here. The situation could unbearable. Where the heck was it? Think, think, I kept telling myself. He could be here any second. In my side pocket, I felt a hard piece of plastic. I grabbed it, stuck it in the key slot and pushed the door open, stepping inside. "Don't just stand there," I said in a panic, "get in here!"

A bemused expression on his face, Wolf followed me in, swinging the door shut behind him. He dropped his snorkeling bag and reached out for me.

"Don't touch me."

"I'm sorry, princess. I didn't realize it hurt already."

"Hurt! What are you talking about?"

Wolf glanced at my shoulders and cleavage. "Aloe vera should help your burn."

"I'm not burned. I always look a bit red at first. Besides, I didn't bring any."

Wolf smiled. "You're in luck then. I have some in my bag. Take a shower, Adie. I'll take one after."

"Really? I didn't think I gave you permission."

He grinned. "You wouldn't want me to take you out looking like this, would you?"

I glanced up at him. Bits of sand clung to his wet blond hair and salt had dried on his tanned skin. His eyes were as clear and blue as a deep, fresh-water stream. I ran the tip of my tongue along my lip. He looked delectable. I realized then that a cold shower might be just what I needed.

As I gathered a change of clothes and made my way to the bathroom, Wolf opened the patio door. Soft Latin music drifted up from the bar below. A woman sang something about *pesos* and *queso*. Money and cheese? But whatever she was all excited about, it sounded smoothly sexy.

Wolf stood looking out at the ocean, his hands resting on the balcony railing. Although he was lean, his shoulders were wide and his back was muscular. That pulsing was starting—like a motor that had revved up and was ready to roar down the highway. The longer I stared it occurred to me that I should stay as far away from him as possible. My body wasn't to be trusted.

I clicked the bathroom door shut, stripped off my soggy things, and let them drop to the floor. I adjusted the water and stepped into the warm spray. Memories flooded back. He was so different from other men—so impulsive and exciting. He was under my skin.

As I worked shower gel over my body, I thought of how his hands had touched me—how his tongue had sent me into an indescribable state of ecstasy. But I couldn't just forgive and forget, could I?

The salt washed off and my hair began to feel soft and clean. When I dried myself it somehow seemed right to be putting on a dress.

He was sitting out on the balcony when I came out. My clingy blue dress had a v-neckline that showed cleavage. My sandals gave me those extra few inches that I needed when I was with a tall man like Wolf. I must be a glutton for punishment. Silently, I watched him.

At that moment he swiveled around. "Ah-hh, Adie!" He stood up, his eyes taking me in. "Did I ever tell you how sexy you are?"

I could feel my cheeks flush. Quickly, I said, "You can take a shower now."

"Come here, Adie."

I'm an independent type of woman, but when he had that tone… I stepped up to him, more out of curiosity than obedience.

From the table he picked up a small bottle and poured some green liquid into his hand. "This is the best aloe vera you'll ever

find. With a little of this, your skin should feel fine by tonight."
Wolf smiled slowly. "We don't want you in pain, later, do we?"
He pushed one of my straps down and gently spread the aloe vera
lotion on my shoulders and down to the rise of my breasts. It felt
cool and pleasant. His fingers stroked my skin lightly before he
returned my strap to its original position, and then he slipped my
other strap down and did the same.

"How's that?" He placed the bottle back on the table.

The aloe vera chilled my skin, pleasantly so. I sighed.

"That good? You're getting easier to please." His voice held a
deep, velvety timbre and when his mouth came down on mine, his
kiss jolted my body; the burning that started at my lips flashed like
electricity, hotly igniting every nerve ending I had. He was a
magnet and I was like a metal that couldn't resist. My mouth
parted to taste him again. Slowly, his tongue slid over the inside of
my lips, spreading liquid heat. Unexpectedly, he stopped. With one
swift motion, he picked me up and carried me over to the bed
where I was gently placed, my head resting on the pillow.

I closed my eyes, waiting for him to join me. Hot lips lightly
brushed my throat. His silken tongue feathered down to the hollow
of my neck where he paused there to kiss the pulsing spot. My
heart raced with his touch. When his kisses moved to that fleshy
sensitive area where my arm meets my chest, I moaned softly.

His turn. I wanted to give him something back. Nuzzling his
neck and ear, I blew in and licked the ridges. A delicious salty
flavor. Again. He groaned softly.

I'd pressed his button. Wolf pushed me down. His hand
slipped under the halter. He explored over the delicate fabric of my
bra, sliding over the swells of my breasts. His fingertips pushed
under the lacy material and made contact with my skin.

"Soft, beautiful…"

I shuddered. Tingles worked their way down my body, and my
sunburn was forgotten.

He undid the straps fastened at my neck, sliding my dress
down, all the while teasing my neck with his tongue. Unfastening
my bra was a brief stop before a train of kisses journeyed to the
valley between my breasts. When he pushed the bra away, he
lightly teased and stroked until my nipples hardened into taut buds.
As he leaned on his elbows, his dark blue eyes met mine. My

fingers dug into his firm biceps and held him tight, wanting him never to stop.

"Princess, I missed you," he whispered, his voice husky. Letting go, he tugged off his T-shirt. Firm, muscular shoulders narrowing to a slim waist. Every shadow of his chest was familiar to me—the sea god, in all his glory. But when he threw his shirt on the floor, it was like a wave splashing right over me. A reality check. Everything I didn't want to remember bombarded my brain. Those phone calls and those women. I forced myself to douse the fire in my body. Abruptly, I shoved him away and covered myself.

"Adie?" he said, confusion written on his face. His hand stroked my cheek. "What is it? Are you all right?"

"This shouldn't have happened...I....I can't..." I broke off, flustered by my conflicting emotions.

"Tell me what's wrong."

"No." I stood up, gripping my dress tightly to me. "Not now."

Wolf stared at me a moment as though looking for answers and not seeing what he wanted. He got up. "Okay—I'll take a shower and then we'll talk."

I watched him close the bathroom door behind him before I fit my bra over my breasts and did it up. Methodically, I tied up the halter closing of my dress and straightened my skirt before I picked up the novel from the bedside table.

Out on the balcony, I took the rattan chair, and leaning back, tried to get comfortable. I didn't know why I'd given in. Obviously, I was losing it. I rubbed my temples, thinking what a mass of jelly I was when it came to Wolf Du Lac. And he didn't seem to know why I was so angry. It was almost as if he were innocent.

I started reading distractedly, hardly understanding the words. If I'd been in the mood, the brooding hero in my book would have been fascinating—almost as compelling as the naked man in my bathroom. A vision of Wolf clad in a towel appeared in my mind.

When I heard the creak of the bathroom door, my eyes riveted on Wolf entering the room, a towel slung low on his waist. He ignored me. Through the glass, I watched him walk over to his bag and take out his clothes. Straightening up, he showed off his perfect six-pack before he slowly undid his towel.

My eyes widened. The male strippers at the Flying Horse hadn't mastered a routine like this. The towel took on a life of its own, seductively covering and uncovering his package and butt, until he moved out of sight. Was he deliberately tantalizing me? I turned away and glanced at the pool bar where I could see a few people having some liquid lunch.

Soap and balmy ocean breeze. Soft lips nuzzled my neck. I felt my book slip through my fingers.

"I'm ready, Adie." Wolf picked up my book and set it on the table.

Ready? I blanked out.

"Let's go."

Go where?

My Hormone Voice got excited. To bed of course—he wants you now. He's being macho. The cave man thing. My body charged up.

But My Logical Voice was angry. Get a grip, Adie. You told him no, and he knows he has to explain everything. He's taking you out to eat, you idiot!

My Hormone Voice squealed—Yes! He can be the dessert—chocolate layer cake, substantial and firm but with a bittersweet chocolate icing—layer after layer, after layer.

Wolf took my hand, pulling me up. His black T-shirt contrasted dramatically with his blond hair, which was messed up as if a woman had just had her way with him. He was so hot he sizzled.

"We'll get a taxi," he said.

"You didn't park your Jeep at the hotel?"

"Yeah, but you know what the parking is like. It might not be a good idea for you to be walking, Adie. The sun is a killer right now."

I nodded. I stopped at the closet and grabbed my gym bag.

Wolf raised an eyebrow.

"I thought I'd go to the karate club after lunch."

Wolf frowned, but he took my bag and carried it.

I didn't protest when he held my hand going down the stairs. It felt good, somehow. I paused to peek over the railing. The coast was clear—no George.

As we reached the lobby, a throaty voice called out, "Adie!"

It was Fern, in beach attire, her sun-kissed dusky skin glowing. Dark eyes sparkling, her tongue poked out, tracing her lower lip. "You must be on your way to lunch, eh?"

Wolf's eyes scanned her voluptuous curves. A skimpy white paraeo covered the bottom of her green print bikini.

"Hey, I'm Fern." She extended her hand to Wolf and smiled.

"Wolf." He shook her hand.

"Will you be coming out to the Hotel Maria with Adie tonight?"

"No, he's busy," I said quickly.

"Not too busy for you, Adie," Wolf said evenly.

"Fashion shows aren't his thing."

Wolf glanced at me appreciatively. "But a beautiful woman is."

"I'll look forward to seeing you again tonight." Fern called out to Bryan standing by the white board, "Can we go now?"

Bryan's head was bent, engrossed in the Mayan sightseeing brochures. He flipped over a brochure. Fern rolled her eyes. Walking over to him, she nudged his arm. Reluctantly, Bryan picked up the brochure and they headed down the corridor to the rooms on the lower level.

* * *

"She a friend?" Wolf asked, as we made our way outside. The heat was rising from the sidewalk in a steamy haze.

"I haven't seen her for years, but we used to be friends in college. They're in my tour group. She likes you."

"Nothing wrong with that," Wolf said causally.

I frowned. "Where are we eating?"

Wolf motioned to a taxi sitting in front of the hotel. When it pulled up to the curb, he opened the door and I slid in the back seat.

"*Hola.*" Wolf said to the driver as we got in. "The Mission, *por favor.*" Wolf closed the cab door.

We pulled into the main street and eased into the traffic. I glanced at Wolf just as he turned to me.

His brow was furrowed. "Tell me about the dinner tonight."

"It's a dinner-fashion show. You remember Carmelita, Diego's sister?"

Wolf nodded.

"She's holding her own fall fashion show, her designs mostly."

Wolf frowned. "You're not meeting Alvarez there, are you? Is that why you didn't want me to go?"

"Diego gave me tickets for the tour group but he can't be there."

"Getting brownie points, is he?"

We were nearing the center of town and I could see the Mission restaurant ahead.

"No, he's worried."

"About what?"

"Carmelita."

Wolf handed the driver a few dollars, then gave me his hand and helped me out. We were at the entrance of the restaurant.

"*Hola, buenos tardes*. A table for two, Señor?"

"*Si.*" Wolf motioned in the direction of the tiny bridge curving to the other side of the restaurant. The maître d' led us to a table. Lush foliage from the plants gave us a secluded area away from the rest of the diners. A waiter brought us menus and glanced at Wolf.

"Dos Equis."

The server nodded and waited for me.

"A piña colada, *por favor*."

The corners of Wolf's mouth turned up. "Bored with the daiquiris, Adie?"

"A change is necessary when the familiar becomes disagreeable," I replied, staring significantly at him.

Wolf propped his elbow on the table and rested his chin on his hand. "Good thing I haven't seen you for months then."

The waiter brought over our drinks, corn chips and salsa—red and green. An orange flower and a slice of pineapple adorned the rim of my goblet, filled with a creamy mixture.

"Have you decided?" the waiter inquired.

"Quesadillas for me." I fingered a corn chip and maneuvering some salsa on top of it.

"Chicken fajita, *por favor*," Wolf said. "Why is Alvarez worried?"

"Carmelita is being threatened."

"Yeah?"

"Really! She got a rat delivered to her in a box. One of her fashion brochures with her picture on it was minus her head."

"What does he want you to do? Round up a psycho?" Wolf scooped up some of the extra spicy green salsa with a corn chip.

"Talk to her. Find out who might be doing it. He thinks Carmelita would open up to me."

"With all the muscle he has, he should be able to track down the nutcase in no time. That's just an excuse, Adie."

"What do you mean?"

"I noticed a red rose in your room—his bait."

"I'm not a fish waiting to be reeled in," I said, my temper flaring.

"Guys like fishing," Wolf said calmly.

"He's not asking a lot from me, Wolf."

"He can't be trusted. You know that. Alvarez always has something up his sleeve."

"You're the last person that should be criticizing him!" I straightened up. "Anyway, I don't see how you can say that. He wanted my help and I like Carmelita. I don't want anything to happen to her."

"All he needs to do is get his men to threaten a few people and he'd have the answer."

"You mean he should get Eduardo to..." I trailed off. I'd never seen Eduardo, but I did know that he got whatever he wanted.

"But, no problem, Adie. I'll help you check this out."

"You really want to come to this fashion show?" I was a little relieved. Carmelita might be in real danger and Wolf was resourceful.

"How's your tour going, by the way?"

"Okay."

"What's with the strange name?"

"The Days of the Dead Tour?"

"Right. Is there a connection?"

I dipped a chip in the salsa. "With Dias de los Muertos? My group is interested in how Cozumel celebrates the three days—the dead infants, adults and Hallowe'en. So the plan is shopping, Mayan food and I'm introducing them to the ruins at Coba with a bit of snorkeling."

"Sounds interesting."

"It has been. You wouldn't believe what happened. With it being Oktoberfest and all, I thought we'd give them a party—free beer and food, but it didn't get a good start."

Wolf took a sip of beer. "Why?"

"The manager at Fleischer's," I ran my finger over my bottom lip, "fell off the table."

"The table?" He grinned. "That's crazy. Were you up there with her?"

"No." I flicked my swivel stick. "Bernie Scharf, you know, the reporter from *Kitchener Today*? He found her."

"He was with you?"

"No, he saw me that night and asked to join us."

"So the woman had a few too many. It happens. It's not your fault, Adie. Everyone gets drunk at Oktoberfest."

"It was worse than that. She died, Wolf."

"Alcohol poisoning?"

"No, I'm not sure what caused it exactly but Ilya is investigating."

"Yea-hh, one of your friends."

"Yes, he is," I said tightly.

"I notice you have very few female friends."

"Unlike you."

Wolf grinned. "I've saved myself for you, Adie."

I scraped some dry skin off my lip.

"Hey," Wolf tore my hand away, "don't ruin those luscious lips. I have plans for them." He sat back in his chair and met my gaze. "Look, Adie," he said, still holding my hand, "this isn't a game. Let the cop solve the murder. Stay out of it. You should know it's dangerous to be involved in a murder investigation."

"He thought I could help. The murderer usually knows the victim and if that's the case, it could be someone I know."

"You want the killer to think you're after him?"

"Everyone at that table that night is on this tour, Wolf."

"Anyone up to anything suspicious?"

"There is something..."

"George."

"Yes, but he's not..." Should I tell him? Diego had said not to talk about it. But Wolf wasn't just anybody. I could count on him to keep it quiet. "I shouldn't say anything." I looked at him from over the rim of my glass.

Wolf considered me thoughtfully. "Alvarez has you involved in something."

"It's Ingrid. She wants me to help her find a Mayan statue."

The waiter appeared with our meals. "Is everything all right, *señor*?"

Wolf nodded, waiting for the man to leave. When he did, he asked, "Who's Ingrid?"

"The owner of Fleischer Travel."

"And you need to help her because?"

"I have a contract with her."

"You're friends?"

"No, I don't like her."

"Then why help her?"

"It's business. If I help her, I get to go to Jamaica."

"Nice." Wolf leaned back and gazed at me. "But?"

"I've been wondering why she wants this Mayan art. And I just found out something else that blew me away."

"What?"

"She's married and has a boyfriend that's been contributing to her finances big-time. You've heard of him."

"Who?"

"Jordan James, the billionaire."

"Advertising tycoon."

"You know anything else about him?"

Wolf shifted and rubbed his chin reflectively. "Collects aboriginal art."

"So Ingrid might have learned about art from him. She's been to art auctions and seems to know what things are worth." I thought back to what Ingrid had said about my frog sculpture.

"What's she like?"

"Ingrid? There's no kind way to describe her. She's a devious and vengeful woman."

"That bad?"

"Um-mm. It doesn't take much to rub her the wrong way. A friend of mine, an older travel agent didn't say hello to her one day. Ingrid transferred him to her London office. He didn't want to move so he had to quit. It wasn't easy for him to find work again."

"And you get along with this woman?"

"Usually. She knows she can't hassle me like she does everyone else."

"She must be intelligent then."

"Ingrid's got money and she doesn't play by the rules. You'll see her tonight. She can charm a snake when she sets her mind to it."

"Good looking?"

"Once upon a time. With all the smoking, drinking, and overeating, she doesn't look as good now. If I were her personal trainer I'd change her diet and put her on some weight machines. But I'm not doing her any favors. Sadly, everyone that comes in contact with her hates her, except for those she hand-selected, employees from her church. They're even tired of her manipulating ways."

"A religious woman?" Wolf said, amused.

"Oh, yes, or claims to be. Her family and employees put up with her preaching, but I doubt if she ever practices anything her church has ever told her. Her daughter can't handle living with her." I remembered that Maureen had run away from home a few times. "And her husband..."

"She's married?"

"Not for much longer. The guy's divorcing her. Everyone's always felt sorry for the poor guy."

"How long were they married?"

"About twenty years."

"Long time," Wolf expressed slowly.

I finished my quesadilla. Wolf had been married for two years. Had it been a bad two years? "Morris took her abuse for years and then one day he decided to call it quits."

"And the reason was?" Wolf downed his beer before he ate the last bit of his fajita.

I shrugged.

Wolf gazed at me. "What time is dinner?"

"Around seven. Are you really coming?"

"Definitely." His deep blue eyes met mine. "You want to talk now?"

I frowned. My stomach would get all upset and besides, Wolf would only think I'm jealous and possessive. I tapped my fingers on the table in frustration. I didn't know what to do about him. But I'm a fighter and...I glanced at my watch. "I've got to go." I stood up. "I need to get a taxi."

Wolf got up. "I'll get one and drop you off at the dojo. I need to see someone anyway." He motioned for the bill.

We headed back out to the front of the restaurant where there was a taxi waiting. He opened the door. I slid down and across the seat to the window.

"*Hola.* Do you know where the Maple Leaf Martial Arts Academy is?" I asked the driver.

"*Si,* Señorita." He eased the cab out into the street and headed away from the waterfront.

"I've thought of you often." Wolf gazed into my eyes. "Your eyes are still turquoise. You know, a workout may do you some good. Get rid of that pent-up anger."

"Hm-ff!" I sniffed. Every time I was upset with him he said my eyes turned turquoise. I don't know if that's true, but I knew my anger was justified. He deserved all the resentment I could shovel at him. He was worse than a rat! He was an animal—no, I had to think about this. I liked animals. It wasn't fair to insult animals by calling him one, but I couldn't think of a word that described him and his treacherous activities.

Wolf stroked my cheek gently. "You've been away too long, Adie."

"I'm sure you were busy enough without me in your life."

Wolf's expression was inscrutable as we pulled up to the training hall. "Do you want to go snorkeling tomorrow morning?"

I shook my head. "I'm working. Taking the group shopping."

"What about the evening?"

"I'll talk to you about it tonight, if you come."

"I said I would." He put his arms around me. Wolf's full lips moved slowly on mine, charging my batteries until I felt like sinking back on the car seat with him and enjoying the full treatment, but my brain went into overdrive.

Are you crazy, Logical said? He still hasn't explained anything to you. What are you, a doormat?

My Hormone Voice had something to say, but there was no time and the taxi driver was staring oddly at me.

59

Seeing the Martial Arts Academy entrance, I gathered up my things. Wolf helped me out and handed me my bag.

"See you soon!" he called out after me, forcing me to think about the night that had started it all.

4

The stairs were narrow going up to the karate dojo. Two guys stood behind the counter, one medium-height, lean and dark, and the other tall and stocky. The smaller of the two was Steve Vidjik. The big guy was Joe Brick. They were both sixth degree black belts from Toronto.

I approached the counter. "Hey."

They checked me out. Recognition dawned on their faces.

Steve smiled. "Hi, Adie! Long time no see."

"Training today?" Joe grinned broadly, probably thinking it would be a sight to see—me wearing three-inch heels and a dress, doing high snap kicks.

"Can I join a class?"

"Sure," Steve picked up a water bottle, "go get ready. I'm having one for the advanced belts in ten minutes."

I nodded, my jaw tightening. Steve's class might be tough. Joe looked more sympathetic to someone a little out of shape. But I had to work off some of my stress, so I made my way down the corridor to the change room. I focused on getting ready as quickly as possible. It was customary to get pushups for being late.

I bowed before I entered and lined up beside two men. They ignored me and stood stiffly, eyeing the entrance to the room. Seconds later, Steve appeared.

He yelled out, "*Skie!*

We completed the bow-in-ritual before we were told to run around the training hall, spinning at the corners, until we were breathing hard. From there on, we did everything from pushups, to crunches, and finally ended up using the punching bags. When the phone rang, Steve told the black belt to take over and he started counting our kicks. After we did one hundred, he told us to practice. I grabbed a jo, a weapon that resembles a four-foot long broomstick, and did my form. Blocks and strikes. A jo packs quite a wallop.

At the end of the class, I was glad to get changed. There were no showers so I went into the washroom and splattered water on my face before I put on my clothes. After reapplying some makeup, I picked up my bag and trekked over to the front counter.

"How much for the class?"

Joe looked up from his paperwork. "Eight dollars, Adie. You comin' back?"

"Maybe, depends. I brought a tour group with me. I'll try but you know…"

"Last time you had major problems. You don't have a mystery to solve, do you, Adie?"

"Life is a mystery, Joe."

Joe chortled loudly.

"Could you call me a taxi, please?"

"Sure. If you go out now, the taxi will be there soon." He picked up the phone.

"Thanks." I waved and took the stairs down. At the bottom I waited inside the doors until I saw a cab approach.

The sun broiled my skin. It was a relief to get in the taxi. "*Hola*, Hotel Don Juan, *por favor*."

"*Si*, Señorita."

He was a man of few words or his English was limited. He left me to my thoughts. It would have been easier if he hadn't. I didn't want to think about Wolf, so I focused on Ingrid. Why was she so interested in Mayan antiquities? And Suzanne thought she was stressed out. Were there problems with the divorce? Morris had a good lawyer—could he get a share of her business? Wolf would know. I would have to ask him, privately, of course. Too bad I was so busy tomorrow, with the shopping and the lunch at Diego's beach house. Maybe I'd have to agree to see him for dinner.

Who are you kiddin'? My Voice said. "You just want to forgive him and forget what he did to you."

When the taxi arrived in front of my hotel, I paid the driver and got out. I rushed to the entrance to escape the sun's heat. It was all my fault of course that I had this burn on my chest. If I hadn't been so distracted by Wolf, I would have loaded on sunscreen and stayed out there fifteen minutes max. I would have tanned. Now I had to watch that I didn't turn into an ugly peeling mess. Hopefully, Wolf had left that bottle of aloe vera for me.

* * *

I stepped into the lobby of the Don Juan. It was busy with a group of divers gathering near the beach door, waiting for their guide to take them out. I weeded through them to the elevator. The stairs are a good workout but karate had my muscles screaming.

When the door slid open, a scruffy man, straw hat pulled low on his forehead, entered. Beard stubbled a dirty face. My nose twitched from his unpleasant fishy cologne. I was glad when he turned away. I distanced myself, keeping to the back of the elevator, my eyes averted. Vacations were when men had the morals of alley cats, carousing around for females in heat. I was not that desperate. When he got off, I had another look at him. Athletic and trim, but that eau-de-tuna was a definite turn-off.

I padded to my room and shoved the key in the slot. It's always a good idea to be aware of your surroundings. Down the hall, the man stopped just past Ingrid's room to look out over the balcony at the golf course. A maid's unattended cart was parked at the end of the hall.

I shut the door behind me and scanned the table for the aloe vera. Yes, it was there. That was considerate of Wolf. I guess he wasn't all bad.

I'd have to hurry if I wanted to talk to Carmelita before the fashion show. After I unzipped my dress, I tossed off my bra and panties and showered. With makeup and hair done it was time to choose a dress.

With deep pink skin it had to be white. I checked my closet and dug out a figure-hugging patterned dress—V-necked, the straps crisscrossing in the back. I opened my drawstring jewelry bag and examined its contents. It wouldn't be smart to wear my pendant with the bright blue topaz, my present from Wolf. If he saw it on me, he'd figure I had forgiven him. No, instead, I decided I'd wear the intricate silver necklace scattered with turquoise that Diego had given me. Turquoise protects the wearer from harm and I needed to protect this deceitful body of mine from Wolf.

Ready to go, I gathered my purse and stepped into the hallway. At the top of the stairs, my cell started buzzing.

"*Bueno?*"

"Adie, you need to get over here." It was Ingrid.

"Why?"

"Please, Adie. Are you in the hotel?"

"I have a meeting in five minutes."

"Come to my room, Adie. I have to show you something."

"Bring it with you."

"Ee-eh! No way! Come here, Adie."

Was the woman on drugs? She should take it easy. It wouldn't be easy to nab a new man with that crazy attitude. I didn't want to see her but Jamaica beckoned. Reluctantly, I headed to her room. I spoke into my cell. "Okay, Ingrid, but only for a minute. As it happens, I'm right outside your room."

The next moment Ingrid's door swung open. She grabbed my hand and pulled me in, slamming the door behind us.

She was as pale as fresh snow.

"Look at this thing!" Ingrid yanked the lid off a black box.

I gasped. A bloody heart filled the bottom of the box. The side of the box dripped bright red droplets onto Ingrid's carpet.

Mesmerized by the dark red stains, Ingrid's lips flapped like a fish out of water. "It's a heart."

"An animal heart."

"I'm not an idiot, Adie. There's a note, too." Ingrid's trembling fingers set the box on the coffee table.

I was breathing normally now. "What does it say?"

She tugged a crumpled piece of paper out of her pocket. It was a yellow stick-it note with a message in block letters: YOU'RE NEXT.

I could see beads of sweat dot her face. Leading her over to the couch, I sat her down. "Have you phoned the police?"

Ingrid shook her head. "There's something else, Adie." She indicated the lid of the box on the floor.

Curiously, I picked it up, remembering too late that maybe the police would check for fingerprints. Well, then again, the evidence was already ruined with Ingrid touching it. When I turned it over, I saw the box was painted with a picture of a skeleton resting in a lounge chair on the beach—a female wearing a sun hat and bathing suit. The skeleton's grin was an orthodontist's dream—a wide Miss America smile with a set of identical white teeth.

"They sell these boxes in the gift stores." Tomorrow, I was taking the group shopping in the stores that specialized in the very same souvenirs. "After you call the police, you might want to call room service and stay in."

"No way, Adie! I'm not staying here alone." She stared at me expectantly.

I wasn't about to spend the evening babysitting this woman. "I have a meeting to go to. See you at the fashion show."

Setting down the lid on the table, I strode purposely to the door. As I left, I overheard Ingrid on the phone ordering the police to come immediately. She'd drive them crazy but she was their problem now.

Carefully, I made my way down the stairs on my high-heeled sandals, holding onto the railing. At the foot of the stairs, my cell buzzed again. "*Bueno?*"

"*Hola*, Adelina."

"Diego?" He didn't sound himself. His voice was too quiet and tense. I was having trouble hanging on to my phone and my purse. I stopped and set my purse down on a table in the lobby.

"Adelina, Carmelita's upset. I told her you'd speak to her. I can't get there right now and she refuses to have Churo or Luis help. I'm still in Cancun."

"What happened?"

"Someone poured blood all over the dress she was planning to wear for the show."

"I'll be there in ten minutes, Diego."

"Thanks, *mi amor*. I'm in your debt. Could you phone me later and let me know how she is?"

"Certainly. Goodbye, Diego."

"*Adios*, Adelina, and thanks."

Blood, again. Now at the fashion show. Wolf must be wrong about Diego. He wasn't manipulating anything. Things were seriously getting worse for Carmelita. But I was glad I wasn't in this alone. When Wolf was around I felt secure, although how I could possibly feel that after what he'd done was beyond me. It was just something about him. He was so confident and in control.

As I walked across the lobby, I remembered I had to update the white board for my Days of the Dead Tour. Pushing my cell into my miniscule evening bag, I failed to notice a woman crouched on the floor. My foot slipped out from under me. It took me by surprise. I righted myself quickly but bumped her.

"I'm so sorry." I stared down at the woman, sprawled on the floor.

The bewildered redhead sat up. I reached to help her and in so doing, my makeup bag dropped out of my purse.

"Oh, no! This is all my fault." She grabbed my bag from the floor and handed it up to me. "I'm such a mess today."

In a print trapeze dress that flounced too wide giving her a pregnancy bump and with that disheveled red hair, I agreed, but I didn't think she was referring to her appearance. "It's not your fault. I should have noticed you were searching for something on the floor. I think I tripped on it. What was it you lost?"

"My ring. An emerald."

My interest piqued. I saw a glint of gold by the foot of the Fleischer Travel board. "There it is." I scooted over and picked it up. It was a magnificent square-cut emerald surrounded by diamonds set in a thick gold band. "Beautiful." I handed it to her.

"Thanks." She beamed, placing the ring back on her finger. "Present from daddy."

I extended my hand. "Adie Sturm."

"Janice, er-rr, Jones. Are you staying here at the hotel?"

"Yes." I gestured to the Fleischer board. "I'm in charge of the tour group."

Janice glanced over. "A fashion show at the Hotel Maria? Wow! Do you know if they have any more seats available?"

The fashion police should have cuffed her and tossed her in solitary confinement. This woman was badly in need of a makeover and I hadn't helped her much by knocking her down. Guilt set in. "I'll give you a ticket. Our group has a table reserved."

"Thanks!" she said excitedly, and then frowned. "But my brother is with me. I'd actually need two tickets."

"Not a problem. Just tell them at the door that you're with the Fleischer travel group."

I turned to the board and wrote: Tuesday, Days of the Dead shopping. Lorita's (main square) at ten am. And then I remembered I'd better update the group on the Coba outing. Quickly I printed the information for Wednesday.

Janice smiled happily. "I'll let my brother know. See you there," she called over her shoulder.

I was relieved. She was a happy camper now. I checked my watch and noted it was six-fifteen. Carmelita would be waiting. I needed to hurry.

Intense heat filtered through the clouds. I proceeded on the side of caution and hailed a cab.

The Hotel Maria was a switch—five stars and looked the part. Prints and oil paintings hung on terra cotta walls behind floral print couches. Several groups of furnishings were situated under a cathedral ceiling with a skylight. Soft light poured into the room.

A pretty brunette perched on a bar stool, staring desolately into space. She smiled when she saw me. "Adelina!" Carmelita called out.

When I strode over, she got off her stool, pulled me close, and kissed my cheeks in the Spanish way.

"How are you, girlfriend?" I studied her down-turned mouth.

She shrugged her shoulders. "So-so, you?"

"It's been quite a day." I ordered a daiquiri. "Diego told me about the blood on the dress."

Her emerald eyes sparkled angrily. "Someone is out to ruin everything, Adelina. It was the show-stopper." She brightened. "Fortunately, I got a hold of another dress, which is now being altered to fit me."

"Why don't you want Diego to help you? He has the man power."

Carmelita sipped her margarita before she answered. "Some things are too personal. And you know brothers, Adelina."

I nodded. I could relate. Mine always got his knickers in a twist about something. A misguided sense of responsibility, I guess, when it came to a younger sister with a mind of her own. "Do you know who's behind all this?"

"I've got some thoughts on it." She stared at the guy who sat a few stools away from us. He winked.

I nudged her to get her attention. "Well?"

"Here you go, Señoritas." The bartender placed two drinks in front of us. We looked down the bar at the stranger. He lifted his glass and saluted us. Carmelita pursed her lips and blew a kiss. What could I do—she was incorrigible. I eyed my drink and hesitated.

"Come on, Adelina, drink it. He's just being polite."

"Sure, you're going to get ready for the show and I'll be left sitting here with him. I've got enough men to handle right now."

Carmelita's laughter carried over the music. But when the

singer sang a raspy blues tune, we listened, swept into the melancholy of his words.

A deep voice spoke up behind us. "You staying here, ladies?" Bright brown eyes in a rugged face.

He held out his hand. "Jeffrey."

Squeezing his hand quickly, Carmelita smiled seductively. "I'm Carmelita." Her silky voice sent him messages. She waved her hand in my direction. "My friend, Adelina."

"So what do you two do?"

Carmelita tossed her head back and shot him a sexy look. "I'm in charge of the fashion show and Adelina's a tour guide."

Jeffrey turned to me. "Adelina? Adie? You with Fleischer Travel?"

"Um-hum." I wondered how he knew that.

"My sister just phoned and said to meet her at the door for the fashion show. She said a blonde gave her some tickets."

"Janice?"

"Yep." He checked out Carmelita over the top of his beer glass. "You model?"

She nodded.

He set his empty glass on the counter. "I thought as much, with those fabulous legs." Then he turned to me. "Not that you aren't attractive, Adelina, but you're rather a small package." He pulled cigarettes and lit one. "I run an ad agency."

A small package?

Jeffrey placed some bills on the bar. "Nice meeting you. See you later?" he asked, his eyes on Carmelita.

She gave him a sultry look.

We watched him head to the elevator.

I patted Carmelita's arm. "As you were about to tell me..."

Carmelita frowned. "It could be Fede. He wants me to stay at home while he's with his whores."

"Could it be someone else?"

She shrugged her shoulders.

"Have you been doing anything you shouldn't be doing?"

"Like?" Carmelita grinned impishly.

I rolled my eyes.

"Well, I did have a little dalliance."

"You mean it's over?"

"Not entirely. It's lost some steam."

"Could it be a jealous girlfriend?"

Carmelita twirled her stir stick, considering the ramifications. "Wife."

"Maybe worse—is that why you didn't want to tell Diego?"

She pursed her lips. "He thinks he should have all the fun."

I shook my head. "Diego isn't married, Carmelita."

Carmelita got up off the stool. "So-oh? I could get a divorce. Fede is pond scum, Adelina. Low on the ladder of microscopic plant life." She picked up her beaded bag. "I've got to go. Come by after the show, room 102, okay?"

I nodded.

She waved and rounded the bar, disappearing from view.

I motioned the bartender. "The bill?"

He shook his head. "The señor paid."

As I took in that information, I felt a hand at my waist. Soft lips nuzzled my neck.

"Fast work, princess," Wolf said softly in my ear.

I swiveled around. "He's Carmelita's, not mine. The man's into models."

"Poor guy."

"Why?"

Wolf's deep blue eyes sparkled as he glanced from my face to my body. "You're a real woman—curved in just the right places."

5

When I told the maître d'I had a table for the Fleischer Travel group, he was impressed. "You have the best seats in the restaurant, Señorita Sturm." He gestured to the raised stage that was built in a t-shape. "The models will be coming down the aisle right in front of you." "Some of your party has already arrived. *Señor* Alvarez has provided daiquiri pitchers."

"How sweet of him."

Wolf gave me a black look.

Leading the way, the maître d'said, "Is that good for you, *señor* or would you prefer something else?"

"Sol, *por favor*." Wolf took my hand and led me to our table.

I sighted Ingrid approaching from the opposite direction. She had decided to come after all. We sat down a second before Ingrid arrived. She eyed Wolf like anyone else would a piece of chocolate layer cake before she plopped herself down beside him. I took the seat next to Wolf, beside Fern.

"Hey, Adie! This was a fun idea. And the daiquiris are delicious."

I nodded in reply, watching Ingrid bringing herself in closer to Wolf. She stared at his black shirt a moment before grasping his bicep for a quick grope. "Nice guns!"

"Watch that woman, Adie," Fern warned before her eyes shifted to Wolf. "He's a firecracker all right, but, Adie, I don't get it. What's going on?"

"What do you mean?"

"Who's the hottie you left with last night? And if he's your lover, why are you here with the sexy Wolf?"

"Diego's a friend. This is his sister's fashion show. That's why we have this table."

"Ah-hh. I'm impressed, Adie. There must be a story in this— you and two sexy men?" She stroked her lower lip thoughtfully. "Diego is the ultimate in male perfection but on the other hand, Wolf is pure animal. But," her eyes twinkled, "you know that, don't you? My bet is you're involved with both."

"It's complicated." I reached over for a goblet of strawberry daiquiri from the tray.

Fern patted my arm. "Can't wait to hear the juicy details. We're still on for breakfast tomorrow at Lorita's?"

"Sure, at nine. The shopping tour's at ten."

"Days of the Dead stuff—so cool."

The waiter set several trays of bread on the table. Each loaf was oval with interesting knobs on the surface.

"Those look like skulls, don't they? Days of the Dead food?" Fern stared at the bread. I picked up a tent card on the table.

"You're right. The show's called Festival of the Dead Fashion." I glanced at Wolf but he was listening to Ingrid's story. She trailed her long claws over his arm—crimson red enamel on super length acrylic nails. When he shook her off to reach for some bread, I grinned.

Wolf laid down his butter knife and whispered into my ear, "Adie, we really need to meet alone. You said you were busy with the tour group tomorrow but I know something you can't say no to."

I got uneasy at his words. He couldn't be suggesting a long, leisurely session of lovemaking, could he? He'd be right. I'd have a hard time resisting that sort of activity with a man like him.

"Let's go to dinner at the Grill."

"Um-mm." Food was always a good start.

"Then we could go dancing."

He was on the right track. "Okay…" Wolf was so firm and tall. I could put my hand on his shoulders and he'd hold my other hand pressed close to him. Our bodies would meld like heated chocolate.

Wolf searched my face. "We need to straighten out your problem, Adie."

What! Where did he get off saying that? He was the one that had loused up big time, not me!

"But not now. Right now let's get some food." Pulling out my chair, he assisted me up. "The buffet's over there." He indicated with his chin as he steered me to the buffet table.

Two women stood in front of the buffet. The platinum blonde's hair was a man-cut, squared at the back and spiked at the front. It did nothing to enhance her wide face and pig nose, although she ill-advisedly had taken the trouble to coat her eyelids with green shimmer and wore a matching floral dress. She nudged her fashionably thin friend. "Jocyline, I don't see any steak, do you?" Her thick pink lips twisted. "What is it with Mexico, anyway? Look at that red sauce. They need labels on this food. The captain said this was the best hotel on the island?"

"I doubt that, Charlene." Her lace-collared silk navy-blue dress matched the metallic blue of her hair. Her complexion was paler than white bread. "It's always tomatoes and peppers. You'd think they'd have chefs with more flare." She gestured with a bejeweled hand in a queenly fashion as she sneered, "Foreign food. I think we should have stayed on the cruise ship."

With them kvetching about whether to stay or go and my stomach rumbling fiercely, I was ready to step in and help. I pointed. "That one is cockroaches, fried in a hot sauce. Terribly spicy. Considered a delicacy in Mexico. Or, you could always go for the goat entrails." My eyes flicked ahead. "The sauce is delicious. I've heard they use minced sea worms to get it thick and brown."

Jocyline with the diamonds nudged Charlene. "This is outrageous." Her elbows flipped up and down like a nervous pigeon preparing for flight. "Let's find a proper restaurant."

I heaved a sigh of relief when she flew off with her friend.

Wolf handed me a plate. "Cockroaches and entrails?" His eyes danced.

"Maybe, who knows?" I shrugged nonchalantly. "That one is probably shrimp, don't you think?" I ladled some chicken in an orange sauce on my plate along with a little rice. "I just get annoyed with tourists who can't keep an open mind about a country's culture. Here they are in this perfect paradise—why do they leave if they don't want a new experience?" I picked up a radish and bit into it. "Besides, I was starving and they were taking way too long." I touched Wolf's arm. "Did you know this food is Mayan to go with Carmelita's theme?"

"Which is?"

"Festival of the Dead Fashion."

Wolf spooned up the shrimp. "A unique concept."

"It's brilliant!" I touched his arm at the sound of the band. "I think it's starting. We should hurry."

Plates in hand, we negotiated our way through the crowd and took our seats.

Wolf's husky voice whispered into my ear, "It won't be easy to watch this show with you sitting beside me—you are smokin' hot tonight, babe." His breath sent a shiver down my body. No man should have that kind of power—magic that captured a woman's soul. But I had to be strong. I couldn't let him do this to me again.

Red flashing strobe lights. A shapely brunette—hair drawn back, strutted out on stage. She wore red platforms and a slinky black dress. Dramatic black eye-liner and a white face. The beaded bag she carried was in the shape of a skull. As it swung from side to side, the eyes in the skull glinted red. The audience gasped.

The lights flashed to gold. Crimson ruby jewels lit her hair like a flame. A hiss of fire-tinged smoke rose from her feet.

Two statuesque blondes, distinctly Nordic, marched out together, in body-hugging dresses, synchronizing their steps. One wore a floor-length silver-sequined dress. Tiny black skulls fringed the low back. A scarlet mini-dress clung to the second model. Skull flowers adorned their hair and skeleton pendants dangled from their necks. In a haze of burgundy smoke, the models twirled around and marched back to the curtains like soldiers in a procession. The audience applauded wildly.

A waiter came around and filled our wine glasses. I pulled on Wolf's shoulder. "Aren't those dresses gorgeous? Carmelita's show will be a success for sure."

Wolf's tone was seductively low. "That red dress has your name written all over it."

I sipped the red wine, distractedly. Was he thinking about that special night when I'd worn a red dress? I sighed. But it was too late for us. There was no hope. Our relationship was over.

I gazed down the rectangular table. Fern and Bryan were on my right and then George. His mouth hung open as he took in the scantily clad models on stage. Janice at the head of the table rested her hand on his arm. Occasionally, she'd stretch up to his ear and whisper.

Next to her, Lola slugged back a daiquiri, eyes slightly glazed. I think she recognized Wolf from the beach. But it was Janice's brother, the ad-man who interested me. Jeffrey flashed an even

Colgate smile on Ingrid, seemingly having forgotten his interest in models. She had the height but there was an extra twenty pounds parked on her middle.

Soft Latin music and yellow strobe lights changed the scene. Two trim brunettes, in bikinis, posed. A black skull bikini on white for one and the negative image in white for the other. The filmy translucent coverings glinted with sparkling red beads. Fern patted my hand, diverting my attention from the show. "Who is that woman anyway, Adie?"

I followed her gaze. Janice nodded as George pointed to the dry ice machine almost hidden behind the lighting. Her frizzy red hair was piled high but she looked somehow wrong. The beige lacy dress did nothing but bleach out her pale freckled features. I wondered if she'd picked up any fashion tips from the show. "Oh-hh. That's Janice. Just met her today. The man on the other side of the table is her brother, Jeffrey."

"Why are they here with us?"

"I met her in the lobby. She'd lost her ring and was scrambling on the floor to find it. I ended up tripping on her. I felt bad so I gave her tickets."

"Tripped over her? That ass is kind of hard to miss, Adie." Fern smirked. "You must have been partying early, or what?" She cocked her head to see past Bryan. "What about him, the brother? He's not bad lookin'. Hardly like the jaundiced Janice. He seems to know Ingrid...does he?"

"I don't think so, although I was wondering what was up. He's into her, I'd say."

Fern shook her head. "Can you believe it—like a bitch in heat. Odd though that Jeff would come to a fashion show, isn't it? Definitely not a faggot."

"No, I wouldn't think so from the way he was hitting on my friend earlier. Not that that his orientation matters. Diego wouldn't care who came."

Fern smirked. "Probably not, or he would have made sure Wolf wasn't on the guest list." She looked over at Wolf. "Will he be here tonight?"

"Who?" My eyes focused on Wolf's messed up blond hair. I wanted to ruffle it up some more and then unbutton his shirt.

Fern laughed. "Diego, of course."

I frowned. "I sure hope not. It could get uncomfortable with both of them in the same room." It was pleasantly cool in the restaurant but I felt a bead of perspiration on my forehead just thinking of it. Taking a last sip of my daiquiri, mostly ice crystals now, I felt some relief.

"Ha, maybe for you." Fern snickered. "I'd love to have both of them in the same room."

"Ye-ss, the bedroom." I fantasized. Then seeing Fern's strange expression, I said, "Not at the same time."

"No? I would." Fern giggled. "It would be like a chocolate fondue. Delicious to the last lick."

I could see it. "White and brown chocolate swirling. Imagine the steam..." I trailed off as Wolf glanced over.

"When do you think we can leave, Adie?" Wolf's lips were turned up at the corners. He must have overheard our conversation, or at least part of it. I flushed, thinking of my flippant remarks about him.

Fern stared hungrily. "You can't go yet, Wolf. It's still early and frankly, we women need some eye candy."

"Adie needs some exercise."

"What are talking about?" Surely he didn't mean...

"A walk, Adie."

"Oh-hh." I was vaguely disappointed with his explanation. But he wasn't about to say what he was really thinking in front of Fern anyway, would he? And then I recalled why I was here. "Sure, later. Carmelita asked me to see her after the show. I have to check whether it went well."

With a clash of cymbals, music reminiscent of conquistadors and bullfights rang out. Ethereal with her long brown hair backlit, in a translucent jaguar print dress, Carmelita sashayed out onto the runway platform and twirled flamboyantly for the audience. Her belt and necklace were made of jade and silver, cut into skull shapes. Carmelita's lips were scarlet red against a powdered white face. Green eyes glittered cat-like with exaggerated black liner and silver shadow—a vampire coming to life.

When she reached the end of the runway, a spooky voice-over intoned, "Fashion of the Dead welcomes you at the Hotel Maria Boutique. *Buenas noches.*" The lights flashed red one last time as Carmelita struck a pose and then swung around. Stepping back on her turn, she swayed uncertainly for a moment and then plummeted off the runway. A seven foot drop. Something nicked my temple sharply as Carmelita swept by and landed in Wolf's outstretched arms.

Shrieks rang out. I'd say it was a showstopper all right. The show was over.

* * *

The management covered up the botched finale with the band playing some lively mariachi music. My eyes searched the stage for the culprit but I saw nothing that would have caused the accident. Wolf set Carmelita down on his chair and I asked, "Are you okay?

Carmelita lifted her bare foot. "I'm fine, thanks. Lost my sandal when the strap broke."

Wolf spotted her shoe lying on the floor under our table. He picked it up and brought it over. Wolf ran his finger over the patterned leather. "The strap was deliberately cut." He handed it to me. I had to admit it looked suspicious.

Carmelita took the shoe from me. "What's this?" She pointed to the red blotches on the metallic sheen. Suddenly aware of the ache at my hairline, I touched the area. Blood covered my fingertips.

Wolf lifted my bangs. "Adie, we need to take at look at your head in the light." He helped me up.

"The dressing room," Carmelita said urgently, "102."

A small group started to gather around us. A slim elegant man, apparently the manager, appeared and held back the crowd while we made our way to the hotel room with Wolf lending each of us an arm.

The room we entered had been designated for Carmelita's use. A young, attractive brunette was placing dresses carefully on hangers as we came in.

"Tina, quickly," Carmelita motioned to the girl, "bring us the first aid kit!"

Tina looked startled. "Are you all right, Carmelita?"

"My friend, Adelina, has been injured. Quickly, *por favor!*"

Wolf and I sat down on the couch. Carmelita threw the sandal with the torn strap on the floor in disgust. "I can't believe this! Someone must hate me. Why are they doing this?"

"I think you need to get some protection, Carmelita," I said. "Diego can give you one of his bodyguards."

"No, if I do that, Fede will insist I stay home and that's the end of my career." Carmelita picked up her hairbrush and started combing out her hair methodically, gripping the brush so tightly her knuckles appeared white.

Wolf sat back, studying Carmelita. "Do these things only happen when you're out modeling?"

Carmelita frowned. "The dress with the blood was here when I arrived this morning, but that rat and the headless picture were delivered to my gate at my house."

Tina, a box in hand, entered the room and set the first aid kit down on the dresser. "Where is your cut, Señorita?"

"It's all right," Wolf said. "I'll take care of it."

"Leave us." Carmelita gestured. "We have things to discuss."

"Certainly." Tina's eyes narrowed. "I'll go home."

We waited until she left the room. Wolf found some antiseptic and some cotton balls. I winced as he dabbed at the wound. "The cut's long but not deep. Do you want to go to the hospital?"

"You don't think I need stitches, do you?"

"There's a gap, but it's small. I'm sure I can close it up." Wolf selected a band-aid and glanced over at Carmelita. "You okay?"

"Physically, yes." Carmelita's eyes shot nervously to the far corner of the room as if she expected someone to jump out at her. "But I don't want to go home to an empty house. And staying here at the hotel would be worse. I feel like someone is watching me."

I gazed at Wolf. "Who do you think could be behind all this?"

Wolf stuck a band-aid securely on my wound. "A jealous wife, or...."

I jerked at the firm contact. "Or what?"

"Has Alvarez been involved in anything that could have made someone angry?"

"Diego?" Carmelita dropped her brush abruptly on the dresser. "You think someone may be seeking revenge on my brother through me?"

"It's possible. Your brother has a way of making enemies."

I hated to admit it, but Wolf could be right. Diego was always into something and his deals made millions or lost millions. Some investors could get resentful if they were counting on a big profit. "But it could be that wife, couldn't it, Carmelita?"

Carmelita nodded. "Ricardo has a spiteful wife."

"Ricardo?" Wolf raised an eyebrow.

Carmelita glanced at him. "I trust you will keep this to yourself?"

Wolf nodded.

"I've been having an affair. Fede was whoring, so I took up with one of Diego's associates, Ricardo Montalvo, a very attractive man but...I was thinking of breaking it off."

"You're getting a divorce, aren't you?" I asked.

She studied her toes, checking the silver nail polish. "I'm not sure any more." Carmelita stood up and started pacing back and forth, across the tiles. She stopped in front of me. "I know this is a lot to ask, Adelina, but I feel we are good friends." She met my eyes.

I nodded. Carmelita picked up a pair of sandals and slipped them on. "I don't want to be alone and Fede is away. I'd like to spend the night with you. Diego must not know what happened. He'll want to send Churo over to guard me and then it won't be long before Fede knows. You understand, don't you?"

"My hotel room is rather small."

"You own a condo, Adelina, and it's extremely spacious with two bedrooms. Haven't you seen it yet?"

"No," I said nervously. Wolf might not be pleased to hear this.

"Condo?" Wolf's brow furrowed. "This has something to do with Alvarez, doesn't it?"

"Um-mm." I wasn't sure what my spin should be.

Carmelita explained, "Diego was grateful. When Adelina saved his life he gave her a condo." She turned to me. "Please, Adelina," she pleaded. "It will only be for one night. Tomorrow I'm going to Cancun anyway. I would be forever in your debt."

Wolf's expression was unreadable. I remembered I had the key in my bag. "Okay, but I'll need to get some things. I have to be at Lorita's by nine and I don't have time to go to the Don Juan and change."

Carmelita smiled secretively. "There's no need for you to get your clothes, or for me either, for that matter. Everything is there."

She yawned. "With a sleeping pill, I might be able to forget all this."

"It's late. Let's go." Wolf held the door open. "I'll drive."

He surprised me—not in the least angry about the condo. Wasn't he even a teeny bit jealous?

Outside, a balmy breeze ruffled my hair yet it felt calming. It was a beautiful starry night.

The Jeep was parked on the street. Carmelita took the seat in the back and I sat in the front.

"Where are we going?" Wolf asked.

"Not far. Take Melgar north," Carmelita said softly.

* * *

The building was walled—security at the gate.

"*Buenos noches.*" Carmelita indicated me with her chin. "Señorita Sturm is staying in her condo tonight."

The security guard nodded and opened the gate.

We followed Carmelita up the stairs. At a heavy oak door, she stopped. "Do you have the key, Adelina?"

I nodded. "And if I didn't?"

She smiled. "No problem. I have one too. I've been checking the housekeeping and periodically stocking the condo."

I glanced at Wolf. His mouth formed a straight line.

When I flicked on the lights, I was taken aback. White leather couches were situated around an oak table. Jade statues, delicate lamps, paintings, and green ceramic bowls decorated the room. Gauzy green curtains covered the multi-paned, double windows in the living room.

Carmelita sauntered over to the coffee table, picked up a decanter of red wine, and poured each of us a glass.

"This room is beautiful, Carmelita." I wandered over to the bathroom, glass in hand. Black and white marble tiles lined the floor and walls. There was a long counter with a double sink and a vase of red roses off to one side. I hastily backed off and bumped into Wolf who looked over my shoulder.

The bedroom was splendid. White floors and, as was the fireplace across from a four-poster brass bed covered with an aquamarine satin spread.

"To match your eyes, princess." Wolf's glance took in the king-sized bed. "Alvarez is nothing if not predictable."

Silently we entered the living room where Carmelita stood sipping her wine. "I just want to thank you, Adelina. And you too, Wolf. Who knows what would have happened if you hadn't caught me when I fell."

"No problem." Wolf looked serious. "I'm glad I was there to help. Do you mind if I speak to Adelina alone?"

Carmelita nodded. "Of course not, I'm off to bed anyway. I'll see you tomorrow, Adelina?" I think she meant at Diego's beach house but I didn't want to ask with Wolf there. Carmelita closed the door quietly behind her and we were alone. I picked up the controller on the table and switched on the CD player. A tango instrumental played softly. Romantic under other circumstances. I leaned back on the couch, my wine in hand, and braced myself. I waited for the shoe to drop.

Wolf joined me on the loveseat, angling his long legs away. He lifted his wine glass and examined the hue. "Knowing Alvarez, this should be an exceptional vintage." He held his glass up to mine. "What should we drink to, princess? It would seem ironic to drink to us, wouldn't it, considering we're drinking his wine?"

"To new beginnings then."

He clicked my glass. "Beginnings." Wolf tipped his glass back and then placed it on the table. His eyes locked with mine. "We might as well get right to it."

"What?" His rolled up shirtsleeves revealed strong forearms and with the buttons at his neck slightly undone, I glimpsed a muscular chest, just as I remembered.

Wolf tapped his leg. "Why didn't you return my calls? Is there someone else in your life?"

"In my life?" He had to be kidding.

"Tell me why you're so angry."

I had to bite the bullet. Where to begin? I took a deep breath. "Well, you know I went on a castle tour a while ago, don't you?"

"Yeah. You told me you were going to get in touch with me when you got back, but you didn't return my calls."

I remembered sitting in my living room, listening to his messages. I bit my lip. "I did phone."

"And?"

"The first two times a woman answered. She said you were sleeping and she didn't want to wake you."

"She have an accent?"

"Um-mm."

"Juanita, my housekeeper."

"She sleeps with you?"

Wolf showed his even white teeth. "Not yet."

My mouth dropped open.

He stroked my cheek. "Of course not. She's married."

"That would stop you?"

"With children."

I raised an eyebrow. "So?"

"She's not my type."

"Ah-ha." That was different.

"So is everything okay now?" He tilted my chin up. His lips worked on mine, sending a delightful shiver down my body.

I jerked away, spilling a drop of red wine on the white leather couch. I set my glass down. Hastily I snatched a tissue up from the box on the end table and swabbed up the spillage.

"Is it?"

I threw the tissue on the table and glanced at him.

"Your eyes are getting turquoise again."

I glared. "And for good reason."

"There was something else?"

"You don't know?"

Wolf sat back and studied me. "Explain."

I picked up the wine glass and had another sip before I started. "I phoned late one night. A woman answered. She said you were in the shower and did I want her to go in and get you."

Wolf sat silently a moment. "Was there more?"

"Yes. I tried the following morning and the same woman answered. She said you were too busy to talk and she hung up." I stared at him expectantly.

"This was in the fall?"

I nodded.

"You want to know who the woman was?"

I shrugged. "Obviously, one of your girlfriends because she did it again."

"Hung up on you?"

I nodded. "This time I didn't get past asking for you."

Wolf rubbed his chin reflectively. "Not a girlfriend, Adie. Daniella. We'd been working on an expansion project, talking to the owner of the adjoining property."

I frowned at the mention of that barracuda and tipped back more wine. Predictable. She'd made her move after I'd left Cozumel.

Wolf took my glass away from me and set it on the table. "She was way out of line, I know, but please try to understand, Adie. She's an excellent real estate agent and knows the ins and outs of Cozumel."

"Hah!" I huffed. "I'll bet she does. And a deal takes all night?"

"I let her sleep in the guest room. She'd had too much to drink. I was tired and didn't feel like driving her back."

"And she doesn't like taxis."

"In her state, I couldn't just dump her in a cab. It was late and she'd done well. I owed her. Daniella knows the language and the ins and outs. Please, understand. You know how she is, Adie." He shifted back in the couch. "Look, now that you know it was her—there's something else that's more important for us to talk about."

I sipped some wine. Daniella had an I-don't-give-a-damn-attitude. As far as hanging up was concerned, she knew it was me and had done it deliberately, although I wouldn't put it past her to hang up on any female phoning Wolf.

"Let's talk about Alvarez." Wolf stared at me expectantly.

This was the other shoe dropping. I knew he wasn't going to like what Diego had done. I hadn't told him about the condo or other gifts, for that matter. But it wasn't like he'd told me anything.

Wolf glanced around the room for a moment before he spoke. "Are you two involved?"

"Huh?"

"As in, having an affair?"

"We're friends."

"I think he has other ideas."

"Well, he's grateful."

Wolf smiled slightly. "He's fishing, and he's got all the bait set up." He glanced around significantly.

"I didn't expect to be staying here."

"Funny that you are."

What was he saying? That Diego was behind the threats to Carmelita?"

"Don't you wonder that you were let in so easily?"

"Diego must have told the guard I'd be here."

Wolf stood. "Will you have dinner with me tomorrow?"

I got up and stepped to him. With my high-heeled sandals on, this man was still taller by a few inches. As I placed my arms on his shoulders, my fingers also noted how strong he was. I kissed him lightly on the lips. "Thanks for being with me tonight. But before you leave I need to ask you some questions—about divorce."

"We aren't married, Adie." Wolf grinned. "No need to rush into divorce details."

"Not for me, Wolf. It's about Ingrid."

"Why?"

"I don't really think her divorce has anything to do with this, but so much is going on, I thought the more I knew…"

"Why don't we talk divorce when we have dinner tomorrow?" Wolf stroked my cheek. "You look tired and you've had a shock. I'll call you. You still have the cell I gave you?"

"Um." Wolf was always a good person to bounce ideas off of. "Listen, I need to tell you something. It's important."

"What is it, Adie? You look upset."

"It's about Ingrid. Just before the fashion show she sent for the police."

"Police?"

"She called me to her room to show me this box someone had dropped off at her door. There was a bloody heart in it with a note." I touched his arm. "A death threat. It said she'd be next."

Wolf's eyes narrowed. "A bloody heart—something to do with sacrifice?"

The memory of the blood on the note flashed before my eyes and a chill swept my body. "We're in Mayan country, Wolf. The Mayans believed blood-letting was needed to give the gods energy."

"Yeah, Mayans. babe, I'd be more inclined to be worried about the note. What did the police say?"

"I don't know and I didn't get a chance to ask her tonight. She and Jeffrey were busy talking."

"The guy who likes models?" Wolf grinned widely. "She's not exactly his type, is she?"

"Something appealed to him." I twirled a strand of my hair. "Hey, you spent a long time talking to her. Did you figure out why she came to Cozumel?"

"Besides looking for a man to satisfy her?"

I frowned. "She was coming on to you?"

"You sound surprised." Wolf's dark blue eyes inspected my face.

"Charming, was she?"

"She tried."

I slid my arms around his waist. "But you're keeping yourself for me?"

Wolf grinned. "Always." He stroked my cheek tenderly. "I've got too much energy for a woman like her." Sliding into his arms came easy—the silk shirt smoothly sexy. He lowered his head. When I felt his lips pressed firmly on mine, I forgot everything and everyone. I breathed in his soapy ocean scent, wishing I were back in my hotel room. This time I wouldn't stop him.

I sighed when he released me.

"Keep me posted on the Ingrid situation, eh?" He opened the door. "I'll call you."

I watched him make his way down the stairs. He turned around at the landing and our eyes met one last time before he disappeared out of view—a black figure disappearing into the shadows, like a panther springing into the night.

6

The mattress was right out of *Goldilocks and the Three Bears*—not too firm, not too soft. It was just right. I glanced over at the clock. Seven-twenty...plenty of time to get ready and meet Fern. But what if Carmelita was wrong?

I got up to check my treasure chest—a heavy oak cabinet, drawers filled with lacy panties and bras. Amazing colors. Flimsy under-wire with lacy straps, convertible bras with sparkly straps, as well as patterned pushup bras. I was Alice in Lingerie Wonderland. Excited, I ran to the closet and slid open the mirrored sliding doors.

Dresses of every description—skirts, jackets, tops, all neatly arranged and color coordinated. A rich girl's Christmas! Then I got worried. What if there weren't any bathing suits? I knelt down and pulled open the bottom drawer. Eye-opening string bikinis along with matching paraeos!

What else? I raced back with my bounty and checked the closet for beach bags. Carmelita had forgotten nothing. I snatched up a black tote and tossed in the clothes. And that's when I glanced down.

Shoes! Rows and rows of them took up half of the walk-in closet. I picked one up...Steve Madden. Designer labels. No discount bargain shoes here. I spotted a pair of wedged sandals with Jessica Simpson printed on the insole and slipped them on. Perfect! On a hanger a frilly print top caught my eye. I grabbed it.

And what about shorts? Back at the dresser I rummaged around until I hit pay dirt. With all my clothing items spread out ready on the bed, I headed to the bathroom.

Similar to the main bathroom, it was larger with white tiled walls, a shower and a marble counter. Was Diego thinking we'd share that one? I could picture his dark eyes sparkling mischievously. He was such a devil.

Shampoo, conditioner, hairspray, gel and cosmetic—everything. Diego was spoiling me.

When I stepped into the shower, I avoided water on my cut, glad the band-aid stayed on. With a fluffy white towel wrapped around me, I styled my hair and applied makeup before I went back into the bedroom to dress.

I hadn't heard any noises in the condo, so I assumed Carmelita had already left or was still sleeping. Not knowing which was the case, I made sure I was quiet as I padded around the place.

I found a container of orange juice in the fridge and water bottles but no food. Not a problem. I wasn't planning on staying. When I glanced at the kitchen table I was surprised to see a note folded over. Adelina was written in a flourishing style.

I hope you like everything. The clothes are bits from the last two collections. I phoned Diego and told him where you were. He said the driver would pick you up at 13:00 at the entrance to the condo and you can have him drive by the Don Juan to pick up your friends. See you there. Thanks for staying with me. C

I found a glass in the cupboard over the counter and poured myself some orange juice. I'd forgotten to phone Diego and I wondered what story Carmelita had told him.

Shutting the door behind me, I headed down the stairs to the entrance. The security guard greeted me politely. *"Buenos dias, Señorita Sturm."*

"Hola."

He smiled and opened the gate.

The streets were filled with bicycles, motor scooters, trucks, and cars. Shops had opened. Some of the owners stood outside beckoning tourists to enter and sample their wares. I passed by a window where an old man sat weaving a blanket on a large loom. Across the street, people were wandering in and out of a busy bakery.

The cobblestone street was meant for pedestrians only. It had the usual jewelry stores, gift shops, and craft stands. The prices were better here than on the main waterfront street, mainly because the cruise ship passengers were warned to stay away.

Lorita's at the square was busy. Fern was sitting close to the entrance under the awning. When she saw me she waved.

"Hey, Fern." I sat down across from her with a view of trees and a statue.

"How're you doing?" Her eyes searched my face.

"Okay, why?"

"No effects from that shoe?"

I touched the Band-Aid at my hairline. It felt slightly tender. "Not much."

"I gathered you knew the model."

I nodded. "Scrambled eggs and coffee, *por favor*," I said to the server and waited as he turned to Fern.

"Waffles, please."

"She's Carmelita Alvarez, Diego's sister."

"Get out! You mean Mr. Perfect?"

"I can't vouch for perfection as far as character is concerned."

"Character is only a necessity for ugly men, Adie."

I grinned. "He's certainly not that. By the way, did Ingrid leave with Jeffrey?"

"She sure did...such a slut. But, I'd say she did well for herself, considering how she's let herself go."

"Do you think they slept together?"

Fern sipped her coffee slowly. "She was all over him when they walked out the door."

The waiter returned with a mug of caffeine fix. "*Gracias.*" I poured in some milk and a generous amount of sugar. "You knew her years ago, didn't you, Fern?"

Her hand clenched tightly on her mug. "I worked for her."

"There must be a story in that." I eyed Fern's pursed lips. "Not a good experience, I'd guess."

"No, it wasn't." She fingered her brooch, anxiously. It was that intense color that only jade had, shaped into a cat form.

"She's not a popular woman at the agency in Kitchener."

The waiter returned with our orders on a tray. He set them down on the table. Fern seemed to welcome the interruption.

"How long did you work for her, Fern?" I dug into my eggs.

"A few months."

"Did you quit...or?"

"I quit, all right!" Fern's voice snapped.

"Sorry, I'm being insensitive."

Fern's large brown eyes met mine. "It's okay, Adie, you didn't know."

My gaze fell to the brooch on her neckline of her blouse. "It's beautiful. Jade isn't it?"

She nodded.

Now I knew what it was. "A jaguar? According to Mayan beliefs, jaguars held up the sky. They were associated with strength, bravery, and power."

"You've done your homework." Fern looked impressed. "The Jaguar God was the god of the underworld and a powerful animal guide. I bought this piece at an auction. It's not one of my animals but I liked the design."

"Your animals?"

"Animal guides protect you. If you know what your animal is, you can wear it for good luck. They'll tell you what you must do."

Fern had always had an interest in the occult but I was mystified by this revelation. "You're saying we have animal guides that protect us?"

"We do. You know unconsciously what animals they are." She looked serious. "Sometimes they come to you in your dreams." Unclasping the brooch, she placed it in my hand. "Touch it."

I stroked the smooth jade. I didn't care for the elaborate look of the jewelry, too fussy, but there was a strange warmth about the jaguar. The shape was sleek and strong.

"You're getting vibes from it, Adie, aren't you?" Fern stared, her gaze burning into me. "Your animal is," her eyes grew spacy, "the jaguar. It's your talisman."

I smiled, thinking how Fern hadn't changed after all these years. I gave her back the brooch. "And what's your animal, Fern?"

She laughed derisively. "I'm definitely snake material." Her eyes searched my face. "Eat your breakfast, Adie. I didn't mean to shock you."

"Not much shocks me anymore."

Fern grinned and picked up some waffle with her fork.

I let her get in a few mouthfuls before I changed the subject back. "I can understand anyone quitting when they've worked for Ingrid, but why didn't you get a job somewhere else? You wanted to be a tour guide, didn't you?"

Fern looked away at some children playing in the square

before she answered. "Ingrid claimed I was coming on to the clients on the Grand Canyon tour." Fern cut into her waffle. "She made sure other agencies believed her story."

"Why would she do this?"

"Jealousy."

"Ingrid was jealous of you? You were just starting out in the travel business. What was she afraid of?"

"Nothing to do with travel, Adie. It had to do with her boyfriend."

"Wasn't she married then?"

"True, but Ingrid had a lover on the side. This guy was wealthy and helped her start up her business. She was afraid of losing him and he was paying too much attention to me," she said, adding hastily, "not that I was interested."

"Jordan James?"

"Um." She gazed intently at me. "You knew about him?"

"What did he see in her?"

Fern swept away a long strand of hair. "She was attractive back then and young. It was about the time she won the Miss Oktoberfest award. She had the world by the tail."

"And what did Jordan James think about you?"

I was a distraction, nothing more, but Ingrid didn't think so." Fern's eyes studied me. "I wonder why she'd let you work for her with him around. You're—a sexy woman."

It wasn't the compliment as much as the wording she'd used that confused me. I wasn't sure what to say. "Thanks." I picked at my eggs. "I've never seen James with her. I just heard they've been together all these years. Do you know what's happened to him?"

"I thought he retired."

"What happened to his business?"

"He had children. They must have taken over." Fern stared at me. "Are you having problems with Ingrid?"

"No, but someone hates her."

Fern laughed. "News flash. The woman is poison. Who doesn't hate her?"

"Someone wants her dead."

Fern froze, fork mid-air.

"A bloody heart was delivered to her with a death threat."

"Ingrid has a serious enemy."

I nodded. "The police know."

"Enough about that bitch. Honestly, I'll get indigestion if I have to think about her. Let's have a pleasant lunch." Fern sipped her coffee. "Speaking of gods and sacrifices—how's the godelicious Wolf?"

I ran my finger over my bottom lip reflectively. "I got some answers last night but I'm still worried."

Fern took my hand and squeezed it reassuringly. "Love can be confusing. You know you can talk to me about anything. My room is down the hall from yours, 206."

"Um-mm." I withdrew my hand and finished my eggs.

Fern smiled. "Maybe, I should have asked how you are juggling the Wolf-Diego situation?"

Before I could answer that, Jim and Tom trotted up.

"Hey, Adie!" Tom adjusted his glasses. "We're early. We'll wait over there." He pointed to a park bench in the square.

"The others should be here any moment, Fern." I waved over the waiter for the bill. As I laid the money on the table, Lola and Dan arrived with Ingrid and Jeffrey.

"That answer your question?" Fern's chin indicated Ingrid and Jeffrey, arms linked, heads conspiratorially close in conversation. Fern glanced down the street. "Hey, isn't your puppy coming?" She checked her watch. "It's ten after and George is either late or..."

I smiled happily. "I think we've waited long enough. Haven't we?" I stood up. "Let the tour begin."

* * *

The clouds were moving in as we approached the tour group gathered in the park. Lola looked concerned. "You okay, Adie? I thought that model was going to knock you out flat last night!"

Dan guffawed loudly. "Little thing like you needs a big man to protect her." He swiveled around. "Speak of the devil. Guess George couldn't miss this." Fern's eyes met mine. We looked past Dan and saw George, trotting up, puffing and panting. He was in baggy brown shorts and a loose white T-shirt, Corona embossed on the front.

"Hi, George," I said, in what I hoped was a friendly tone.

"Hey, Adie. Have you arranged for me to meet with your friend…the one that has the investment company?"

"Ingrid?" I made sure she was listening before I said, "Diego's driver will pick you two up at the Don Juan shortly after one. Dress for a party." I turned to the rest of the group. "We'll be stopping at three stores for the Days of Dead souvenirs and there are silver shops all along this street. Remember you can bargain for your purchases but please don't be insulting to the merchants."

"What would you call insulting, Adie?" Dan asked.

"If you want an item, ask the vendor what price they want and then make a lower offer. They'll give you a counter offer but you need to meet them in the middle."

Dan had his chance to try bargaining when he picked up fancy black box with skeletons decorating the exterior. The formally attired skeletons were getting married.

Ingrid's face was white as a sheet. I looked over at the box she was holding. A female skeleton wearing a bathing suit, was sitting in a lounge chair was painted on the front. Jeffrey patted her shoulder consolingly.

I hadn't taken Jeffrey for the gigolo type. He looked too well off. Why would he spend the night with Ingrid—a woman that wasn't his type? Then again, maybe he hadn't.

"Jeffrey…can we talk?" I turned to Fern and whispered, "Could you keep Ingrid busy?"

Fern nodded and grabbed the paraeo Ingrid was now fingering. Ingrid squawked in protest.

Jeffrey smiled. "What's up?"

"I thought you liked models."

"I do, usually, but I get tired of these beautiful airheads. Besides, I enjoy Ingrid's company. We talk business."

"Does she have a deal in mind?"

"Possibly."

I lifted an eyebrow.

"She's interested in antiquities."

"That must make some interesting pillow talk."

"The best." Jeffrey smirked. "You think I could meet your friend?"

"We're talking big time money."

"How much?"

I shook my head. "Ingrid's the expert. Ask her."

Lola touched my arm. "We're all done, Adie. We're going to the shop across the street. Dan wants to get me some jewelry."

"Meet you at the pottery shop up the street." I signaled the others that we were leaving.

* * *

Our last stop was Pedro's Donkey. It had everything from a jewelry shop at the entrance to numerous rooms with carvings, clothing, and furniture at the back. Off to the right there was a restaurant. I told my group that there was a table reserved for them. Everyone headed over except Jeffrey who mentioned something about the cash machine. Ingrid stayed with me to browse. I could hear Dan's loud laughter from the entrance of the restaurant.

It was half past eleven and I knew I had to get back to change, but each room had interesting objects that I wanted to see. Colorful blue and red traditional Mayan pottery caught my eye. I fingered a vase, intrigued by the detail. In a bin nearby, I found a box with prints from a local artist that I flipped through.

From the beaded curtain of the doorway, Ingrid called out. "They have Days of the Dead souvenirs here?"

"There's a room that has them."

"Where, Adie?" She poked her face in and jerked her chin. "That one has furniture."

"And if you go through, you'll see another room behind the Turkish carpets." The room I was in had rattan furniture—cozy couches and chairs with plump pillows. While I tested one, Ingrid went ahead.

With Ingrid leaving I was curious to examine what the bin in the corner held. "Rain sticks," I said out loud. "Cool!" I glanced around to see if anyone had heard me talking to myself.

Picking up a long one, I turned it upside-down. It sounded like a light rain shower at first but gained momentum suddenly, the raindrops pounding down, like a heavy tropical shower. The tag said Authentic Mayan Rain stick, made with corn pebbles. I was still holding the rain stick when something crashed in the next room, followed by a scream.

Sweeping the hanging rug aside, I ploughed through the beaded curtain. My eyes darted to a masked pony-tailed man in a baseball cap. Waving a knife, he charged straight at Ingrid.

She had knocked over a table in her retreat, but having nowhere left to go she stood frozen on the spot. A second more and she'd be skewered. Adrenaline surged through my body. Leaping past her, I elbowed her back. With the rain stick I blocked him, knocking the knife out of his hand onto the floor. Butting the rainstick full-force to his face, I made contact. Blood gushed over his chin and T-shirt. He grunted, gripping his bleeding nose. When I came at him again he kicked over a bin of hats before swinging open the fire exit door and racing out.

The alarm sounded.

We stared at the gaping door—a hot breeze blowing in. Ingrid wedged her fingers into my arm, her face white as a ghost. "Adie!" she gasped.

In the noise and confusion a distinguished gray-haired man in a suit rushed in with two security guards. "Señorita what has happened here?"

I took a deep breath before I explained. "Señora Fleischer," I indicated with my hand, "was attacked by a man with a knife. He set off the alarm when he ran out."

The manager looked stricken. "In my store? How can this be?" Forehead furrowed, he motioned for the guards to wait as he strode over to the open exit. He surveyed the street a moment before he got on his cell and motioned for the guards to check the alley.

My body legs trembled from the adrenaline rush. I was still shaking when Lola and Dan appeared.

"What happened, Adie?" Lola asked.

"Ingrid was attacked. He ran out that door."

Dan led Ingrid over to a rattan chair where she plopped herself down, her face blanched of color.

Two police officers in taupe uniforms and caps arrived as I took a chair next to Ingrid. A serious man in his thirties introduced himself. "*Buenos tardes.* I am Officer Hernandez of the Cozumel Policia." He gave me a curious look. "Do you remember me, Señorita Sturm?"

"Officer Hernandez, yes." The last time I was in Cozumel, Hernandez had been on the Mexican end of a murder case.

"Can you describe what happened?"

"I heard a noise. I was in the other room. When I ran in, I saw a man with a knife threatening Señora Fleischer. I stopped him with the rain stick."

Hernandez's eyes lit on the rain stick propped up against a woven basket. "Stopped?"

"Well, I struck the knife from his hand."

He spotted the blood on the tiles.

"And whacked his nose."

"Broken?"

"Most likely."

"Can you describe the man?"

"Blond hair in a ponytail, baseball hat. He had a black mask that covered part of his face."

"A mask?" Hernadez.furrowed his brow. "A Carnaval mask—shiny?"

"No, it was plain black—like a Zorro mask."

"How big was the man?"

I rubbed my eyes, trying to remember. "Medium height, maybe taller but stocky. I'm never sure about height because," I glanced at my high-wedged sandals, "I usually wear heels."

Heranadez took in my legs. "Moustache or beard?"

"Yes."

"Which?"

"Both." My eyes swept the floor and stopped at a shiny glint of steel almost covered by a black box. Hernandez tracked my gaze. He tugged out a pair of latex gloves and reached over and picked up the knife. Lola gasped. The blade was long and thick.

"Is this the knife, Señorita?"

I nodded.

Hernandez dropped the knife into a plastic bag and handed it to one of the other officers. He glanced down at me. "The man left through the exit?"

I nodded.

"Señora Fleischer." He turned to Ingrid. "Did you recognize this man?"

"No, it all happened so quickly." Tears welled in her eyes. She gulped before she continued. "I didn't see him at first. He came at me from behind the rug. Officer," Ingrid bolted up on her feet and clutched his sleeve, "you must find him! He could be the one that brought the bloody heart to my hotel room!"

"Certainly, Señora. We'll put this information together in your file," Hernandez said calmly. "We'll watch for him. Have no fear. We want our tourists to feel safe in Cozumel." Hernandez turned to Dan. "We're done here, Señor. Perhaps you can bring her back." He added to Ingrid, "If we have any information we will contact you, *señora*."

Dan helped Ingrid up and steered her to the front of the store. I followed behind with Lola. Ingrid turned to me, digging her nails into my forearm. "Adie, I can't go with you to the party."

"That's okay, Ingrid. Go back and try to relax."

She grabbed my arm. "You must make the deal for me."

"What?"

"Excuse us a minute?" Ingrid called out.

Lola and Dan stepped out on the sidewalk. Dan held his hand up for a taxi.

Ingrid took an envelope out of her purse and handed it to me. "Show Diego the photos and see if he can find one for me. I'll pay up to nine hundred thousand, but, Adie, try to get it for less. I know you can..."

I searched her face. "Can't this wait? I feel awkward about this."

Ingrid shook her head. "Time is of the essence. If he can get the antiquity I want, I will arrange the payment. But tell him I will need to examine it personally before we finalize the deal. My contact information is on the back of the card." She squeezed my hand. "Do me this favor, Adie, and I'll give you a month in Jamaica."

* * *

The condo was a block away from the store. The security guard greeted me politely. "*Buenos dias*, Señorita Sturm."

"*Buenos dias.* Did Señora Bolivar Alvarez come back?"

He shook his head. "She left early this morning."

"Could you please buzz my apartment when the limo arrives?"

"*Si,* Señorita." He tipped his hat.

The lobby was cool and luxurious with the variegated ivory marble continuing from the stairs to the next landing. I pulled out my key and let myself in. It was an aesthetically pleasing room with the neutral tones accented with green—calming, after the encounter with the thug.

Once in the bedroom, I slid open the door and scanned the closet for something casual but stylish for Diego's luncheon. I found a lemon-yellow halter dress, which clung to my waist and hips and flared down to an irregular hemline. Very flattering, I thought, admiring myself.

I stepped back into my sandals and found the beach bag and opened it. I threw in two more string bikinis, just in case. After freshening my makeup, I went back into the living room and waited, eating a few grapes from a bowl the housekeeper had set on the table, and thought about the attacker at Pedro's Donkey. He seemed somehow familiar.

The intercom buzzed. I clicked the switch near the door. "*Bueno,*" I answered.

"Señorita Sturm, the limo is here."

"*Gracias.* I'll be right down."

I grabbed my beach bag and put on a pair of sunglasses as I made my way down the stairs to the lobby. An older well-dressed couple had just come in from outside. They were busy talking, but they took a moment to exchange a greeting in passing. Wealthy retired Mexicans on holiday, I guessed. Diego's parents probably came to Cozumel for their holidays. Life would be hectic in a highly populated place like Mexico City. His father had an import-export business and Diego must have his hand in it to be able to locate antiquities.

Was I doing something illegal? Who was I kidding? I didn't just fall off the turnip truck here. I knew this skirted into a gray area. Were three weeks in a five star all-inclusive hotel worth it? I thought back to the ice-storm I'd left behind. That would only be the start of a Canadian winter—freezing temperatures and snow in January, all of which I would miss.

The sun peeked from behind fluffy white clouds as I trekked out to the limo parked in front.

"*Buenos dias,* Señorita Sturm." The driver nodded politely and opened the door.

I recognized him from my last visit to Cozumel. "Ernesto?"

"*Si.*" He grinned. "You remember my name? Good. Last time, I was privileged to bring you to Señor Alvarez's yacht. Today you will be sure to enjoy his beach house."

"What's it like?"

"Very grand."

A mansion most likely. There were sure to be many important wealthy people at this gathering. I glanced down at my yellow designer dress. I couldn't be better dressed than this. Even if I didn't know the rest of Diego's clique, I knew Diego and his sister. I could handle this. My biggest concern was George and his social behavior—or should I say, lack of it.

I was beginning to regret the idea of George accompanying me to Diego's beach house. For once I regretted not having Ingrid along. I frowned, recalling his rude leer. But I had to get past that. It was par for the course when it came to being an attractive tour group leader—at least to some men. A job was a job. No matter what creeps became part of my group, it was important to leave them satisfied by the end of the trip. The last thing I needed was a bad evaluation from a disgruntled client.

By the time the limo pulled up in front of the Don Juan, I was feeling at little bit down in the dumps. Under an awning, George leaned against the wall, waiting. When he saw the limo he trotted up to my window. I pushed the button to lower the glass. George stuck his face in.

"Adie, if it's all right, I'll follow you in my rental."

"Sure." I sighed inwardly with relief.

"Another thing, Adie. Do you think Mr. Alvarez would mind if I brought Janice?"

"Janice?" Whoa! What a break. "I'm sure it would be fine. Is she ready?"

George gestured to someone behind the heavy sliding doors and Janice stepped out slowly, squinting into the sun. Her outfit was not what I expected. An elegant pink sundress cinched at the waist and flared to the knees. And her jewelry was amazing—a thin tennis bracelet, a diamond pendant and matching earrings.

I instructed Ernesto to wait for George while he helped Janice into his rental Ford. Admittedly, I was puzzled. Yesterday, Janice was a fashion disaster and today she was dressed to the nines.

A memory flashed before my eyes. The emerald ring surrounded by diamonds. This woman had money—lots of it and here I'd thought I was doing her a favor inviting her to the fashion show for some pointers. What was she up to?

The driver was heading down the southern coastal highway past Chankanaab Park towards the fabulous San Francisco Beach. At a fork in the road, we veered off down a quiet road. After a short drive we turned into a narrow driveway, coming to a stop at a high iron gate. The guard at the gate let us through. Behind us, the Ford was still at the gate.

Ernesto swiveled around. "There's a problem."

I peered out the back window. George got out of his vehicle and bellowed at the guard in the booth.

"Ernesto, I need to talk to the guard."

"Would you like for me to accompany you?"

I opened my door. "No, it's okay. I'll only be a moment." I swung my legs down on the pavement. The sun beat down through the palms as I started my trek back to the entrance. In the trees, the birds shrieked to join in with George's shouts.

As I got closer to the gate, I noticed a tall, thin man stepping out of the gate. His face flustered and red, George stood rigidly, shoulders raised, in the kind of posture men get in before a brawl. The guard waved a wicked-looking knife just short of George's belt. The steel caught the light—gleaming brightly in the sun. I didn't wait any longer. As fast as my heels would allow, I skittered over the gravel to the gate. "No!" I shouted.

The guard jerked about. Brown hair swept his high fore-head. Sideburns bordered a narrow face. I would have considered him attractive except for the jagged scar that crossed his cheek-bone. But it was more than that. His coal-black eyes chilled me more than any winter's storm.

I stopped in my tracks. A film of sweat coated my skin under my bangs. Behind me, I heard shuffling footsteps.

"Eduardo!" The chauffeur trotted up. "This is Señorita Sturm."

Eduardo's eyes journeyed down my body. "Señor Alvarez's lady?"

Ernesto nodded.

"Señor Alvarez wants no mistakes."

Ernesto said something in Spanish.

"And what about this *cabrón*?" Eduardo spat through his teeth. "He claims to be an investor here to discuss real estate with *señor* Alvarez."

A mosquito hummed around my face. I swatted it away. "It's true! Señor Alvarez told me to bring him."

Eduardo's eyes riveted on me.

"*Si,*" Ernesto agreed nervously. He lapsed into Spanish.

Whatever he said must have had some effect. Swinging the gate open, Eduardo called out, "You—go," gesturing with his finger to George.

I'd never seen George move so fast. He hopped in the Ford, slammed the door shut, and gunned the engine, zooming through the gate to stop behind the limo.

The sun beat down on our heads as Ernesto and I hiked back. It was a relief to get into the back seat still cool from the air conditioning. The plush white leather felt pleasantly smooth on my skin.

For a minute there, I'd thought George was a goner. That frigid look in Eduardo's eyes pierced like a sword. I don't know how I would have defused the situation if Ernesto hadn't been there.

On the way up to the house, Ernesto spoke on the car phone. I breathed deeply in an effort to calm down. Too much happened today. A day of knives. A close call for George. And someone wanted Ingrid dead.

7

Cars lined the circular driveway. Sleek, expensive European imports in unobtrusive shades of silver. Towering emperor palms partially obstructed my view of an ivory mansion with a red-tiled roof. On the right, a six-car garage—through the lime trees, tennis courts and the glint of blue from a pool. The scent of bougainvilleas in the garden wafted in the warm moist breeze. From somewhere within the grounds, I heard soft guitar music and the garble of voices.

I was on pins and needles about this whole thing—my stomach in knots. As Ernesto helped me out of the limo, I was pleased to see Diego waiting, leaning languidly on a pillar near the side of the house. He gazed out past the trees to the turquoise waters of the Caribbean, his expression faraway and dreamy, unaware of my approach.

I watched him for a moment. His white shirt, open at the neck, was tucked into a pair of jeans. As the wind picked up, his medium length brown hair fell down on his forehead. Spotting me, he smiled, his hazel eyes startling me with their changeable depths.

"Adelinita." Diego pulled me close and kissed my cheek. A subtle hint of citron assailed my nostrils. I returned his kiss. "Ernesto told me there was a problem. You're not upset, are you, *mi amor*?"

What could I say? I was. Eduardo was a mean SOB. "My client was taken aback, to say the least. Eduardo threatened him with a knife."

Diego shrugged his shoulders. "He follows my orders, *mi amor,* but you," he said smoothly, putting his arms around me, "must not feel distressed. No one will ever hurt you. Eduardo has been told how important you are." His eyes flicked to the approaching Ford. "Ah, here is your client." He whispered in my ear, "Is there anything I should know before I do business?"

I shook my head. George was one-of-a-kind.

The blue Ford parked. George and Janice got out. Janice, the klutz of the other day, had apparently turned over a new leaf. She glided up as confident as any prom queen. She didn't quite have the looks to match but she was definitely a contender with the dress and jewelry. "Adie, hi!" She tittered, her eyes glued on my handsome companion.

"Diego, I'd like you to meet Janice Jones."

"Diego Bolivar Alvarez." He took her hand and lightly kissed her wrist. "It's a pleasure."

The red-head sighed.

"This," I said, turning to the big man, "is George Vandomheit." With a social moron like him, it was dubious if he would remember the required etiquette. Luckily, Diego reached out his hand first and George clued in.

The billionaire eyed Janice speculatively. "Are you the client that is interested in art?"

"Janice is George's friend. Unfortunately, Ingrid was unable to make it, Diego. She wanted me to handle it. Could I speak with you about that privately?"

Diego nodded. "Of course, *mi amor*." He gave each of us an arm and said, "Ladies, shall we?" leading us around to the other side of the house. "Most of my guests have arrived and the barbeque is ready."

Hibiscus trees with tangerine flowers were scattered randomly between short spiky palms along the winding gravel pathway to the ocean side of the house. "It's lovely here, Diego."

"Your beauty enhances my garden, Adelina." Diego's eyes swept down my dress, pausing a second too long on my legs.

"Your gardens are spectacular." Janice piped up enthusiastically, fluttering her eyelashes.

"You are too kind, Janice. George is a lucky man," Diego said smoothly.

Janice smiled smugly at me. But before I had time to puzzle this out, we neared the patio.

The party was in full swing, music and laughter rising over the rush of the sparkling waves against the shore. A long table had been set up buffet-style near an enormous built-in barbeque. George caught up with us and sensing Janice's fascination with Diego, hastily claimed her. "Will you be free to talk later, Mr. Alvarez?"

"Certainly, George, and please call me Diego. In the meantime, perhaps you and Janice would like some drinks?" Diego snapped his fingers for a waiter before he brought me over to the bar.

Perched on a wicker barstool, sipping a margarita, Carmelita swung her crossed leg back-and-forth to the music. A dashing bartender in a black vest and white shirt was shaking a frothy mixture in a rhythmic motion, all the while conversing with the willowy Carmelita. When she caught sight of me, she smiled broadly and stepped down. Artfully she sent me air kisses before she whispered excitedly, "Ricardo is here, Adelina!"

I checked out the patio and saw several men in casual clothes chatting with a few fashionably dressed women in staggering heels, flaunting flashy jewelry. "I'd like Adelina to meet my friends. Do you mind?" Carmelita captured my hand, drawing me away from Diego.

"But first she must have a drink, Carmelita."

"Of course. How rude of me." She said something rapidly in Spanish to the bartender. Diego frowned, adding a phrase and I was given a margarita with a white hibiscus adorning the edge of the glass.

Diego absently ran his fingers down a strand of my hair, his gaze intense. "See you in a while, *mi amor?*"

I nodded. His gaze lingered on me as he reluctantly joined a group of partiers. I sipped my drink slowly and complimented the bartender. "This margarita is perfect."

"*Gracias,* Señorita Sturm."

I was mystified. "Seems everyone knows who I am," I said to Carmelita.

"Diego told them." Carmelita laughed. "My brother is so in love. He lies in his bed at night fantasizing about you."

My cheeks grew hot, but I had to admit there was a certain part of me that was very curious about him too.

I looked around. Diego seemed to have disappeared and I couldn't see George either. Janice was carefully examining the cold buffet table and helping herself to some salad. I couldn't get over the change in her.

Carmelita snapped her fingers. "I'm losing you again." She waved over two slim women. One was a dusky-skinned beauty and the other a blonde stunner. "These are my models and friends, Belinda and Lourdes."

They greeted me with kisses.

Carmelita chatted softly to them in Spanish. They smiled at us in parting and wandered off. "That was just an excuse, Adelina. I really wanted you to meet Ricardo." She indicated a man standing near Janice. He was a tall, handsome man with gray streaks in his thick dark hair. "That's him. Wait 'til he's done talking."

He looked to be in his forties. Warm brown eyes and full lips—a George Clooney clone. "Is it still going strong then?"

Carmelita ran her tongue over her lips. "Mm-mm. But we need to be careful. Gloria's here." Her eyes roamed over to the barbeque where a trim blonde woman in a tight black dress was loading up a plateful of shrimp.

"His wife?"

She nodded.

"What about your husband? Is he here, as well?"

"Luckily for me, my father wanted him to stay in Mexico City a while longer. He doesn't know anything about the incident on the runway." She gripped my hand. "Diego doesn't know either. Let's keep it that way, all right?"

I touched Carmelita's arm. "Why?"

"These are Spanish men, Adelina. They aren't liberated. The last thing I want is for one of them to ruin my career." We strolled over to the buffet table, where she handed me a plate and took one for herself. "Those are grilled sea scallops and that," she pointed to the next platter, "is calamari."

"Scallops, I like but," I spotted another platter, "oh, there's lobster."

The chef, seeing my interest, said, "Would you like some, Señorita Sturm? Señor Alvarez said you would prefer the rock lobster."

"And he was right." I gave him my plate on which he placed a cracked lobster tail." I thanked him and added some rice and a bit of salad. "So, what's his wife like?"

"Gloria? She's a dragon. I'm so fortunate his daughter takes after him."

"Oh?"

"You met her last night. Tina. Does odd jobs. When I feel she's ready, she'll model."

"Has she worked for you long?"

We sat down at a table overlooking the far side of a kidney-shaped pool. A bridge in the shape of an arch crossed the pool near the center.

"No. Ricardo asked me to give her a job. Apparently, Gloria was opposed to Tina modeling but Ricardo likes to irritate her." Carmelita sipped her margarita, her eyes drawn to the dancing on the other side of the pool. "Ricardo's in the import-export business. Weren't you bringing a buyer for some antiquities?"

"Diego told you?"

"Is it that one?" Carmelita's eyes fell on Janice.

I shook my head. "Ingrid was taken ill. I'll be opening the deal."

Carmelita's laughter tinkled. "Really? I'd love to be a fly on the wall to see you wheeling and dealing with my brother." She sipped her drink. "And how did you make out with the sexy Wolf?"

"He told me Daniella wasn't involved with him. Is that true?"

Carmelita popped a shrimp into her mouth. "There's a lot going on between them, but I'm not sure it's romantic."

"Does Diego know?"

"Hh-mm, probably. The slut stops in to see him every week." She forked up a scallop. "You know, Adelina, I'm glad they broke up. Imagine Daniella for a sister-in-law."

My cell buzzed. "Excuse me." I flipped it open. *"Bueno?"*

"Very sexy. My spicy woman has outdone herself." Wolf's voice was seductively husky.

"Oh?"

"Yellow is your color, princess."

Whoa! How did he know what I was wearing? "Where are you?"

"Close. Are we still on for dinner?"

"Yes, but I have questions, Wolf." I glanced around the pool area but didn't spot him.

"I do too…what are you wearing under that dress?"

My eyes shot down. I was wearing panties but my bra was built into the dress. I jerked my head up, peering into the sun at the windows of the house, but the drapes were all drawn shut. He was nowhere in sight. "How did you know what I'm wearing? Where are you?"

"Calm down, princess. You are way too stressed. But not to worry, I can help. I think you would benefit from one of my special massages, don't you?"

His strong, sensitive hands all over, relaxing and soothing my tension until tantalizing tingles charged every nerve ending in my body. I sighed.

"Should I pick you up from the condo tonight?"

When I thought of the closet full of fabulous outfits waiting for me in the condo compared to my pathetic suitcase full of year-old discount clothes at the Don Juan, making a decision was a no-brainer. "Yes."

"Six?"

"Where are we going?"

"You like surprises." I heard the phone click.

"That was Wolf, wasn't it?" Carmelita grinned.

My eyes narrowed. "He's here, isn't he?" I could see it in her face. "Tell me."

"Ah-hm."

"Where?"

"I don't know for sure, Adelina." Carmelita tossed her hair back impatiently.

This woman was maddening. "When did you see him?" I demanded sharply.

"He arrived at the same time as Ricardo and disappeared shortly afterwards. Really, Adelina, I don't know where he went. I was trying to keep my cool around Gloria. The witch knows just how to press my buttons." Her eyes followed Ricardo. "Wolf had a meeting with Diego about something."

"I didn't think they liked each other."

Carmelita laughed. "Business is business. None of these people here like each other, with the exception of my models and us." Her eyes swept to the dance crowd on the deck. Gloria and the handsome Ricardo swayed sensuously in a slow rumba. Carmelita's jaw clenched. "Look at her, Adelina. She knows I'm watching them. Not that she gives a damn about Ricardo. They haven't had sex for a year."

"Is that what he told you?"

"Hm-mm. He was talking about divorcing her. But they all lie, don't they?" She stared, her eyes dreamy. "He sends me flowers and jewelry before each show. And then, he comes by afterwards and we make love."

"He sounds very romantic, but please be realistic. Don't forget he's married." I tapped the tabletop. "Listen, Carmelita. I'm worried about you. Do you think you'll be okay in Cancun?"

"Everything has happened here in Cozumel, so far. But if Gloria is behind this, who knows? She has the money to hire anyone."

"You don't think the saboteur is an enemy of Diego's?"

"I think anyone foolish enough to irk Diego isn't looking for a long life," she remarked dryly.

"You think Diego is that vengeful?" I bit my lip anxiously. "He wouldn't send someone after Wolf, would he?"

Carmelita smiled. "No, of course not."

"Why are you so sure?"

"Diego thrives on competition."

"They couldn't be business rivals, Carmelita. Most of Wolf's holdings are in Canada." I poked around for some more lobster hidden in the shell.

"And most of Diego's are here, but he's expanding his operations in Canada—Toronto and Montreal."

"So are you saying they are helping each other?"

"Business allies, but in the romantic sense, amiga, they are rivals."

"How is the lobster, *mi amor*?" Diego said, from behind us.

I turned. "Excellent!"

Diego sat down at our table between us. One of the waiters brought over a plateful of grilled scallops and a salad. A dark beer in a pilsner glass was set before him by another waiter. He lifted the beer to his lips, his thick gold bracelet sparkling in the sunlight. "Did Carmelita introduce you to Ricardo, by chance?"

"No, but she pointed him out to me. He's involved in the import-export business?"

"Yes. After we've finished eating, we'll meet in the house. He'll be helpful in your inquiry for your friend."

A waiter hovered behind me ready to whisk my plate away as I placed my fork down. My eyes searched the pool area but still no sign of Wolf.

"I hope you brought a bikini."

"Um-mm." I wondered where Wolf was hiding.

"Right after the meeting, would you join me for a swim?"

"Sure… You haven't had much chance to enjoy your own party, have you?"

Diego flashed me a dazzling smile. "Don't worry, *mi amor*. I will eventually."

Carmelita chuckled. "You will have to be extra attentive to Adelina or she will likely disappear on you."

"I'm way ahead of you on this, Carmelita." Diego turned to me. "Are you interested in the Days of the Dead?"

"Very much. Did I tell you that it's the theme for my tour?"

"No, I don't think you had." He called out to a waiter in Spanish. A minute later, a silver tray with candy skulls was placed in front of us. "These are made especially for the Days of the Dead. Try one, Adelina."

White skulls with green or pink eyes and yellow skulls with red eyes winked conspiratorially at me, their sparkly eyes glittering in the sunlight. Green lines and blue stars decorated the face of a skull I picked up. "Almost too pretty to eat." I bit into the little candy. "Pure sugar with a hint of vanilla."

Diego pushed a strand of my hair away from my cheek. "You were expecting chocolate?"

"No…"

"Yes, she was." Carmelita's eyes twinkled. "Don't worry, *amiga*, this is the land of the Mayans, in other words, chocolate country. And we both know how Diego likes to please you. He'll find you some. You know how he is."

A passing waiter swept up Diego's plate.

With lunch over, I was feeling a bit nervous about this deal. I wished I hadn't gotten myself involved.

Diego finished his beer and set it down. "Shall we?" He glanced at Carmelita. "Tell Ricardo to meet us in the office."

Carmelita nodded and got up with us.

Diego put his hand at my back and we walked to the side entrance of the beach house. The hallway was dark and quiet. My heels clicked on the marble tiles as we passed two closed doors. He paused at the next door and slowly opened it. "There's something here I wanted to show you."

My curiosity was piqued. Inside a spacious square room, wide wood-framed landscapes in rich autumn shades hung on walls painted a deep lemon color. Ivory drapes were tied back to let in the afternoon sun. A round oak table dominated the room. Yellow marigolds in an oriental vase had been placed in the center of the table and a photograph in a gold gilt frame was placed near a decanter and glasses.

Diego led me over to a leather loveseat. From the table he picked up a photograph. It was a sepia print of three small children, two boys and a girl. Laughing and holding each other, the threesome faced the camera. The boys had light-brown wavy hair and the girl's hair was blonde.

"What adorable children." I noticed their eyes. "This boy is you, the little girl is Carmelita but who is the other boy?"

"My older brother, Amancio." Diego's eyes looked sad. "He had a quality about him that set him apart from all of us. We were as close as two brothers could be. It devastated all of us when he drowned in a diving accident a couple of years ago." Diego's forehead furrowed. "They never found his body. My father wanted him to take over his empire but," he shrugged his shoulders, "it became my responsibility to run our Cozumel operation, to my father's disappointment." Diego filled two glasses with a golden amber liquid and handed one to me. He grinned ruefully. "You can't always have what you want. The old man realizes now that I was more suited for the job and he seems to be happy with the way I have directed the company."

He clicked my glass with his. "To Amancio. May he visit us soon." Diego smiled slightly. "You'll find it of interest that people set up altars for the dead at this time, do the traditional baking and decorate the gravesite of their relatives—all in preparation for the return of the spirits. The Days of the Dead are a mixture of Mayan and Spanish cultures. I'm afraid this," he waved his hand, "isn't typical of Dias de los Muertos and certainly not as elaborate as some. We've never done this before—a special circumstance. Last year, my nanny, after the death of her husband, asked to stay and supervise the servants here at the beach house." He eyed his glass. "Mama was actively involved in the family business, so Alva was always like a mother to us. She's the one who decorated the room."

My eyes settled on the china vase filled with yellow marigolds. "The flowers?"

"Ye-ss. Those particular flowers signify death and rebirth. I believe we usually have roses at the mausoleum. But, no, it's not just the flowers." His eyes flicked over to a brass candelabrum at the corner of the room. "Alva set out the candles and the photograph. None of us do this sort of thing normally. I mean," he shrugged his shoulders, "we do honor the dead at the cemetery, but that's about it. There's an altar at the family mausoleum. We have an attendant do the upkeep. Some people wash the stone and keep a vigil on the night of the Dead." He shrugged. "Our family is not superstitious that way. It is a custom of the ignorant but when Alva insisted, I let her go ahead and encouraged Carmelita to help her.

Carmelita was in need of some sort of distraction from her god-awful marriage." He lifted his glass, admiring the hue of the tequila. "I told them if they were to do this right, Amancio should have his favorite tequila."

"How sad about your brother." I stroked Diego's arm.

Diego took up my hand and kissed it. "The dead are not unhappy, Adelinita." He brought his glass to his lips and drank. "This was his favorite—Reserva Antigua 1800 Anejo. Aged in the barrel for many years. What do you think?"

"Soft, very smooth."

"And the flavors?"

"Honey."

"This is a complex blend."

"It has..."

Diego smiled encouragingly. "Have another sip."

I closed my eyes and let my taste buds take over. "Not chocolate?"

Diego looked pleased with my summation. "Nice, isn't it?" He glanced back at the altar. "In Mexico, people set up food for the dead with some favorite objects the loved one enjoyed. You see," he pointed to a silver case, lying next to the candles, "his cigarettes. Tradition has it, the spirits return to us on the night of November first. Many visit the cemetery that night in hopes of seeing the dead. Families have dinner on November second to feed the dead. There's a lot of hocus pocus associated with it. Butterflies are the spirits returning to visit, and such." He smiled, as if amused by the whole thing. "Take your glass, *mi amor.* Ricardo will be waiting for us by now."

The office was near the end of the hall. The door was open. Ricardo relaxed in a green leather chair, his feet outstretched on the ottoman. Seeing us, he stood up politely and waited as Diego introduced us.

"Adelina, may I present Ricardo Montalvo— Señorita Sturm."

"Nice to meet you." I shook Ricardo's hand.

Diego guided me to a creamy leather chair. He himself decided not to sit behind the massive oak desk. Instead he opted for a cushiony settee directly across from me. The men eyed me as I got out the envelope. I passed Ingrid's photos and Diego, in turn, gave them to Ricardo.

"The Jaguar God in jade. Late Classic period, I would say," Diego said, his voice just above a whisper.

After a quick study, Ricardo nodded imperceptivity. "I can get one for you. How much is this lady willing to pay?"

"A fair price."

"Nine hundred thousand," Diego suggested.

I sipped my tequila and said nothing. The men exchanged glances.

"These are all rare pieces, *mi amor*," Diego explained slowly, as if I were a child with an attention deficit disorder needing some repetition in order to comprehend the complex mechanisms of the art world. "Fortunately, Ricardo knows a collector who is willing to give one up." He poured some tequila from a decanter he had set on the coffee table and handed a full glass to Ricardo.

I tilted my snifter, deliberately watching the amber liquid flow to the other side of the glass, glinting gold where the filtered sunlight hit.

Impatiently, Ricardo shifted in his chair. Diego cleared his throat to get my attention. I stared at them.

"A fair price."

Speaking rapidly in Spanish, Ricardo clarified something. Diego examined his pinky ring reflectively. Ricardo suggested, "We can perhaps obtain it for eight hundred and ninety-eight thousand. The collector needs the money."

"Seven hundred and fifty thousand is doable as long as the statue is acceptable to my buyer."

Diego's smile didn't reach his eyes. "You amuse me, *mi amor*. This is a Classic piece."

I crossed my legs, displaying some thigh. Their eyes traveled up my leg.

"Ingrid might be persuaded to pay seven hundred and seventy thousand." I smiled encouragingly.

Diego tapped his fingernails impatiently on the wooden armrest.

Ricardo leaned forward. "We need to make something on this deal, Señorita Sturm. Eight hundred and fifty would be our best price."

"I am taking your word that it is an authentic piece."

Diego threw up his hands, exasperated. "I would not cheat you! She will have the opportunity to examine the piece and refuse it if she wants. Be reasonable, *mi amor*."

"Give the collector less. He wants the money badly, you say."

Diego leaned over and poured me some more tequila. "Surely, you can do better?" His brandy eyes crinkled at the corners as he smiled.

"Eight hundred thousand is my best offer." I stood up and walked to the doorway, swiveling back towards them at the last moment. "Think about it." I stepped into the dark hallway and started towards the door.

"Wait!" Diego pursued me down the hall. "Adelina, come back. "Eight hundred forty thousand. It's a fair price for valuable Mayan art." I let him escort me back. Settling myself in my chair, I said, "Eight hundred and twenty thousand. My final offer."

"Eight hundred and twenty thousand, under one condition."

I regarded him suspiciously. "What condition, Diego?"

"I would like very much to take pictures of you in your bikini."

Ricardo kept his face impassive.

"By the pool?"

"I have a better place. Do we have a deal?"

"Eight hundred and twenty thousand and two pictures."

Diego nodded solemnly.

I got up and shook hands with both of them. "It will be delivered?"

Ricardo nodded. "I have her contact information." He pocketed the picture of the Jaguar God and placed his snifter back on the table. "*Con permisso*," he said politely before exiting the room.

"Where?"

"In the bedroom." He put his hand up. "You can trust me, Adelina."

"You promise, otherwise…"

Diego regarded me seriously. "You have my word." He took my arm. "Come, Adelina, we should do this before you swim."

"No messed up hair, you mean?"

Contemplatively, he fingered a stray strand of my hair. "Your hair has a lovely abandoned appearance. I'd like to capture that…" He stopped abruptly as a massive man came out of one of the rooms and ambled towards us.

"*Señor* Alvarez." He inclined his head respectfully before continuing quickly in Spanish.

Diego listened and nodded. He turned to me. "You can change in that bedroom at the end of the hall. I'll be there shortly with my camera. I need to make a call but I won't be long."

I watched them go back to the office and I continued down the corridor to the bedroom. Inside, a king-sized, brass poster bed, with a silky black spread, dominated the spacious room. Ivory marble tiles covered the surface of the floor and an immense floor to ceiling window met a vaulted ceiling. French patio doors opened onto a small private courtyard filled with flowering plants and patio furniture.

Seeing the mirrored doors on one side of the room, I peeked in. A walk-in closet. From the assortment of men's clothing I guessed I was in Diego's bedroom. Curiously, I felt the fabric of a white shirt. Silk. I brought it to my face—a scent of citron.

Aware he might be displeased to find me snooping, I slid the doors of the closet shut and padded over to the bed. I stifled a yawn. I needed to get changed, but first, I should lock the door. At the oak door, I found a keyhole without a key. I was beginning to feel like a fly caught in spider's web. A sexy spider.

I'd have to hurry. Snapping myself into gear, I picked up the beach bag and dug out a white and black print bikini. Slipping off my dress and my panties, I tossed them on the bed. My metallic high-heeled sandals unfastened, dropped to the floor. After I tugged on the white print bottoms, I pulled out the top and was tying on the halter when the door creaked. The straps slipped through my fingers and the top slid up, uncovering my breasts. I sensed, rather than saw, the flash of a camera.

"Stop that!" I said through my teeth, seeing Diego with a camera from over my shoulder. Capturing the delinquent bikini strings, I tied the bikini in place.

"Don't be upset, *mi amor*. Your pose was so classic. Degas painted it."

"You are not Degas, and I am not your model!" Great, I thought angrily. He's got this risqué photo that he could post on the net. That would be the end of my career. "Delete it!"

Diego flashed a white grin. "But you promised me a photo."

"You heard me."

"All right, Adelinita, but let me take one with those high heels."

"Okay, but that's it." I picked up the sandals and perched myself on the bed. Diego placed the camera on a green silk-upholstered loveseat at the end of the bed. From an oak table he picked up a decanter filled with an amber liquid and poured two glasses.

"If that's tequila, Diego, I don't know if I'm up to it."

"We just completed a deal, *mi amor*. We must seal it with a drink. That's how businessmen do it here—but if you can't, that's understandable."

He didn't think I was up to snuff with his macho male associates? "Pour me one," I said tightly, taking a seat on the couch.

Diego handed me a snifter and proposed a toast. "To more lucrative deals." He clicked his glass to mine.

I drank the sweet nectar and eyed Diego. "You think it was lucrative for you? Are you saying I lost out?"

Diego patted my hand. "You didn't lose anything, Adelinita. It wasn't your money to lose."

I sipped the tequila and glared at him. "It was my client and if I am to bring any more clients to you, I want to be sure that you are dealing honestly with them."

"Rest assured, she will not complain."

"You don't know Ingrid. She's evil."

"Hence the underworld Jaguar God is her favorite?"

"Death is attracted to her."

"How so?"

"A bloody heart in a box with a death threat was delivered to her and today she was attacked in a store—a man with a knife." I took up my sandals from the floor and put them on, while Diego's eyes watched me.

"The woman has a serious enemy."

"You can see why she was too stressed to come here today."

He shrugged his shoulders, dismissively. "Just as well, *mi amor*. It was far more fun doing business with you. You need to stay here in Cozumel." He leaned back, and stretched his legs out, scrutinizing me. "I could give you your own travel agency."

"You know I can't do that, Diego."

"But you will think about it? Now, finish your drink, Adelinita. You said you'd indulge me with another photo. Lay on the bed. It will be a sensational shot."

"With my heels on?"

"Definitely." Diego took my glass and placed it on the table. In one sweep he lifted me in his arms and the next instant I was perched on his bed. "Lay back and spread your hair out and bend one leg." He picked up the camera and started to adjust the focus.

Whoa! I was floating in space. The room did a complete three-sixty. I had been weaned on schnapps—that's practically pure booze. If I were a boy, I would have had a heavy growth of chest hair by now. A real man, according to family tradition, knows how to consume schnapps—but at this point, I was wondering if I'd had enough practice.

"Adelinita, give me a sultry look."

The pillow was so soft—sleep would be so easy right now. I stretched out one leg, wishing I'd taken off the shoes.

Sit up! My Logical Voice ordered. Don't let him know it's hitting you hard.

"Let's try another one in case that one isn't good."

I sat up and leaned forward on my elbows.

"Nice!" Diego said enthusiastically.

Exhausted by the effort, I rolled over on my back and shut my eyes. The bed moved as Diego lay down beside me. "Adelinita, I've missed you."

"You have?" I murmured, glancing up at Diego. The greenish tinge in his hazel eyes dazzled me. A delightful shiver ran down my body as my hormones recharged.

My Logical Voice started screaming in my brain—I told you to get up when you had the chance. You are such a fool, taking him up on his dare. He's got you now, doesn't he? Meanwhile my Hormone Voice kept coaxing me—touch him, he wants you to.

I reached out and ran my fingers through his wavy dark hair. Leaning in, he lowered his lips on mine, his kiss tender. My mouth pressed into his. Burning heat from his body to mine. His tongue played on my lips. I had no options left. My mouth parted for more. His touch made my body quiver.

Diego pushed a stray lock of hair away from my neck before he pressed his mouth lightly on my throat. His fingers stroked my hair. With each feather-light kiss, I sighed and let my fingertips explore his warm strong arms.

Suddenly he sat up, unbuttoned his shirt and tugged it off. His body was as delicious as I remembered, a strong chest and six-pack worth broadcasting to my friends. Lowering himself beside me, he said in a smoky voice near my ear, "Why don't we go visit the collector tomorrow? You'll find the Mayan pieces intriguing." Nuzzling my neck once again, his hand skimmed the base of my breast.

"How long would it take?" I asked distractedly, wondering where his hand would go next and whether I should stop him.

"My pilot can fly us." He kissed my throat, sucking my skin into his mouth. "It would be better to stay overnight."

"I don't know about that," I said breathlessly.

His fingers stroked my skin where it met my bikini top. "Your skin is so smooth," he said softly, before bringing his lips down to caress the object of his interest. His thumb pulled the bikini lower, exposing more to his lips.

I struggled to control my urge to push him in closer. Summoning up all my strength, I pulled away. "Diego, you know I'm involved with another man."

Caressing the palm of my outstretched hand, he drew me in with his brandy eyes, searching for something I had and he wanted. "Only temporarily, Adelinita. You'll soon see him for what he is really is. He has no time for you—too busy setting up deals. Moreover, there's Daniella. She must be sleeping with him by now. You've been gone for a while and a man has needs."

How could I have forgotten about that barracuda and her underhanded ways? It upset me so much to think of her, Diego easily guided me back down onto the silky surface.

"Sweet Adelinita, stay here with me." His hair brushed lightly against my cheek as he closed into my neck and kissed me once again. "I want to get to know you better."

"No, Diego. I should go." But his bed held me there—a haven of comfort. I was floating on a cloud, one of those big, fluffy ones you see on a sunny day in a bright blue sky.

"But you must see the ceiling."

What was he was talking about? Diego must have had too much tequila himself. But I didn't care…he was so sweet and such a devastatingly handsome man. Lying here on the bed was bliss. My thoughts became wicked. Why shouldn't I have him? After all, Wolf was a wild card—always had been. Besides, he was sleeping with Daniella. I had the opportunity to have this man—*carpe diem*. Should I seize the day…and Diego?"

Pushing a wayward strand of hair from my eyes, Diego whispered, "Look up."

It was a ceiling fresco in the shape of a wheel. Mayan Gods in traditional Mayan headdresses scattered about the wheel. The more I looked, the more it blew me away—the figures were nude in kama-sutra positions.

Diego pointed to one portion of the painting. "There's the Jaguar God—the sun deity during the day and the patron of war."

I peered at it, The Jaguar God wasn't making war—no, I'd say he was getting it on with a cutie with a round behind. The sex looked a little uncomfortable and I couldn't see myself getting what I needed from those positions. "And my frog god?"

"There." Diego waved his hand upwards to the west point of the circle. "He's holding a lightning bolt, a stone ax and a serpent. See the cave? That's his home."

My eyes fixed on a beautiful naked goddess beckoning the frog god to her. The mural was kinky but why bother with visuals? Were Diego's partners so bored they needed an interesting ceiling to look at? I giggled.

Diego smiled, bemused. He leaned over and brought his hand to my waist. His eyelids lowered and his lips moved smoothly on mine. I felt his fingertips lightly stroke my waist and slide down to my hip, to the curve of my butt. Liquid fire torched my center. I was so wrong. Diego was a master at lovemaking.

"You're a woman made for love." His silken tongue awakened my neck and trailed down to the rise of my breasts. I pulled him closer, my hand skimming his waist. Diego reached for the strings of my bikini.

Loud voices and a commotion carried from the corridor—a man's guttural tones followed by a high-pitched woman's protests. There was a quick rap on the door. I sat up.

"Just a moment," Diego called out gruffly. Getting up, he opened the door.

"*Discúlpeme*, Señor Alvarez. There is a problem." Diego's massive bodyguard stepped into the bedroom.

Annoyance displayed itself on Diego's handsome visage. "Churo, surely this can wait."

Churo's eyes appraised his boss's situation. I saw a flicker of a smile. "There is a lady, Señor Alvarez, in your office. She said she wanted to speak with you. I let her wait but I caught her searching through the papers on your desk."

Hastily, Diego got up. I swung my legs off the bed and reached down for my bag. The room spun. I sat back down. I spotted my dress and panties on the floor. Slowly, I scooped up my clothes. I took a moment before I pulled out my paraeo. While I tied it on, I was intensely curious as to what the situation with the woman was.

"Pardon me, Adelinita, but I need to deal with this."

I nodded.

I heard Diego talk to Churo as they made their way down the hall. I waited for their voices to grow fainter before I peeked into the hallway. I couldn't see anyone but I heard more Spanish followed by a woman's high-pitched squeal. "Get your hands off me!"

Gliding against the wall, I made my way to the office.

Diego's voice was harsh. "What is it you were looking for?"

"I came in here looking for you, Diego."

"Oh?"

"It's true. I am interested in antiquities and Ingrid had mentioned that she was making a purchase."

"So you found it necessary to search through my papers?"

"Not searching, merely looking. The folder on your desk was labeled Mayan Art. I didn't think you would mind. I was told to wait for you to return. Ask him."

"Janice, I would be happy to discuss this with you if you have the money," Diego said smoothly.

"Rest assured, Diego, I do."

Whoa! This was klutzy, little Janice? She was slicker than oil. But who was playing whom? Before I could hear more, Churo and Luis came out. After they saw me, the game was over. I had no choice but to continue on out into the bright sunshine.

* * *

The pool was busy. The water sparkled in the sunshine but somehow it didn't attract me. Past the trees bordering the property, a gate opened to the beach. The powdery white sand and the sparkle of sunlight on the surf's aquamarine waters beckoned to me. I had a longing to feel the sand between my toes. Through the gate, I headed away from the party.

The hot ocean breeze filmed my skin with salty moisture, awakening my body. I breathed in the air to clear my head.

White chaise lounge chairs were lined up in a row close to the shore. A round beach bar with a palapa roof stood next to the gate. A couple of partiers were standing around having some beer. I set my bag on a chair and perched myself on the end to unfasten my sandals. Kicking them off, I stood up and pulled off my paraeo, dropping it on the chair.

His approach was silent. I was startled to feel his breath in my ear before his tongue flicked down my earlobe to the nape of my neck. "Gorgeous woman," Wolf said, "you taste so good." When his lips nuzzled my neck, a pleasurable rush flowed down my body. Powerful arms encircled my waist and his lips caressed my shoulder. "You're always surprising me, princess. What brings you to the fox's den?"

I turned to towards Wolf. "Tell me your secret and I'll tell you mine."

His enigmatic blue eyes searched my face. "I have many. You'll have to spend more time with me and everything that is important will be revealed."

"We're still having dinner tonight?"

"Sure are." Wolf's eyes took in my bikini. "Your assets have never looked better. Should I be thanking Alvarez for his contribution to your allure?"

I stiffened. Diego hadn't bought me. "The clothes are a loan. I won't be taking them with me."

Wolf stroked my cheek. "You can be so very naïve for such a sophisticated woman. You're telling me he doesn't want to get more involved?"

"Why the sudden curiosity? You were way too busy to e-mail. Which reminds me—your mother."

Wolf frowned. "What about my mother?"

"Before I left, my mom said Erika's upset you haven't contacted her."

"Business. I'm involved in a deal. She worries too much. You know mothers." He directed his attention to the ocean and then swiveled about and scooped me up in his arms. In a few strides he stood at the water's edge.

I clung to his neck in alarm. I was not keen about a sudden cool drop into the ocean.

Wolf smiled and slowly put me down into the gentle breaking waves. "Join me?"

"I wouldn't miss it for the world."

* * *

If it wasn't for the remnants of tequila in my system I could have caught up to him. Okay, I'm kidding—this guy was a bullet. Without my fins, I was a passable swimmer but by no means strong. I was way more confident snorkeling with the buoyancy of salt water with fins and a mask keeping me afloat, but the warm, clear water was a gift of nature I couldn't refuse.

Eventually, all good things came to an end. We let the waves push us back into shore and as the water got shallower we stood up. In the distance I could see a hotel further along the bend in the bay. In the other direction a white cruise ship glistened in the sun.

"Wolf, do you think Diego would try to cheat me?"

He grinned. "Yeah, sure, if he could get away with it. Oh, you said cheat you. Maybe not, but cheat on you...I have no doubt in my mind."

I poked his ribs. "I bought a Mayan God for Ingrid. Would he try to rip me off?"

Wolf appeared amused. "He wants to win you, remember?"

He pushed his wet hair back. "Besides, you're no amateur when it comes to bargaining."

"Um-mm." He was right about that. My pop had trained me well. I tried to comb my hair with my fingers but the salt water had glued it together.

"Let's rinse off," Wolf said as we neared the beach shower just outside the gate. The cold shower was a shock to the system but it did the job.

"Wait for me," I called out over my shoulder, running back to get my beach bag and sandals. I carried them along and joined Wolf at the gate.

"Adelina—Wolf!" Carmelita waved to us. "Where have you been?" Carmelita asked when we got back on the patio. She sat down on a lounge chair.

Wolf wandered over to the bar as I took the chair beside her and fastened my high-heeled sandals. "Business with Diego and then…" I said, as I tied on my paraeo.

Carmelita interjected, "Monkey business with Wolf." She laughed. "I wonder which one got the better deal?"

An exquisitely fine-boned blonde, with a perfect do, poked her way out from the crowd and stopped before us. "Carmelita, darling, Diego has outdone himself. What a lovely party." She stared at me. "Have we been introduced, my dear?"

"No, I'm Adie Sturm."

"Gloria Montalvo." She leaned over to kiss my cheek. "Strange name you have." She frowned at my wet hair a moment, before asking, "Is that what you Americans call a nick name?"

"Adie is short for Adelina and I'm a Canadian."

Wolf came up and handed me a strawberry daiquiri. In his other hand, he held a bottle of Dos Equis, his favorite beer.

Gloria shot a look at Wolf, her attention straying to his hair, almost dried to its streaky blond state. "Ah-hh, Wolf, you are a tricky one. Daniella should watch it. She's been fretting. And she should, shouldn't she? If she knew you were intent on the lovely Adelina, she'd be seething." Gloria tittered. "But don't worry about her, for now. I told her to look for Diego. She seemed to know you were in a meeting." A look of confusion appeared on her face. "*Dios mio,* how stupid of me—Adelina Sturm, of course. How could I forget? I should have recognized your name." She smiled triumphantly. "You are the American he's been raving about—his latest conquest."

My cheeks flushed in embarrassment. Carmelita came to my rescue. "Perhaps you misunderstood, *amiga*. Diego is extremely fond of Adelina, but his acquaintance with Adelina is yet young."

Gloria's eyes narrowed as she watched me tug a comb out from my bag. "What a lovely bikini, Adelina. From Carmelita's show? Diego has such good taste, doesn't he?"

I set my drink down, before I became tempted to throw it in her face. I struggled to comb my hair. Ignoring Gloria, I glanced at Carmelita. "Do you have a hat I could borrow?"

"Certainly, Adelina. I'll get one for you. Gloria, have you met my designer?" She took the dragon's arm and led her over to a slim stylish young man in tight jeans.

Wolf joined me on the chair and slipped his arm around my waist. "Forget about her. She talks too much."

But I was upset—seething inside. I picked up my daiquiri and slowly sipped my drink, deliberating about what the woman had said. She thought I was Diego's mistress and if I accepted any more gifts… Absentmindedly, I watched Carmelita heading over to the house. Gloria was at the pool, wiggling to a salsa beat with Carmelita's young designer.

"Guess who?" Out of the corner of my eye I saw a delicate pair of hands with long pink nails cover Wolf's eyes.

The return of my nemesis. Daniella. Thick-lashed brown eyes and an upturned nose in a heart-shaped face. Her round hips were tightly encased in a black dress slit high and cut low over her apple-shaped breasts. She deliberately ignored my presence, leaning down to whisper into his ear. "Things are going well, *mi amor.*"

"Daniella, you remember my friend?"

"Ah, yes." Her eyes flicked over to me. "Aggie, isn't it?"

"Adie."

Daniella stepped around the chair and plopped herself down on Wolf's lap, stroking his cheek in a familiar manner. "We need to confirm it."

Wolf's eyes narrowed in annoyance. He shoved her off and stood up.

Seething inside, I rose to my feet. "I'll leave you two to

whatever," I said, grabbing my bag before I stalked away toward the house in search of Carmelita.

As I neared the entrance, I heard a scream from within the house. I picked up my pace and raced down the hall. Sighting an open door, I stepped cautiously towards it. Footsteps. Diego and his bodyguards came running from the far corridor.

"What happened, Adelina?" Diego called out, when he saw me.

"I don't know. I came looking for Carmelita when I heard the scream."

From inside the room, we heard hysterical weeping. Diego hurried to open the door. I pressed close to him to see around his arm.

The flowers and candles were strewn everywhere amongst pieces of broken china. Carmelita was down on her knees. In her hand she held a photo of her dead brother.

8

Carmelita's gaze flicked up to us. "Someone wants revenge," she said quietly. "They knew I'd helped Alva set this up."

I knelt down and put my arms around her. "Is the photo intact?"

Carmelita nodded. "It was disrespectful and wicked."

I squeezed her shoulders.

"We'll find the vandal, *mi amor*," Diego assured her. He shot a glance at Churo who nodded. "Come, don't be upset." He pulled her up and gave her a quick hug. "Maria will clean up the mess. Go with Churo. Rest awhile. Everything will be as it was before in no time." Churo led Carmelita down the corridor to a room I assumed to be a bedroom.

My heart went out to Carmelita with the mess strewn on the floor. "I'll be going now, Diego. With this happening, I think you need to know about the sabotage at the show. Ask Carmelita. She didn't want me to say anything, but I think it would be best that you knew. Besides, everyone saw it. She can't keep it a secret."

"Now I am concerned. I will handle it diplomatically, of course. I will insist she has a bodyguard." Diego kissed me on the cheek. "We'll go tomorrow morning as planned. I'll phone you with the details. The driver will take you to the condo."

"A driver is not necessary," Wolf spoke up behind me. "I'll take Adie."

I don't know why I agreed to go with Wolf, especially after seeing him with that barracuda. On the other hand, I felt especially pleased that he had decided to abandon Daniella.

His face solemn, Diego nodded. Wolf took my hand. We walked down to the side entrance. As we entered the crowded patio, I asked him dryly, "Should you be leaving your date?"

I waited for a quip but instead his jaw clenched. At the driveway we stopped in front of his black Jeep.

As Wolf unlocked the driver's door, a raspy voice called out. "Señor Du Lac, you take good care of Señorita Sturm, *si*?" On a small wooden bench under a tall palm, smoking a cigarette, Eduardo stretched his long legs. His piercing brown eyes stared penetratingly. "A woman like her needs a strong man. But before you decide you are that man, you would be wise to remember she belongs to *señor* Alvarez."

Wolf's dark blue eyes met his, glittering dangerously. Eduardo curled his lip in an evil smile, exposing teeth studded with sparkling gold fillings. He spat on the grass, guffawing loudly. His rattling smoker's cough took over and ended in a retching choke.

Wolf opened the door for me before I got in. I heaved a sigh of relief when he started the engine and the Jeep eased into the road.

"That man scares me," I said, thinking how he had undressed me with his eyes. My skin crawled at the sight of him.

"Better stick with me, princess. Alvarez has some ugly bodyguards."

"And you have some sleazy groupies."

The corners of Wolf's mouth twitched as he stared ahead at the road. A couple of cars joined us on the main road back to San Miguel. "Daniella is putting something together for me." He reached over and touched my hand. "I'll explain it tonight."

I jerked my hand away. "What should I wear?"

Wolf glanced sidelong at me and said, "Something to match your eyes. The Caribbean blue ones, not the turquoise. I'd hate to have you angry with me."

"Then you should stop irritating me, shouldn't you?"

"I know how to make you purr, kitten."

"This cat is more likely to scratch than purr," I snapped.

Wolf smiled slowly. "Intriguing…" His clear blue eyes studied me for a moment as we came to a stop sign. "You'll have to come and see my cottages."

"They're all renovated?" Before I left Cozumel, Wolf had bought a property with several cottages in San Miguel.

"Not all of them but the one I'm staying in is." Wolf steered the Jeep alongside the yellow painted curb and parked in front of the condo. "I'll be back in about an hour to get you. Does that give you enough time to get ready?"

I nodded, and stuck my fingers in the semi-dry rat's nest on my head. As I was contemplating how many bottles of detangler I'd need, Wolf got out and came around to open the door for me. He helped me out, glancing appreciatively at my outstretched legs revealed by the paraeo as I jumped down. Shoving the car door shut with one hand, he joined me on the sidewalk. The late afternoon sun streaked the sky crimson and gold as it crept down behind the brightly painted stucco buildings across the street.

Wolf tilted my chin up to him. "Don't ever doubt I care for you." His mouth pressed firmly on mine, burning with an inner fire. Eagerly my lips parted for his enticing tongue. It was like a bolt of lightning shooting through my system.

"See you soon, princess."

Our eyes connected momentarily, my dark lust reflecting in his sapphire depths, before I picked up my beach bag and headed towards the condo.

The guard unlocked the wrought iron gate, greeting me politely. "*Buenos tardes,* Señorita Sturm." He kept his face expressionless as his eyes shot to my salt-clogged coiffure.

"*Buenos tardes.*" I trekked down the quiet hallway and up the marble stairs. Tugging out the key from my beach bag, I unlocked the door and kicked off my sandals. The diaphanous olive green curtains were tied back with a braided gold rope, allowing the sun to lend a rosy glow to the room. The air-conditioning was set on low but it was much cooler inside the condo, a relief from the humidity outdoors. This apartment was much larger than my house back home. Diego was grateful for saving his life. Surely, it was okay to stay here? Padding silently into the bedroom, knots formed in the pit of my stomach.

In the mirrored doors of the closet, my reflection was tanned, the redness gone, my eyes bluer than ever. Peeking in the closet was like peeling back the wrapping of a much-desired gift. Happily, I rummaged around and found a bra-top halter dress in cobalt blue with narrow strands of emerald green zigzagging through the weave. In the shoe rack, I tugged out peep-toed green sandals with ankle ties, matching the texturing of the dress. Digging around in the lingerie drawer, I located a lacy pair of panties.

Taking everything with me into the ensuite bathroom, including my beach bag, I hung up the silk dress and placed the other things on the counter. This bathroom had it all—fluffy white bathrobes, heated towel racks, luxurious bath towels, and a fabulous shower with fifteen jets ready to massage any part of my body. Puzzled by the switch located next to the lights, I curiously flicked it on and was soothed by an easy South American tango that filled the room with romantic ambiance. How like Diego to arrange this.

I ran the shower to a comfortable temperature and stepped in. Shampoo and conditioner got the sea salt out and body gel softened my skin. After I dried off, I smoothed a peach lotion all over. According to my watch, it was twenty minutes to six.

Hurriedly, I applied makeup and styled my hair. I needed to look fabulous. When I finished I checked myself out in the elaborate gilt-framed mirror. In karate the motto is *never give up*. I needed to recapture my man. Daniella had to be defeated and annihilated. Not an easy task but I had the advantage. I knew him better than that man-eater ever would.

My cell intruded on my thoughts. I shut off the music and clicked open the cell. *"Bueno."* I inspected myself in the mirror again as I listened.

"Hola, mi amor. Just calling to confirm."

"It's not a long trip, is it, Diego? I need to be back by one-thirty. I've scheduled a trip to Coba for my tour group."

"Certainly. We shall return by then."

"Is Carmelita all right?" I straightened my dress with one hand before turning the knob on the door.

"She's fine. Churo will go with her to Cancun. How about I pick you up at seven?"

"That's early."

Diego laughed. "To compensate for the obscene hour, we shall have breakfast and a pleasant lunch. The trip will be worth your while."

"Okay, that will work. Could you pick me up from the Don Juan? I need to be back there tonight."

"Certainly. I'll look forward to seeing you. *Adios, mi amor."*

"Adios, Diego." I smiled, thinking of how his eyes change to green so suddenly. Did it have something to do with me? It was kind of cool to have such power over a man.

On entering the bedroom, I ended the call and would have dropped it in my purse, but I froze in shock. My fingers lost their grip, the cell slid from my hand onto the marble tile where it skittered across the floor before friction stopped its momentum.

The room was in chaos. While I had been showering, someone

had come in and thrown the exquisite designer dresses all over the floor and then finished the job by wetting them with a pale liquid.

I knelt down and picked up a jersey-knit dress and smelled the fabric. Sweet. I touched it. My fingertip felt sticky. Orange juice. Thank God for small miracles. My eyes shot to a plastic orange juice container flung behind a chair. There, beside it, I saw a magnificent tangerine-colored gown strewn on the marble floor, viciously slashed from the neck-line to the hem.

My gaze fixed on a serrated knife which lay on top of the torn fabric. My heart pounded. I listened, thinking rapidly. A weapon would help. I glanced at the steak knife but I decided against it. I didn't have any experience with knives. It had to be something else.

From where I stood, the living room was visible, palely lit by the setting sun. Had someone set about destroying the whole condominium? More importantly, was the intruder still here? My eyes lit on a four-inch patent leather stiletto lying next to the torn dress. I picked it up, readying it as a weapon for an encounter. Tiptoeing through the doorway, I peered into the living room. Surprisingly, the luxurious leather couches and chairs remained immaculately intact in their positions around the glass coffee table where the maid had thoughtfully placed a vase filled with yellow, long-stemmed roses.

The intercom buzzed loudly in the silent condo. I ran over to the button and clicked it upwards. "Yes," I said, my voice sounding strange, even to my own ears.

"Adie? Is something wrong?" It was Wolf.

I pressed the buzzer. "Come up. Hurry!"

I opened the door and stood halfway into the hallway, waiting. I was so glad when he appeared at the top of the stairs, I rushed to him.

"What's going on?"

I stopped him, placing my finger to his lips to caution him. "Someone broke into the condo while I was in the shower. The clothes are a mess," I said in a low whisper.

"Have you checked the rest of the condo?"

I shook my head. "He may still be in there."

Quietly, Wolf pushed the door open and stepped into the living room. His eyes surveyed the area that continued into an open concept kitchen. I pulled his hand along to follow me in. Wolf frowned as he surveyed the mess in the bedroom, his eyes finally lighting on the long, jagged knife. He took my hand and we went back into the lounge.

Wolf's eyes shot to the guest bedroom with its closed door. "Stay here," he said softly, before he crept up to the door and slowly turned the knob. He stepped back before kicking the door open. The room was neat as a pin. No one had been in there since the maid had cleaned earlier today. Without another word Wolf retraced his steps to the entrance door and examined it for signs of a forced entry.

"Nothing here, Adie." He ran his fingers down the doorframe. "This person either was let in or had a key."

He glanced at the large picture window but dismissed that as an unlikely possibility.

I felt a chill. This intruder with a knife had been busy right outside my door while I was showering.

"I'm calling the police." Wolf pulled out his cell and punched in the number. He asked for Hernandez.

I waited while he spoke. When he ended the call, I said, "Diego will have to know."

"I thought it was your condo," Wolf said pointedly. "The police need to start an investigation." He led me out into the hallway, pulling the door shut behind us. We took the stairs to the lobby and then Wolf stopped, peering out into the twilight. There was no sign of the guard at the gate.

"Was there a guard there when you came in?"

Wolf frowned. "No, but he could be on a break somewhere."

We fell silent, waiting for the police to arrive. Wolf gave me a comforting squeeze as a police car pulled into the curb. We watched them park behind Wolf's black Jeep. Two uniformed police officers got out. The taller man undid the latch and swung the gate open, proceeding up the cobblestone walkway to the lobby, followed by the other cop. When their eyes adjusted to the dim lighting in the lobby, they spotted us and approached.

"*Buenos tardes,* Señorita Sturm, Señor Du Lac," Officer Hernandez said politely, while the other cop stood nearby, waiting. "What's the problem?"

"*Buenos tardes*, Officer Hernandez. You'll need to come up to my condo and see," I said, leading the way back. When I flicked on the lights, Hernandez's eyes widened appreciatively.

The kitchen separated itself from the living room by a black granite counter-topped bar with built in oak cupboards. A few high stools were placed on either side of the bar. Nothing seemed amiss.

Everything seemed so normal I half expected to see the clothes all tidied up and put away when we came to the bedroom. But it was the same scene of destruction I had shown Wolf earlier.

"Someone broke in here and did this, I assume?" Hernandez asked, his eyes darting to the closet.

I nodded.

Hernandez rapidly ordered the other officer to search the condo or that's what I assumed since they spoke in Spanish. The officer checked the windows and latches while Hernandez questioned me. "These are your clothes, Señorita Sturm?"

"Señora Bolivar Alvarez brought them here for my use while I stayed in Cozumel. The clothes are from her fashion show." It then occurred to me how upset Carmelita would be to see the clothes trashed like this. I would have to phone her.

"She has a key to this condo?" Officer Hernandez pulled out his notebook and scribbled some notes as I replied.

"Yes, and Señor Alvarez has a key as well, but they wouldn't do this," I said emphatically.

Officer Hernandez pursed his lips as he thought this over. "Pardon me, Señorita Sturm, for being so personal but is Señor Alvarez staying here?"

I felt myself flush. "No, I was here last night with Señora Bolivar Alvarez."

Officer Hernandez looked puzzled. "Are you living with Señor Du Lac then?"

"No, Officer."

Wolf explained, saying, "Señorita Sturm was here temporarily. From now on she will be staying with me at my cottage."

"What!"

Pulling me closer, Wolf whispered in my ear. "You're not safe here, Adie. It's for your own protection."

I shook his arm off. "Wolf, I can't. I have to be back at the Don Juan tonight to make arrangements for the tour group. I thought you could drop me off at the hotel after dinner."

Wolf ignored me and spoke to Officer Hernandez. "My address is Casa Rosita, 10 Avenida Norte, Calle 2 y 4. You can reach me on my cell at 88-3666."

"Señorita Sturm. I will make a report of this incident and I will question the guard. Perhaps he saw the intruder. Does Señor Alvarez know?"

"No, but I'll tell him tomorrow when I see him."

"Has this incident got anything to do with Señora Fleischer?"

"I don't know. It could, but it might have something to do with Señora Alvarez." I thought of how the blood had ruined the showstopper dress.

"How so?" He poised his pen, ready to record the information.

"Señora Alvarez didn't want me to say anything."

Hernandez shut his notebook reflectively and then he re-opened it. "I will need your phone number and your residence."

"This is my condo but it's more likely I'll be at the Hotel Don Juan, Room 202. My cell is 66-9090." My number was Wolf's idea of a joke when he gave me the cute little Blackberry a few months ago. And then I remembered something. "Officer Hernandez, I'll be in Coba tomorrow night."

"I must warn you, Señorita, if this has anything to do with *señora* Fleischer, you should be very cautious. Someone wanted to kill her and perhaps they find you a problem since you came to her rescue."

"I will be with Señorita Sturm in Coba," Wolf said.

"You're coming with me?" I was astonished by his announcement.

"Um-mm. You need a knowledgeable guide." He smiled. "We can go snorkeling in a cenote on the way."

"And this is because you think I need you to protect me?"

"For sure." And then seeing my frown, he said, "Besides there's almost nothing you like better than snorkeling with me."

"Oh yes, there is…"

Wolf shot me a lustful look.

"Food. I love to eat."

"Ah-hh, a pointed reminder. It's time for you to be fed, isn't it?" Wolf turned to Officer Hernandez who was grinning broadly.

"Señorita Sturm and I need to go. We have a reservation."

* * *

When we got into the Jeep, I tossed my skull beach bag into the back seat. Carmelita's designer outfits in the bag weren't damaged and I wasn't about to let some perverted fashion predator ruin my yellow dress or the snazzy string bikinis.

"By the way, I'm not your pet, Wolf."

Wolf's eyes glinted wickedly. "You are much too wild to be a pet." He maneuvered the jeep into traffic and turned down Avenida 10, stopping at the light. "I think cat when I see you," he said, reaching over, a finger stroking my cheek, "jungle cat." He pulled me close and his lips pressed on my mouth, awaking my desire. I felt deprived when he released me and placed his hands back on the steering wheel. After we turned right on a side street, he parked on Rosada Salas near the corner and said, "I hope you like La Choza."

It was busy and full of people but our table was situated alongside the garden courtyard away from the crowd. It was famous for its authentic Mayan cuisine and had won numerous awards, yet it was a simple place. The atmosphere was relaxed— on the wall an underwater mural of sea turtles swimming around a coral reef. At the far end of the room a Mexican trio softly strummed a ballad.

Wolf pulled out a chair for me and seated himself, his leg brushing against mine. I felt the heat from his jean-clad leg. His nearness was giving me thoughts beyond food. When he turned to summon a waiter, I admired his broad shoulders, covered by the black silk shirt, unbuttoned to glimpse the shadows of his muscular chest. "Ah-hh," I said softly.

"Don't worry, he's coming. Your usual?"

I didn't have a usual with him. He was a man of imagination and high sexual energy. Then, I clued in. "Yes, a strawberry daiquiri, please."

In San Miguel for several months now, Wolf had picked up some Spanish. When the waiter arrived, he ordered our drinks and entrees. Wolf was deciding what I should eat?

"Adie, I ordered the house special for us. It's Mayan. I thought you might want to try it."

"How do you know I'll like it?" I asked, as the waiter

appeared with a huge goblet filled with a crystallized crimson potion.

"You will. It's called *pollo de mole rojo.*"

I had a sip of my strawberry daiquiri and sat back in my rattan chair, watching the wicked gleam in his eyes, while attempting to translate. "Rubbing it in, eh, Wolf? Well, I know a little Spanish, too. *Pollo* is chicken!" I said, pleased with myself.

"Your knowledge is ever increasing."

"You noticed, eh?"

"Your knowledge needs more testing," he said softly.

Somehow, I knew this had nothing to do with Spanish. "There's a lot I need to tell you."

"Oh? Nothing disagreeable, I hope."

"What I have to tell you isn't, but maybe you won't like the questions I'll ask you later."

"Start with the good part then," Wolf said. He drank his beer, eyeing me from over the rim of the pilsner glass.

"Nothing is too good about this. It's about Ingrid."

Wolf lifted an eyebrow in response.

"Tomorrow I'm going with Diego to pick up the Jaguar God for her."

"You aren't helping her transport it, are you?"

The waiter carried two plates to our table and set them in front of us. "No, and neither is Diego's business associate."

"The Canadian government isn't as particular as the Mexican government."

"What do you mean?"

Wolf leaned back in his chair, brought his beer up to his lips, and drank deeply. "There was this tourist who bought some Pre-Colombian art in the jungle somewhere and when he got to the border he was afraid he was being ripped off, so he asked the border guard if the old man in the jungle was selling authentic antiquities." Wolf had a mouthful of his chicken entrée and then continued. "The border guards arrested him and put him in jail."

"Jail—a Mexican jail?"

"You got the picture." He ate a forkful of the entrée and then had another sip of his Corona. "It took his family months to pay off the officials to return to Canada."

"Don't worry, I'm not going to jail for that woman." I

tried a mouthful of the *pollo de mole rojo* and savored the delicious essence of the sauce combined with the chicken. "This is so good, Wolf."

"There's something you like in the sauce."

"What?"

"What do you like more than anything?" Wolf smiled slowly at my expression.

"Not—chocolate?"

Wolf grinned. "Just for you, baby."

"You remembered how much I like chocolate?"

"You and me both—releases those powerful endorphins." He stroked my hand, meeting my eyes.

"So the *pollo* is Mayan. Is *mole* chocolate?"

"It means mixture. This one is with tomatoes but many also have the component of chocolate." Wolf signaled the serenading musicians who had just finished their song at a table in front of the mural. They came over with smiling faces and asked if he had a request. "There's a song I heard in Cuba. Do you know *Dos Gardinias?*

"*Si, señor.*" The musicians strummed a rumba beat and the tenor sang the poignant lyrics in Spanish. Wolf held my hand as I attempted to understand the meaning of the words. It was definitely something about love. I understand *te quiero*, which means I love you, but I didn't want to read too much into this. When the musicians bowed, Wolf extended his hand with some bills.

"That was lovely, Wolf. I like Cuba, do you?"

"Um." Wolf's eyes met mine. "Maybe we'll be able to see it together some day."

I wondered if that trip had been with his ex. "Maybe…"

"Tell me about why Hernandez thinks you are a threat to someone."

"I know you don't think much of my karate skills."

Wolf put his glass down. "Why would you say that?" He rubbed my hand reassuringly. "I know I've kidded you about it, princess, but it takes getting used to—having my woman so kick-ass."

His woman? Did I hear that right?

"What happened with Ingrid?"

133

I forked up some more chicken. "I took the tour group to find some Days of the Dead souvenirs, you know, like skeleton boxes and figurines. We were in the back of Pedro's Donkey. I heard something fall and went to investigate. This guy was about to knife her. I knocked it out of his hand and cracked his nose, but he made a run for it into the alley."

"With your hand?"

I grinned. "No, picked up a rain stick. It was perfect."

"So she's lucky she's alive because of you?"

"Um-mm, but she was so stressed out after that she couldn't come out to Diego's house to talk to him about the statue. That's why I negotiated her deal with Diego."

"How much did she pay for the art?"

"We agreed on eight hundred twenty thousand dollars." I didn't think he'd want to know about the bikini shoot so I kept that little tidbit to myself.

"She's got money to throw around." He pushed his plate away.

I twirled my fork around thoughtfully. "Remember when I wanted to ask you about divorce?"

Wolf smiled slowly. "And I told you we had to get married first."

"An unlikely possibility."

"Afraid of commitment?"

"Hah, and you aren't?" I laid my fork and knife down on the plate and a passing waiter swept up the plates on his way to the kitchen. "Anyway, what I wanted to ask you is, when someone gets divorced do you get a share of your marital partner's business?"

Wolf sat back in his rattan chair, his fingertips steepled together reflectively. His mouth twitched. "You want to know what my assets are before you consider marriage?"

"No, this has nothing to do with you and me, Wolf." I tugged on his sleeve. "Ingrid has been a mess ever since her husband said he wanted a divorce. She has loads of money from her lover."

"Jordan James." Wolf's eyes roved lazily to my cleavage.

"Exactly."

"Did her husband have a business?"

"No. He was an accountant, I think, but," I wet my lips,

134

admiring his strong tanned forearms, "he did some work for her."

"I can see why she might be getting stressed. If he was involved in her company, he might be entitled to a share."

"In that case, she's more likely to want to murder him. Then, she wouldn't have to pay him anything."

Wolf's eyes shimmered blue like a fast-moving waterfall somewhere high in the rain forest. "Would he have reason to hate her?"

I let loose a laugh. "The poor guy had to live with the most manipulative control-freak I've ever met. Twenty years of it, Wolf."

"Do you know of anyone else that would want her dead?"

"Everyone who ever worked for her."

Wolf grinned.

I picked up my glass. "I wonder if she had a falling out with Jordan James."

"And he decided she should die?"

I had a last slurp of strawberry daiquiri and set it down. "It's a thought. He could have hired hit men."

"It's a possibility."

"Do you remember Janice?"

Wolf shook his head.

"You saw her at Diego's party and at the fashion show. Average-looking, red hair."

"Oh, yes. There was a tall red-head at Alvarez's house but she was better than average." He cocked his head. "Big boobs?"

"You would notice that," I said, in annoyance.

"I'm a man, baby."

My eyes raked his broad shoulders and strong chest. He was that. Um-hmm!

"What about her?"

"Her dress! It looked like high-end designer. And did you notice the jewelry?"

"No." Wolf grinned. "That's your department."

"The girl has money. You remember her at the dinner-fashion show?" Wolf looked puzzled. "That's understandable. She was badly in need of a makeover then. Janice has been conning me."

"You?" Wolf teased. "She's been trying to pull the wool over your eyes? But you didn't fall for it, did you?"

"I'm not going let her think otherwise at this point. If I confront her, I won't be able to find out what she's up to."

"And you know this because?"

"Churo caught her rifling through Diego's art papers."

"That would have riled the fox," Wolf said dryly.

"It did at first, but he called her bluff."

"How?"

"She said she was interested in Mayan antiquities and that Ingrid had told her about them," I said. "Then Diego took her in to his office to see what kind of money she was talking."

"You think she was lying?"

"She's rich enough, I'd guess. But there's something suspicious about her and her brother." Noting Wolf's puzzled expression, I explained. "Jeffrey. He's the one that bought me a drink at the Hotel Maria. The guy that prefers models."

"He's the one that had the hots for the willowy Carmelita and then spent the evening with our couch-potato friend, Ingrid."

I smirked. "More than that."

Wolf lifted an eyebrow. "He slept with her?"

"He said he did." I tapped my finger on the table, expounding further. "But get this. He said he spoke to Ingrid about antiquities, implying maybe I should get him in on a deal."

"What did you tell him?"

"Something vague. I have no idea what Mayan art is worth. I know Pre-Colombian is a lot less than Classic, but it's expensive. I'll ask Diego when I see him."

"Why are you going with him anyway?"

"He said I would learn a lot if I went."

Wolf grimaced. "I'm sure he's willing to show you more than what you need to know." He signaled the waiter for the bill. "Where does the collector live?"

I shrugged. "Couldn't be that far. He said I'd be back by one-thirty." I decided not to tell Wolf about going there in Diego's plane.

Wolf gave the waiter his credit card. "What time do we leave for Coba?"

"We should be on the two o'clock ferry for Playa." I cocked my head. "Aren't you busy working tomorrow?"

"Taking some time off to be with you." Wolf signed for the

check.

"If you don't mind, I'd like to skip the dancing. I'll have to get up early."

"I'll take you back to…where?"

"The Don Juan—but wait. Do you mind if we stop at the Internet Café? I need to send an e-mail."

* * *

We were lucky it was open. The adjoining department store was still humming with activity as Wolf parked the Jeep and helped me out, his eyes on my dress. "Very hot. The blue compliments your eyes, princess, and," he stroked my cheek, "at the same time, highlights that mischievous glint that makes you the spicy woman you are."

"Is that right, handsome?" I slid my fingers down his shoulder over the hard muscle underneath. "Nice."

"There's more of me," Wolf suggested seductively, his eyelids lowered.

"Um-mm, I'll bet there is."

Wolf drew me close, and his lips caressed mine, creating a rhythm of their own, until I was caught up in their music.

"*Con permiso*." A scowling hatchet-faced woman headed out the door. We separated to let her through. The woman's broad frame forced me to back up against the door. I choked down a laugh.

Wolf's eyes danced. "They should consider installing a wider door."

I'm not sure if she understood his remark, but she shot us a look of disgust as she brushed by.

Luckily a computer was available. In a few seconds I was ready to send my e-mail.

Hi, Ilya. Something strange is going on. Some-one wants to kill Ingrid Fleischer. This must have something to do with Telly's death. What did the autopsy show on Telly? Adie

Wolf stood looking over my shoulder. "Coincidence?"

I looked up. "I don't believe in coincidence, do you?"

* * *

The streetlights illuminated the sidewalks dimly. Wolf decided to leave the Jeep there so that we could walk the short distance to the Don Juan. The irregular surface and the cracks and were enough of an obstacle course even without the three-inch stilettos. I held tightly onto Wolf's arm on the way back to the hotel.

"You're okay leaving the Jeep there?"

"It should be fine for a while." He shot a glance at me. "Or should I have figured on a longer time?"

My hormones soared. I could almost feel his skin against mine, his warm breath at my ear as his fingers touched my body. I shouldn't though, should I?

So what's stopping you, my Hormone Voice said. He's into you.

My Logical Voice argued—If he knew how much you wanted him, he'd treat you no better than Daniella, his lust-deprived groupie.

"Adie," Wolf whispered in my ear, lightly running his hand down my waist. "Do you want to go up to your room?"

"Mm-mm…" His touch triggered delightful tremors through my body. "But first I need to check the Fleischer Travel board and make a few calls."

Wolf nodded, but I detected a flash of disappointment in his eyes.

At the front desk I asked for my messages. Leafing through I noted all were from my tour group. Janice was coming along to Coba. That meant she and George must have hooked up last night.

The other missive from Ingrid commanded me to get a suite for her and Jeffrey. I grinned. She was out of luck. No such thing in a hotel in the jungle. She'd have to get cozy in a double bed. That would put a kink into her sexual repertoire. I didn't imagine we'd need any more rooms since each had a double bed. There had been only one room available with a queen and I smiled, thinking how wise I'd been in following my intuition on booking it for me. Daniella could spend the evening alone—painting her claws.

There was also a note from Professor Hidalgo saying he would meet us at the ferry dock in Playa del Carmen at two fifty-five. Good, I thought. I didn't want any glitches in this plan. I rubbed my forehead, aware of the tension above my eyebrows. I searched the lobby for Wolf. Had he disappeared on me?

This was my chance to escape to my room and put on some sexy lingerie, or would my guy prefer to take off my dress? Which would excite him more? The man was unpredictable, to say the least. I glanced around. No sign of Wolf. I started to get worried. Had he left?

At the elevator, the doors slid apart. Bryan, wearing shorts and a T-shirt with a Corona logo, walked out reading a pamphlet.

"Hey, Bryan! All set for Coba?" From his well-developed arms and legs, I could tell he worked out. I hadn't noticed that before when he wore his buttoned-up shirt and Dockers.

Bryan jerked his head up from the brochure he was absorbed in reading. "Hey, Adie. I'm looking forward to Coba. Two-ten?"

"Yep. There'll be shuttle at the front of the hotel."

"See you tomorrow!"

I waved and entered the empty elevator. What had Fern said he did for a living, or hadn't she? When I stepped out, I headed to Ingrid's room. At the door marked 204, I knocked, waited, and knocked again.

Suddenly the door jerked open. Ingrid's dark shoulder-length hair was standing on end. She was wearing a transparent black negligee. "Adie, I'm busy. We'll talk tomorrow." She pushed the door shut.

I knocked again.

She swung the door open. "I said tomorrow."

"You don't want to hear about your…"

Grabbing my arm, she pulled me in. The room was a mess. A pair of panties, a dress, and a bra were scattered on the rattan couch. Two half empty cocktail glasses filled with a murky green liquid stood on the maple coffee table. I had the distinct feeling she wasn't alone.

"Ingrid?" a masculine voice called out from the bedroom.

"Just a minute, darling." Her words came out sweet as honey. Then in a harsh undertone, she said, "Well?"

"Eight hundred-twenty thou."

She sighed in relief. "When do I get it?"

"I'll have it for you at one-thirty tomorrow." I gripped the doorknob and swung the door ajar.

"Come here. Move your sweet ass!" A male yelled from the bedroom. "Let's get this paperwork done and then we'll get back to pleasuring you."

Ingrid flushed. "Coming, honey," she called over her shoulder before shoving me into the hall. "Good work," she said as an afterthought, before slamming the door.

I clenched my jaw. Why had I ever signed a contract with her? As I wandered down the hall to my room, I searched my purse for the key. At my door I glanced down the hall. Still no sign of Wolf. Had I managed to mess this up? He should have understood about business, since he was so driven when it came to his own projects.

My room was clean and neat. Quite a contrast to the sleek Italian leather couches and the silk covered king-sized bed in my condo. It was modest with a rattan love seat and two chairs which were arranged about a tiny coffee table. However, positively speaking, my clothing was safely hung in my closet and there wasn't any sign of a nutcase with a knife.

I unlocked the sliding door and drew it aside to stand on my balcony. The moist, evening ocean breeze brushed my skin. The white caps glinted on the crests of the waves, now darkly shadowed with lavender. The sensuous beat of Santana floated up from the busy bar below.

A knock on the door was followed by a masculine voice shouting out, "Room service!"

Obviously a mistake. I peered into the peephole. The waiter stood out of view. Picking up my umbrella, I readied it and slowly eased the door open.

"Martinis for Señorita Sturm."

I started, "I didn't order..." before I spied the speaker. Wolf was balancing a tray with two steaming glasses filled with a brown liquid, topped with whipped cream. He placed the tray on the coffee table and turned to me quizzically. "I thought you'd be in bed by now."

"And that would be a disappointment?"

"Only if you didn't let me in." He grinned. "But this is even better. I can help you get ready." Santana's Latin bass-line drifted up with the tropical breeze as Wolf handed me a drink.

"What's all this?" I sat down on the bed. The sprinkle of cinnamon on the whipped cream gave it a festive appearance.

"You'll have to try it. Toast?" He lifted his cup.

"To Mexico?"

His eyes glinted wickedly as he sat down beside me. "And to you and me."

"Only in Mexico?"

The tip of his finger traced my cheek. "Life holds many surprises."

My pulse raced as I met his gaze. "To surprises."

Wolf clicked his cup to mine. I sipped tentatively, expecting some sort of coffee but I was wrong. It was a perfect surprise for a chocoholic. "Nice." Chocolate does strange things to me and from the look in his eyes, I think he knew that.

"Kahlua with cocoa."

"Chocolate creates a state of..."

Wolf's lips softly brushed my neck. "Euphoria."

"Yes-ss," I murmured weakly, as his tongue feathered to the hollow of my throat.

"Drink, princess."

I let the warm liquid ease its way down. Wolf took my cup and set it beside his on the bedside table. When he turned back to me, I saw something in his eyes that made me melt. I reached up. My hand brought his head down. Sensuously, his mouth moved on mine and our lips, coated with potent chocolate, played. When he gripped me closer, I felt his warm breath on my ear. I shivered as his tongue ran over the contours of each ridge, ending its journey at my earlobe. Arousal charged my body and I pulled him tighter, wanting more.

The musical tune from my cell tore us apart.

It could be Diego about our trip tomorrow. "Sorry, it could be important. I have to get that." I reached over and held my cell to my ear. "*Bueno.*"

"*Hola,* amiga. Where are you? The guard told me the police were at the condo."

"Carmelita." I could feel Wolf's hand on my calf, lightly stroking my skin. "I'm sorry I just left it like that. I would have phoned you about the mess but you'd had such a bad day—I didn't want to ruin your evening." I fell back on the bed. Wolf eased down beside me, his arm crossing over my stomach, resting on my hip, lips trailing down to my shoulder. I let my hand holding my cell rest on the pillow. Carmelita's voice was faint. I started drifting away with the heady sensations he was invoking.

"Tina told me. She went over to pick up a dress she thought we should bring and the police were there."

"A dress? I thought they were all my size."

"One of the models must wear petite."

Only half listening, I focused on the heat of Wolf's tongue arousing the tender part of my forearm and its journey up. But my brain wasn't entirely jelly. I connected with something she'd said. "You didn't leave anything in the guest room for yourself, did you?"

"No, not this time. Adelina, I must confess—I've stayed at the condo before."

"Oh?" Then I clued in. "Oh-hh…"

"Yes, you must understand love is difficult when the two of us are married. The condo was perfect for us to get together. But, amiga, do you think it's my sabotager? I can't believe this has anything to do with you."

"I don't know, Carmelita, but I didn't want to stay there alone after what happened. Did Tina tell you about the knife?"

"Yes, she was very upset when she found out you'd been staying there. She's removed all the dresses and is busy cleaning them. The little dear has been extremely helpful."

"I know I should have contacted you, Carmelita, but I didn't have your number, and I didn't think I wanted to involve Diego."

"You're right. It's better he doesn't know. Do you have a pen?"

I pushed Wolf away and reached for a pen on the night table. As she gave me her number I scribbled it quickly.

"Where are you, Carmelita?"

"Cancun, but just for the next couple of nights. And you?"

"At the hotel. I'll be in Coba tomorrow night. I'm not sure if they have cell reception there."

"Don't worry about me, Adelina. Luis is with me. I didn't tell Diego about the condo but he'd heard about the fashion show disaster and insisted I take security with me."

"Good. I won't worry so much then. Be careful, Carmelita."

"I will. *Adios,* amiga."

"*Chao,* Carmelita." I programmed in her number before I shut my phone. An idea bubbled in my brain—I was beginning to think I knew who was behind the fashion sabotage.

Wolf handed me my drink, reminding me that I had this sizzling man with me. Seeing him empty handed, I asked, "You finished yours?"

"I like it hot."

"So do I…" I stroked his cheek. "Sorry about the interruption, but I have to take my calls, just in case it's from a client."

"But this was Carmelita?"

"Yes. I should have phoned her but I didn't want to upset her further after what she went through at the beach house. She's the one that helped set up that room in memory of her brother."

Wolf's forehead furrowed. "I heard it was a diving accident."

"Right. Three years ago."

Wolf kicked off his slipons and swung his long legs up on the bed, leaning his back against the pillows, his arms stretched out on the headboard. "Come to think of it, I heard something about him. Both he and Alvarez were educated in Europe, although he was being groomed to run the family business. Trouble was…he didn't want the job."

"And when Amancio died, Diego took over."

"Apparently they were running Royal Investments together for a few years after Papa Bolivar went back to Mexico City."

"Something like you and your brother, eh?"

Wolf grimaced.

"You aren't getting along?" Not bothering to take off my high-heeled sandals, I relaxed back against the pillows, cozying up against Wolf, sipping my drink, feeling the warmth of his body through his shirt.

"Mike came down here with all kinds of half-baked ideas. Then a few weeks ago he chucked it all in and flew back, leaving things wide open for me to finally put my plan in motion. Tonight I finalize the deal." He stared at the ceiling distractedly.

From the downstairs bar, Santana's sultry beat became more intense—a song about a bad woman. I closed my eyes and lay back. I was ready to throw caution to the wind and be seriously bad. I rolled over my hand drawn to his hair like a magnet is to metal. My fingers dug into his ruffled hair.

My action startled Wolf, who glanced at me with renewed interest. "Blue like the Caribbean, always changing—mysterious eyes." Taking my goblet, he set it on the table. "Spicy woman…" His voice was husky and low. As he glanced at my scooped neckline, his eyes traveled to my dress, hiked up high over my knees. Leaning on one elbow, he let his hand stroke my arm lightly. "Your skin is smooth—like silk," his voice husky.

When he pulled me down, I couldn't resist him. My body was my mistress. His full lips assaulted mine. It took an inner strength to withdraw and I did but only to tease him. Tiny nibbles on his lower lip.

The music from the bar told the woman's story. I could have been her. No, I was good—my breasts against his chest, my hands wrapped around him. Slowly I licked his lip.

His eyes gleamed. When he pressed on my mouth until my lips parted, I let him enter. His tongue seared like a burning poker. A flame lit inside me. It danced wildly. No one could ever put out this fire.

My pulse quickened. The heat inside me radiated down. I wanted to tear his shirt open and feel the warmth of his chest. I started to unfasten the buttons. Before I reached the second, he took over. When he yanked his shirt open, his chest became my toy. My hands slid across his hard muscles—down to his taut abs. My fingernails scraped lightly. Wolf caught his breath. I brought my lips to his chest and kissed my way to his nipple. I let my tongue tantalize him. Tiny butterfly flicks. One more nibble and I released him. Glancing at his face, I saw the intensity in his eyes. A quick intake of breath. Encouraged, I licked his chest until he whispered, "You make me hot."

But Wolf was never passive in anything he did. "Come here, princess." Undoing my halter tie, he brought his lips to my exposed neck. Sweet kisses—more delicious than chocolate. At the base of my throat he paused before his mouth gripped my skin an instant, sending darts of fire to my core.

His lips eased off and moved to my shoulder. My pulse raced. With each touch of his lips I burned for him. When his tongue flicked over the rise of my breasts, I pressed and held his head down. My fingers threaded his hair—soft waves that shot me into a swirl of bliss. My breathing became ragged. In his heavy lidded blues I saw a spark that spoke of his need.

Wolf slid my dress lower and captured my mound, his fingertips teasing my nipple. Molten lava spread down to my thighs.

My hand glided over his jeans. He groaned deep in his throat. Restlessly, he shifted and brought his other hand up. My breast molded to his hands. I met his eyes and saw his passion.

He stroked my belly. I sighed deeply, swept into a dreamy space. When he licked the tender skin, I pulsed with the heat of his touch. "Wolf..." I whispered, not really knowing what I wanted to say except what he was doing to me was mystical magic and I needed him more than I needed any man.

He brought his hand to my thigh. The heat of his fingers was like a match set to oil—flames brilliantly exploding.

When a droning noise reverberated from his pant pocket, we froze. His eyes met mine. "I'd ignore it, but it could only mean something has gone wrong. Believe me, if it weren't so important..." He pulled out his cell from his pocket "Yeah?" he said gruffly.

I waited impatiently. His caller had too much to say and was taking too long saying it. Giving up, I tugged up my dress, tied it, and sat up at the edge of the bed.

"Why don't you get in there and talk him out of it?" Wolf said in a growl. "Daniella, this is not a good time." His jaw clenched. "All right...all right, stay there. I'm coming." Clicking the phone shut, he pressed it back into his pocket. He stroked my cheek tenderly. "Don't be angry, Adie. There's a screw up. Someone else must have heard that I was interested in the adjoining property. He's there now meeting with the bar owner, trying to buy it out from under me. Daniella was to make him an offer but she's afraid to go in with all the men in there. If it weren't so crucial to the project..." Wolf stood up, pulling his shirt back on. "I'll make it up to you, princess, I promise." His last kiss, soft and sensuous, hinted of pleasures to come, before he reluctantly released me and buttoned his shirt.

At the doorway, he grinned. "We had that purring going, but I have a feeling we'll need way more time to get to those scratches."

The acrylic glass I threw clipped his shoulder and stopped any further annoying remarks but it didn't change the fact he'd left me stirred up and unsatisfied in an empty room.

As I sat back against the pillows, something else began to nag me. From the table by the bed, I picked up my cell, pressed Carmelita's number and waited.

9

Hey, Adie. Henderson's death was most likely murder.
Autopsy showed she ingested a drug cocktail. Do you have any
reason to think she might want to commit suicide? Her co-workers
think she was happy about the promotion. These attacks on
Fleischer are likely connected. Can you think of anyone who'd
want her dead? Ilya

PS: Have some margaritas for me, eh?

I was sitting in the Internet Café at the Chedraui Plaza with a
few minutes of leeway until the arrival of the limo. Diego said he'd
meet me at the airport so I thought I'd better take advantage of the
time I had. There wouldn't be any internet in Coba.

So why attack Ingrid? What was the connection between Telly
and the boss from hell? Did someone have something against
Fleischer Travel? The thing was Telly hadn't been hated like
Ingrid. Her ingratiating attitude had only been annoying to the rest
of the staff. She did whatever Ingrid wanted to get a promotion and
at the end she had it made. Unfortunately, all her hopes and dreams
drowned in a slurp of beer.

I clicked reply.

Hey Ilya. I'm checking out the tour group for you. If you find
out anything else message me. Adie

PS: Had a margarita for you.

When I glanced outside I spied Diego's Mercedes parked in
front of the café. Ernesto in his white uniform got out and trotted
up in time to open the glass door for me.

"*Buenos dias,* Señorita." Ernesto smiled broadly.

"Good afternoon, Ernesto. *Como esta?*"

"Very well, thank you. It is a beautiful day for your flight."
Ernesto swung the door of the sedan open and assisted me in. I
lifted up a tad to spread the skirt of my cotton dress before I sank
down into the leather seat. This time I was prepared. My dress fit
snugly, but with the flaring skirt it was definitely not trashy. Diego
would not get the wrong impression.

I looked at the sky. Sunny, but it could turn cloudy or even rain by the afternoon for my trip to Coba. The weather was totally unpredictable during the rainy season. Hopefully, the ferry crossing to Playa del Carmen would be a calm one.

The drive was short. On our arrival Ernesto escorted me down a long corridor which led to the airport runway. He pointed ahead to a white-striped plane. Two men stood together talking. The taller one smoking a cigarette was Eduardo.

An arm encircled my waist. A whiff of citron. "Adelina, how beautiful you look!" Diego's hair brushed my face as he whispered in my ear. I turned. Clad in a white linen shirt tucked into tan casual pants, Diego looked exceptionally edible. "Do you like my jet? But, wait, I shouldn't ask you until you've seen the inside."

He took my arm and led me to the waiting plane. "*Hola!*" Diego greeted the men standing by the stairway. "Ah, Tomas," he said to the man in a white pilot's uniform. "Let me introduce you to my friend, Señorita Sturm." Diego signaled Eduardo's dismissal with a slight twitch of his head.

"*Buenos dias,* Señorita Sturm. I am Captain Ortega, your pilot today. Hopefully, you will enjoy the flight."

"I'm sure I will, Captain."

"The weather is unsettled, Señorita. If we experience turbulence, the seat belts may become necessary."

"I understand. Is it a long flight?"

Tomas pursed his lips and nodded respectfully to Diego. "Señor Alvarez will fill you in. You will excuse me?" He made his way up the stairs into the jet.

I looked expectantly at Diego.

He explained as we headed up the steps. "Collectors hesitate to broadcast their whereabouts, Adelina, for numerous reasons. The major one is art thieves and then there is the annoying agreement of seventy-two."

Diego motioned for me to go ahead of him. Eduardo and Tomas had already disappeared into the cockpit. We were alone.

"I'd like to hear more about this agreement." I stopped at the leather chairs, wondering if this was where he wanted us to sit. Halfway down the aisle, there was bar and galley area. At the back, a three-seat ivory leather divan. The door at the end was undoubtedly for the washroom.

"Have you had breakfast, *mi amor?*" Seeing me shake my

head, Diego handed me two mugs from the galley and carried over a tray with sugar, cream, and croissants. He set the tray down on the mahogany table. "Could you please bring over the coffee, Adelina?"

I picked up the carafe and placed it on the table. The seat belts sign flashed red in three languages. I sat down beside Diego and fastened my seat belt.

Diego had a whimsical expression on his handsome face. "I like the concept of having breakfast with you." The engines revved louder as we took off. When the plane started to level out, Diego picked up my hand, stroking my palm with his thumb. "You know you are special to me."

"Yes, I know, but I can't possibly keep the condo and the clothes."

"It's all right for you to accept gifts from me. Remember you saved my life and I owe you. Won't you pour?"

I nodded. "We've gone through this before. You know you don't owe anything." I set the mugs in front of us and poured the coffee. "Cream or sugar?"

The seat belt sign flickered off.

"Cream, please, Adelina."

I poured cream into our china mugs. I then added three spoonfuls of sugar into mine. I hesitated. The silver spoon was awfully tiny. I tossed in two more and stirred my coffee.

Diego's expression was amused as he cocked his head. "You like your coffee sweet, I see."

"It's a Canadian thing."

"Um-m." Diego nodded. "There's so much I need to discover about you. Do you like the clothes?"

"Carmelita's collection is amazing." I looked out the window as I decided how I should tell him. "There was a reason I slept at the hotel last night. Did Carmelita talk to you?"

"No, why?"

"While I was in the shower, someone doused a good portion of clothes with orange juice and one dress was slashed down the middle. I contacted the police but they couldn't turn up any clues as to who did it."

"Why didn't you phone me? I wouldn't have wanted you to be alone. I could have picked you up and taken you back to my house.

I have a good security system as well as several reliable employees."

I shuddered, thinking of Eduardo ready to carve a hole in George's belly.

Diego said with a smile, "My bedroom is particularly secure and you would have had your every need provided for."

"We are friends, Diego, not lovers. Besides, as it happened I wasn't alone."

Diego rubbed his index finger on his chin, frowning. "Wolf?"

I nodded. "We had dinner plans."

Diego commented dryly, "You, Wolf, and Daniella?"

"No!" I said sharply. "What are you implying? Is there something I should know?"

"Pastry?" He offered me a plate with an assortment of baked goods. "These have chocolate fillings."

"Diego, you're avoiding the subject. What about Daniella? Tell me!"

He selected a pastry and bit into it, chewing thoughtfully. "Have you seen them together lately?"

"Yes, I did. At your beach house. I admit she was all over him, but they're putting together some sort of deal."

"And this involves a great part of his day and night." Diego grinned mischievously. "Daniella can be very helpful." He brushed a crumb off his pants. "She likes to please a man."

"He cares about me."

"Caring is an emotion. Sex is a need." He took a chocolate pastry and brought it to my mouth. "Try it, Adelina. You like chocolate."

I bit into the pastry and considered his observation. Was he talking about Wolf's sexual needs or was he speaking about Daniella's? I had needs too, and this chocolate pastry was scrumptious. So was the man seated beside me. I took the pastry from his hand and had another mouthful, admiring his chest where the shirt gaped open. And then there was my hottie, whom I wasn't so sure about. Did Daniella conduct her skanky business with him after hours? "So you're saying Daniella, is what, insinuating herself into Wolf's life and there is no place there for me?"

"I've known Daniella for two years. Believe me, that's what she does."

"She tried to manipulate you?"

Diego flashed a white grin. "Unbeknownst to me, she arranged our wedding. I told you that story, didn't I?"

I sipped my coffee, watching him from behind my cup. "Yes, but it didn't happen."

"True, but the woman is bull-headed. If she wants something or someone, she gives it more than a college try. She elbows out all her opponents and charges the goal line to make the winning kick herself. She has numerous skillful techniques and is a player to be reckoned with. Barbara never knew what hit her."

Barbara? Who was she? "Just how is Daniella helping with Wolf's business?"

"Ask him, Adelina. This can be a way for you to test his commitment to you."

I nodded, wondering why Diego was so close-mouthed about Wolf's business. I would find out about Daniella tonight, but for now, I should be focusing on business—Ingrid's business. Could the statue have had anything to do with the attacks on Ingrid? "When do we land?"

"It's not a long flight." Diego glanced at his watch. "Twenty minutes."

"Which brings me to my next question." I wiped my fingers on the linen napkin and looked back at Diego. "Where are we going?"

"The mainland." Diego set his coffee cup down and pulled me to my feet. "I haven't shown you the rest of the plane." He placed his hand on my back, leading me aft to the divan. "Let's sit here, *mi amor*. We'll be far more comfortable."

"Mexico?"

Diego edged nearer to me. "The collector wants it to be kept a secret, remember?"

"Okay. Now tell me about the agreement of seventy-two."

Diego placed his hand on the skirt of my dress, his fingertips stroking my knee. "Very becoming, Adelina. Not from the collection, I'd guess. Carmelita's designer goes for slinkier dresses." His eyes lowered to my cleavage. "Modest but pleasing."

Impatiently, I tapped his hand to get his attention. "The agreement? You were about to tell me."

"Ah-h, yes, but you are distracting me." Diego's hand

wandered to a strand of my hair, pulling it through his fingers. "Several countries have signed an agreement that prohibits export of Mayan antiquities out of the country of origin."

"And Mexico is one of them, eh?"

"Yes, *cariño*. That's why Ingrid would have to pay more if she expected the statue to be delivered to Canada. But it's not a problem either way." He brought his finger up to my lips, tracing the outline of my mouth. "Such pouty lips—so ready for…" Diego lowered his mouth to mine, pushing me down on the divan. With one hand he scooped up my legs onto the couch and brought himself down beside me.

The couch was wide and soft, but Diego must have thought I needed an extra pillow. Reaching above me, he placed a pillow behind my head and brought his tongue to my parted lips. My hormones reacted like a confused mess of merengue dancers trying to outdo themselves in a club competition. Diego's hand moved along my hip and his lips caressed my shoulder, sending shivers down my body. I knew I should stop him, but I couldn't see why. I was so unsure of Wolf. Was he allowing Daniella to lure him in on the pretense of a business crisis? My hand gravitated to Diego's wavy brown hair, weaving my fingers through and then letting them slide slowly to his neck.

"Adelinita," Diego whispered, his voice deep with passion. His kisses left my shoulder and wandered to my breasts exposed by the low neckline. His brandy eyes shimmered as he glanced up. Did I want this to go further? Diego and I were friends—very good friends, maybe, but I hadn't given him the idea we would become intimate, had I?

"You drive me crazy, Adelina. I want to make love to you." His hand shoved my skirt up and lightly stroked my thigh.

"No, Diego. We shouldn't." I placed my hand on his to signal him to stop. Diego's eyes flickered green with lust. His hand moved over my dress, fingers caressing my body. Pushing the material at the neckline of my dress down, he exposed more. He bent his head to kiss the valley between my breasts. My body tingled.

I barely felt his hands untie my straps, his lips on my shoulder. My dress slipped down.

The pilot's voice crackled as it came on the intercom abruptly.

"Señor Alvarez, we are coming down for a landing. Fasten your seat belts, *por favor*." Red lights flickered on.

Diego sighed with annoyance. I was a mixed bundle of emotions—guilt and disappointment heading the list. Hastily, I pulled up my dress and tied my straps before taking Diego's offered hand. Helping me up, he led us back to our seats.

***

A couple of Jeeps waited where we disembarked. A red-hot breeze blasted out at us, like burning furnace heat. We had landed on a runway located in the middle of a farmer's field—sugar cane as far as the eye could see. Eduardo and Tomas jumped into a yellow Jeep driven by an enormous man with a bald head. Diego led me over to another Jeep where a brawny man wearing a black leather cowboy hat sat waiting.

"Hey, dude!" The stranger in a black T-shirt with *Sol* in yellow lettering, snickered. "Got yourself a new lady, eh?"

"*Hola*, Reese! This lovely lady is Adelina Sturm from your part of the country." Diego helped me in and then slid in beside me in the back. "But you have it wrong—we're just friends."

Reese chortled. "Yeah? Gotta see that to believe it." He punched Diego lightly on the arm before he reached over and firmly shook my hand. "Reese Goldane, nice to meetcha, Adelina. So you're a Canuck, too, eh?"

"Call me Adie. I'm from Kitchener, and you, Reese?"

"Windsor. How about that?" The engine turned over and he drove out onto a dirt road bordered by small spiky palms and tall eucalyptus trees. He flicked a glance over his shoulder at Diego. "Treating her good, are you?"

"She has my undivided attention." Diego winked.

That could be a problem, studying my sexy companion. He was the stuff fantasies were made of.

Go for it! My Hormone Voice yelled.

But my Logical Voice started arguing with Hormone. And what about Wolf? He could be hers if she tried. She's got more going for her than that barracuda, Daniella.

Hormone laughed. That's not a problem. She doesn't have to give up Wolf to have Diego. She dated Pete from Detroit and Peter from Amsterdam at the same time and managed to juggle them with no problem.

Logical spoke up. This is different! She's a mature woman now, with a biological clock—it's time for her to pick a man for the future.

Hormone wasn't about to give up. She shouted back. Boring, boring, boring!

"Stop it," I said, forgetting I was talking out loud.

"She's right," Reese said. "We should take her seriously. If you brought her with you to see the Mayan art, Diego, she's not an idiot, and," he glanced back at me appraisingly, "she's sure not a bimbo either."

Reese steered the jeep to the right and we entered a cleared area with a high wire fence and a gatehouse. A guard opened the gate and we drove in followed by the yellow Jeep with the bodyguards. A large house loomed ahead at the end of a curved paved driveway, emperor palms in front of a terra cotta stucco mansion with a red tile roof. "I'm sorry for offending you, Adie."

"No, Reese, don't be. I'm being too sensitive." I didn't want to admit I was crazy enough to be talking to myself. On the other hand, what I'd said had put the boys club in its place. Women are everywhere including politics. These men should get used to it and quit talking about us like we're sex objects. "What type of business are you in, Reese?" I looked over at him.

He had a husky build but no excess fat. His T-shirt was tucked into a pair of loose-fitting black jeans, tightened by a leather belt, turquoise stones inlaid into a silver buckle.

"Retired for now. I made my money with internet gambling and got out when the going was good."

"Have you been collecting art for long?"

"About ten years now. You like art, Adie?"

"I do. I took a course in art history but I'm more familiar with European artists. I'd like to learn more about Mayan culture and how it's depicted in the Classic and Pre-Classic periods."

"I'm impressed with your choice, dude." Reese parked the Jeep, and got out, kicking his door shut with his boot. The yellow Jeep pulled up beside us and the bodyguards and Tomas got out. "I was right, eh?" Reese shot Diego a look. "Adie is not like your last *friend*."

"You mean Barbara?"

We made our way up the cobble-stoned walkway to the front door.

Reese scratched his head. "Oh, I forgot about Barbara." He chuckled. "Hard to forget Barbara with that wild, red hair, but no, I was thinking of the other one."

"Celese...the blonde?"

Reese grinned widely. "Gorgeous but a real ice princess." He laughed. "Bet you melted her icicles in no time, eh, dude? No, I was thinking of the South American, the one with the super tight outfits." He scratched his head. "Oh, yeah, I know now...Daniella. That one was hot."

Diego grinned. "Daniella is an outrageous flirt."

"And did she ever have it bad for you." Reese glancing surreptitiously at me, and said, "But I sense a dangerous undercurrent with this lady—a smokin' volcano. A come-and-get me, if you-dare look." Reese swung open the heavy oak door. "So you thought you needed a change, a bit of class, dude? Or is it the fire beneath the surface that turns you on?" Seeing my drawn mouth, he said, "Oh, sorry, Adie, I'm doin' it again. Forgive me. I'm just a stupid man not used to intelligent women, I guess."

Hardly stupid. Someone with a house like this? I was awed by both the grounds and the sheer size of it. As far as Reese was concerned, I figured it's too hard to teach an old dog new tricks. I'd let sleeping dogs lie. "Is living in the interior an isolated life?"

Reese motioned for us to go first. He guffawed. "You mean do I have women?"

The wide dark hallway was cool after the humidity from outside. My high heels clicked loudly on the marble tiles as Diego and I led the way to a wide door halfway down the corridor.

"Now that you've had a look at the house, I think you know the answer to your question." We followed him into a lounge furnished with several sofas and reclining chairs around an oak table.

"When you got the bucks, they stand in line—models, actresses, you name it. Women love rich men. They don't give a damn what I'm really like." Reese poured red wine from a crystal decanter into three glasses. He handed us each one. "*Salud.*"

"*Salud.*" Diego and I clicked our glasses to his.

My eyes wandered around the room. Paintings depicting Mayan life hung at three levels on the burgundy walls. The dark oak tables scattered around the room had a variety of jade and clay statues, mostly Mayan gods.

I studied Reese. "You don't want a more permanent relationship, then?"

"Every man wants to have heirs eventually, especially when you have money to leave behind, eh, Diego?"

Diego smiled slightly in agreement.

"Why don't we start with the statue you purchased and then I'll show you some of the other art, Adie." Reese gestured to an opulent leather couch. "Make yourselves at home."

He ambled over to the far corner of the room, picked up a figurine and returned to plop himself down on a reclining chair. He held up a jade statue. I could still see the distinctive features of the Jaguar God's face.

"This is the Sun God. The story is K'inich Ahaw becomes the Jaguar God of the Underworld when he travels beneath the earth after sunset. He's taking a severed head as an offering."

"May I?" Diego asked.

Reese set the statue on the table and shoved it towards us.

Carefully, Diego picked it up and placed it on the table. He glanced at me. "When the Sun God becomes the Jaguar God, he's also the patron of war. Many of the Mayan rulers assumed the identity of the Sun God. See the detail in the clothing, Adelina?"

When I touched the cool jade statue, sliding my fingers along the ridges, I shivered involuntarily.

Reese leaned forward. "You're feeling it too, eh, Adie?" His gray eyes watched me intently as I checked the statue for possible flaws.

Diego smiled in a superior way, amused by his friend. "Reese tends to be superstitious when it comes to art. He's glad Ingrid is buying the statue."

Reese pursed his lips and offered Diego a cigar. When Diego shook his head, Reese snickered. "Don't want any cigar breath, eh?" Choosing a small metal device from the same box he snipped off the end of the cigar before he picked up a heavy crystal lighter. He inhaled as he lit the cigar.

"Something bothers you about this statue," I said.

Reese glanced away but not before I caught his worried expression.

A rap on the door sounded and a stout ebony-haired woman

entered carrying a tray with appetizers, salsa and nachos. "Señor Goldane, I have made you appetizers. I thought you would like to share them with your guests. *Buenos dias,* Señor Alvarez," The lady smiled broadly at Diego before she added, Señorita."

Diego flashed her a show-stopping smile. "Ah-h, Goya, how considerate of you to bring my favorite tamales."

"How did you know I made your favorites?" Goya said shyly, setting the tray down.

Diego got up and caught her hand kissing her wrist. "Because you're the chef from heaven."

Goya giggled and pulled her hand back. "How gracious you are, *señor* Alvarez."

"Let me introduce you to my friend, Señorita Sturm."

"Nice to meet you and to have my first taste of tamales."

"*Mucho gusto,* Señorita Sturm."

"It is pleasure to serve these to you and Señor Alvarez."

Reese chuckled. "I think you'd work for Diego for free, eh, Goya?"

Blushing a dark red to the roots of her coal black hair, Goya made a quick exit leaving the tray.

Glancing at Diego, I said, "Another woman under your spell."

Diego ran his fingers slowly down my shoulder. "But it is your love I need, Adelinita."

I shook my head. And you have it, Diego." This guy was too sexy for womankind.

Smiling broadly at our exchange, Reese urged. "Have a nibble, Adie. Goya makes the greatest tamales."

Diego handed me a tamale on a napkin. "Seared scallops in a spicy papaya sauce."

"Wait." Reese stopped us. "We need to celebrate. Now what should we have?" Suddenly the door swung open and a slender blonde wearing a rose-silk, baby-doll outfit and four-inch stilettos sauntered into the room. "Hey," she greeted us lazily. Wandering over she pecked Reese on the cheek. "When did you get up, babe? Missed you…you know I had bad bad dreams about you." She winked at Diego. Seeing the tray of tamales, she grabbed one. "Ouch! Hot!"

Reese patted her butt and snickered. "Nothing compared to you, Nikki. How about you fix us some ryes neat, eh?" He glanced at us. "Met Nikki in Lauderdale. She's a damn good bartender."

Nikki scowled at him and trekked over to the bar. Moments later she appeared with a tray and set it abruptly on the table, the glasses rocking dangerously. Grabbing another tamale, she shot Reese a *you're dead-meat glance* and clicked out of the room, snapping the door shut noisily behind her.

"Don't mind Nikki, Adie. She's temperamental but a nice person. Right now she's between jobs." He handed us both shot glasses filled with a dark amber liquid, and then picking up the remaining glass, he lifted it high. "To money and art."

We clicked our glasses and I sipped the liquor a bit apprehensively. Rye is as Canadian as bacon but it didn't always like me. Still I couldn't wimp out now. "So you were about to tell me what bothers you about the statue, Reese."

"Un-hmm. It's just a feeling."

"What kind of feeling?" I exchanged glances with Diego.

Reese studied the liquor. His left eye twitched. "It's unlucky."

"How so?" I dipped a tamale in some red sauce.

Reese went back to the bar and brought back the Seagram's, refilling our glasses. "The day I got the statue my brother was in a car accident." He slugged the rye back. "Then my girlfriend left me. She said she didn't like the way the house felt." He rested his chin on his hand.

"That's awful!" I said.

Reese stared at his empty glass. "It got worse. I became really sick. Had to go for tests. They found I had cancer." He refilled his glass.

"I'm so sorry!" I felt bad I'd asked.

Reese chugged down another glass of rye. "Intestinal cancer...had surgery and so far I'm okay, but I don't want it coming back. I need to sell the statue ASAP, you understand?"

I nodded. Bad karma. I'd give the statue to Ingrid and let her deal with it. Ordinarily I'm not so superstitious, but I'd learned to follow my instincts to be safe and I was getting strong negative vibes.

Diego picked up a double-chambered pottery vessel. "Quetzalcoatl." He eyed the creature perched on the pot. "Where'd you get this one from?"

Reese gathered his strength and refocused. "Just south of

Merida. Adie, you said you wanted to know more about Classic period art. This here is one of them. That's the Feathered Serpent God and those things above him are bats. It's probably not the best work but it kind of caught my fancy. If you've had enough to eat, why don't I show you some of my plaques?"

Together we walked over to the wall.

Pointing to two jade plaques hanging low, Reese said, "Those are Early Classic period. The Bird Monster God is represented in profile and that's the Maize God in the next plaque. See how his head is flattened to represent an ear of corn. Cool, eh?"

Diego said, "They're small but valuable, *mi amor*. See the relief painting above? The bird's a quetzal."

"The national bird of Honduras?"

"Almost right," Diego whispered in my ear. His hand brushed my hair aside, before his lips pressed against my neck. "Costa Rica, Adelinita."

I caught Reese watching us. "Over here, you love birds…we have the bloodletting plaques. The sea urchin spines were used to pierce the body." Reese paused at a low oak table. "Now here's a real woman for you."

I was a bit put off by the gory art and was relieved that the figurine Reese picked up from a table was a female. A substantial bare-breasted one.

"Ixchel?"

Reese nodded. "Mayan blue clay. You know about the Moon Goddess, eh?" He turned to Diego. "Adie's an okay chick. You lucked out with her. So what do you think buddy? I mean about Ixchel. She turn you on?"

Diego grinned. "Almost as much as Adelina."

I don't know if it was the booze or what, but Diego was getting to me too, and that was a signal with a bright red light. I glanced at my watch and touched Diego's arm. "I'm sorry, Reese, but I have get back to Cozumel. I still need to pack a bag and gather up my tour group."

"It would have been so romantic to stay here in the jungle together tonight, wouldn't it?" Diego sighed. "But we will have other opportunities, I'm sure. How about a box for the statue?"

Reese picked up the phone on the bar and spoke to someone. "They're ready to go. Bring a box for the jaguar." He set the phone down. "Trev's bringing the packaging. It was great that Diego brought you along, Adie. Too bad you have to leave so soon." He grinned. "You're welcome to stay longer next time." Reese passed me his business card.

I glanced at it. There was only his name followed by a cell number.

A heavy knock and the massive bald man from the Jeep, entered. Reese gave him the jade statue. Quickly, Trev wrapped it with a thick cloth before he dropped it in a velvet bag and gave it to Reese.

"Good idea, Trev. A box is too bulky. Handle it with care."

I nodded. "Thank you for having me for lunch. Tell Goya her tamales were fantastic."

"I'll tell her." Reese smiled, and then he became more serious. "Will you forgive me if I don't go outside with you? I'm feeling kind of tired."

"Sure, it was nice to meet you."

"You too, Adie. And remember if you ever want to come and visit…" He winked conspiratorially.

Diego gripped Reese's arm affectionately as they shook hands. "Take care, my friend."

His hand still on Diego's shoulder, Reese replied in a low undertone, "This sale may not have been the best deal I've ever made, but I'm sure my luck will improve as soon as it's gone."

The velvet bag in one hand, Diego guided me down the corridor to the front door. In an undertone he said, "Reese had his first chemo treatment last week."

"Poor guy." Money couldn't buy health or luck.

***

A gust of hot, moist air hit us on the way to the Jeep. It had been pleasant inside but with the mid-day sun and the alcohol, my stomach was rebelling.

The yellow Jeep headed down the road in a cloud of dust. Diego opened the door of the other jeep. Assisting me up, he strode around to the driver's side and jumped in. The Jeep exposed us to the heat of the noon sun. I was glad when we got moving.

With it being the tail end of the rainy season, the vegetation along the road was lush and green. The towering eucalyptus trees alongside the road filtered out some of the rays as we drove to the landing strip where the jet waited for us.

Heavy dark clouds gathered overhead as Diego swung open his door.

"Did I tell you that it's a Challenger 600—a little larger than my Leer."

Sometimes I forgot how much money Diego had. "It's beautiful, Diego."

He looked pleased by my comment and took my hand. Together we climbed the steps.

Eduardo stood at the landing. "*Buenos tardes*, Señor Alvarez. Tomas has been told." He stepped back allowing us to pass.

Diego nodded. "We'll need to sit forward in the jet to start," he said to me. "Once we're on our flight route we can move aft."

Uh-oh! Diego wanted me to get *comfortable* with him again. I was feeling way too laid-back right now to be handling Diego if he decided he wanted to take our relationship up a level.

"Relax, *mi amor*." Sitting beside me, he slid his fingers through a strand of my hair, his brandy eyes glinting green. "I'll bring us some drinks."

He called back from the galley, "We need to toast our very successful day together."

Moments later, he slid in the seat beside me bringing with him two snifters of a coppery cognac. Diego grinned wickedly. "Ingrid has made a good deal and so have I, thanks to you and Reese." He clicked his glass to mine. "*Salud!*"

"*Salud*," I said, less enthusiastically. Two shots of rye and now cognac?

"Try the Remy, Adelina. It is exceptionally smooth."

If Ingrid changed her mind about this and that was a distinct possibility, everyone would blame me. That woman was as changeable as the weather.

Flecks of rain coated the window as the engines got louder and the jet started its take-off.

I felt Diego's fingers touch my face, and I turned to him.

"Don't frown, Adelina." He traced the lines freshly formed on my forehead. "Surely you are not worried about the legality of this deal?"

I searched his eyes. "I don't want to end up in jail."

Diego patted my hand reassuringly, flashing his heart-breaker smile. "No one will arrest you no matter what you've done. It always pays to have friends in high places."

"You?"

"The Bolivar Alvarez family is extensive. Money buys silence."

"What about Ingrid? Will it be difficult for her to get the art out of Mexico?"

"No. Eduardo will make sure your tour group is only superficially checked." Diego glanced out the window as the jet taxied up the runway. "Come on, have a sip. With your excellent palate you should detect numerous flavors," he said cajolingly.

A shiver ran down my spine. Maybe I did need something to fortify me. And once I got back, all my responsibility for the jade statue would end. I peeked past Diego as the jet lifted up in the air. Down below, jungle edged the cane fields. I sipped some cognac. "Honey, oak, cinnamon, and fruit, for sure."

"And something else you love…"

I took another sip. "Ah-hh," I sighed with pleasure, "Chocolate." I turned to him with my question. "Is this deliberate, Diego?"

"What?" he asked innocently.

"Cognac with a chocolate undertone."

"Chocolate was the invention of the Mayans. You want the full experience, don't you?"

I laughed. "Cognac is hardly Mayan."

Diego rested his hand on my skirt covering my thigh. "I want to satisfy your cravings, Adelinita—whatever they might be." Then he frowned. "But I am concerned about your trip to Coba. Someone wants to kill Ingrid and you've stood in the killer's way. Eduardo should take this trip with you."

"No thank you. You forget I am an advanced student of karate."

"I would never forget that, Adelina." He chuckled. "I will always remember how you hit me where it hurt. But you are a woman and there may be a killer out there who is also a martial artist."

"True." I nodded. "But Eduardo is not necessary, Diego. Wolf is coming with me."

Diego frowned. "Wolf may not be a match for a hired killer."

"I'm not so sure they are hit men. They were shorter than Wolf."

"Hit men can be any size or sex and height has nothing to do with killing."

I hadn't thought of that. Then something else occurred to me. "Why do you think someone wants to kill Ingrid?"

The plane vibrated ominously as we ascended higher over the clouds.

Diego glanced at the rain flicking the window. "What is that they say? Follow blood or money."

"Well, she sure has money."

The jet shuddered and the seat belt sign flashed back on. Diego sighed.

"I hope she doesn't mess things up with this sale." The cognac hit my stomach spreading its warmth.

"She can't. Eduardo collected the money last night."

"Oh? Do you know if she was with a man?"

Diego smiled. "Eduardo did remark that for a woman that has seen better days, she had a willing man waiting for her in the bedroom."

"Did he see the man?"

"You're very curious about Ingrid's sex life. Why is that?"

"Just a conversation I overheard. The man in the bedroom asked her to sign something and she didn't want me to see him."

"Perhaps she was embarrassed?"

"Ingrid? Not likely. She was hiding something."

Diego swirled the amber liquid in his glass before he took a sip. "Do you think she knows who wants to kill her?"

I picked a fleck of dry skin off my lips as I thought about that. "If she does, why wouldn't she tell Officer Hernandez her suspicions?"

"She could have. Did Hernandez talk to you about Ingrid?"

I nodded. "He thought the vandalism in the condo could be something to do with her."

"Or Carmelita. Hernandez doesn't know anything about the sabotage at the fashion show, does he?"

"I didn't think you wanted him to know."

"Good. Carmelita has Luis with her. What's going on with her, Adelina?"

Should I tell him? Carmelita may not like it, but things were escalating and she could be in danger. "She's having an affair, Diego."

"Damn! What is she thinking?" he said tightly. "She's married."

"She thinks Federico is busy with other women."

Diego stared at me. "She's trying to make Fede jealous?"

I hadn't thought of that. "Could be. Does Federico know about the fashion show sabotage?"

"No," he smiled slyly, "and maybe he should be told."

I put my hand on his arm. "But, Diego, Carmelita will have a fit if anyone stops her from having her career. And she'll blame me."

"Not if I tell the idiot to be reasonable. He will comply if he knows what's good for him." Diego sipped the cognac. "This could work out for Carmelita. Fede could start acting like a man for a change." He stared out the window. We had hit a storm.

Rain pelted the pane like thousands of tiny bullets. It was impossible to see anything except heavy dark clouds. With the turbulence, I was glad we weren't sitting in the rear of the plane. The plane pitched up and down. I checked my watch. It was nearly one-thirty. I'd really have to rush it to be there in time. And what about Wolf? He hadn't phoned. Had he changed his mind?

My thoughts were interrupted by the crackle of the intercom and Tomas.

"*Señor* Alvarez, I am trying to get clearing but there are some problems. Please remain in your seats until after we have landed."

Diego took up my hand, kissing my wrist as he looked earnestly into my eyes. "I'm afraid our trip has been somewhat ruined. Would you come to my party as my date—I've reserved Lorita's. There'll be a show for my guests with a Day of the Dead theme. You'll like the entertainment."

I nodded unable to speak, feeling strangely queasy.

"If you were ready at seven, my driver would pick you up. But you'll have to tell me where."

I tried to concentrate on Diego's hazel eyes and what he was saying but I was dizzy. The inside of the plane took on its own motion.

"Adelina?" Diego's face seemed too close. "You're pale. Are

you all right?"

I shook my head awkwardly. My stomach was turning somersaults. I tried to undo my seatbelt but I fumbled badly, my snifter still in my hand. Diego caught on. He snatched my glass and set it on the table. I undid my belt and stood up unsteadily. The jet shook.

Diego shoved a napkin in my hand just in time as some of the cognac started to make its way up my throat. I brought the napkin to my mouth. Placing one arm around my waist, Diego picked up speed, to the lavatory at the back of the plane. He cranked the washroom's folding door open. "Do you want me to stay with you?" he asked anxiously.

I shook my head and shut the door behind me. I knelt down by the toilet, willing myself to get control but it was not to be. The lid of the toilet wavered in front of my eyes and I heaved up my cognac followed by a second rush of bile. I waited. My stomach was better but did I dare stand up? Unsteadily I shoehorned myself up, holding onto a silver bar on the wall by the sink as the jet jiggled. I shot a glance at my face in the gold gilt mirror. Who was that sallow-complexioned zombie? I ran some water and filled a crystal glass to rinse out my mouth. Luckily it was Diego's washroom, equipped with mouthwash, brand-new toothbrushes in wrappers and toothpaste, which I took full advantage of. Another drawer had blush. After applying a rose shade, I rolled on a pleasing peach lipstick.

Feeling almost human, I lurched up the aisle to rejoin Diego. The jet was in its descent and the wind currents were buffeting the plane on its way down. He got up to steady me as I sank down in the wide leather chair. "I'm sorry, Adelina. Tomas should have avoided the storm." He took up my hand. "Are you feeling any better?"

I gave him a weak smile. "I'm okay, but I can't say I look forward to the ferry crossing to Playa del Carmen. Do you know the time?"

"Don't worry about being late, Adelina. The ferry will be delayed."

The jet's engines revved louder. The wheels hit the runway with a jolt, bouncing on the surface a few times before it slowed and stopped. I breathed a sigh of relief. After a moment the seat belt sign turned off and we got up.

Diego went ahead of me down the stairs. At the bottom he held out his hand to assist me. "Here is the bag. Ernesto will take you back. I'll phone to confirm our plans."

10

The front desk was crowded with a newly arrived tour group from Italy. I bypassed them and flew up the stairs to my floor. I needed to give Ingrid the jaguar. At room 204, I knocked and waited. With no response, I tried again. Where was she?

I couldn't hang around any longer or I'd be responsible for the whole group missing the ferry. How annoying that woman was! First she told me to bring the statue and then she doesn't bother to be there to get it. I raced to my room and inserted my key, all too aware I was running out of time.

The maid had tidied up. Everything was neat and orderly. Too bad she wasn't my own personal maid. If she'd packed for me, I wouldn't have been so stressed right now.

From the closet I dragged out my red carry-on, whipped out my karate stuff, and threw in my snorkeling equipment along with clothes and a few other essentials. Hurriedly, I changed just as my cell started to vibrate. I dug out my phone. "*Bueno?*"

"How's my sensuous woman?" Wolf said in his husky voice.

"I'm good," I said breathlessly, my body responding as if by magic. "You?"

"Turned on, whenever I hear that sexy voice of yours."

"Are you coming?"

Wolf laughed.

I blushed. "I meant to Coba."

"See you soon, baby."

I clicked the phone shut, feeling giddy after that exchange. But I couldn't go yet, no matter how much I wanted to see him. There was still the statue and what to do with it.

My room safe was too small and it was no use waiting in line at the front desk to get to the hotel safe. I eyed the velvet bag. The statue was bulky, not easy to hide. As I checked the room an idea flashed in my fried brain. It wasn't foolproof, but it would work. Snatching up the velvet bag, I hid it. With a last glance at my watch, I grabbed my carry-on, locked the door behind me and raced down the stairs to the lobby.

Outside the clouds were no longer black—blue patches in

between streaks of gray. The storm had passed. Just then, the shuttle pulled up. Everyone was there, except Ingrid and Jeffrey. If she didn't come soon, we would have to leave without her or miss the ferry.

"Hey, everybody! All aboard for Coba!"

On my signal the folding door of the shuttle opened and the group boarded. Nervously, I checked the street for Ingrid.

"Wait!" Janice nudged my arm. "Look…there they are."

Two people in matching safari outfits were running straight towards the shuttle. It was them alright—Jeffrey panted, taking on the task of dragging Ingrid up the steps. When they took a seat near the back, I gave the driver the go-ahead. A strange pair. For the life of me, I couldn't see the attraction. Ingrid was an overweight alcoholic. And that wasn't taking into account the fact that she smoked like a chimney. And yet this attractive man in his thirties, who had a thing for models, found *her* desirable? It didn't add up.

The sun was peeking out now, filtering into the van, the light picking up the sparkle from Ingrid's earrings. Diamonds. Large stones. I wasn't the only one who noticed.

Janice couldn't take her eyes off Ingrid. "Beautiful earrings. Where did you get them?" She leaned in for a better look."

Ingrid flicked a glance at Janice. "They were a gift. Unfortunately, I had to part with the necklace."

Janice's face paled, freckles noticeably pronounced.

"Hey, Adie," George piped up, "when do we get there?"

I held up a finger to stall him and picked up the microphone to announce, "Welcome to the Days of the Dead Tour to Coba." I paused to see if everyone was listening. Seeing their eyes on me, I said, "Shortly, we'll be at the ferry dock. I've prearranged our tickets. You'll be able to board the ferry as soon as I've spoken to the cashier. Seats on the main level are enclosed but if you want the sea air, you can go up on the upper deck. It's also a better choice if you're inclined to feel seasick.

Professor Hidalgo from the Museum in San Miguel, will be traveling with us. He's an expert in Mayan history and will be at your disposal during the entire trip. Once we arrive in Playa del Carmen, I have arranged for us to take Jeeps to Coba with a brief stop at a *cenote* on the way. Meet me at the white pillar at the end of the wharf, next to the La Rosa Restaurant. From there we'll walk to our Jeeps. Any questions?"

"When do we go snorkeling?" Jim shouted out.

I adjusted the microphone. "We're stopping at a *cenote*. Even for those not interested in snorkeling it's a great photo op."

"What the hell are these sin-notes you're talking about, Adie?" George shoveled handfuls of chips into his mouth.

"*Cenotes* are sink holes or caves. They're all along the coastline here because the limestone surface cracks. They form above the underground rivers."

"Will we see Coba tonight, Adie?" Bryan spoke quietly from across the aisle. It was hard to hear him above George and Janice who had started arguing about something Janice forgot to bring.

"Yes, we should have a good hour and a half to see the ruins." Bryan was holding a thick paperback that didn't look much like a beach novel. I peered to read the title, but at the angle he was gripping the book, I could only read the word *Mayans*. Fern, sitting next to him, wore a large brimmed straw hat. Very Scarlet O'Hara—a southern plantation mistress with her liquid brown eyes and flowing raven tresses. To my relief, she hadn't made the mistake of wearing a flowing long dress. My eyes shot back to Bryan. "Professor Hidalgo will explain the history behind the pyramids at Coba."

Bryan nodded thoughtfully.

With everyone busy talking I sat back down in my seat, my eyes searching the dock for Wolf. The driver slowed and pulled in alongside the curb. A crowd gathered on the wharf for the two o'clock boat to the mainland. Diego was right. There was a ten minute delay.

But where was Wolf? I didn't notice anyone who vaguely resembled a sea god. Did this mean he wasn't coming? More trouble with his business deal? Maybe Diego was right about Wolf. I was nothing to him—a fling, no more. He didn't value me the way he should. I would always be disappointed with him in my life.

Annoyed with myself for being so gullible, I picked up my bags and made my way to the door. The driver pulled a switch to open the folding door. When I edged up, he scuttled out to help me down with my bags. The clouds were drifting east and the rain had passed, leaving us with a sunny humid day. I picked up my bags and led the way to the ticket booth with the group following.

The ticket booth cashier checked my prepaid tickets and signaled for us to proceed. I wanted to call Wolf, but I knew better. Men get bored when women are too available. Honesty is a mistake when it comes to love. I learned that the hard way back in college.

Most of my tour group opted to sit on the enclosed area on the main level where the seats were spaced in rows. I had to get some fresh air. Taking the stairs to the upper deck, I strolled over to the railing, set my bags down and watched the turquoise waters of the Caribbean brush against the rocky shoreline of Cozumel.

A whiff of soap and balmy, ocean breeze. Warm arms encircled my waist and drew me close. His lips nuzzled the base of my neck, sending waves of pleasure down my body. "You should never wear clothes," Wolf whispered, "your skin is made for touching."

I glanced over my shoulder up to his dark blue eyes, more intense than ever with his tanned face. "You're here after all." I took in his ruffled blond hair, all natural, just like him.

"Close your eyes," he ordered softly, loosening his grip.

"Why?" I was somewhat annoyed by how insecure he'd made me feel.

"I have something you'd like, princess."

Something? More like everything. This man couldn't get any hotter with his broad shoulders and narrow waist set off by the black T-shirt not to mention his blue jeans tight over his butt. And then there was the glint in his eyes. He must put love potion in his coffee in the morning to come on with this primal vibe, still going strong into the afternoon.

I closed my eyes. A delicate chain tickled my chest and a smooth object settled in my cleavage. I waited while Wolf did up the necklace at the nape of my neck. I glanced down. The pendant was a startling green, highly polished and attached to a slender, twisted-strand of silver. A jade figure hung from a loop. "It's beautiful, Wolf!" I fingered the jade. "Who is she?"

"You've spoken to her at her shrine."

I cocked my head up at him. There was only one major Mayan female deity, Ixchel. The moon goddess brought fertility. "Isn't this a bit of a risk?"

Wolf smiled slowly. "She'll protect you too. But not too safe, I have plans for you that call for some risk." His mouth moved sensuously, parting my lips for his tongue. My body thrilled to his touch, but my mind swirled in confusion—I didn't think I'd want handcuffs or whips if that was what he was thinking.

Wolf laughed, seeing my expression. "Nothing you wouldn't like."

"Good. I thought you might be getting bored with our activities."

"Snorkeling? We haven't done any yet."

I frowned at his deliberate misunderstanding.

He smiled slowly. "With you taking off with the fox, I've hardly had a chance to be with you, let alone time to get bored." Wolf handed me my purse, grabbed my bags and took my hand, leading me to a deck chair. "How did that go, anyway?" Placing my things on the deck, he sat down and stretched out his long legs.

"We flew to some place on the mainland." I positioned myself in the chair next to him.

"Yeah?" Wolf raised an eyebrow.

"We met with his collector, had some interesting tamales and flew home."

Wolf stared out at the Caribbean. Through the haze Playa del Carmen appeared in the distance. He stroked his finger down my cheek, smiling slowly. "So Alvarez plied you with tequila, took you on a tour of the house and showed you the bedroom."

I blushed guiltily. "No, he didn't."

"And?"

"Nothing," I said, a little too sharply.

Wolf met my eyes. "There's a bed in there somewhere."

Wow! He was good, although I don't know if the divan counted as a bed. "Let's not talk about Diego." I touched his hand. "You have so much to tell me." I remembered what Diego had warned me about. Would Wolf keep me in the dark because he didn't want a commitment?

"I do?" He put his arms around me.

"Daniella's phone call last night. How did that end up?"

"Better than I would have thought."

"She plied you with beer and took *you* to bed." I speculated on how the Daniella would maneuver to advance her battle.

"There was some beer and she wanted to, but I kept my virtue."

"She exaggerated the situation?"

"Not really. Apart from the owner's wife, I didn't see any other women. The place was going strong and I could see she wouldn't want to go in there on her own with all those guys checking her out.

Hah, typical man. He was blind when it came to Daniella. She thrived on male attention but this time the stakes were too high for her to risk showing her true colors.

"And you're plan—what is it? You didn't bother to tell me."

Wolf grinned. "I was trying to when you started to seduce me."

"Oh? You think you're so hot, don't you?"

Wolf's mouth twitched. "You wouldn't be spending any time with me if you didn't think I was."

"I'm not a completely shallow individual. I like a man to have personality." And he was kind of beautiful on the inside—at least what I knew about him. He was fun and romantic. Not that Diego wasn't. I couldn't help it if I was attracted to both of them, could I? Personality was only a small part of the equation when it came to Diego or Wolf. They were hotties like no other. Chocolate truffles—one with a hint of rum and the other definitely mocha. Both enticing to a chocoholic and severely addictive. I shook my head and sighed. Too many choices.

Life was a massive maze. Sometimes you drove down a road, took a turn and what you wanted wasn't right there. Other times there'd be an unexpected detour and you'd have to start all over again and think up a new strategy. I took his hand. "Tell me about your plan."

"I'm expanding. I have this vision of a larger resort right in the town without the frills."

"You mean like a two-star?"

"No, I don't want anything like a hotel. I want atmosphere—a real laid-back sort of place. There'll be a pool and spa, but the guests will have an authentic Mexican cantina and restaurant."

"Adult only?"

"Maybe…I'll have to think that through a bit more." Wolf's eyes scanned the Playa del Carmen coastline. "Daniella was trying to get the cantina owner to sell it to me but he was having a change of heart when someone else came up with a better offer."

"Or so she said."

"It all worked out in the end. He signed the papers, but," he considered, "I guess it wasn't too good for us." He pushed a strand of my hair back. "Tonight, babe, you'll have my complete and undivided attention."

"Promises, promises," I said dryly.

He ran his hands slowly down my arms, sending shivers of excitement to my hardening nubs. His eyes exuded sexuality in their electrifying gaze. "Alvarez is the one to watch. He'll probably land his helicopter on the nearest pyramid and drag you away to his house in the jungle."

I smiled in amusement. "Like Tarzan? Not Diego, he's far too classy for that sort of behavior." I ran a finger down his cheek. "But if you want to stop me from running off, you'll have to cater to my whims, won't you?" I glanced at the shoreline. "We're coming into Playa del Carmen. I need to go. I don't want to keep the group waiting."

"Sure." Wolf picked up our bags. I carried my purse. It would have been a bit much to expect him to walk around with it too. But I could see the bags weren't any problem for him—a man that lean and powerful.

The ferry had stopped and the passengers wandered in between a winding roped-in area to get off. I told Wolf we had to meet my group in front of the La Rosa Restaurant. We trekked down the wharf, dodging children running about and people coming from the opposite direction to meet the arriving ferry passengers.

La Rosa was a busy place. Tourists and Mexicans lined up to get a table. Fern and Bryan stood at a pillar waiting.

"Hey!" I said. "You remember my friend, Wolf?"

"Um-hmm." Fern smiled like a cat spotting a mouse.

"Wolf, could you wait here with them? I need to get our lunches."

A good tour guide never forgets the food. I bypassed some tourists waiting to be seated, who favored me with some unpleasant stares and situated myself in front of the maitre'd. "*Hola*, I'm Señorita Sturm. I ordered lunch for my tour group. Is it ready?"

"*Si*, no problem." The man bowed slightly. "I'll have one of the waiters bring them out. Is that your group there?" He pointed to the pillar, where the rest of my group gathered.

"Yes. We'll be at the parking lot." I dug out my wallet and gave him my credit card. I glanced back and saw the group was all there. An ancient, little man in a tan suit had joined them.

"Professor!" I made my way over and extending my hand, I said, "I'm Adie Sturm."

"Ah, Señorita Sturm. It is indeed a pleasure."

"You will be traveling with me in the lead car. I am so glad you were able to come with us." I motioned for the tour group to come closer.

"Everyone, this is Professor Hidalgo. He's an expert on the Mayans. He'll be telling us about the *cenote* on the way to Coba. You will find the history behind it fascinating. Please," I gestured to the group, "follow me."

Wolf took my hand as we strolled along the sidewalk, the group behind us. Bryan caught up with the professor and started to quiz him about *cenotes*. Half a block away, the Hertz man waited in the parking lot with our rented Jeeps and the keys for each vehicle. Jeffrey, Wolf, and Dan had agreed to do the driving. While the designated drivers were busy signing insurance papers, the rest of the group placed their luggage in the backs of the Jeeps. I directed the rest of them to their vehicles.

Fern, Bryan and the wizened old professor got in the back seat of our black Jeep just as the waiter arrived with a box of tacos and water bottles. I was glad Wolf was driving. Mexican roads and drivers didn't faze him. "I assume this *cenote* is off the main road," Wolf said.

"It is. Take the highway to Tulum and turn off to Coba. At that point watch for the side road."

Fern opened the box and passed around tacos. "How is the snorkeling there, professor?"

"It's spectacular. No doubt about it."

Wolf swung the Jeep out onto highway 307. Bryan shoved his hat low over his eyes. "Adie was telling us about the limestone and the formation of the sinkholes, Professor."

"This area near Tulum has the two longest underwater cave

systems known on earth. It is believed that fewer than ten per cent
have been explored as yet." He squared his shoulders. "The
Mayans called them *Dzonot*, but the Spaniards thought they said
cenote."

The hot afternoon sun uncomfortably heated the interior of our
jeep. Once out on the highway, the flow of air picked up and it
became more bearable. I passed Wolf an open bottle of water and
took one for myself. Glancing back at Fern and Bryan, I thought
how little I knew about them. This would be the perfect time to
satisfy my curiosity. Imprisoned inside the Jeep, they wouldn't be
able to escape any of my probing questions.

"I'm really interested in the Mayans, Professor Hidalgo." Fern
said enthusiastically. "One of the college courses Adie and I took
was about cults. I did a paper on ancient religions."

"Ah-hh." Professor Hidalgo nodded his head in approval.
"You are interested in the sacrifices at the *cenotes* then?"

Fern's eyes sparkled. "How common were they?"

"Very. Skeletal remains of men, women and children have
been found in all the *cenotes*." The professor took a big bite of his
cheese taco and chewed reflectively.

I shuddered. This conversation was too much like Reese's
ghastly art—nobles piercing their penises and tongues to collect
blood for the gods. "Are you interested in Mayan culture, Bryan?"

"Yup. Glad Fern suggested this trip."

The Jeep slowed as we came to a *tope*, one of those tricky
speed bumps on Mexican roads. Fern had always been artsy, but
Bryan didn't look the type with his preppy shirt and baggy shorts.

Wolf spoke up. "Do you two snorkel?" He shot his question
over his shoulder.

"We want to try it this trip," Fern said. "I've got a desk job
and I want to do something physical."

I grabbed my sunglasses and pulled them on. "What company
do you work for?"

"Actually, it's an art gallery."

"Oh?"

"Nothing important, Adie—basically paper work. I might take
some courses if I continue on there but for now, it's a job."

"What about you, Bryan?"

"Flamboro Downs."

"Harness racing isn't it?"

"Yup."

"In what capacity?" Wolf slowed down for a truck turning off the road.

"Security." Bryan shifted uncomfortably. "Isn't that the road, Wolf?" He pointed to a sign ahead.

"Yes…" The professor bopped up and down excitedly. "That's it!"

Wolf made a right and drifted over to the side of the road. I took advantage of the moment to check if the other jeeps had followed us. "We're okay, Wolf. They're behind us."

The jungle vegetation was becoming more tropical as we drove inland. It was oppressively humid. No breeze. Potholes more than road. In fact, I wasn't sure we were on a road anymore when it suddenly ended.

"Is it far?" I asked the professor when everyone congregated.

"Approximately fifty yards down that path."

What path? I scanned the area. Surrounded by foliage, I barely made out a narrow dirt path that wound its way into the jungle. In single file we followed behind the professor. A cocoon of heat and humidity—mosquitoes swarmed, attacking exposed flesh. Hidalgo's dry wrinkled skin worked like a snake skin, shielding like an armor. My eyes flicked from the ground to the bushes on guard for snakes.

Above us, we heard a sharp squawk and a flit of emerald in the trees—a macaw. Hidalgo pushed aside a branch and we stepped into a clearing with three sinkholes. A breeze kept the bugs at bay. Standing at the ledge, the water sparkled below us. One large pool, about thirty feet across and two smaller ones made up the *cenote*. A thick jungle canopy shaded part of the cave but at the same time, contained the moist heat. A misty haze surrounded us.

When the whole group had gathered the professor began. "This is the *Calavera of the Jaguar*. Some call it the Temple of Doom. Probably for good reason. *Cenotes* gathered rainwater for the people. Because of that the Rain God needed to be kept strong with human sacrifices. If you walk up the path, you'll see how the arrangement of the sink holes appear to resemble the eyes, nose and mouth of a skull."

"Cool!" Fern squeezed Bryan's hand excitedly.

"This place creeps me out," Ingrid grumbled. Swatting a mosquito she said to Jeffrey. "I don't want to stay. Come back to the car with me."

Jeffrey must have tuned her out. He strode over to the limestone overhang thick with tree roots and focused on a brown iguana sitting in the sun.

"Anyone for a swim?" Dan joked.

"Fortunately, I brought this rope ladder. I will fasten it here." The professor bent down to tie it to an iron ring at the edge of the *cenote*, triple looping it with sailor's knots. "There was a ladder here but it seems to have disappeared."

"You're wearing a bikini aren't you, Adie?" Wolf fingered the narrow strap that peeked out past my top.

Was he out of his mind?

Wolf kicked off his Nike runners. "Don't worry. I'll take you down." Tugging off his T-shirt, he flung it down on a patch of grass.

Her fears temporarily forgotten, Ingrid's jaw dropped. When Wolf's jeans landed, Lola's eyes started to bug out.

I couldn't believe he meant to do this. And I was to come with him? Wolf drew me in closer and undid the buttons on my top. I froze. He smiled and yanked it off, throwing it on top of his clothes.

Dan chortled. "You got Adie speechless, Wolf. That's a new one!"

George snickered.

Wolf unzipped my shorts and pushed them off my hips. "You can do this," he whispered. "You're my mermaid, remember?"

Jim piped up enthusiastically. "If you two go, Tom and I will." He jabbed Tom in the ribs.

"How about you, Fern?" Tom said flirtatiously, kicking off his Adidas runners.

"Maybe." Fern shot a glance at Bryan but he was wandering to the other pool and didn't take notice.

"I could go with you."

Fern fluffed her long waves and smiled mysteriously.

My shorts hit the grass and as I stepped back to pick them up, Wolf grabbed them and tossed them on the pile. Jim and Tom started to strip off too but they weren't getting the attention Wolf's buff bod got. With his washboard flat abs, broad shoulders and muscular chest, he was pin-up material—a sea god ready to return to the water.

Someone sharply jabbed me on my shoulder. I jerked away from Ingrid's scarlet talon. "What the…"

"Adie," Ingrid hissed out her words. "Where is it? If you don't come back alive, I need to know where it is."

"Ss-hh!" I silenced her, noticing Fern and Janice listening. "Later, Ingrid." Ingrid frowned but pressed her lips shut.

Glad I had put her off I took a moment to admire the curve of Wolf's firm butt in his boxers. When he grinned, I knew then I should have made a run for it.

Too late. Wolf had me. At the edge of the *cenote* realization struck me like a bolt of lightening. He really meant to do this—not only that, but I was coming along.

"Stop, don't go!"

Distracted, I looked back but saw it wasn't me Ingrid was yelling at. "You leave now and you'll regret it, Jeffrey." She threatened loudly.

I didn't get to hear the rest because at that moment Wolf lifted me up to the rope ladder. I can swim but this was a twenty foot drop. Fear knotted in my stomach.

"Hold tight to my neck and lock your legs around my waist. Think of it as an inner thigh workout in the gym." Seeing my expression, he said, "You'll be fine, Adie."

Wolf gripped the rope with me hanging on to him. The descent into the *cenote* took only moments but it seemed endless, with my sweaty, slippery hands interlocking to keep myself from losing my grip on Wolf. This was worse than those twirling-shaking-stomach twisters at the fair.

"When I say, now—hold your breath. We'll be hitting the water."

I barely heard the word before I was launched into the cool cave water. The chill enveloped me in a tight embrace. Water so clear and compelling, I could see the tips of long, sharp stalagmites from the bottom. Tiny silver fish shot out around me. I kicked my legs to propel myself up and popped my head out. A second later, Wolf was there too, grinning mischievously.

"What?" I grabbed on to his shoulders, pulling him to me.

His glance swept down. "Your top is off."

"Not funny!" I glanced down. It was true. I clung to him and shrank down.

Treading water, Wolf put one arm around my waist and said, "Calm down, babe. Grab the strings and tie it. I'll keep you floating."

Above us, I could see a heads peering down before a splatter of water hit my eyes. Water swirled where someone had jumped in. Just as Jim's head sprung back up, I engaged both strings and tied them.

Jim popped up. "Isn't this awesome?" Not waiting for a reply he dived back down into the *cenote*.

It was a mystical experience. From above the hot sun filtered through the foliage into the *cenote*. The thick roots of the trees sparkled gold. Rust had penetrated the chamber of the cave. Everywhere the water shimmered an enchanting cerulean blue. It was no wonder the Mayans considered *cenotes* a sacred place—a connection to the gods.

The trip back up the rope was hard on Wolf but he took it as a personal challenge to climb up with me hanging on like a monkey. At the top he sat down on the limestone overhang. "Was it worth it?"

"Was it ever! It's like the place hasn't been seen by humans since the ancient Mayans." My eyes studied him. "Did you know it would be like this?"

Wolf shook his head.

"Then why?"

"Why?"

"With me tagging along?"

Wolf ran his index finger over his bottom lip, as he watched Tom climb up the rope. His eyes shot back to me. "I want to do things with you."

"Is this the risk you mentioned before?"

"Part of it."

I stretched out my legs and leaned my back into his arm. I twisted my head to search his eyes but I couldn't find any clues as to what his thoughts were. "Thanks. You took me somewhere I wouldn't have gone on my own."

The trees rustled as two green macaws flew up higher in the

foliage. Wolf bent down and gently kissed my lips in reply.

A branch snapped. The mood was shattered by the hasty arrival of Fern, looking a bit worse for wear. "You've got to come, Adie. The bitch queen is freaked."

I got on my feet. "Something wrong with Ingrid?"

"She's nuts. If you don't calm her down, I'll throw her into the *cenote*."

I tugged my shorts and top on over my wet bikini. The dry clothes stuck like glue. Wolf had zipped up his jeans and was stepping into his loosely tied Nikes by the time I was ready.

"Let's go." I jerked my chin to the path.

When we arrived at the clearing Ingrid was hunched over sobbing in Lola's maternal arms. Most of tour group was there near the vehicles talking amongst themselves. Jeffrey stood beside Lola smoking distractedly.

When she saw me, Ingrid shook off Lola. "It's about time! Where in God's name have you been? Didn't I tell you this place is evil? Didn't you hear what the professor said? There are spirits of priests and sacrificed people at this place. We need to get the hell out of here!"

"Calm down. Tell me what happened."

Ingrid's fingernails dug into my arm. "I went down the path to the other entrance. I could hear all of you swimming. Your voices carried. Jeff was with me, but he left to take some pictures of the eyes of the skull on the outside. There was some light from the crack in the cave wall but apart from that it was dark and misty. At first, I thought it was you people swimming in the water, shouting at me but I didn't see anyone. But I felt someone watching me. I turned around and saw..." Her voice shook. "I'm not sure what. It was definitely a person—a primitive, wild-looking creature speaking gibberish." She stabbed her finger in air. "This thing came after me...with a knife!"

11

Lola gave me a fearful wide-eyed look. This was bad. Ingrid's crazy imagination could ruin this trip. I had to distract them. "Listen everyone. It's getting late. Gather your things we need to continue on to Coba. To your Jeeps, please!" Wolf and I escorted Ingrid over to her vehicle and thankfully she got in.

The others sat waiting for us. When I gazed over my shoulder, Fern looked a bit droopy. Her shirt had a few dirt stains and she her face was shiny with sweat. I, on the other hand was refreshed from my swim but stressed from dealing with Ingrid. I dug out my bottle of water and took a long swig. "Did you have a good time?" I asked Bryan, as Wolf swung out onto the road.

"It was fascinating, Adie. We saw spider monkeys and with some luck we'll see some others in Coba."

I swiveled to Professor Hidalgo. "Ingrid said you talked to her about spirits at the *cenotes*."

"*Si*, she heard the voices," he said, in a hushed tone. He pushed his wire-rimmed glasses higher on his nose. "But they could have been birds or animal noises or even someone from our tour group, heh?"

"And the vision?"

"The Mayans believed in multiple souls. Only one would die at the *cenote*. They'd find a new soul—some sort of animal." Seeing a captive audience in the back seat, he added enthusiastically, "But the rulers were special. They could take on the spirit of the jaguar."

Fern fingered her jade pendant. "That would be so cool."

The professor nodded reflectively. "Yes, the jaguar can triumph over all the others." He noticed Fern's pendant. "Jade was meant for the nobility—the rulers. You aspire to greatness, Fern?"

Fern smiled surreptitiously.

On both sides of the road, we passed wild undergrowth and a few small houses. Bryan made a quiet comment to the Professor in Spanish and he replied pointing to the potholes filled with muddy water. I got the gist of it—something to do with the rainy season. But glancing up at the sky, I was optimistic about the rest of the day. It was bright and sunny—no clouds and hopefully no more rain today.

On entering the village of Coba, we drove straight ahead past a restaurant until we sited a still blue lake dotted with soldier-straight reeds, reminiscent of the bayous of Louisiana. Cormorants flecked the lake. I strained to see the alligator Professor Hidalgo pointed out. Passing a few restaurants, we entered a dirt parking area and Wolf pulled the Jeep in under the shade of a papaya tree.

"Should I rent bikes?"

The professor nodded. "It is a ways to the Nohoch Mul pyramids. We could walk but our time is limited. Bikes would be better."

I got out just as the other Jeeps pulled up. An old man sitting on a bench in front of a shed had some bikes for rent. After I paid I returned to catch the tail end of the professor's lecture about the history of Coba. "The word Coba means 'water stirred by wind'. The city stood in the midst of five shallow lakes. This was one of the grandest cities of the Mayans, with a population of seventy to one hundred and twenty-five thousand at its height in AD 632. Until the rise of Chichen Itza, it was the most well known Mayan site."

I touched the professor's arm. "We need to go." I turned to the group. "I've arranged bikes."

Ingrid made a face. "Adie, you don't really expect us to ride those rickety things, do you?"

"There's a special bike available that has a carrier for a passenger. You can pay for a driver or maybe Jeffrey..." I glanced over to a bike with a contraption attached to the back. Jeffrey frowned and someone snickered.

"Do you want me to me take you up in one of those, princess?" Wolf's eyes glinted in amusement. "You could just sit back and I'd be your slave."

"Slave, eh? Interesting idea but I think I'm fit enough to handle a bike."

"You're better than fit." He smiled lazily.

Ingrid's voice took on a superior tone. "It's not a matter of fitness. Seeking a little comfort is not an unreasonable request for anyone."

"The only other choice is walking and we don't have the time." I threw my leg over the bike. "Professor, will you lead the way?"

With everyone already on their bikes Ingrid gave in and got on hers.

The trees, tall and heavy with foliage, shaded a surprisingly wide dirt path. The screeching of birds in the jungle and the chattering of the monkeys distracted me for a moment and I narrowly missed hitting a rock in the road. I didn't dare glance back to check on the boss. Now, if she got lost...I grinned, thinking what a break that would be.

We biked down one road and turned right. Before long, we veered off and stopped. The Mayan ball court in front of us was I-shaped with sloping high walls on either side of a dirt playing field.

The professor eagerly went into his lecture. "The exact game rules are uncertain but the goal was to propel a rubber ball, made from the sap of a rubber tree through the ring on the wall. The players deflected the ball by hitting it with various body parts, including their hips and shoulder, but couldn't use their hands or feet. For protection they wore leather belts or yokes and padding on their forearms and knees."

Jeffrey slid his hand on the wall. "Sounds rough."

"It was. Often warriors played the game to reenact a war." Throwing his arms up, his voice rose feverously. "The leader of the losing team would be dragged forward, his playing equipment pulled roughly from his body. Bound head and foot by ropes he would be taken to the high priest and decapitated!" After someone gasped, he smiled smugly. "The leader of winning team, on the other-hand, would be presented with a necklace of jade beads."

"But, professor," Bryan rocked back and forth on his heels excitedly, "I read that the winner would be sacrificed because it would be an honor to die for the god."

The professor grunted. "There are many versions. No one is sure of what actually happened." He gestured at the stone ring. "The ring was in the shape of a portal."

At this point I lost my focus. The professor's lecture had become a blur. We were standing behind our group, Wolf's hand stroking my lower back while his lips brushed my shoulder. The nerve endings in my body quivered.

"I want to mingle with a lady whose flavor I can't resist," Wolf said softly in my ear.

I looked up. "And what flavor would that be?"

His eyes flicked down. "Spicy-hot."

A surge of arousal sparked my nipples. I glanced down to see if anything showed and saw a dirt stain on my pale-pink top. Come to think of it, my hair was probably messed up too and...

"Don't worry, babe, you're just the way I like you—wild hair and slightly dirty. What I'm looking forward to is the cleanup. A nice long shower, slicking you down with soap, and washing off every little part of you."

As the professor droned on in the background, I had this intense craving, stronger than a chocolate urge—if I didn't have him, I'd go crazy with lust.

The yellow butterfly that fluttered in front of me brought my attention back to my job and the reason I was really there. My brain cells regrouped. I waited until the professor came to a finish and took that opportunity to direct everyone to their bikes.

Our next stop was an impressive, towering pyramid called *La Iglesia*, the temple of the church. This was a definite photo opportunity. "Fern, could you, please?" I handed her my camera and grabbed Wolf's hand, drawing him close. His arms encircled me as Fern aimed the camera.

"I have the temple in the background." Fern centered the shot. "Smile! Don't look so serious."

"How about this, then." Wolf swung me up high in his arms and held me up like a trophy."

Fern clicked the shutter. "Not boring. Take a look."

Wolf put me down. I took the camera and held it up. "My hair is a mess and I have this stupid expression."

Wolf leaned in to look. "Wicked eyes, spicy woman."

Fern laughed. "I think you two are in heat."

Embarrassed, I asked. "Where's Bryan?"

"He dragged the professor off to climb the pyramid. Hope the little guy doesn't die of a heart attack. But it's hard to put off Bryan. Once he gets an idea he's really gung-ho." Fern checked out the pyramid in the distance. "It's high, isn't it?"

"It was used as a watchtower. But it's way smaller than the one we'll see at Nohoch Mul." I glanced at my watch. "We need to move on. Can you tell them to come down, please?"

"Sure. Looks like the rest of them are ready to move on." Fern glanced at Dan and Lola sitting on the steps of the pyramid. She called over her shoulder "I'll get them, too."

"Wolf, could you round up those guys over there, please?" I motioned in the opposite direction where Tom and George stood checking out some female tourists.

"No problem. Where're you going?"

"There." My eyes flicked to a flash of orange in the underbrush. "I think that's Janice. I need to get her."

I took a grassy path that wound around a thicket of bushes. She was walking with someone. I chugged along quickly to catch up.

Janice's voice was raised an octave higher than usual. Shrilly, she objected to a person I couldn't see. "You can't keep them! It's not like you need the jewelry, is it? Besides, I'll compensate you."

"Oh, is that right?"

"Sixty thousand. I'll pay you when we get back to the hotel."

The other woman laughed contemptuously.

Janice's words snapped out. "How much do you want?"

I sneaked up but something rustled in the grass. I jumped back crying out as a banded snake, black-red with a repeating pattern disappeared into the thicker grass behind the tree.

It was obvious I had overheard them. Janice scowled. "What are doing here, Adie?"

"We're having a private conversation." Ingrid glared at me her hands on her hips.

"Sorry, I didn't mean to interrupt. I only came to tell you that we're leaving.

Janice shot Ingrid a murderous look. "We'll discuss this later."

Without another word Ingrid turned on her heel and strode in the direction of the clearing. Elbowing me out of the way, Janice stalked down the path.

The diamond earrings. Janice wanted them. Why were they so important? I followed them to the bikes.

"Hey, Adie!" Fern tapped me on the arm. "We're ready to roll."

"Thanks, Fern." I noticed the professor had ridden off with the group. But Wolf had waited for me. Together we caught up to the others. It wasn't long until we saw why El Castillo was the most famous of the pyramids of Coba.

Professor Hidalgo stood quietly until the group settled down. "The pyramid directly before us, El Castillo, is the tallest pyramid in the Yucatan with the exception of a structure in Calakmul. It is even higher than the more famous pyramid at Chichen Itza.

"Why here?" Bryan peered up at the ruin. "It looks like we're in the middle of nowhere."

"Yes, indeed!" The professor virtually glowed with that question. "Coba, although larger than any other location of Mayan ruins, has had very little reconstruction done but it was a major center at one time. Mayan roads, crossed here." He gestured to the left where a white surface appeared through the dirt. "One of them went one hundred kilometers to Uxmal and if you climb to the top, you should be able to see all the way to Tulum, a seaside Mayan village on the coast."

Tulum was beautiful. Diego and I had spent a day there a few months ago—a day that had bonded us. That was the beginning of the rivalry between Diego and Wolf. I was a prize they were willing to fight for, or so they claimed.

At first, I'd been flattered. Who wouldn't want two sexy guys in pursuit? But what if I committed to one of them? Would they become bored and move on to a new woman to battle over? Daniella had been Diego's fiancé and now she was Wolf's business partner? Or was it more? Was that why Wolf found her so attractive?

"Let's go, baby." Hearing his husky voice caused me to forget everything except his eyes.

"Wow!" I stared up at the steps to the top. "One hundred and twenty-four, Wolf."

"Adie," Dan called out to me as we started our climb. "Lola and I are exhausted. We're sitting this one out. The professor said there's something he'd show us."

We started the climb. I was better at it than Wolf—small feet come in handy when the steps are narrow. I weaved my way up between people going up. A glance down was enough to make me remember how much I hated heights. To keep myself balanced, I kept my eyes focused on the other climbers ahead. With the narrow steps and the intense afternoon heat, it was getting hotter, the higher we climbed. I recalled that the Mayan men were small—a tall man barely five feet. It was hard to imagine. Because I'm petite, I had to be unpredictable in my moves to gain the advantage with my sparring partners. If nothing else, I was that.

When we finally made it to the top, Wolf hugged me to him. "We made it, babe."

I looked down. The thick green forest canopy was dense with vegetation. We were perched like birds above it. In the distance, the gray stones of an unexcavated ruin, mysteriously untouched for centuries, stood partially hidden in the greenery.

Jim and Tom's triumphant shouts as they reached the top were overpowered by a tremendous growl from the jungle below us.

I clutched Wolf's arm excitedly. "Look! It's a howler monkey!"

Wolf grinned. "Mating call?"

"It's territorial," Jim said from behind us. "Watch the trees."

I saw a black shape swing from branch to branch below us. "Did you see it, now?"

Wolf's eyes flicked over to another black shape skimming the tree tops. "Do you think he'll catch her?" She likes to give him a hard time."

Surveying the area, my eyes dropped to Ingrid, Fern, Janice and Jeffrey making slow progress. Hidalgo and Bryan were just above them. As they slowed down other visitors brushed by. Ingrid suddenly sat down. She wasn't the only one. Others had climbed less than half way before they gave up too.

How had the priests had managed this trek every morning and evening? High as we were, the breeze was just that—a light puff of air that did nothing to alleviate the oppressive heat. "Let's go inside." I indicated the stone arch of the temple.

Wolf stooped in ahead of me. Inside it was cooler and darker. The thick walls provided relief from the heat. Alone in the temple with Wolf, I became aware of the power of the ancient structure. It was deadly quiet, like the inside of a tomb.

"It gives you a strange feeling, doesn't it? The magic of the ancient Mayans."

Wolf placed his arms around my waist and pressed himself

close. I felt his hardness against me. "Yeah, magic all right." He breathed the words into my ear. "Powerful magic that's just for you."

His warm lips kissed my neck and as I stared out at the awesome view, I forgot about everything except him. He was stoking my fire and if there had been a door in that temple, I would have shut it and let myself capture the passion. Before I could speculate on what we could be doing a sharp cry, almost animal, sounded from outside.

I rushed out the doorway and looked down. Near the bottom of the steps, a familiar figure lay awkwardly sprawled on the narrow, stone steps.

12

Fortunately, Ingrid had not made it up too far before she slipped. She was hurt, but curiously subdued. In the lobby of the hotel Ingrid took me aside to whisper, "I was doing fine, Adie, taking it slowly, until someone pushed me." She glanced around. "No one believes me. I know it was one of them."

"It's the heat, angel. You got dizzy." Jeffrey squeezed Ingrid's hand. "Let's get you settled in the bedroom. I'll order some margaritas." Jeffrey placed his hand at her back and directed her away down the hall.

I heaved a sigh of relief as they took the corridor on the left and disappeared.

"Forget about her. She's trouble with a capital T. Why don't I arrange dinner for us?" Wolf handed me a key. "See you in the room soon, babe?"

"I'd like to take a quick swim first. Meet you back here, okay?"

"Sure, princess." Wolf smiled slowly. "Keep that bikini on for me. I like seeing you slick and wet all over."

I stepped under the overhead ceiling-fan for some breeze to calm my jumping hormones and looked around. The room was better than I'd expected. We had a pool view which put it up a notch but when my eyes lit on the queen-size bed, I couldn't help but grin like a fool.

Digging around in my bag, I found a blue string bikini and slipped it on. Critically, I glanced at myself in the mirror. Trim and toned except for that difficult area on my belly. I sighed. Someday...

From my bag, I got out a container. Treats—he'd want some sweets with his dessert.

***

In the warm water, I relaxed, swimming on my back. After circling around I climbed out. Perched on the ladder, I let my legs dangle down.

The sparkling water shimmered from the lamps bordering the pool. Off to one side, fronds from the palm trees swayed with the evening breeze. Shadows interplayed with the flashes of light filtering in through the palms. From behind, I heard footsteps.

"Daiquiris, Adie," Fern bent down and handed me a frosty glass filled with a strawberry mixture. Her skimpy brown bikini blended in with her dark skin tone, almost as if she were nude. Sliding her legs down, she sat next to me. Tilting her glass back, she sipped her drink before she set it down. "Pretty, isn't it?"

From my position, I could see the window of my room but not into it—the fading light of the setting sun glimmered on the surface of the glass.

Fern followed my gaze. "Don't worry, you've got time. Your hottie is busy rounding up some food. Saw him when I got these." She pushed back a long, black tendril hanging over her eye. "How's your drink, babe?"

"Great," I said, feeling the burn of the rum as it hit my empty stomach. Cold and satisfying.

Fern gazed into my eyes. "You know, we really had a good time in college, didn't we? Remember when you came out to the farm?"

"You mean when we'd had all that wine?" I laughed ruefully, thinking of how wasted I'd been.

"Um-mm. You were hilarious." Fern patted my thigh for emphasis. "And my boyfriend Rick thought you were *so* hot."

Memories of Fern and her boyfriend sifted through the dustbin of my mind. That night they'd both been refilling my glass while we sat around the coffee table, all of us sprawled on pillows listening to Rick's wild stories—his affair with his male high school teacher and then his fling with his girlfriend's mom. After his confessions I'd started to have a creepy feeling about him.

"Rick and I wanted you to stay but you took off."

Liquored up to my limit I'd driven off, lucky to have made it out of there. I tipped back my glass and clumsily missed my mouth, spilling some of the daiquiri mixture on my chest.

"Ooops!" Fern set her drink down. "Let me help." She took her finger and traced the dribble of crystals and liquor on my breast. Lifting her fingertip to her lips, she said, "Tasty with that bit of salt."

Taken aback, I stared at her.

"Salt—just a bit of glow. You know women don't sweat, or perspire…we glow. Don't we, Adie? That's what's nice about women—they don't have those powerful sweat glands that men have." The tip of her tongue skimmed her lips before she spoke again. "Not that I would toss a man as succulent as Wolf out of bed. He looks like he's made for lovin'." Her fingers trailed on my thighs. She sighed, "you are so lucky, babe." She giggled. "Remember when we were talkin' chocolate fondue?"

I nodded.

"You could have that and more."

I set my glass down nervously. I stood up. "Got to go, Fern. Wolf should be back by now." I glanced at her—beautiful, dark eyes sending me a message. "Thanks for the drink."

Hurriedly, I shot down the hall to my room and unlocked my door. Wolf wasn't back yet. I had time. Inside, the room was dim. Dusk had set in. I closed the blinds and turned on a table lamp. Taking candles out of a box in my overnight bag, I lit each one and placed them strategically about the room. I decided I'd leave the door open a crack for Wolf.

And now for the hors d'oeuvres. Taking a baggie of Hershey's kisses with me, I reclined on the bed, my head resting on the pillows. Very carefully I placed an arrangement of chocolate on my belly, a few on my thighs and the rest over my breasts. I closed my eyes and waited.

I heard a rustle and the clink of glasses but lay quietly, pretending to sleep. The bed sagged on one side with his weight. I felt his lips suck up a chocolate chip on my belly. I tingled when he sucked up another. I sighed and brought my hand down to his hair.

"Omigod! What the…" I sat up, scattering the chocolate chips all over the bed. "Fern!" I stared into a pair of long-lashed brown eyes.

Fern smirked. "I know I'm not Wolf, but Adie, you have to admit, you liked the way I sucked up those chips." She found a chocolate chip that had rolled off my belly and put it to her lips.

"Fern, you need to leave. I'm not gay and I sure didn't think you were."

"No?" Fern grinned. "You're not that naïve. Besides, babe,

I'm bi, not gay. My lascivious thoughts about those two guys of yours are real and definitely x-rated. So I thought, since we've always connected so well, you wouldn't mind sharing Wolf and at the same time I could—" she squeezed my hand and went on, "satisfy your secret fantasies, Adie." Fern laughed. "Think, Adie, you could have us both and we'll make you melt like jelly. It will be all about you. Who could ask for more?"

"I'm not bi. You should go."

"How do you know Wolfie didn't send me here to be your appetizer?"

My jaw dropped. "He wouldn't do that."

"Jordan James did." Fern got up and went over to the table, poured us tequila and handed me one. She clicked my glass. "What did you mean? Jordan James sent you to Ingrid?

Fern nodded. "Mm-mm!" She tipped back her drink. "You really want me to leave, babe? It's quite the story."

This might be the break I needed. I shook my head.

She smiled knowingly. "I thought not. Drink up, Adie."

Tipping back my shot glass, I sat back against the pillows.

"In those days I was a little wild, eager to try anything. My needs were strong. Ingrid was attractive in a blowsy-sort-of-way—not like now. Jordan James was turned on by the thought of a three-some. He wasn't good-looking but he was generous with his money and I had a loan to pay off. We were at a conference. And if you ask me, Ingrid was hot for me. Jordon went all out and bought me high-heeled shoes and a lacy outfit from Victoria's Secret. Told me to meet him in Ingrid's hotel room. Said he'd get the champagne." She glanced at the last chocolate chip. "Didn't think of chocolate, though. No one knew about chocolate power except the Mayans."

"And Ingrid? What did she think about a three-some?"

"She wanted it, but got jealous when James started on me and ignored her. Deprived of attention the bitch queen devised a careful well-thought-out plan to end my career, in case James was thinking of trading-up." Fern picked up a chocolate chip and sucked on it slowly. "Ingrid had to get rid of me or face losing her cash cow." Fern chuckled. "Or in this case, cash bull."

"So she started rumors about you coming on to clients."

"She lied, Adie. To make things worse, she told everyone I

was hassling the rich female clients." Fern knocked back the last bit of tequila. "So you can see why no one hired me after that."

"What about Jordan James? Didn't he help you?"

"The man had no backbone. When I refused to have sex after that, he blew up. He had a few loose screws." Fern laughed derisively. "But the nerd had it bad for Ingrid. Gave her his wife's jewelry, stock in his company, not to mention tons of money."

Worriedly, I tossed back some tequila, thinking how I'd helped Ingrid find the Jaguar God. Hopefully, it wouldn't have any negative after effects. I didn't want to be implicated in anything illegal. It was getting dangerous. She could have been pushed off the stairs and the attacker with the knife was real enough. "I need to go find Wolf." I tied on a cover up and opened the door, waiting expectantly.

Fern winked. "Okay, no problem, babe, but," she said softly, as she sashayed out the door, "don't knock it 'til you've tried it." She blew me a kiss.

I watched her make her way around the corner before I headed to the restaurant. Halfway down the hall, I heard raised voices coming from the open door of a room at the end of the corridor. Afraid of being seen, I edged against the wall close to the room.

"I gave you all the sex you ever wanted!" A man shouted. "That's more than the old man ever did."

"Maybe so," a woman's voice snarled, "but he compensated by giving me stocks, didn't he?"

"That was his mistake—losing his marbles after he screwed you."

Ingrid laughed scornfully. "Now I know who you take after. Could it be mama dearest was a sleaze? Seems to me Jordan said she had a boy toy on the side."

"Leave her out of it." Jeffrey softened his voice persuasively. "Janice wants the diamonds and she'll pay you more than they're worth. As for the stocks, just sign here."

"First tell me what you've done with Jordan? Afraid he'll leave me money before he dies?" Ingrid's voice faded momentarily. I heard water running and I crept up closer to hear what she was saying. "If he's in a home, I want to…"

Pain exploded in my head. A kaleidoscope of colors flashed in front of my eyes. Bringing my hand up, my fingertips made contact with a sticky mess at the top of my head, before everything went black.

****

"Adie?" Wolf's distorted voice vibrated like he was talking from the entrance of an empty tunnel and I was far, far, away.

My eyes were glued shut. I couldn't open them. My head was drumming insistently like the bass notes pounding from a macho guy's sound system in his fully loaded Camero. I struggled to get up, but a heavy hand kept me down.

"Just rest, baby. Can you tell me what happened?"

I opened my eyes a slit to see Wolf staring at me.

"Don't move. There's an ice bag balanced on your head. We want that bump to go down."

"Bump?"

"Someone knocked you out."

I brought my finger to the sore spot on my hairline and touched it tentatively.

"Leave that alone," Wolf said brushing my hand away. "It's a cut. I thought you'd want it stitched up. The village nurse took care of it. You spoke to her, so she figured you'd be okay as long as I wake you up every few hours."

"Oh-hh." It hadn't been a nightmare—that woman peering into my eyes. "Wolf, who found me?"

"I did. When you weren't in the room, I backtracked to the pool and not seeing you there either, I checked the hall to the restaurant."

"There was no one in the hall?"

"No. It was quiet. Do you remember why you were there?"

I rubbed my eyes, hoping to ease the pain. I jerked up suddenly, unbalancing the ice pack and sending it flying to the floor.

Wolf gripped my hand. "What is it?"

"I remember now. I was outside Ingrid and Jeff's room. They were arguing about the stuff they wanted from her."

"They?"

"Janice wants the jewelry."

"Why?"

"I think Jeffrey and Janice are relatives of Jordan James. They're young enough to be his kids."

193

"What are their last names?"

"Jones…but I didn't see any ID."

Wolf picked up the ice pack and placed it back on the top of my head. "So Jeffrey sleeps with Ingrid and…"

"Persuades her to give him the stocks," I finished and then reconsidered. "Or does he?"

"Let's say, she refuses…" Wolf ran his fingers through his hair, giving it that messy just-done-it bedroom look.

"So he tries…" I lost my train of thought watching him. Whoever clobbered me hadn't destroyed my libido but had managed to ruin what would have been a sensuous night with a steamy hot man. I had more motivation than ever to find the creep.

"To kill her in the shop."

I ran the scenario in the shop through my mind. The scene flashed before my eyes. "He'd already left when she got attacked at Pedro's Donkey."

"What did the punk look like?"

"A pony-tailed guy with a baseball cap and a three-day stubble. He had a mask on. A Zorro-type thing. And you know, Wolf, the guy trying to get into Ingrid's room had a hat and a beard."

"Coincidence?"

"Maybe but there's something else…"

"What?"

"These two had the same body type—stocky. And their faces were square and wide."

Wolf stroked his chin as he listened.

I grabbed his hand. "They could be the same man in disguise. Don't you see?" I closed my eyes, willing the pain to go away.

Wolf handed me a glass of water and two Aspirins. "Take these. We'll talk later. Relax. You're safe and that's all that matters."

Safe wasn't so bad if it included snuggling up. I rested against the pillow once again. The bed sagged as Wolf climbed in beside me. I opened my eyes a crack to see him studying me before the room went dark with the click of the lamp. The sweet smell of cranberries from the candles lingered in the air but now Wolf's scent of soap and balmy ocean breeze assailed my nostrils in the most enticing way. I turned to him and felt his lips on my shoulder…tiny soft kisses.

"It's okay for you to sleep, princess. We've got tomorrow."

The last thing I remembered was a hand stroking my cheek and a kiss on my cheek.

13

Wolf held the door open for me, smiling mysteriously as he gazed into my eyes. "I have a foolproof plan for us."

We were at the Don Juan. Wolf set our bags down before he picked up his phone and worked on a text message. He passed it over for me to read. "See that?" he said, angling the screen. "Daniella knows I'm not working today under any circumstances." He ran a finger down my cheek. "Nothing will stop us now, baby, except," he clicked his phone off, "technology."

"And," I said, grabbing my cell from my purse, "our stupidity in bowing into it." I turned the sound off, shoved it back in the zippered compartment and looked around.

It wasn't as if I noticed anything in particular, but the wrong things looked neat. My papers on the dresser were stacked in a tidy pile, my clothes had been folded and placed on a chair and my shoes were lined up with exactly the right amount of space between them. My maid had cleaned and made a few swan-shaped towels to decorate my bed, but she had made sure my personal possessions were exactly where I had tossed them.

"What's wrong, Adie?" Wolf's sapphire eyes regarded me intently.

"The room," I mumbled, "it's too neat,"

"You think you've had a visitor?"

"Yes, and there's only one reason why." I dropped my purse on the table and ran over to the air conditioning unit, a clunky, archaic cooling system enclosed in a cabinet. I wretched open the lower portion and sighed in relief when I saw a small velvet bag. "It's here!"

"Strange place for a valuable antiquity."

"I had no choice. Ingrid wasn't there and I was in a hurry to get the group to the ferry. My room safe is too small and they were too busy at front desk to put it in the hotel safe." Carefully, I unwrapped the statue and gave it to Wolf.

He handled the jade carving of the Jaguar God curiously, eying the craftsmanship. "So this is Ingrid's little investment."

"Small but very expensive."

I took the statue back from Wolf and wrapped the cloth around it before I placed it back in the bag. "If you can believe it, Ingrid's paying Diego eight hundred twenty thou—and that's a sale price!" I nodded contemplatively. "She got a good deal."

"According to Alvarez."

"Someone else must think so."

"Someone who knows about the statue. Could be Alvarez didn't really want to sell it."

I shot him a look. "Just because you don't like him doesn't mean he would steal it back. Don't forget Ingrid has enemies. As far as bad luck is concerned, dropping this off in Ingrid's room should be the end of mine." I crossed my hand over my chest and let my fingertips slide down a loose tendril, my thumb stroking my skin. "And then you'll have to work on your plan."

Wolf's eyes followed the movement of my fingers. "We'll be there, soon." He stroked my cheek. "Bring those sexy gold shoes of yours and some of your lacy under things."

I studied his sensuous mouth that begged to be kissed. My brain was rapidly losing its functions. I had to get a grip. "That's all?"

"I've taken care of the rest."

I tossed everything in my bag and took Wolf's offered hand.

We made our way to Ingrid's room. I knocked.

Ingrid swung the door open. Seeing Wolf, she gave him a hungry glance. "Ah, hello, handsome!" Her eyes swept to me. "Adie, you brought it?"

I nodded and handed her the bag.

"Good." Her eyes traveled down his body. "You know, Wolf, Fleischer has other exciting tours you'd like. Book with us when you get that adventurous urge." She beamed up at him in a suggestive manner. "Stop by my office."

Wolf grunted something that sounded like, "Sure..."

"Call me." She winked before she clicked the door shut.

I was *so* ready to leave. Seeing my expression, Wolf squeezed my shoulders. "We have better things to think about."

"You're right." The statue was no longer my concern.

I stopped at the Fleischer Travel board and added tonight's event in the city square. I rubbed my neck easing out the tight knots that had gathered there from a minute with Ingrid. "You sure I shouldn't bring anything else?"

Wolf stood there grinning, his thoughts obviously not on Ingrid. "Only you, my spicy woman."

***

The street, Avenida Benito Juarez in the town of San Miguel, becomes the crossroad that traverses the island to the east coast. That's where we went—the wild part of the island known for its high surf, wide sandy beaches and unbelievable beauty. Uninhabited on the whole, a few restaurants take care of the adventurous visitors who want to escape the maddening crowds on the west coast which is beehive busy on the days the cruise ships dock.

None the less, I shot a glance at Wolf when he swung past Coconuts, a popular restaurant on the cliff and drove further south, wondering where our destination was. The island itself is only twenty-eight miles long and the east coast road is about half of the length—the northern part of Cozumel inaccessible. From his smug lazy smile, I clearly surmised this man had something up his sleeve.

When he finally pulled up on a hilly dirt driveway, I saw a large ivory Spanish-style building perched on the edge of a cliff overlooking the Caribbean. Wolf came around to help me out of the Jeep.

"You let me down today," Wolf said.

"What do you mean?"

"Don't get me wrong, you look great in shorts, but it's always a pleasure to see how you modestly maneuver yourself out of my Jeep wearing a slinky short dress and high heels." He grinned. "Somehow, I still manage to get to see a teasing flash of thigh."

"Then you'd better be good if you want any of those sort of treats."

"I plan to be. You'll get so much goodness you'll be begging for me to be bad."

My body sparked—like a match lit near a container of highly flammable oil.

Wolf smiled slowly and took my hand, leading me to a heavy

oak door. Stooping down, he took out a key from behind a clay flowerpot and inserted it in the door.

"You bought this house?"

"Rented."

Inside, a marble floor in the entrance hall led to an enormous room with windows facing out to the Caribbean. An oak dining room table stood in the center of the room surrounded by high-back wooden chairs. Set apart, to one side, low green couches and armchairs with multi-colored pillows were arranged around a square coffee table. Heavy wooden framed oil paintings hung on the ochre walls.

"What a lovely room." The eclectic combination of traditional and modern Mexican furniture was pleasing as was the view. It was a secret place dreams were made of. Savage rough surf ravaged a jagged outcropping of coral, spraying a foamy froth onto a powdery-white shore obscured from the road by a dense grouping of palms.

Wolf placed his arm around my shoulders. "A very private beach," he said softly, "for us."

"Empty and yet," I glanced at the marigolds in a vase on the table and back to the cooler set at the door opening to the deck, "it's as if someone has recently been here." I glanced up at him. "Your handyman?"

Wolf's finger traced the outline of my lips. "Sometimes I forget that your detecting skills exceed the average. In fact, you are exceptionally perceptive, Adie Sturm."

"If only that were true! I'd know who the murderer is. There's a connection to Telly's murder but I can't put my finger on it. Things are worse than ever with Ingrid being attacked and now me." Tentatively, I touched my wound.

"That's my fault. I'm sorry, Adie." Wolf kissed my forehead, below the cut. "I shouldn't have let you out of my sight last night. Believe me, I would have been right back but..."

"What?"

"It was busy in the restaurant—everyone and their mother getting takeout. It was almost my turn and then things got bad."

"How?"

"Janice was just ahead of me ordering food but every time she ordered she changed her mind. After she did it for the third time the people behind me were getting annoyed. But that wasn't the worst of it. The chef got so pissed off, he threw a lobster tail at her and quit.

My mouth dropped open in astonishment. "A lobster tail?"

Wolf grinned. "Temperamental types, these chefs."

"Janice got hit by a lobster? That's bizarre!"

"I don't think it really hurt her but she cried. Nobody was sympathetic so I calmed her down until the owner came and took over. That's when I finally got our dinner." Wolf shook his head. "Waste of time, though. You didn't get to eat." He drew me in his arms and whispered into my ear, "I can't say I ever expected to see you lying in that hallway. How're you?"

I pulled back and gazed into his dark blue depths. "The fajitas you plied me with today definitely helped. They're just what a food-deprived woman needs."

"I have the feeling you've been very much deprived in other ways—ways I need to rectify." Wolf released me and strode over to the cooler, picking it up. With one hand he held the back door open for me to go out. A small deck with a short flight of wooden stairs zigzagged down to the beach. An orange blanket had been spread out on the sand and a closed woven basket was set next to it under a flowering red hibiscus tree. It was a patch of paradise, just for us. Wolf set the cooler beside the blanket and smiled winningly, taking my hand, assisting me down.

From out of the cooler, Wolf seized fluted glasses and a bottle of champagne. He handed me the glasses to hold while he popped the cork.

"Are we celebrating the Days of the Dead?"

"We can, but I'd rather celebrate that you're alive," Wolf said, pouring the golden bubbly.

"Seriously?"

"For sure, baby—I don't want a repeat of last night."

"Alright," bringing my glass up to his, "to life and to those spirits that return tonight."

Wolf's eyes fixed on me. "You returning to me is an even more important cause for celebration. To adventure."

I clicked his glass and swallowed the champagne gratefully, the bubbles tickling my suddenly dry throat.

"Close your eyes and finish."

"Why?"

Wolf placed his finger on my lips and leaned closer. "Be patient, my curious lady…you'll soon find out."

I let the golden nectar flow down, closed my eyes and waited.

"Now open those luscious lips."

A sweet smelling firm fruit. Wolf's mouth brushed mine and my eyes flew open in surprise. A chocolate-coated strawberry was deposited in my mouth. My taste buds jolted awake with the incredible flavor before I swallowed. And then, once again, his mouth met mine, his tongue tickling the inside of my mouth where traces of champagne, chocolate and strawberry mingled.

"Soft, succulent sweetness," Wolf whispered in my ear, his breath sending a pleasurable shiver down my body. "But there's more—you'll need to indulge me again."

I watched him fill our glasses. "How?"

"Drink."

I let the champagne wet my mouth.

"Close your eyes, Baby."

I leaned back on my elbows, totally relaxed with the sun filtering in through the trees and the warm Caribbean breeze blowing gently on my face. I remembered I had a bikini on under the shorts and T-shirt and if I just slipped them off…"

"I have something for you—open."

A smooth, creamy chocolate truffle landed on my tongue, melting slowly with the warmth of my mouth. The potent flavor of chocolate rose above the rest, strongly conquering them all. "Delicious."

"Anything to please my princess."

I sank down on the blanket, my head falling back as Wolf's lips lightly brushed my throat, every kiss igniting spark after spark. His tongue, silken and hot, feathered down to my shoulder and to the tender sensitive skin on the inner part of my arm. Being kissed there was somehow extremely intimate, even more arousing than anywhere else.

Hearing my sighs, Wolf released me and slid my top up and I, seeing his intention raised my arms and freed myself of the thin cotton garment. Eyes, liquid with passion, met mine before his head bent to my cleavage and lightly licked my skin.

"Adie Sturm, you are a delicious woman." He stroked my

belly so tenderly my skin quivered from his touch.

"Better than chocolate?"

"Much more edible and chocolate's hard to beat." Sitting back up, he pulled off his T-shirt. Strong, broad shoulders, a well-developed chest and a washboard-flat six-pack. I kissed his chest and let my lips trail to his abs before I sat back on my heels taking in every detail of his powerful body. I closed my eyes a split second to regain my sanity. He was driving me so crazy I couldn't think straight. But that was a fight I couldn't and didn't want to win.

I pushed my hands down to rid myself of my shorts but he touched my hand to stop me, "Lay back, my spicy woman, and let me do everything."

With my hips raised, he removed my clothing. The warm Caribbean breeze caressed my body and I stretched my legs out, completely relaxed. He brought my foot to his mouth and slowly sucked each toe in turn. I wavered between begging him to let-up and pleading with him never to stop. My eyes met his and I knew this was part of the adventure he wanted for me.

Furthering his exploration, his hot tongue meandered up my leg, periodically stopping to capture my skin in his mouth on his way up to my inner thighs. My hips squirmed in their eagerness for more but he surprised me by suddenly sitting up. Picking up his glass, he smiled wickedly, before he spilled cool fizz over my sun-warmed belly. I gasped, taken aback at this sudden torture that was quickly replaced with pleasure as Wolf's attentive tongue licked up the champagne. My skin sizzled with the combination of chilly, effervescent liquid and Wolf's smoldering flicks. Fiery hot with desire I cried out at his touch and dug my fingers into his unruly hair, holding him to me until he took in every last drop.

Wolf glanced up. "This champagne has an excellent finish. More?"

"Not yet…another truffle?"

"An easy request."

Wolf dug out a truffle from the cooler and brought it to my lips, but I shook my head and took it in my fingers, placing it under my bikini top. "For you."

Wolf's eyes focused on the lump under the flimsy material. "I like treasure hunts," he said, before he pushed my top lower exposing a truffle perched on my mound. "Especially tasty ones." Sucking up each flake of the decadent candy, he said in a husky voice, "May I have another?"

I sat up and reached into the cooler and came up with another dark chocolate truffle that I placed inside my bikini on my other peak, and then lay back to watch him. He started his journey. His tongue wetly circled the hollow of my throat. Lips nuzzled my skin. I waited with more anticipation than a child on Christmas morning.

Reaching around to untie my bikini strings, he pushed it away. A balmy breeze caressed my breasts. Over one smooth mound his kisses journeyed and into the valley between. Involuntarily, a moan escaped from somewhere deep inside me. Cupping my breast, his tongue licked up the chocolate.

I wanted to give him as much pleasure as he gave me. I touched him in way I knew he liked. A groan sounded deep within his throat. Wolf was no quitter. Lips tasting of chocolate, tortured and teased. Our tongues danced a sensuous tango, over and under each other. Unexpectedly, he pulled away. I sat up in surprise.

Wolf reached into the woven basket removing a clear bottle filled with a golden liquid. Squeezing out a few drops into his hands, he raised an eyebrow in a silent question.

A massage? I smiled a *yes* before I rolled over on my stomach, bringing my arms to my sides. The oil felt wonderfully warm and I knew Wolf must have heated it in his hands before he smoothed it over my shoulders. Lightly he stroked the oil over my back. When his fingertips encountered the small triangle that covered my bottom, he undid the strings, exposing my skin to the sun and his magic touch. Circular motions spread liquid heat. Sudden tremors shot down—miraculous messages zapped like high voltage electricity.

He set the oil down and let his tongue and fingers caress my aching body. My breathing became ragged with the flick of his tongue and I became conscious of a floating sensation. I turned around and pressed myself against his steamy body as the fire in me surged.

When he suddenly tore away from me, I opened my eyes. Wolf stood before me. Slowly, he undid the string of his bathing suit. The sunlight lent a golden glow to his tanned body. My eyes took in his athletic form. Wide shoulders and a well-defined chest tapering to a narrow waist and hips. His legs long and powerful. Every part of him thrilled me. He was everything that mattered—a man like no other.

His face looked serious. "Happy?"

Speechless, I shook my head. "Come here…I want you."

He got down and stretched out beside me. Turning his head, he smiled devilishly. "Sure about that, Adie?"

Two can play that game. Casually, I sat up to pour myself a glass of bubbly. I gazed at him steadily, bringing the flute to my lips. "Hm-mm…maybe."

Wolf's eyes connected to mine, a wicked glint in his. "You seem satisfied now that you've had an appetizer, almost complacent, I'd say. Have you forgotten I have an entrée waiting for you?"

"You first!" I poured the glass of bubbly over him. Tossing the empty glass aside, I kissed his chest. My tongue swirled over his nipples until I heard him catch his breath. He let out a low moan. This was my signal. I snatched up the massage oil and squirted the liquid on him. I stroked up and down everywhere until he groaned his lust for me. "Adie…"

It was my turn to make him happy. I blew light deliberate breaths into his ear while my tongue flirted with the ridges. My hands, slippery with oil, started high and worked their way down his firm body. He groaned. I could tell he could hold off no longer. Our massage was over.

We clung to each other wetly…the sweat and oil coating our bodies. My tongue licked him again until smoldering signals from his heavy-lidded eyes reflected my own internal fire. I fueled his every need. Like a pebble sucked into a flow of molten lava, Wolf pulled me down onto the blanket and we rolled together, my fingernails scraping his chest. As the moist ocean breeze scattered tiny sand crystals onto our damp bodies, our lips melded and a magnetically powerful force streamed through me. The sunlight gleamed silver through his streaky blonde hair and I reached out to seize the strands tugging wildly, my breathing erratic. Wolf's mouth torched my lips once more, before he propelled me around against his chest and shoved his rock-hard member against me.

Wrapping his arms around me, he whispered, "Your entrée is

here," and he entered, his rhythm, vigorous and strong. Soap and balmy ocean breeze lingered and I breathed him in. The surf rushed and crashed with each push, his fingers urging me into a dreamy state of euphoria. In sync, we breathed as one.

I needed to feel him like I never felt him before. When his hands closed around my hips, I lifted myself, but I was totally unprepared for the wave of pleasure. Riding the surf, we shot over the crest. I shuddered, my cries blending into the wind. And still we rocked, each of us prolonging the ecstasy.

Reaching back, my fingertips pressed, spurring him to his peak. He groaned bringing me down with him as he fell back, still embracing me, bodies slippery and wet. I twisted to look over my shoulder at my exhausted lover. His lips turned up at the ends. He looked so satiated. I pulled away. "A delectable entrée."

Wolf touched the scratches I'd made. "I think you liked it. You sure dug in."

"And you didn't?" I glanced at my bruised breast.

He stroked me lightly. "Enjoyed every single, delicious bite. But, I promise I'll take it easy with dessert, princess."

"Dessert!" My eyes widened. "Now?"

Wolf laughed. "No, later. We'll have to hold off until tonight." He ran his fingertip down my breast. "Not that I'm not tempted." He brought his lips down on the soft mound in his hand. "I'm never tired of making love to you. And we never have enough time, do we? Unfortunately, we need to get back. It's party night, remember?" He grabbed his T-shirt and tugged it over his head.

I picked up my bikini and tied it on. "I don't recall saying I'd go anywhere with you. Come to think of it, I don't remember you inviting me, either." I pulled my top over my head. What had I told Diego? The last leg of the flight was a blur with my stomach doing somersaults. I vaguely recalled Diego's invitation.

"Alvarez?" Wolf's voice had an edge.

"I…I'm not sure."

"Elusive woman." Nonchalantly, Wolf got up and motioned for me to pick up the edges of the blanket. Together we folded and gathered it up, neither of us speaking.

He handed the blanket to me to carry and picked up the cooler and basket. "Fortunately, I anticipated your reluctance to commit and have provided you with some incentive." He took my hand on the way up the stairs.

"And what would that be?" I swung the door open and held it for him.

He laughed. "Patience, woman. You'll know soon enough." Wolf carried our cooler in and set it down. He motioned to my carry-on. "Don't forget your bag."

"Where are we going?" I locked the door.

Wolf leaned over. His sensuous lips caressed mine. "Surprise."

14

"Fern could have done it."

"She couldn't have disguised herself as a bearded man no matter how hard she tried, baby." Wolf massaged my foot, paying special attention to my toes.

I was sprawled back against an oversized orange pillow on a comfy rattan couch in his cottage. A Mexican blanket hung on the wall behind us. Across the room, the watchful eyes of a spotted jaguar peeked out from behind tall grass in a vibrant oil painting. The mixture of marble flooring, oak and rattan furniture gave it a comfortable feeling. I sighed in contentment. It was an exceptional massage but I didn't want to let myself become distracted. A murderer was still out there.

"Fern had opportunity and motive." I waved a finger in the air. "She hated Ingrid for ruining her career and she was the only one of my suspects who was at Oktoberfest and here in Mexico." I shook my head. "She sure threw me for a loop when I found her sucking up those chocolate chips on my belly."

Wolf grinned. "And you were worried she liked me."

"And with good reason. Don't forget, she was expecting *you* to join the party."

"What about Bryan?"

"She didn't mention him." I giggled. "Maybe he was with the professor."

Wolf squeezed my little toe. "I meant as her accomplice. He could have attacked Ingrid. He's a powerful guy and with a disguise…"

"So they wanted to poison Ingrid but Telly foiled their plan and drank Ingrid's beer. Ye-s-ss!" I sat up triumphantly. "That's it! No, wait," I sank back, "there's still Janice and Jeffrey. They could have been in Kitchener. Toronto's only an hour's drive away. And they definitely would have liked Ingrid out of the way."

"But wasn't Jeff with Ingrid at the store?"

"He left. And the guy that attacked her had a cap, beard and a mask on, remember?"

"Wouldn't you think she would have recognized her own lover?"

"That disguise could have hidden anyone." I grinned. "But you don't know Ingrid. She probably paid more attention to his package than the rest of him."

Wolf laughed and stroked my leg.

I brushed a damp strand of hair away from my eye. "Do you think the stocks could revert back to the company if she dies?"

"It's possible."

"Or they could go to her estate."

"I thought Morris divorced her?" Wolf grabbed my other foot and massaged my arch.

"Not yet. That's why she's buying up Mayan art."

"Hiding her assets, is she?"

"He'll get nothing from her when the divorce is final. She's eager to buy up a collection of jaguar pieces."

"And Alvarez is providing them."

"Only one of them, so far." I withdrew my foot. "I need to check my messages. I left my number for my tour group in case they had questions about the Day of the Dead celebration in the square tonight." And Diego? Who knows what he was thinking. My queasy experience on the plane could have put an end to that relationship anyway. And then there was the condo damage. Would he blame me for that? But it was my condo, not his, I told myself.

Logical broke in: It isn't really yours. You know that. He gave you that condo so he could set you up as his mistress. You did the right thing moving out. Had you stayed there who knows what would have happened. That man gets everything he wants and you topped that list.

Wolf jarred me out of my thoughts. "You'll be at the square anyway—with me of course." He stood up. "Do you want your present now?"

My ears perked. "Present?"

From a drawer in the side table, Wolf brought out a package wrapped in gold paper and tied with a glittery bow. "I thought you'd like this and I *know* I would."

"You said it was for me."

"It is." He handed it to me and gazed at me expectantly. "I

know you can't wait. Open it."

I didn't want to appear too eager and I hated to mess up the sparkly paper but when I found he'd fiendishly taped it securely on every corner, I ripped the paper forcefully and once I started, there was no stopping me.

Wolf grinned, watching my progress. "I couldn't resist the extra tape."

I rolled my eyes. "You like watching me destroy this lovely paper?"

"I like seeing the true Adie Sturm."

But I had already tuned him out. Right before my eyes was the most gorgeous dress I'd ever seen. The scarlet dress from Carmelita's fashion show.

"Omigod! Thank you—it's…"

"You. A sexy dress for my spicy woman." Wolf picked up his cell. "We'll stop at Alvarez's party and then we'll do up the town, okay?" He pressed a number. "I have to make a few calls. Go ahead and take a shower. I'll join you in a couple of minutes."

I nodded, watching him head into the kitchen still in his bathing suit. I closed my eyes and sighed, imagining how he'd feel—wet and lathered, his skin slippery-smooth.

When I turned on my cell, my phone flashed. Text messages. I'd get to those in a minute. I clicked contacts. I had my own messages to send.

Something was really bugging me. Because I was on tour a lot, I'd spent relatively little time at Fleischer's Travel. As hard as I tried, I couldn't recall what Morris looked like. He'd come by a couple of times over the years but he wasn't the kind of man a woman would notice or remember—square glasses, short brownish hair and a blah sort of face.

I texted Ilya Kharkov. *Hey, check Morris Fleischer TY*

Next, I clicked on Slick, my reporter bud. He would be just as anxious to get the scoop on the murder and he'd want to help. *Send me a pic of Morris Fleischer PLZ*

When my cell flashed, I saw a text from Diego. *Lorita's at 8 call me xoxoxD*

That was clear enough. Diego would be at Lorita's and he wanted to send his driver to get me. I had stupidly made a date with both hotties. I rubbed my forehead in frustration—when I made a mess I really dug myself in deep.

I took the coward's way out and I messaged Diego. *CU there xoxA.*

That way he knew I'd be coming but if I came with Wolf, what could he say? I hadn't confirmed it with him or had I?

Carmelita had sent a text as well. *Good news C u 2nite.* Was that about Ricardo? Was she planning to divorce Fede after all?

I scrolled down to Ingrid. *D has another jaguar. I need u. Meet us at the cemetery at 9.*

I didn't want any part of that. I could feel the tension building up already. Meet her at the cemetery? No, way! The whole thing was odd. Why would Diego want to make this deal at the cemetery, unless he couldn't fit her into his plans otherwise? I thought about that. Yes! That's it. He'd said he'd been close to his brother Amancio. He'd want to go to the cemetery tonight even though he was hosting a party. But why did Ingrid think I needed to come? The woman was enough of a wheeler-dealer to take on Diego. I got on the phone and speed-dialed her number but got her voice mail.

"Ingrid, it's Adie. Go ahead and make the deal. You'll be fine without me." With all my thoughts about the Diego dilemma, I didn't notice Wolf behind me. Unexpectedly, he snatched my cell from my hand, lifted me up into his arms and carried me to the bathroom at the end of the hall.

"Shower time, baby. We've got to get rid of that beach look. Not that it doesn't look hot on you, but it'll be time to go soon." Wolf ran his finger down my cheek. "You will sizzle in that dress."

"Where're we going?"

"The square."

That's what I was afraid of.

"Alvarez said to bring a date to his fiesta at Lorita's."

I stared at him. This would have been the time to tell him Diego had already asked me but he started taking my clothes off and flinging them on the floor. With his hands all over me I quickly forgot I had a brain or a mouth to speak with.

The shower was a large marble tiled affair with jets on every wall shooting gentle spray on my salty body, a mixture of perspiration and salt from the ocean air. Wolf's lips caressed my shoulder and I leaned back against the wall to allow him access to my neck.

"Salty woman. You taste like more." His lips drew in the skin at my throat.

"Slow down, tiger, we have a night ahead of us." But his soapy hands on my breasts were driving me so crazy I forgot all about my screwed up situation. I grabbed the soap and smelled it. Now I knew why Wolf had that unforgettable scent of ocean breeze—my clean, natural man. He was the fishing and hunting type guy—an outdoors' man from his teens. There was nothing wimpy about him.

While Wolf shampooed, I spread the soap over his firm body with my hands—starting at the shoulders, down the chest to his six-pack and then…

"Take it easy down there, princess. I won't be able to get my jeans on." He tilted my chin up. "Or is that what you had in mind?"

I dropped my hold on him. My hormones were more active than usual—sending out those *let's have sex* vibes.

"Don't get all embarrassed, Adie. There's nothing wrong with you wanting to touch me. You know I love to be with you—it's more than sex."

"Oh? What is it you feel?"

Wolf ran his fingers through my hair and tilted my head up. Meeting my eyes he said, "You know when we were teens and we hung out together?"

I nodded, recalling the time we'd spent on the lake—that hot, sultry day when he'd suggested we get it on. I had been totally in to him but I knew once I began, I'd want to do more. I was one horny virgin.

"You were irresistible."

"If that was the case, why didn't you phone me? Why did you wait so long to ask me out?" I asked puzzled.

"You know Erika."

"You mean she stopped you?"

"Your dad had made such a big stink about us having sex that Erika believed him. Anyway, my dad said if I ever had sex with you again, I'd have to marry you."

"What! They thought we'd had sex? We hadn't even kissed!"

Wolf looked away his eyes distant. "After that massage, I'd thought you might have wanted to…" He grinned ruefully. "I was wrong," he said hesitantly, "or was I?"

I stared at him silently.

"It wouldn't have been easy to sneak around without a car. Erika thought I was too wild to be trusted driving the Cadillac. By the time I bought a motorcycle, you'd gone to college."

"So all this was going on and I knew nothing about it?"

"Yeah, but I didn't tell you this just to clue you in to what happened back then."

"Why are you telling me?"

"I think what we have is bigger than chemistry."

That was so true! Wolf and I were fantastic together. Who was I to stop whatever was happening? "How big?" I asked breathlessly, my heart pounding faster.

Wolf glanced down. His ram-rod stiff tool brushed against my belly in greeting. "Huge," he said grinning.

"Get serious!"

"I'm a guy, Adie. This is normal—especially when you're so wet and sexy."

"Tell me." I poked his chest. "I want to know, Wolf."

"Okay, it's like this, Adie…" His cell clamored for attention. "Sorry, baby, got to get that. Something I'm working on." He stepped out of the shower, grabbing a towel on his way out.

That was no surprise. He had a lot of fish to fry, most of which I knew too little about. Probably the barracuda, wanting to get her teeth into him, was using a business tidbit as an excuse. Disappointed, I showered off and dried myself.

Wolf popped his head. "Princess, check the bottom cupboard. It has everything you might need to make yourself sizzle—at least, I hope so. I told Juanita to equip the best for you."

I opened the door to the cabinet taken aback by the display of cosmetics and hair styling supplies. Okay, I was a little suspicious, remembering Diego's warning about men and their needs. I took out a bottle of foundation and checked the skin hue—medium, that was right. Daniella would need dark. The perfume was Mania, a soft spicy scent I sometimes wear. That was perceptive of him. Daniella favored a floral scent of some kind. I sighed with relief— he wasn't trying to pull the wool over my eyes after all.

Unwrapping the mascara, I brushed a coat, waited and brushed on a water-proof coat. Why was I born with blonde lashes, I muttered to myself in frustration. Think of the money I'd have saved on mascara if I'd inherited my dad's lashes. But we all have our cross to bear, none of us perfect, and of course, some things we can't change.

With humidity heavy in the air, I pinned my hair in an up-do and sprayed it in place. I didn't want Daniella to make me look bad. With her big hair helmet glued with heavy-duty hair spray, she was probably prancing around Lorita's in a super tight dress coming on to every male in sight. I had my work cut out for me. Curling a few loose tendrils around my face, I spritzed them lightly before I walked out to get my underwear and my new red dress. I could hear Wolf talking and assumed he was still negotiating whatever. I grabbed my things and proceeded to make myself enticing for both of my hotties. The mirror told me I had done well. I was ready to knock 'em dead.

Have you ever been caught in a sudden downpour? My mood was light. I was ready to frolic until I made the stupid mistake of entering the living room. I couldn't believe what I saw.

Daniella stood in front of Wolf. He was in jeans, no shirt—she was practically naked, clad in a skimpy thong and low-cut pushup bra, her black dress slung over a chair.

Hearing me enter the room, she froze momentarily but recovered quickly enough. "Aggie! What a surprise! I thought you'd be at Lorita's dancing with Diego, by now." She placed her hands on her hips and cocked her head to the side, staring at me. "Have you been leading him on, *amiga*? He was fretting about your whereabouts before I left. Poor dear is hopelessly smitten with you." She eyed me jealously. "Diego gave you that one from the collection, I see." She slid the door open. "Wolf and I were about to have a little skinny dip. I'd ask you to join us but I know you're in a hurry." Daniella slid the door open and stepped outside.

My cell beeped with a message and I turned to pick it up, distractedly. I felt Wolf's arms around me before he whispered in my ear, "Ignore her. She's had one too many. I didn't know she was going to do this—she stripped off before I came into the room. I swear I didn't tell her to come here. I had no idea, Adie. Don't be angry." He stroked my arms. "We'll get a taxi and get out of here."

"And leave her here?" I swung around to glare at him.

Wolf shrugged his shoulders. "We could drop her off at her

house. Let's not let this spoil our night."

I grabbed my purse from the table as Daniella called out from the patio. "Don't be such a stick-in-the-mud, Wolfito. Hurry, *mi amor*, the water's heavenly!"

15

I was seething—my cell fell out of my hand, clattering loudly as it hit the tile floor. Wolf's grasp was tight, but I was having none of it. It's not easy to run in four-inch heels but I managed, right after I shot my fist into his solar plexus. I didn't wait to see if I'd really hurt him. It was more a jab than a strike anyway so I wasn't too concerned. He deserved it. That phone call he'd had earlier must have been from her.

Out on the street, I saw a taxi and headed straight to it. I could hear Wolf's footsteps gaining on me but I dropped myself into the backseat and shut the door in the nick of time.

Wolf shouted at me to stop but I ignored him. "*El parque, por favor*," I said to the cab driver. When he pulled out into the street, I sighed in relief.

"I'll need to go around the back way. I'm sorry, Señorita, but the street has been closed off for the *fiesta*."

"That's okay. Is there a lot going on?"

"They have displays, a show and I think fireworks. I will join my family here in a while." The driver spoke, his eyes on me in the mirror.

"I hope you have lots of fun. It's nice to have a family." I was surprised I said that. Maybe it gets better when there's someone special and children.

I sat back in the vinyl seat thinking not so pleasant thoughts about my sea god, wondering if we could have any kind of future with Daniella bouncing into our lives like a yoyo. When the taxi came to a stop, I paid and waited for him to open the door. Interesting how cab drivers do that for the ladies in Mexico. Made me feel better—like I was important to someone.

"*Gracias*," I said. "Have a good night."

The cobblestone street was filled with pedestrians shopping. I couldn't resist a quick look at the bead stand. I smiled at a lady checking out my outfit and heels. She gave me a toothy grin of appreciation—unlike some of the disapproving, old biddies at home. I reached up to examine a white and brown shell choker and saw something strange. *"Las mariposas,"* Two large spotted brown butterflies, their wings folded perched on the stand next to the necklaces.

She nodded.

"Buena suerte?"

She nodded. Good luck came with butterflies—returning spirits of the dead. I could use some of that. I dug up two dollars and took a necklace. After she wrapped it in tissue, I placed it in my purse and glanced back at the butterflies. One of them suddenly opened its wings, revealing a brilliant azure trimmed with black.

"Hermosa!" I marveled at the startling blue.

"Come back to us, Señorita," she said as I left. "We'll bring you luck."

After I entered the square, I was hit with the scent of pine incense wafting in the air. Altars to the dead had been set up with dishes of corn, bread, candles and vases filled with marigolds set on either side of a short length of carpet. The townspeople standing around weren't exactly happy but there was a feeling of anticipation—perhaps for the returning dead or for the special foods and drinks laid out by the vendors.

"Come try, Señorita." A young guy invited me to come closer. He was selling some sort of drink. "No alcohol, but it's good."

"What is it?"

"Atole." He handed me a small plastic cup. "It's made of corn."

Handing him some coins, I sipped it slowly. Pleasant, I thought setting the empty cup back on his table. *"Gracias."*

"De nada." He checked me out. "You make me *nervosa—* your eyes are so blue. I will be done soon, would you dance with me tonight?"

I shook my head. *"No, gracias.* I am meeting someone."

"This is my sister's stand. I'm a dive master. Will you dance with me tomorrow?"

"If I'm here you can ask me." Seeing his satisfied look, I took that as my cue to leave and trekked over to Lorita's.

A mariachi band blasted away from the interior of the restaurant and a fashionably dressed crowd milled about holding martini glasses. On the patio tables, candles and flowers were artfully arranged. I spotted Carmelita right away in among a group of admiring males. In a leopard print gown and four-inch stilettos, she looked devastatingly lovely, her light brown hair flowing in waves down her back.

"Adelina!" She pushed aside one of the men to bring me into her circle. Kissing my cheeks in greeting, she said, "I'm so glad you came. I was afraid something had happened to you." She drew the handsome man to her left closer. "You remember Ricardo?"

"Yes." I gave him my hand.

Ricardo drew my hand to his mouth and brushed his lips on my wrist. "Señorita Sturm. You are radiantly beautiful tonight." His eyes swept down my dress. "Is your friend happy with her acquisition?"

"Very much so. She wants another." Ricardo's eyes were so huge and brown I got lost in their luster. Pulling myself together, I said, "Please call me Adie. I take it you have found her another piece?"

"No, not I." He frowned. "I did recall her mentioning she was looking to collect more when I spoke to her." Remembering his manners, he indicated the younger man by his side. "May I present my brother, Guillermo?"

"*Encantado*." Guillermo took my hand and lightly caressed my wrist. "Have you come alone, Adelina?" He was a younger version of Ricardo, a bit slimmer but the hottie gene was abundantly evident.

"He takes after you, Ricardo—always an eye for a beautiful woman," Carmelita flashed a hundred-watt smile. "But, you are too late, darling. Adelina has other fish frying. Have you heard the Spanish expression, *pescado*, amiga?"

"No, what does it mean?"

"Well-ll, a *pez* is a fish and *pescado* is dead fish—hooked so to speak, and you," her eyes twinkled in amusement, "have managed to hook a couple of fish on your line."

"I don't see any *pescados*."

Carmelita gestured over to the far side of the patio to a drop-dead sexy man in a white shirt and tan pants, speaking to a curvaceous redhead in a figure-hugging gown. "There's one now. Poor Barbara is out of luck now that you've arrived." She whispered conspiratorially in my ear, "Diego has been salivating in anticipation of your arrival." She grabbed my arm, apologizing to the men. "We need to speak privately. Excuse us?" Blowing them both a kiss, she steered me away to a table close to the sidewalk. "Now tell me about your other fish—what did you do about Wolf? I was afraid the Brazilian bitch had scratched your eyes out, but I should have known you would annihilate her."

"What Brazilian bitch are we speaking about?"

"Daniella, of course! You didn't know she was Brazilian? She has the manners of a jungle woman, doesn't she?"

"She's far worse than a primitive cannibal—she's a spitting cobra." I gritted my teeth thinking how I'd love to get revenge but then something clicked. Diego was the puppet master in this. "Diego had something to do with Daniella coming to Wolf's cottage, didn't he?"

Carmelita grinned. "My brother, sly fox that he is, thought he'd eliminate the competition. Wolf is investing in his resort so he called him on that pretense but in reality he wanted to pinpoint your whereabouts." Her laughter tinkled merrily. "Diego is *so* devious. He sent Daniella over there knowing it would rile you so much you'd appear at his *fiesta* without him." She squeezed my hand. "And he was right, wasn't he? Did you break up with Wolf?" She was a tad too interested.

"No, we're not through. He'll show up here after he drags that man-eater out of the pool."

"Hopefully, before she's had a piece of him."

I frowned, thinking Carmelita could be right. Daniella could have lured him into the pool with her to have some hot sex.

"You know, I think I could take a lesson from you, *amiga*." She stopped and stared straight ahead and then flicked her eyes back to me. "Perhaps, there would be no need to drop Ricardo while I acquaint myself further with Guillarmo, unless of course you fancy him?" She caught my astonished expression and smirked.

I rolled my eyes. "You said you had good news. Something happened? Are you and Fede splitting up?"

"No, nothing that dramatic. Fede and I are still together." She laughed. "And so are Ricardo and I." She tossed her bangs away from her eyes. "The good news was about the saboteur."

"You caught him?"

"I did exactly as you suggested and your hunch was correct."

She squeezed my arm affectionately. "While the fashion show was going on, Luis hid in the dressing room where the dresses were kept. Sure enough, Tina showed up. She was about to cut up the show stopper, when Luis stepped out from behind the curtain and detained the little mosquito."

"Wow!"

"She screeched and howled but she settled down quickly enough after he cuffed her." Carmelita ran her fingers through her hair thoughtfully. "By the time I got there she was swearing like a fish wife. Called me a whore etcetera. She has quite a mouth, little Tina does."

"Did she say anything in her defense?"

Carmelita yawned, covering her mouth delicately with her hand. "She didn't have a defense, with Luis witnessing it all. She admitted everything, including the condo sabotage. That part was easy for her, with me stupidly giving her the key. She was upset that Ricardo and I were having an affair and naively believed he'd divorce Gloria to be with me." She signaled for a waiter carrying around a tray of daiquiris to approach us. Picking up two, she handed me a goblet. "You must try these, *amiga*, they are exceptional."

I sipped the frosty scarlet drink. "You're right. They are."

"Tina has ambitions to be a model and wants her parents' marriage to stay intact. But I think she was more concerned about social embarrassment than anything else—typical teenager." Carmelita tipped back her glass. "I reassured her. The solution is simple. I told her I had no intention of taking her father away— perhaps her uncle." Carmelita giggled at her witticism. "And my intentions are strictly dishonorable. A woman has her needs, after all."

I grinned. "True enough. It's when they get out of control…"

"Let me take you out of control, Adelinita." A husky voice seduced my nerve endings. I swung around to look up at a pair of brandy eyes in a handsome face. "Adelinita, you are ravishing tonight, as always." Diego kissed my cheeks.

"And you have been," I poked my finger into his hard abs, "bad—worse than usual."

Diego's fingers slipped through my hair slowly. "Bad, I like that. Imagine all the bad things I have yet to try with you."

A twinge of arousal shot through my body. "Why did you send Daniella over to Wolf's?"

"I was anxious to see you. Unfortunately, you were occupied with Wolf." Diego smiled smugly. "So I thought, why not expedite the process? All is fair in love in war, isn't it?" He shrugged. "Wolf doesn't appreciate you. I'm the one you should be with."

Carmelita grinned at our exchange. "I'll leave you two." She glanced in the direction of Ricardo's table where he and Guillermo sat smoking, both of them coolly watching us. "Save me a seat," she called out airily, before turning on her heel, returning to her admirers.

"Diego, darlin'." A woman's voice drawled. A fair-skinned redhead in a tawny silk dress came up behind Diego and rubbed his shoulder in a familiar manner. "You left me so suddenly, I was worried. Come back to my table, darlin'. We have so much to talk about."

"You must excuse my rudeness, Barbara, but it was unavoidable. My date has arrived." Diego smiled engagingly at her. "Let me introduce you to Adelina. She's from Toronto."

Barbara's mouth formed a straight line but she extended her hand politely. "Hi ya'll. Visitin' Mexico?"

I nodded.

"Barbara has a house in San Miguel." He turned to Barbara. "You bought it last year, didn't you?" Not waiting for a reply, he said, "Adelina has a condo not far from here."

"Oh? Since when?"

"Not long—a few months."

"Ah'm in Corpus Cristi and ya'll?"

"Near the museum."

"Ah like to get to know all the ex-pats but," she smiled confidently, "I haven't seen ya'll befo'."

I smiled my most mysterious smile. "No? Maybe, you will. I plan to visit frequently now that I've made friends here."

"Why don' we do lunch sometim'?" Her smile didn't reach her eyes.

"Sure." I smiled to show my sincerity but I didn't think I'd quite convinced her.

Barbara dug around in her bag and pressed her business card in my hand. "Call me."

My attention wandered to a grassy knoll near a statue of San Miguel's mayor. I spied a woman that looked remarkably like Fern. Her long black hair was distinctive as was her voluptuous figure. It must be her, I thought seeing a stocky blond guy with her. The guy had to be Bryan.

"Honeh?" Barbara repeated.

Not having a clue as to what she had just said, I gazed at her blankly, shoving her card into my purse.

"Ya'll come, won't ya? It's only a lil' soiree. It's not necessary to bring a date, unless, of course, ya'll wanna."

"I may be working." I caught the drift of her question. "But it's sweet of you to invite me."

Diego took this opportunity to kiss Barbara's wrist. "Enjoy the party, Barbara. We'll speak later," he said, before his eyes flicked to me. "This table has the best view of the show." He pulled a chair out for me and we sat down.

"I thought the show would be over there." I pointed to the center of the square.

"The city will have a Mayan play there. See, they are starting," he pointed at the smoke, "but for this *fiesta* I hired another group of actors to perform a Mayan show right here. You like fireworks?"

I nodded.

"There should be plenty tonight." Diego motioned for a passing waiter carrying appetizers to approach. The waiter set a plateful of *tapas* on the table. The choices were varied—seafood, chicken and cheese, wrapped in tortillas. I placed a napkin on my lap and picked out a *tapa.* Glancing around, I thought how mysterious the square looked at dusk, with the smoke hazy in the air.

"Simple fare, *mi amor.*"

After an afternoon with Wolf, I had worked up an appetite. "Excellent," I picked up a *tapa* and took a bite, "but not typical of Day of the Dead food, is it?"

Diego snapped his fingers to get a passing waiter's attention. The man hurried over to our table, inclining his head humbly.

"*Si, señor* Alvarez?"

"Señorita Sturm would like to try a *tamale de mole.*"

"Of course." He served one on my plate. "My sincere

apologizes, *señor* Alvarez. It was remiss of me."

"*Tamale de mole?*"

The waiter nodded.

Diego smiled. "You had tamales when we visited Reese but these are different."

"Mm-mm. Chocolate tomales…I think you're trying to seduce me with chocolate."

"And if that's what you're thinking, you'd be right…" Diego's eyelids lowered as his mouth pressed on mine. His tongue caressing my lip pushed his kiss up a notch. I had to force myself to withdraw.

"Loving you is like eating chocolate but with an additional component—you're way more addictive. Every kiss with you makes me want more. Perhaps I'm in love with you."

"Don't say that word, Diego. You know it's not true."

When the breeze picked up and blew a strand of hair in my eyes, his hand was quick to pull the tendril away only to drop down to linger on my shoulder.

"Smooth skin like silk," he bent his head to my ear, "and your hair—it conjures up magical dreams." His eyes took on a dreamy faraway look as he stared into the night. "I see a beautiful princess lying on a four poster bed, her hair spread out on a pillow like a fan. I want to awaken her with kiss—so she'd be mine."

"Dreams are seldom reality."

"But they can become real if one really wants it." Diego brought his daiquiri up to his full lips and I couldn't help noticing his heavy gold ring with the square green stone.

"Your ring is unusual."

"The stone is jade. Remember when we saw Reese's Mayan collection? Many figures use jade for religious statues or jewelry for the nobility." He lifted his hand up for me to see. "The gold *B* stands for Bolivar." He took my hand, his expression intense. "My family can become your family."

"We are friends Diego, no more."

Diego smiled brilliantly. "You deceive yourself. We are well beyond friends." He peered at my forehead. "What's this, *cariño?*" Diego brought his finger to my cut. "You were hurt." His finger grazed my bump and I flinched. "What happened?"

"When we were in Coba, someone hit me on the head."

"Hit you?"

"Wolf found me lying in the hallway. I think it had something to do with Ingrid."

"She has the jaguar and you got it for her. But why would someone strike you?" He frowned. "And more importantly, why wasn't Du Lac there to protect you?"

"Don't be ridiculous, Diego!" I snapped. "I'm not a little girl that needs her daddy."

Diego smiled and patted my hand. "Pardon me, my sweet Adelinita, I forgot you had hand to hand combat skills. I'll never forget that time at Tulum." He gripped his abdomen and faked some pain. "You strike a powerful blow, *mi amor*. Now, about some of those hand skills..." He grinned mischievously. "I know your lip skills are exemplary but I think we owe it to ourselves to investigate further." Seeing me frown, he said, "Adelina, you have to admit your attraction to me." He ran his fingers down a tendril of my hair. "It's attractive like this, but I like it better when it's down." He gazed at me. "You have the power to distract me with those pouty lips and your eyes, so slanty and blue... But believe me, *cariño*, when I say, it's more than your physical beauty. I admire your spirit and I know what you need."

"Oh? What's that, Diego?" I was almost afraid to hear the answer.

"Definitely romance. Yet I know love has not always treated you well."

"Diego, there is something we need to talk about."

"What do you need to make you happy, Adelinita?"

"It's not what I need, it's what I don't want."

Diego took my hand and ran his fingertips lightly over it. "You know I'd do anything for you."

I wanted to be diplomatic but my words sounded awkward to my own ears. "People in your employ and others too, seem to believe I am your..."

"*Novia?*"

"I get the impression they think I'm something other than your girlfriend. They think I'm your kept woman." There, I'd said it. Could he deny it? I was sick of the humiliation. That nasty Eduardo and his insinuations, not to mention the dragon lady. As if I would chose a man for his money in exchange for sexual favors.

Everything I'd ever achieved in life was through my own hard work.

Diego patted my hand in a conciliatory manner. "A fierce woman like you can never be truly possessed by a mortal man. You are no more my mistress than Daniella ever was. No matter what you think of her, Adelina, she is a woman with considerable business acumen."

And that was the problem. I couldn't just tell Wolf to get rid of a woman who furthered his business ambitions. A bitter taste filled my mouth as I thought of that predator taking a bite out of my sea god. I should have joined her in that pool and drowned her while I had the chance. The chair beside me scraped, followed by a familiar giggle startling me out of my dark reflections.

"Guess who's here to join us, amiga?" Carmelita pulled Wolf down into the seat between us.

In a black T-shirt and jeans his athletic body was enticingly svelte, contrasting sharply with his sexy bedroom hair. Wolf smiled wickedly. "You should have waited, princess. I could have done with some help."

Carmelita stroked his arm a bit too intimately. "I can't wait to hear what happened."

"Where is Daniella?" Diego lit a cigarillo. "She so enjoys my fiestas, I can't imagine her missing this one."

"She insisted on changing her dress.'

"You must be joking!" Carmelita furrowed her brow. "She had that sensational black dress from my collection—the slinky, sequined number. My designer was loath to part with it," she whispered in my ear, "especially with the chintzy price she paid."

"Yes," Diego said, "she was exquisite tonight before she left to see you, Du Lac. Why did she decide to change?"

"It was a bit too wet for her to be comfortable in."

"Wet!" I shot him a look of disbelief. "Last I saw, her dress was on the back of the living room chair and she was about to go skinny dipping."

Wolf stroked my cheek. "Those were her intentions—not mine, remember?"

Carmelita chuckled. "The devil sent temptation and you resisted?"

"It must have been *hard*," I hissed through my teeth.

Wolf ignored my remark and waved a waiter over. "Sol, *por favor*." He placed a finger on my mouth. "You doubt me, princess?" He shot a glance at Diego. "Adie and I have history together—a connection. Daniella can't come between us."

Diego traced the edge of his goblet thoughtfully. "A divorce must have been difficult for you, my friend. I've never had that particular problem myself. You must tell us how you deal with such emotional conflict and then move on so easily with Adelina."

Wolf frowned. "Divorce is never easy but Adie and I have a unique relationship that hardly compares to a brief marriage doomed from the start. We've known each other since our teens, and our families are friends. Luckily we met again, here in Cozumel." He stared challengingly at Diego and added, "Adie isn't just a pretty face," his eyes trailed down to my cleavage, "or a sexy body—she's exceptional."

Diego nodded. "True." He took my hand, stroking my fingertips. "A woman like no other, strong yet with a certain vulnerability." He sat back against his chair and remarked smoothly. "She's a warrior in need of a suitable mate."

"An alpha male," Wolf agreed, smiling superiorly.

Diego traced my recent hairline scar with his finger. "Someone who can protect her. Someone with position—a self-made man."

Wolf frowned. "I concur with the first part of your statement, but if you're referring to yourself, wasn't the Bolivar fortune initiated by your father?"

Diego glared at Wolf. "Royal Investments is mine! I built it into what it is after my brother died." He pointed his knife. "And what about you? Didn't your parents give you the financial backing for your company?"

"Some," Wolf conceded smiling, "but only at the beginning." He dropped his arm at the back of my chair. "You've forgotten something essential about Adie. She wouldn't risk her integrity to become a man's possession."

"Adelina needs a man that can provide her with romance."

"Chocolate and strawberries." Wolf's eyes locked with mine. His lips were so sensual, his features ruggedly asymmetrical but together they spewed sexuality. My hormones whirled, my nipples hardened when I thought of the two of us at the beach. How passionate he'd been—how he'd given me so much pleasure. I fingered the jade Ixchel pendant on my neck, his lovely but rather odd gift.

"A romantic like Adelina loves roses and dancing." Diego swept a strand of hair away, his fingers running intimately down my neck.

True. Diego knew what I liked. His rose had been a perfect ending to our romantic evening, the two of us swaying in an Argentinean tango that vibrated to the very soul—a moist ocean breeze cooling our overheated bodies. The dance had been so seductive. When I was in Canada, I'd forgotten Diego's allure but that night at the restaurant my memories had resurfaced in his arms. And then later—his kiss.

Shut up! My Logical Voice commanded. Those two are discussing you like you're a piece of property they both want to buy. You should be angry. Where's your pride?

Logical was right! They were so rude, arguing about what I liked as if I wasn't sitting there between them. What did they think they would accomplish with their negotiations anyway—as if one of them would say—Okay you can have her. You know her better. You're more alpha than I am. Fat chance of that! Both of them thought women keeled over at the sight of them. I frowned. And they were right—Barbara, Daniella and so many others. But what about my feelings? I bit my lip thinking about that. Life was a bowl of cherries with plenty of pits—hopefully easy enough to remove. I glanced sidelong at Diego—sophisticated and devastatingly handsome. I turned to Wolf—unpredictable, sizzling with animal magnetism. I blanked out their words, watching their expressions. They were playing hard and the score was 2-2, going into overtime, their voices edgier by the minute. If this were a hockey game, ice hockey that is, they'd be body-slamming their way into the boards by now, with some punches thrown in, enough to land them both in the penalty box.

Carmelita seeing my clenched jaw, whispered, "Macho male one-upmanship—let it go, amiga. Think of them as matadors with the bull." She giggled. "In this case, it's hard to distinguish the bull from the matador—with so much of it flying around. You have so much to be thankful for. Be grateful that Daniella hasn't arrived to spoil our *fiesta*."

That brought up another point. "So tell me why you came, Wolf?"

Wolf shot me an incredulous look before he said, "I think you already know the answer to that. I brought your cell, by the way." Reaching into his pocket, he dropped it on the table in front of me. "You've got messages from your *friends*."

Our waiter brought over a beer for Wolf and served the rest of us another round of daiquiris. Diego's eyes lit on the waiter's nametag. "*Muchos gracias*, Juan." He held his glass up. "On this special day, *Dia de los Muertos*, I'd like to make a toast to my brother, Amancio. *Salud!*"

"*Salud!*" We clicked our glasses as the actors in Mayan costume took their places for their performance.

"Tell us," Carmelita poked Wolf's arm, "won't you, darling, how did Daniella get her dress wet?"

All eyes focused on Wolf.

Wolf's lips twitched. "When she knew I wasn't going to join her, she was pissed off in a major way. Got her clothes back on and made off but didn't get too far. In her rush, she didn't see the skimmer rod, tripped and landed in the water, only this time in her dress."

"Then you drove her home?" I asked, sure she'd want that. In fact, it could work in her favor. Wolf liked being a knight in shining armor, even if it meant rescuing a barracuda.

"I tried but she got her cell out and in no time a guy arrived to pick her up."

I furrowed my brow at that one. Danielle had an ace up her sleeve or ...

"A *pescado*, a hooked fish," Carmelita commented with an impish grin. "Daniella has her own collection, to be used or abused, when needed."

My phone beeped. I excused myself and headed over to the corner of the patio to take a look, remembering those e-mails I had sent from Wolf's place. Slick might have gotten a hold of a picture of Morris.

I glanced down and clicked the icon. I had a glimpse of his face before my arm got knocked out of position.

"What the..."

"Sorry, Adie," Janice gushed out her words. She was dressed

to the nines in a gold lamé job and were those Ingrid's diamond earrings?

She eyed my dress disapprovingly. "From the show, I see."

"A gift." I studied the earrings. "Those earrings are so pretty. They look just like Ingrid's."

Janice chortled. "That's because they *are*. I finally got them back."

"Back?"

"They were my mom's. She passed away a few years ago. I should have inherited them but my old man went loony bins and gave them away."

"Your father?" I asked curiously. Then I put it together. "Your name isn't Janice Jones, is it? You're Janice James, aren't you?"

"You're smarter than you look."

"Why did you hide this from me?"

"I needed to meet Ingrid and dowdy Miss Jones was just the sort of person the sophisticated Adie Sturm would feel sorry for and invite to the fashion show. But, as you can see," she gestured to her outfit, "I'm not what I seem. Not everyone gets an invite to Diego's parties, do they?" She straightened her shoulders, holding her head high. "Only friends and business associates of Diego's, right, Adie? Well, position is everything in this island, or haven't you noticed? Diego invited me, you know. My family has money and he's smart enough to see how knowing me would be benefit him, especially after I bought myself my own little statue. I have as much right to be here as you."

"I never implied you didn't, Janice."

"No, but I saw the pitiful look you gave me when we first met. Now, perhaps there's just a teensy bit of jealousy?" She tapped her foot for emphasis, showing off her stylish, Italian shoes. She glanced over to the bar where George sat, shooting the breeze with the bartender. "I have to thank you for introducing me to that man. George adores me." She winked. "And he's hot, if you know what I mean? Too bad, Jeffrey doesn't approve."

"That's a brother for you." Mine had ruined my budding relationship with the elusive Alan. "Where is he, Janice?"

Janice absentmindedly ran her fingers around a stray lock of her curly red tresses and twirled it. "Who knows—he's probably with that cow."

"Is he still trying to snap up Ingrid's stocks?"

Janice swiveled to me. "Her stocks! They're ours, not that conniving bitch's." She laughed derisively. "Miss Curiosity got an earful at Coba, didn't she? But I guess someone had enough of you. Knocked you out just outside Jeff's room, eh?" She poked her finger into my arm. "How much did you overhear?"

"Enough."

"Jeff's a fool for trusting Ingrid. He really thinks she'll give in and sign over the stocks because he's such a stud-muffin."

My ears perked. "But she's not going to, is she, Janice?" I felt a hand on my shoulder.

"Well, well, well…" George barked out his words in a jovial fashion, "if it isn't our fearless leader." He peered at my forehead. "I'm surprised you can party after that incident. You look okay, though." His eyes roved to my cleavage and muttered, "Yeah." He glanced over at the head table where Diego, Carmelita and Wolf sat. "I see we have something in common."

"Oh?" I asked.

"You like to make friends in high places, eh, Adie?" He placed his arm around Janice. "Me, too. My babelicious sweetheart here is not only a hunk of woman, but an heiress, no less. Isn't that a shocker?"

"Why didn't you tell me George?"

He gave my butt a quick pat. "Women can't be privy to such top secret info, Adie. They like to gossip. And that was an especially bad idea with Jan and Jeff trying to buy back…Oops!" He noticed Janice's icy stare. "Sorry, sugar cube."

The performers gathered in front of Lorita's. A drummer kneeled down and a man set up a four-foot high incense burner.

"Come on, Jan, we need to get a table," George said hastily, pulling Janice along with him.

I watched the incense being lit. Jeffrey could be with Ingrid right now helping with the jaguar transaction. She'd said she was meeting Diego at nine. I glanced at the time on my cell: 8:55.

In front of the restaurant two men brought in spindly evergreens and set them up as a backdrop for the show. Another man hung skull masks in the trees.

Wait a minute—negotiate with whom? Ricardo knew nothing about it and glancing over to where Diego sat, I could see he was in no hurry to go anywhere.

I gripped Janice's forearm tightly and squeezed. "Where is Jeffrey? Is he with Ingrid?"

"Ow! Let me go!"

I'd had it with her. I squeeze the pressure point below her elbow. "Tell me!"

George scowled, but seemed at a loss to do anything.

"Really, Adie." She squirmed. "I don't know where they are."

I looked in her eyes and saw nothing but fear. She didn't know. I let go of her. Janice stepped back behind George.

A hush came over the crowd at the appearance of five barefoot gods, four men and a woman, all with immense peacock feathered headdresses—black and white bones painted on their bodies.

The men had patterned shields in turquoise and yellow to match their loincloths and bright leather anklets trimmed with feathers. The female with a red feathered headdress and a turquoise and gold gown barely covering her blue-painted thighs sat down in a throne-like chair. She would be Ixchel, the fertility goddess, I surmised, and the others had to be the Rain, Corn, Jaguar and Honey Gods.

I clicked my cell and waited. I tore my eyes away from the show and studied the picture that appeared. I angled the phone and stared hard at the image, recalling the attacker in Pedro's Donkey. Morris's face was square but his hair wasn't blond and his eyes were hidden by black-framed glasses. It wasn't likely him. I squinted to see it better, thinking about Diego. Why did Ingrid think she would see him at the cemetery? He was in the midst of hosting a party. And hadn't he said people of his class didn't go to the cemetery to greet the returning spirits?

Smoke and incense blew over the show as drumbeats resounded steadily in a staccato rhythm. I watched the gods dance for the entranced audience—leaping over a fire they burned in a metal pot. Dragging my eyes away, I read Ilya's message.

No luck in locating Morris Fleischer. Have you found the murderer? What's going on? Get back to me.

Something wasn't right. I rubbed my forehead, conscious of the throbbing tension building behind my eyes. The drum beats resounded louder and smoke shot up, the gods illuminated in a blue haze. Ixchel was being slowly carried over to the Corn god and laid on top of him. If I were sitting there, Diego would be explaining the sexual connotation of the pantomime to me, his eyes shooting off arrows of desire each of them aimed for my heart. And just when I'd feel like leaving with him, immersing myself in a daring new adventure, Wolf would distract me with his nearness, his hand on my waist, his body heat sparking embers of arousal, bringing back all the memories of our love-making.

The cell screen blanked and my brain switched gears. The murderer was here in Cozumel. Telly was the murderer's mistake. Anyone of us in our group could have picked up that beer intended for Ingrid.

Standing on the upper level of Lorita's, staring out at the crowd, I put the facts together. In my mind the puzzle fell into place, piece by piece. Only one thing didn't quite make sense.

The dramatic reenactment flashed to its fiery climax with the flamboyant dancers leaping over flames in time with the roll of the drums. Diego's guests gazed mesmerized as the Rain God lay down, out-stretched on the interlocking stone while the other deities backed away.

The Jaguar God, god of the underworld approached, his face partially covered with a jaguar mask, gold and black body paint patterning his body. His torch flamed brightly. He held it up high before he lowered it to the prostrate Rain God's face. The audience gasped as the god opened his mouth to receive the flame, swallowing it, until only a whiff of smoke remained. All eyes remained riveted and the unbelievable happened—rain fell, sprinkling lightly at first, before it gained momentum, splattering down in increasingly large drops. The wind picked up. A tropical downpour released.

Unaffected by the elements, the Jaguar God stood proudly, spreading his arms out in triumph while I bolted out of Lorita's into the storm. Within seconds I was drenched but my mind wasn't on the Rain God or the fact that I was wet through—I had to get to the cemetery before it was too late.

"Hey, blondie!" a local called out from the protection of his awning as I ran past. Whatever else he said was lost in the rush of the downpour. In and out between those with umbrellas and others that didn't, I wove down the street. Stumbling over a beer can, I righted myself to stop myself from slipping into the flooded street.

High-heels are difficult enough to run in but with the road now inches deep with water it was hazardous. I hopped onto the narrow cracked sidewalk. Rain-ridden gusts plastered me. My dress clung wetly like a limp skin. My fancy up-do had come undone, hanging down to my shoulders, like dead, limp snakes.

I squinted at the signpost through the rain. How much farther? I guessed another block. Out of breath, I leaned against a wall mural. An immense black cat. *Gato* lettered in red. The cat's back was arched, ready to strike, its slanted eyes vicious.

Time ticked faster than the racing of my pulse. I had to get there. If only the rain would stop. In the night air, I trembled as much from the cool breeze on my chilled skin as from my fear—if my hunch was right, it was a setup. Ingrid wouldn't live long enough to see the new jaguar statue.

16

My eyes searched ahead. A hazy mist enveloped the street. It couldn't be too much farther. Wet, dirty and tired, I stopped. Sweat trickled off my brow. I wiped it away—along with the rain. Sweeping my hair back, I scuttled ahead, sidestepping rusty steel rings in the sidewalk. The disrepair of the cement forced me to take to the road. A motor scooter zoomed out from nowhere. I jumped back.

The *avenida* ended. One high white wall met another at right angles. The rain drizzled its last hurrah and then sputtered and spit to a halt.

A wide iron gate at the corner was open but apart from a covered cart filled with marigolds and roses, I saw no one. Not even the vendor for the flowers. A sign posted at the gate in Spanish mentioned the hours the mass would be held at the church and something else beyond my expertise.

I stepped to the gate. Ahead I could see the aboveground mausoleums. Shimmery structures shrouded by mist. My heels sank into the muddy grass. In a few strides I was on a stone path.

The structures were large—each was room-sized with its own individual architectural design. The greater the building, the more elaborate the grilled windows and tropical gardens bordering the gates.

I read *Fam. Alonso Maquieres* on a triangular façade. The shed-like structure was constructed in stone, painted yellow. Through the barred window, I saw an altar. Flickering candles illuminated Jesus on the cross. A vase filled with marigolds was set next to a guilt-framed photograph.

To the right, teal-checked tiles made up the walls of a building topped by a triangular roof. *Emila Reyes* with dates and words was printed on an overhang. My eyes shot ahead but there was no sign of the Bolivar mausoleum.

Glancing from side to side, I checked the names as I walked. Larger mausoleums were now less frequent. In the distance, I could see some women, their heads covered with black lace, in long black dresses. I wandered ahead a few steps more before I knew this was all wrong. These mausoleums were too small...the tombs no larger than the size of a door. These were the resting place of the poor.

The Bolivar mausoleum had to be elsewhere. But where? I retraced my steps to my entry point and took another path but the tombs didn't live up to the grandeur I would have expected. I made it to the last tomb when I realized I was on a dead-end path with no exit.

Dark clouds shifted overhead and a sliver of a moon appeared, casting an eerie glow on the pale wet tombs, their shadows distorted darkly on the grass. On the bed of a low-lying tomb, a candle's light skipped with the breeze. I was never more aware of how alone I was.

Backtracking to the start of the path where I came in, I turned left. The grassy path was muddy and my heels slowed me down, digging into the soft ground as I hurried by a tomb having the appearance of a small house fronted by a door and windows—
Mauseleo de la Familia Pascual

A wreath of roses arranged at an ornate gate, gave me the distinct impression that the Pascual family was one of the well-to-do families of Cozumel. I was close—I felt it. With the streetlights far away, this section of the cemetery was dimly lit with the lunar glow of a fickle moon flitting between the clouds. The bark of a dog startled me and I turned in the direction of the sound only to plow into a solid figure robed in thick cotton.

A hand steadied me and I gazed up at a handsome face—full lips and a patrician nose, slightly curved. In perfect English, he asked, "Are you lost, Señorita?"

"I am looking for a mausoleum." He wasn't a mugger, unless muggers in Mexico wore monk's clothing and carried large, china vases filled with orchids.

"Perhaps, I can be of assistance." His hood fell back, revealing long, wavy black hair.

"It's the..." for a second my mind blanked. His eyes were dynamic—emerald, framed by dark lashes. If I were Catholic, I'd have need of immediate confession. I wasn't sure what my exact sin was but my thoughts were terribly inappropriate for a man of the cloth. I shook my head in confusion.

"Are you alright, Señorita?" He looked concerned. "During the rainy season we experience tropical storms here in Cozumel." His eyes wandered to my halter-top dress. "You're wet through. And cold." He dug into the pocket of his robe. He pulled out a small towel. "It's clean. Let me assist you." Dabbing the towel on my back and shoulders, he hesitated, seeing my expression. "Would you like to dry your hair?"

I ran my fingers through my tangled soggy tresses. "I really need to go," I said tensely. "Would you know where I could find the Bolivar mausoleum?"

"Certainly. These flowers are for the Bolivar mausoleum. I will take you there." His smile was radiant. "You know the Bolivars?"

"Yes."

"Which ones?"

"Diego and Carmelita. They're friends. And you?"

He nodded. "I have known them many years." He glanced at me. *"What's your name?"*

"Adie Sturm and yours?"

The stranger caught my elbow as I slipped on the wet stone path. Bending his head down to me, he said softly, "Call me Brother Aman. It's a pleasure to meet you. Your name is unusual. Is Adie what you Americans call a nickname?"

"It's short for Adelina."

"A lovely name for a lovely lady." He glanced intently at me. "It's not wise for a woman to walk alone, unescorted, even in a safe place like San Miguel."

"It's an emergency, Brother Aman. I have reason to believe someone I know is in danger."

The monk stopped in his tracks. "Here?"

"Yes, at the Bolivar mausoleum. Someone wants to kill her…"

"In that case, we must hurry!" Brother Aman said, speeding up.

In my heels, I trotted quickly to keep up with the tall man's stride. Through darkness more than light, the mausoleums loomed larger as we came around the bend. Unique with its asymmetrical layout, the cemetery resembled a maze, each pathway having an unpredictable ending.

Abruptly, we stopped. There before us was a magnificent

edifice. A glistening ivory structure had a curved arch over the door and rusty-red trim. The ornately-pillared stone fence in front was bordered by pointy-scarlet plants while palms on the left edged the entrance. Over the door in flowing black letters *Mausoleo De La Familia Bolivar* was inscribed. Next to a tree on the right, a stone plaque was mounted. I translated what I could, making some sense out of it.

Amancio: Juntas à Dios
Viviras siempre
en nuestros corazones

Diego's brother was with God but lived in their hearts. How sad for them, I thought. Even though my brother was a bother at times, siblings have a special bond. There'd be a hole in my heart if he died.

On both sides of the gate, a delicate wreath of roses and orchids had been carefully hung on the posts. Through the glass-paned door, we could see framed photographs of the Bolivars on a table-clothed altar. On a lower level, vases filled with blood-red roses were artistically arranged. Dancing yellow lights from the altar candles hypnotically beckoned us to come closer.

My eyes darted beyond the mausoleum looking for Ingrid, but I saw only the tips of palms fronds swaying in the breeze. Noises in the wind startled me. At first, I thought I had only imagined the voices. I shot a sidelong glance at Brother Aman.

He held his finger to his lips. "Come this way." He steered me into a narrow gap between the Bolivar mausoleum and the neighboring Delgado tomb. "They're at the back."

The passageway was about three feet wide and twenty feet in length. Obscure shadows cloaked the path—it was the last place I wanted to be but I didn't have a choice. With Brother Aman beside me, I crept along, my hand skimming the wall. As we neared the corner of the mausoleum. I heard them talking before my eyes spotted them.

"What are you doing here? Where's Diego?" Ingrid demanded furiously.

I peered out but the recipient of her venom had his back to me, a loose hooded coat covering him. I held my hand up to stop Brother Aman. "Thank you for your help, Brother Aman," I said softly, "but you must not get involved in any of this."

He stared at me intently, nodded and stepped back into the darkness. My eyes fixed on Ingrid and the stranger.

"You have a long wait if you're expecting the hoity-toity Santiago Bolivar Alvarez. He wouldn't be caught dead here." The man chuckled. "News flash, honeybunch! No one is bringing another statue…not tonight—not ever."

"So you tricked me into coming." Ingrid sneered. "Quite an achievement for a scumbag like you. Well I've had enough. Stay here with the dead people or better still, why don't you crawl back into the hole you crawled out of?" Ingrid plodded past him.

His hand shot out and grabbed her arm. "You're not going anywhere."

"Let go of me, asshole!" Ingrid struggled to pull away.

I inched up behind a palm.

"Hand over that statue."

"I don't have it."

His deep voice was calm. "It's in that bag." You would have followed Alvarez's instructions to the letter. The text said to bring it to compare them."

"Diego's instructions but not yours," Ingrid snarled out her words and flung off his arm. "Take a hike, retard."

"Give it to me."

"I'd say try taking it, but I know you don't have the balls."

"Nobody has balls enough for you. There isn't a man alive that could give you what you need."

Ingrid scoffed. "A real man satisfied me in every way." Her face flushed with anger. "Why do you think I was with Jordan James for twenty years?"

"A woman like you only cares for money. He set you up in business. You didn't really get an inheritance from your aunt, did you?"

"You are so stupid." Ingrid smirked. "You'd believe anything as long as you didn't have to give me any money. You've been skimming money from me for years. What a break I had Jordan."

"Money is the god you worship." He eyed the tote she held.

"So you lured me here to steal my statue. It's not like you were jealous of Jordan. You were probably glad he was satisfying me sexually because you sure had no interest. It's a wonder that I ever conceived, is it? But then it's doubtful you're the father." She chortled. "Once a year is a long shot, wouldn't you say?"

Morris' eyes narrowed but he said nothing.

"Did you ever ask your counselor why you couldn't get it up?" Ingrid laughed. "Or did you know all along you were gay. You're lucky I stayed considering your job paid peanuts. If it weren't for Jordan we'd be living in the slums. So be grateful, you pathetic SOB, that I got us a beautiful old home in Beechwood."

"And thank you, honeybunch, for putting all our money into art—untraceable Mayan antiquities." Morris' voice dripping with sarcasm. "It was considerate of you to leave them at home for me while you traipsed off to Cozumel to get me more."

I could see his profile and mentally matched it with the picture I'd been sent on my cell. He wasn't the attacker at Pedro's Donkey but I was sure he was the scruffy man from the elevator with the fish odor. He looked better than his photo.

"Shut the fuck up! You sent me that heart didn't you? You can't even take a divorce like a man. How infantile!" Angrily she unzipped her jacket. "And I suppose it was you trying to scare me at the *cenote*?" Ingrid swung her hand back and struck him hard on the side of his face. "That's for pushing me down the stairs at Coba."

Morris shoved her away. She flew backwards landing in the muddy grass. "I'll take responsibility for the box. Scared the hell out of you, didn't I?" He stepped forward. "You looked like a piece of shit when you opened the door for the police." He laughed. "Much like you do now. Now give me the jade." With his boot he kicked her. Ingrid screamed.

I rushed out from behind the palm. "Leave her alone!"

Morris whipped around his eyes sparkling dangerously. "Adie Sturm to the rescue? This is a surprise. I'd have thought you would have given up the sleuthing after I cracked that bottle over your head." He rubbed his chin thoughtfully. "Slow learner, eh? Too bad the big guy came looking for you. A sliver from that bottle could have made a nice little nick in your throat. Finished you off and I'd have had time to do my bitch wife."

I shuddered. The man was insane.

Morris spat a glob of saliva out on the grass. "Jeff James wouldn't have protected you, Ingrid." He watched her sit up. "He wanted old Jordie's shares. That's all. If you were dead, he'd be laughing all the way to the board meeting."

I knew now why I hadn't recognized him. He'd always been so clean-cut when he'd come in to the office—bow tie, a nerdy suit and he'd always worn those large black-framed glasses. Now he had five-day stubble and wild long hair.

"Jeffrey is in love with me. He knows a real woman when he sees one."

"You're delusional." He poked her arm with his foot. "Ten years ago, you were a babe, like Adie, here, but you let yourself go. People get what they deserve in life. In your case, *nada*. A fitting end for a scheming woman." He turned to me. "You should have stayed out of it. She doesn't deserve your loyalty. Now you'll have to go down with her."

"You delivered the heart and," I got this mental picture of the man at Ingrid's door. "You were at Ingrid's door when we first arrived, but you had a beard!"

Morris smiled. "Observant of you, my dear, but you're a bit too late to help your boss. True, I grew a beard. A good disguise, right? After I shaved it off I decided I needed some facial hair— you know, that Brad Pitt look."

I glanced at Ingrid who'd gotten to her feet, her bag forgotten on the ground.

From his coat pocket Morris whipped out a knife. "Something for you," he swiveled about, "and for our Adie. What a shame it is you're wasting your life for a user like her." His eyes roamed to the entrance of the alley. "You should have stayed with your boyfriend." His eyes searched in the darkness. "You'd have been safe but now you'll have to join this controlling bitch in hell."

Why hadn't I brought a weapon? Anything. But all I had was my purse looped on my wrist. How could I have been so unprepared? I had to stall him. "Why did you have to kill Telly?" I stepped back. He didn't seem in the least bit alarmed. Didn't he think I'd run?

"Oh yes, Telly. That pathetic alchie." He smirked. "Slurped up my special beer cocktail. Too bad honeybunch got a tummy ache. Such bad timing."

"You couldn't have done this alone."

He came at me from behind. A hairy arm closed around my neck, locking me in a tight hold.

"Sweet timing, eh?" A harsh voice growled in my ear. His breath reeked and his body had the odor of old sweat. "Remember me, cutie?"

I twisted my head about. The pony-tailed assailant from the shop. I let my purse slide off my hand.

"You stopped me from killing her before but now you go down with her." A hard object jabbed into my back. "Feel that?" He let out a high pitched giggle. "Gun power beats karate know-how any day."

"Sorry, Adie but I've got to tie up loose ends. And you," Morris said lightly, "are definitely a loose end. Should I introduce you two? But you don't really have time to become acquainted, do you?" He tittered at his witticism. "FYI—Ron's my cuz and he's gung-ho to help me get rid of my garbage."

"Ron?" Ingrid peered up "that you?"

"Yep. He looks different, eh?"

"Don't listen to this maniac, Ron." Ingrid pulled herself up. "Shoot him—I'll pay you double whatever Morris is giving you."

"Oh gosh!" Ron twittered. "So nice of you, Mrs. Fleischer!" His fingers dug into my neck as his mood changed. "Like I'd believe you." He growled. "I'm a no-account bastard. Isn't that what you called me? My mom's the one that slept around, unlike you." His oily hair brushed my forehead. "Oo-ops! I forgot. You're better than her. You're a high-class whore."

Morris gestured with his knife. "See what your hostility did? He doesn't mind ridding the planet of a worthless cow." He kept his eyes on Ingrid. "But first, Ron boy, it will be Adie. They're having some spectacular fireworks in the square. No one will give a damn about a little noise, will they? It might interest you to know, Adie, that a Luger sounds remarkably like a firecracker."

If someone's about to shoot you, there's no point in standing there and conveniently dying. I screamed a karate *kiai* and stepped down hard on Ron's foot. Taken aback, he jerked and loosened his grip. Twisting my body on an angle and I clenched my fingers into a fist, struck his nose and on the way down, smashed into his forearm. He cried out and dropped his hand. The gun fired. A deafening explosion. The bullet flashed brightly in the dim light.

Ron flung himself down on the ground to retrieve the semi-automatic. On his hands and knees he groped until he had it.

Twisting around, he aimed it at me. I froze. Suddenly I was shoved away and a vase full of orchids slammed hard on Ron's head.

Brother Aman stood back to survey his work. He grinned at the look on my face. "I thought you might need me." His eyes narrowed. "Behind you!"

I swiveled around. Morris was almost at me, his knife held low. Presenting my side to him, I brought my forearm under his knife hand and propelled his arm in a windmill motion before I struck his arm with the hard edge of my other hand. The knife slashed my hand as it dropped. Turning my supporting foot, I got a kick out to his knee. He stumbled backwards.

Ingrid flung herself on the ground and snatched up the knife, eyes glinting dangerously. She charged at Morris. "Bastard!" Somehow she misstepped, tripping on a rock. I watched in horror as her body propelled forward, landing into the knife. She grunted as the blade tore into her. Rivers of red patterned the grass. Ingrid lay motionless. My eyes flitted up. Morris was gone. Only the mist remained.

A hand gently brushed my shoulder. "Are you alright?"

I stared at the blood on my hand, the pain just now starting.

"You're hurt," Brother Aman said softly. From out of his pocket, he pulled a towel and wrapped my bleeding hand, "You'll be okay," he said. "They'll check it at the hospital, but," his eyes shot to Ingrid's still body, "I don't know about her."

"Adie!" I heard Wolf's shout from the alley.

"I must go," Brother Aman whispered urgently, pulling up his hood. "*Adios,* Adelina." He strode to the next mausoleum.

Wolf and Diego broke into the clearing. From the corner of the mausoleum, Brother Aman waved.

Diego's eyes shot to the monk before he disappeared around the tomb. "What happened, Adelina?"

Wolf took hold of my towel-wrapped hand. "You're hurt. It's bleeding. Come on, baby, we need to get you to the hospital!"

"Let's go." Diego took my elbow. "*Cariño*, don't worry, my driver is waiting at the entrance." He glanced at the bodies on the lawn. "I'll call the police for those two," he said, dismissively.

I shook my head, shrugging off Diego. "I'll be okay! Ingrid," I gestured with my chin, "check her, please, Wolf!"

The men stared at the figure lying on the grassy knoll a few yards away. "Adelina," Diego asked in a hushed tone, "is that the Fleischer woman? She's been shot?"

"No." I shivered, my body now reacting to what I had just experienced.

"Take care of her," Wolf ordered Diego. "I'll look."

Diego put his arms around me and held me close. I was beginning to shake uncontrollably. "She had a knife—she wanted to kill her husband."

"Calm down, *querida*. If you shot her, I'll deal with it." Diego stroked my damp hair gently. "I'll explain it to the police. There won't be a problem."

Tears trickled down my cheeks brought on from the soothing comfort of his voice and the warmth of his body. "She thought she had a text from you about another Jaguar God. She came here to see you—make a deal. But Morris, her ex was here. He wanted her dead…"

Wolf turned Ingrid over onto her back. I gasped. Her eyes stared sightlessly. The knife was deeply embedded in her chest.

"How?" Wolf asked.

"There was a struggle. She grabbed the knife and fell." I glanced down at the grass where her bag had been. "The statue's gone!"

"And what about him?" Diego eyes lit on Ron, unconscious on the grass.

I pulled away from Diego and knelt down beside Ron. I took up his hand and could feel a faint pulse. "He's alive."

"What was he doing here?" Diego crouched beside me. With his finger, he pushed aside pieces of the vase embedded in Ron's hair.

"Ron was in this with Morris. They wanted the jaguar. He was about to shoot me when, Brother Aman struck him with the vase."

Wolf came over. "Who's Brother Arman?"

"You saw him go. He helped me find the Bolivar mausoleum. He was bringing the flowers here. If it wasn't for him, I would have been shot."

"Brother Aman, Brother Aman…" Diego repeated in a dazed manner. "My brother's name is Amancio." Diego's face drained of color. "*Mierda*," he muttered softly, under his breath. "Adelina, was it him?"

17

A crimson streaked sunset glowed vibrantly on the horizon. The crests of the waves shimmered pink with the reflected light. I leaned my head on Wolf's shoulder but kept my eyes on the setting sun.

"Do you think we'll see the green ray?"

His eyes sparkled blue like a fresh water stream on a sunny day. "Ah-h, yes...the flash at sunset. It's rare sight but if we do, our wishes will come true. Get a wish ready, princess," Wolf whispered.

As the sun sank into the ocean, the cerulean blue sky lit with color—orange, yellow followed by a glimpse of green. I could hardly believe it. I made my wish. It was an impossible one.

"I made mine," Wolf said quietly, "and you?"

"Um-mm."

Wolf brought his fingers to his forehead. "I predict…they're coming true as we speak."

"And you know this because?"

"I have psychic powers." Wolf gazed down at me, his eyes heavy-lidded. "My predictions are always right." He brought his sensuous lips to mine and worked his magic over my mouth.

Oh yes! My Hormone Voice sighed. His kisses are sweeter than any shiraz you've ever tasted. I let my lips linger on his, savoring the flavor of his kiss. After I tasted him I forced myself away. "So what's my wish?"

"You want love."

"Love is inevitable and unavoidable," I noted, "much like a hurricane in Cozumel." I stroked his cheek and met his eyes. "But let's not confuse it with sex."

Exactly, My Logical Voice agreed. Finally, you're seeing things the way they are. This magnetic man has the power to hook you in with his eyes.

"I'll have to prove it to you then."

"Hey, Adie, Wolf!" Fern called out from her table. "Come join us."

I had invited my tour group for dinner at the fabulous San Francisco Beach Bar, famous for its spectacular sunsets. Fern and some of the others were sitting at tables overlooking the beach.

We headed over. Wolf pulled out a chair for me.

Fern wore a funky black dress and Bryan, sitting next to her wore his usual dockers and golf shirt.

"You look gorgeous in that dress, Adie." Fern leaned back in her chair. "Doesn't she, Wolf?"

"I'm the wrong person to comment." Wolf grinned. "But when I saw it in Carmelita's Fashion Show, I knew it was perfect for her." He signaled the waiter.

"And?" Fern asked.

"He bought it for me. This is its second tryout. Luckily they were able to get the stains out."

"Stains?"

"Blood."

Fern's eyes widened. "Ingrid's?"

I shook my head. "Mine." I glanced at my bandaged wrist that had accidentally met with Morris' knife.

Fern patted my shoulder. "You are brave."

"Adie's a fighter," Wolf said, a hint of pride in his voice. He handed me my daiquiri.

Fern peered at the jade pendant at my neck. "Beautiful jade. Ixchel's power kept you safe."

I rubbed the smooth jade, meeting Wolf's eyes. "She did."

Bryan leaned his elbows on the table. "Have they caught Morris yet?"

I sipped my daiquiri. "Officer Hernandez said they're looking for him but I'd think since he didn't actually kill anyone here, it won't be high priority."

Fern nodded. "I thought Telly's murder had something to do with Ingrid's attacks. Who would have imagined that Morris was capable of murder?" She tossed her mane back. "I met him once about six years ago, when I worked at Fleischer's. He showed up unexpectedly while Jordan was in the office with Ingrid. Cool as a cucumber, Ingrid introduced them. Morris thought Jordan was a business associate." She snickered. "I guess he was, the way she fleeced him dry."

"Fern, before Morris disappeared, he admitted to sending

Ingrid the bloody heart and the threatening note."

Fern leaned back in her chair, her expression smug.

"Sacrificing a heart was a Toltec tradition. Some say the Mayans didn't believe in human sacrifice." Bryan said, slouched comfortably, legs outstretched.

Wolf eyed the golden bubbles in his beer reflectively before he said what I was thinking. "You seem to have more than a passing knowledge of Mayan culture, Bryan. The Coba trip was right up your alley."

"Yeah, I was glad Adie had the foresight to hire the professor."

"He knew his stuff, alright. And you two were really keen about the sacrifices at the *cenotes*." I rubbed my lip. "The cenote was beautiful—excellent for snorkeling yet, neither of you seemed to have any interest." I shot a look at Fern. "I remember from our college days how much you liked swimming."

Fern nodded. "Too many bugs out there."

Bryan gazed out into the distance.

"You saw how clear the water was," I said. "Convenient for you though."

Fern raised an eyebrow.

I sipped my drink and set it down with a dull thud. Fern sat up startled. "You two made the noises to frighten Ingrid!"

"She deserved it after what she did to me."

"And Bryan went after her with a knife."

Bryan laughed. "Wasn't hard to put on the mask and cloak. She ruined Fern's life. The bitch deserved it."

"You did it for Fern."

"Someone has to protect her honor. Jordan James was a selfish bastard." Bryan raised his voice, "Treated Fern like a whore."

"My hero." Fern beamed. "Come on, loosen up, Adie. You know it's all true. Let's drink to the boss from hell, to Ingrid—a dead Ingrid." Fern lifted her glass to Bryan.

"Amen." He clicked his beer can.

"So she didn't imagine someone pushing her down the stairs at Coba?"

Fern smirked. "I'd call it a nudge, not really a push. The fat-ass scrapped her knees, Adie. Hardly a major thing."

"She wasn't my favorite person but you didn't see her die."

The lavender horizon cloaked with glints of red was reminiscent of the blood splashed on the grass. I shivered and crossed my arms, hugging myself to warm the chill I felt inside.

"Let's go for a walk, Adie." Wolf said suddenly, pulling out my chair. "You'll excuse us?"

Bryan nodded.

"Adie?" Fern said softly, her dark eyes sympathetic.

"What?"

"Don't feel bad. Some things you can't change. It was her fate. Karma."

"Bitterness can destroy a person, Fern. Forget and forgive…" That was my advice for Fern but for me it wouldn't be so easy for me. How could I wipe away those blank staring eyes from my memory?

Wolf wrapped his arm around my shoulders and we walked out to the beach, stopping at the water's edge. Pinpoints of lights appeared on the horizon—Playa del Carmen across the bay. Too much had happened since we'd been there. The *cenote*, Coba and the cemetery.

"I hope Ingrid's daughter will get through this." I wet my foot in the salty water.

"Rough for the kid—mother dead, and a father on the run."

"Ingrid's sister and mother live in town. I guess in time, she'll be okay. And Ingrid implied Jordan James was the father."

"Interesting. But what about you?" Wolf asked with concern. "This has been a helluva experience. I wish I'd been there for you."

"You couldn't have done anything. They had weapons, Wolf."

"Hey," Wolf laughed, "I know you're a kick-ass woman but I've had my share of fights. Hung out with some bad types a few years ago."

"And how did you know where I went?"

"Remember when Daniella arrived?"

"Um-mm." I wasn't likely to forget that.

"When she left, I found your cell phone. You had messages. I wasn't sure where you'd gone but I suspected you'd go to Alvarez. When I checked them I read one from Ingrid. I didn't think anything of it at the time but when you disappeared at the end of the show, I knew you must have gone to the cemetery."

"So you decided I needed help."

"Adie…" Wolf said softly, "I didn't want you out there alone. It's not safe."

I'd heard that before—the handsome monk had said as much. Could he have been Amancio? I stared out at the sea. Spirits returned on that special night, but no, it wasn't possible, was it? I looked up at Wolf. "So you thought I needed rescuing."

"With someone breaking a bottle over your head the other night, I think I had good reason to assume that you could be in danger."

"And Diego?"

"He insisted on coming too."

"And he just left his own party? You'd think he'd have taken Churo if he was that concerned."

Wolf ran his hands down my arms. "He wanted to rescue you. If he took Churo, he'd look like a coward."

"A coward?" *Diego?* "Under all that charm, he's a dangerous man."

Wolf pointed to a lounge chair, and he sat down pulling me up against him. "Funny, his charm eludes me."

I leaned on his chest comfortably pulling my legs up close. I tilted my head up to see his face. "If Carmelita hadn't told me that Diego had sent Daniella, I would have been so angry with you."

"I told you I hadn't asked her over."

I glared up at him. "Even so…she decides to go for a nude swim. Who would do that unless she thought you approved?"

"Daniella is a ballsy sort of woman."

"Tell me, Wolf Du Lac," I asked, fearful of the answer, "is she or has she ever been your lover?"

"I've never made love to her, Adie."

I sighed in relief.

"We're lovers—you and me," Wolf whispered in my ear and pulled me closer. "I want you to come back to see where we could go from here."

"You do, do you?" I shot him a look. "And why should I do that?'

His eyes burned intensely. "The Days of the Dead are over, baby." He dug out a paper from his jean pocket and offered it to me. "The living have a lot more to do. I want you to have this."

Stars were popping out like tiny silver pinheads speared into a midnight blue canvas. "What is it?" It was too dark to read the print.

"A lease for two years—my gift to you."

"A lease?"

"Remember the house on the beach?"

How could I ever forget that spectacular powdery beach, lying in the arms of my lover? A place dreams became reality. My heart had pounded with the pleasure he had given me and every fiber in my body had shouted with joy.

"It's yours."

"Mine?"

"Don't worry," Wolf whispered, "I'll take care of it for you. You won't have the responsibility. I just want you to come back and enjoy it." He stroked my cheek. "Will you?"

His windblown hair fell across his forehead. I pushed it away and met his eyes. "Yes."

"Good—let's go for that dessert."

www.AnastasiaAmor.com
Anastasia.Amor@hotmail.com
https://www.facebook.com/Anastasia.Amor.author

http://anastasiaamor1.blogspot.ca

ABOUT THE AUTHOR

OKTOBERFEST WOMAN OF THE YEAR FINALIST and EPIC AWARD NOMINEE, ANASTASIA AMOR is a university psychology and education graduate. Amor believes in balance.She is the proud mother of two, a pet-mom and a teacher. She also speaks German and is learning Spanish. Art and writing are her passions but she loves to dance and is a known chocoholic. Twenty years in Mexico, research of Mayan ruins and Cozumel cultural experiences inspired the popular Adie Sturm Mystery Series. As a martial artist she puts realism into Adie Sturm's fight scenarios. Researching DEAD DELICIOUS she learned to scuba dive. Psychic experiences, Cuban journeys and karate training sparked the fantasy-paranormal HAVANA HEAT. Her Canadian heroines are intelligent and fearless as well as sensual. Amor also writes erotic romance.

Praise for:

A CORPSE FOR COZUMEL: *ADIE STURM MYSTERY*
"…suspense starts in the first few pages…strong, sexy characters and intense sexual tension keep you wanting more…a great read that's hard to put down." —***4 Stars!*** Two Lips Reviews

"…good suspense...expanse of detail of the locations and the plot, creating a vivid world for all..."—***4 Stars!*** Enchanting Reviews

"…hot sexy men... thrilling suspense… You won't guess who the killer is until it's too late." —Night Owl Romance Reviews

THE CURSE OF THE CARNAVAL: *ADIE STURM MYSTERY—*
Epic Nominee 2011

DEAD DELICIOUS—"Highly Recommended !" **Anastasia Amor is truly the queen of steamy mysteries."** — Natalie G. Owens, *An Eternity of Roses.*

HAVANA HEAT*...a paranormal fantasy romance* ***5 Stars!*** "Havana Heat is a sensory experience. It's a sultry pleasure trip that rouses all the senses and won't let go. I think that the best attribute of this novel is its ability to surprise and engage. Every chapter, every scene, thrusts you in a different world, a varied experience that transports you utterly into magical realms and otherworldly adventures. The story has many threads woven into the plot but they are seamlessly pulled into the finish line and tied together. The paranormal aspect is highly original and captivating. Havana Heat makes you breathless. It will take you to Cuba with a one-way ticket and refuse to let you leave. I wanted to be there with Reese and Anise, Francisco and Sylvie. Your heartstrings will be pulled quite ruthlessly and in some poignant parts, you won't be able to stop a tear or two from falling. Fast paced and drop dead sexy… hits all the right spots for me"—*Natalie G. Owens, author of **An Eternity of Roses***

"Twists and turns in this tropical romance make it a paranormal reading adventure that will keep you on your toes until the last word!"—*Barbara Huffert, author of **Linked***

250

EXPLORING IRRESISTIBLE… erotic romance… 5 stars
"Exploring Irresistible is as decadent as fine dark chocolate and tropical drinks. Amor's vivid descriptions put me right there. What I love best is that I can come back and enjoy this story over and over again. This book is sensuous romance at it's best. Hot sultry Puerto Rico. When Aleese sees sinfully irresistible Arman— a man like chocolate...the tiger inside her is unleashed! A fight for control over her life surges into a burning adventure of passion and erotic fantasy…***Irresistible in every way!***"——*Michelle Stinson Ross*